Mary Derwent
A tale of Wyoming and Mohawk Valleys in 1778

by

Ann S. Stephens

Mary Derwent
A tale of Wyoming and Mohawk Valleys in 1778
by Ann S. Stephens

ISBN: 978-93-63052-39-0

Published by

DOUBLE 9 BOOKS

2/13-B, Ansari Road
Daryaganj, New Delhi – 110002
info@double9books.com
www.double9books.com
Tel. 011-40042856

ABOUT THE AUTHOR

Ann Sophia Stephens (1810-1886) was an American novelist and magazine editor who is credited as the progenitor of the dime novel genre. She began her writing career in Portland, Maine, where she co-founded and edited the Portland Magazine. Later, in New York, she served as the editor of The Ladies Companion and adopted the pseudonym Jonathan Slick. Stephens wrote over twenty-five serial novels, along with short stories and poems for well-known periodicals. Her novel "Malaeska, the Indian Wife of the White Hunter" is considered the first dime novel and was highly influential. Stephens also published her own magazine, Mrs Stephens' Illustrated New Monthly. Her works include "High Life in New York," "The Old Homestead," and "A Noble Woman."

CONTENTS

CHAPTER I
THE VALLEY OF WYOMING

Monockonok Island lies in the stream of the Susquehanna, where the Valley of Wyoming presents its greenest fields and most level banks to the sunshine. It is a quiet little spot, lying dreamily in the river, which breaks and sparkles around it with a silvery tumult. The Indians have gathered up the music of these waters in a name that will live forever—Monockonok—rapid or broken waters. You scarcely notice the island amid the luxuriant scenery of Wyoming, it seems so insignificant in its prettiness. Hedges of black alder, hazel branches, and sedgy rushes stand in thickets, or droop in garlands along its shores.

A few miles below Monockonok, between a curve of the river and a picturesque sweep of the mountains, lies the town of Wilkesbarre, a gem among villages set in a haven of loveliness.

Two or three miles higher up may be seen the town of Pittston, with its mines, its forges, its mills, and its modern dwelling-houses, crowding close up to the heart of the valley, in which the Lackawanna and the Susquehanna unite among exhaustless coal beds and the eternal beat of human industry.

For twenty miles below the Lackawanna gap, the valley, though under partial cultivation for nearly a quarter of a century, seemed scarcely more than an unbroken forest. The beautiful river in its bosom was almost hidden beneath the huge black walnuts, the elms and sycamores that crowded to its banks.

But with all this beautiful wildness, the strife of disputed civilization had already been felt in the valley. Indian forages were frequent, and the Connecticut settlers had been twice driven from their humble dwellings by the Pennsylvanians, who were restive at the introduction of pioneers from the neighboring States into this fertile region.

The blackened ruins of a dwelling here and there left evidence of this unnatural contest, while stockades and block-houses of recent erection, scattered along the valley, gave picturesque proofs of continued anxiety and peril.

From twenty to thirty houses occupied the spot where Wilkesbarre now stands, while log-cabins were grouped near the forts, each with its clearing, its young fruit-orchard, and its patch of wheat or corn.

A single log-cabin, sheltered by a huge old elm with a slope of grass descending to the water in front, and a garden in the rear, enriched with variously tinted vegetables, and made cheerful by a few hollyhocks, marigolds, and sunflowers, stood like a mammoth bird's nest on Monockonok Island.

Two immense black walnuts, with their mastlike trunks naked thirty feet high, stood back from the house. The shore was broken up with clumps of sycamores, oaks, maples, and groups of drooping willows, while an undergrowth of dogwood, mountain-ash and tamarisk trees chained into huge garlands by frost grape-vines and wild clematis, were seen in picturesque leafiness along the banks.

This log-cabin had been built years before, by a young man who came with his mother and his two little orphan girls to seek a home, and hide the deep grief occasioned by the loss of his wife in the wilderness. Derwent took up his residence in Wyoming with the New England settlers on their second return to the valley, when it was almost as much inhabited by the Indians as the whites.

Derwent struggled manfully in his new enterprise, but it was with a broken spirit and by stern moral force alone. His health, always delicate, sunk beneath the labor of establishing a new home, and though he worked on, month by month, it was as a Pilgrim toils toward a shrine, patiently and with endurance rather than hope.

Two little girls formed the sunshine of this humble family, and the fairy island was made brighter by their pleasant voices and graceful ways, as it was by the wild birds that haunted it with music. In the great indulgence of the invalid father, and the active love of that dear old grandmother, they had early lost all sense of orphanage, and were happy as the wild birds, free as the striped squirrels that peeped at them from the branches of the black walnut trees where they loved to play.

Very different were these two children from infancy up. Jane, the youngest, was a bright, happy little creature, full of fun, eager for a frolic, and heedless of everything else; endowed with commonplace goodness and a pleasant temper, she was simply a bright, lovable child. But Mary, who seemed younger by half than her robust sister, was so fragile, so delicate, that you dreaded to see the very winds of heaven blow upon her, even when they left the spring blossoms unhurt. Her large wistful eyes were full of earnestness. She was so fair, so fragile, swaying as she walked, like a flower too heavy for its stem, and with that look of unutterable sweetness forever about the little mouth.

With Derwent Little Mary was an object of singular tenderness, while the force and life of his warmer affections went to the younger child. He was their only teacher, and during the years that he lived it was a pleasant recreation to give them such instruction as his own rather superior attainments afforded.

Thus in primitive happiness the little family lived till Mary passed gently out of her childhood. There was little visiting among the pioneers, and a stranger seldom made way to Monockonok. An Indian sometimes touched the island with his canoe in his progress down the river; but this was always a happy event to the children, who received the savages with childish admiration, as if they had been orioles or golden robins. At the sight of a canoe, Jane would run gleefully to the river, waving kisses to the savage with her hand, and flaunting out her apron as a signal to win him shoreward. It was a singular fact, but the Indians seldom obeyed these signals unless Mary was by her side. A single gleam of her golden hair—a glimpse of her bent form—would prove more effectual than all her sister's pretty wiles.

Why did these savages come so readily at her look? What was the meaning of the strange homage with which they approached her? Why did they never touch her dress, or smooth her hair, or give her any of those wild marks of liking which Jane received so cheerfully? Why did they lay eagles' plumes and the skins of flame-colored birds at her feet, with so much humility? Mary could never comprehend this, but it filled her with vague awe, while the savages went away thoughtfully, like men filled with a spirit of worship.

One other person sometimes visited the island, who had a powerful influence over these children. This man was an Indian missionary, who, following the path of Zinzendorf, had made his home in the wilderness, about the time that Derwent entered the valley. He was evidently a man of birth and education, for even the wild habits of the woods had been insufficient to disguise the natural refinement of mind and manners which made the humility of his character so touchingly beautiful.

This man came often to the island. Sometimes he remained all night in the cabin. Sometimes he lingered days with the family, teaching the little girls those higher branches which their father could not control, and planting a thousand holy thoughts in the young minds, that lifted themselves to his knowledge, as the flower opens its cup for the night dew.

Under these beautiful and almost holy influences the children lived in their island home, each taking from the elements around her such nutriment as her nature craved, till Derwent, who had been ill since their first remembrance, sunk slowly to his deathbed.

The last attack came suddenly, while the missionary was absent among the Shawnees, far down the valley; but scarcely had the little family felt the need of his presence, when he appeared quietly and kindly. All one night he remained with the sick man; their conversation could be heard in broken fragments in the next room, where the old mother sat weeping over her grandchildren, holding Jane fondly in her lap, while Mary sat upon the floor, so chilled with grief that she did not feel the tender sorrow lavished upon her sister, as neglect of herself. Like a pure white lily broken at the stem, she sat wistfully gazing in the distance, wondering what death was, vaguely and in dreamy desolation. They were called at last, and with a dying effort Jane was drawn to her father's bed, the last breath, the last blessing fell upon her. Mary had no time; the father's life was exhausted in that one benediction.

The missionary led her forth into the open air. He said but little, and his voice fell dreamily on the senses of the child; but its first low cadence filled her soul with infinite resignation. From that time Mary could never realize that her father had died, leaving no blessing for her. It seemed as if the missionary had inhaled the life from his departing soul, and turned it all to love. The child recognized a double presence in this holy man. Not even her grandmother was permitted to kiss the forehead which his lips had touched. Her brow became sacred from that time, and she would shrink back with a cry of absolute pain if any one attempted to disturb the kiss which was to her the place of a lost blessing.

The missionary had many duties to perform, and his intercourse with the island was sometimes interrupted for months; but the little heart that clung to him could live upon a remembrance of his teachings, even when his presence was withheld. It was a wonderful influence, that which his strong, pure soul had obtained over the child. While these feelings were taking root in the nature of one sister, the other was working out her own life, and the grandmother took up the duties imposed by her bereavement with great resolution.

CHAPTER II
THE CRUEL ENLIGHTENMENT

Grandmother Derwent had contrived to purchase implements for spinning and weaving the coarse cloth, which constituted the principal clothing of the settlers. The inhabitants gave her plenty of work, and produce from her farm supplied her household with grain and vegetables.

Even the little girls, who under many circumstances would have been a burden, were in reality an assistance to her.

Jane was a bright and beautiful child, with dark silky hair, pleasant eyes, and lips like the damp petals of a red rose. She was, withal, a tidy, active little maiden, and, as Mrs. Derwent was wont to say, "saved grandma a great many steps" by running to the spring for water, winding *quills*, and doing what Miss Sedgwick calls the "odds and ends of housework."

Jane led a pleasant life on the island. She was a frank, mirthful creature, and it suited her to paddle her canoe on the bosom of the river, or even to urge it down the current, when "grandma" wanted a piece of cloth carried to the village, or was anxious to procure tea and other delicacies for her household.

When Mrs. Derwent's quill-box was full, and "the work all done up," Jane might be found clambering among the wild rocks, which frowned along the eastern shore, looking over the face of some bold precipice at her image reflected in the stream below; or, perchance, perched in the foliage of a grape-vine, with her rosy face peering out from the leaves, and her laugh ringing merrily from cliff to cliff, while her little hands showered down the purple clusters to her sister below.

Such was Jane Derwent, at the age of fourteen; but poor little Mary Derwent! nature grew more and more cruel to her. While each year endowed her sister with new beauty and unclouded cheerfulness, she, poor delicate thing, was kept instinctively from the notice of her fellow-creatures. The inmates of that little cabin could not bear that strange eyes should gaze on her deformity—for it was this deformity which had ever made the child an object of such tender interest.

From her infancy the little girl had presented a strange mixture of the hideous and the beautiful. Her oval face, with its marvellous symmetry of features, might have been the original from which Dubufe drew the chaste and heavenly features of Eve, in his picture of the "Temptation." The same sweetness and purity was there, but the expression was chastened and melancholy. Her soft blue eyes were always sad, and almost always moist; the lashes drooped over them, an expression of languid misery. A smile seldom brightened her mouth—the same mournful expression of hopelessness sat forever on that calm, white forehead; the faint color would often die away from her cheek, but it seldom deepened there.

Mary was fifteen before any person supposed her conscious of her horrible malformation, or was aware of the deep sensitiveness of her nature. The event which brought both to life occurred a few years after the death of her father. Both the children had been sent to school, and her first trial came on the clearing, before the little log schoolhouse of the village. Mary was chosen into the centre of the merry ring by Edward Clark, a bright-eyed, handsome boy, with manners bold and frank almost to carelessness.

The kind-hearted boy drew her gently into the ring, and joined the circle, without the laugh and joyous bound which usually accompanied his movements. There was an instinctive feeling of delicacy and tenderness towards the little girl which forbade all boisterous merriment when she was by his side. It was her turn to select a partner; she extended her hand timidly towards a boy somewhat older than herself—the son of a rich landholder in the valley; but young Wintermoot drew back with an insulting laugh, and refused to stand up with the *hunchback*.

Instantly the ring was broken up. Edward Clark leaped forward, and with a blow, rendered powerful by honest indignation, smote the insulter to the ground. For one moment Mary looked around bewildered, as if she did not comprehend the nature of the taunt; then the blood rushed up to her face, her soft blue eyes blazed with a sudden flash of fire, the little hand was clenched, and her distorted form dilated with passion. Instantly the blood flowed back upon her heart, her white lips closed over her clenched teeth, and she fell forward with her face upon the ground, as one stricken by unseen lightning.

The group gathered around her, awe-stricken and afraid. They could not comprehend this fearful burst of passion in a creature habitually so gentle and sweet-tempered. It seemed as if the insolent boy had crushed her to death with a sneer.

Her brave defender knelt and raised her head to his bosom, tears of generous indignation still lingered on his burning cheek, and his form shook with scarcely abated excitement.

At length Mary Derwent arose with the calmness of a hushed storm upon her face, and turning to her inevitable solitude walked silently away.

There was something terrible in the look of anguish with which she left her companions, taking, as it were, a silent and eternal farewell of all the joys that belong to childhood. The coarse taunt of the boy had been a cruel revelation, tearing away all the tender shields and loving delusions with which home-affection had so long sheltered her. She did not know what meaning lay in the word hunchback, but felt, with a sting of unutterable shame, that it was applied to her because she was unlike other girls. That she must never be loved as they were—never hope to be one of them again.

The school-children looked on this intense passion with silent awe. Even Jane dared not utter the sympathy that filled her eyes with tears, or follow after her sister.

So with terror and shame at the cruel discovery at her heart, Mary went away. The blood throbbed in her temples and rushed hotly through all her veins. An acute sense of wrong seized upon her, and thirsting to be alone she fled to the woods like a hunted animal, recoiling alike from her playfellows and her home.

Through the thick undergrowth and over wild rocks the poor creature tore her way, struggling and panting amid the thorny brushwood, as if life and death depended upon her progress.

A striped squirrel ran along the boughs of a chestnut-tree and peered down upon her from among the long green leaves and tassel-like blossoms. A flush came to her beautiful forehead, and with a cry that seemed in itself a pang, she tore up a stone to fling at it. The squirrel started away, uttering a broken noise that fell upon her sore heart like a taunt. Why did the little creature follow her? Why did it bend those sharp, black eyes upon her, with its head turned so mockingly upon one side? Was she never to be alone? Was the cruel animal still gibing at her through the chestnut-leaves?

The squirrel darted from bough to bough, and at last ran down the trunk of the chestnut. Mary followed it with eager glances till her eyes fell upon the root of the tree. The stone dropped from her hand, the angry color fled from her face, and stretching out her arms with a cry that perished on her lips she waited for the missionary to descend.

He came rather quickly, and the gentle serenity of his countenance was disturbed, but still a look of unutterable goodness rested upon it. When he reached Mary her eyes were flooded with tears, and she trembled from head to foot. *His* sympathy she could endure. His very look had opened the purest fountains of her heart again. She was not altogether alone.

"Crying, Mary, crying?" he said, in a tone of inquiry, rather than of reproach. "Who has taught you to weep?"

"Oh! father, father, what can I do? Where can I hide myself?" cried the poor girl, lifting her clasped hands piteously upward.

The missionary saw it all. For a moment the color left his lips, and his eyes were full of trouble to their azure depths. He sat down by her side, and drew her gently towards him.

"And this has driven you so far from home?" he said, smoothing her hair with one hand, which trembled among the golden tresses, for never had his sympathies been drawn more powerfully forth. "Who has done this cruel thing, Mary?"

She did not answer, but he felt a shudder pass over her frame as she made a vain effort to speak.

"Was it your playfellows at school?"

"I shall never have playfellows again," broke from the trembling lips which seemed torn apart by the desolating words; "never again, for where does another girl like me live in the world? God has made no playfellow for me!"

The missionary allowed her to weep. He knew that a world of bitterness would be carried from her bosom with those tears.

"But God has made us for something better than playfellows to each other," he said at last, taking her little hand in his.

She looked at him wistfully, and answered with unutterable sadness, "But I cannot be even that; I am alone!"

"No," answered the missionary, "not alone—not alone, though you never heard another human voice—even here in the deep woods you would find something to love and help, too—never think yourself alone, Mary, while any creature that God has made is near."

"But who will love *me*? Who will help *me*?" cried the girl, with a burst of anguish.

"Who will love you, Mary! Do not I love you? Does not your grandmother and sister love you?"

"But now—now that they know about this—that I am a hunchback, it will be all over."

"But they have known it, Mary, ever since you were a little child. Well, well! we must not talk about it, but think how much every one at home has loved you."

"And they knew it all—they saw it while I was blind, and loved me still," murmured the girl, while great tears of gratitude rolled down her cheeks, "and they will love me always just the same—you promise me this?"

"Always the same, Mary!"

"Yes, yes—I see they have loved me always, more than if I were ever so beautiful—they were sorry for me; I understand!" There was a sting of bitterness in her voice. The love which came from compassion wounded her.

"But our Saviour loves his creatures most for this very reason. Their imperfections and feebleness appeal like an unuttered prayer to him. It is a beautiful love, Mary, that which strength gives to dependence, for it approaches nearest to that heavenly benevolence which the true soul always thirsts for."

Mary lifted her eyes to his face as he spoke. The unshed tears trembled like diamonds within them. She became very thoughtful, and drooped slowly downward, coloring faintly beneath his eyes, as maidens sometimes blush at their own innocent thoughts when nothing but the eye of God is upon them.

"But there is another love, my father; I have seen it at the school and in the cabins, I have watched it as I have the mountain flowers, and thought that God meant this love for me, like the rest; but when I go among other girls, no one will ever think that I am one of them—no one but Edward Clark, and he only feels pity-love for me; to all the rest I am a hunchback."

A look of great trouble came upon the face of the missionary. For some moments he did not answer, and the poor girl drooped by his side. The blush faded from the snow of her forehead, and she trembled all over with vague shame of the words she had spoken. His silence seemed like a reproach to her.

"My child!"—oh! with what holy sweetness the words fell from his lips—"my child, it is true; this love must never be yours."

"Never!" echoed the pale lips of the child. "Never!"

"This dream of love, give it up, Mary, while it is but a dream," added the missionary, in a firmer voice. "To many more than yourself it is a hope never, never realized. Do not struggle for it—do not pine for it—God help you! child—God help us all!"

The anguish in his voice thrilled her to the soul. She bent her forehead meekly to his knee, murmuring:

"I will try to be patient—but, oh! do not look at me so mournfully."

He laid his hands softly under her forehead, and, lifting her face to his gazed mournfully upon it, as if his soul were looking far away through her eyes into the dim past.

"Father, believe me, I will try."

His hands dropped downward at the sound of her voice, and his lips began to move, as if unuttered words were passing through them. Mary knew that he was praying, and her face drooped reverently downward. When or how this silence broke into words she never knew, but over her soul went the burning eloquence of his voice, carried heavenward by prayer—by the wind, and the rush of the mountain stream. The very breath lay still upon her lips as she listened, and she felt more like a winged angel close to the gate of heaven than the poor deformed girl, whose soul had, a few hours before, been so full of bitterness.

CHAPTER III
THE FOREST WALK

When the missionary arose from his knees—for to that position he had unconsciously fallen—Mary stood beside him, quiet and smiling.

"Come, my child," he said, taking Mary by the hand, and leading her up from the ravine. "It is almost night, and you have wandered far from the island; see, the woods are already dusky. The birds and squirrels are settling down in the leaves; you would have been afraid to go home in the dark."

"I might have been lost, but not afraid," answered Mary, in a sad voice; "after this, darkness will be my best friend."

"But the forest is full of Indians, Mary, and now, since the English have excited them against us, no white person is safe after dark; I will go home with you; but, after this, promise me never to come alone to the woods again."

"The Indians will not harm me," answered Mary, with a mournful smile; "they pity me, I think, and love me a little, too. I am not afraid of them; their tomahawks are not so sharp as Jason Wintermoot's words were this morning."

As she spoke there was a rustling among the bushes at their right, and through the purple gloom of the woods they saw a group of Indians crouching behind a rock, and glaring at them through the undergrowth. One had his rifle lifted with a dusky hand, creeping towards the rock; the others were poised for a spring. Mary saw them, and leaped upon a rock close by, protecting the missionary from the aim taken at his life.

"Not him—not him!" she cried, flinging up both arms in wild appeal; "shoot *me*! You don't know how I long to die."

The Indians looked at each other in dismay. The threatening rifle fell with a clang upon the rock, and instead of an assault the savages crept out from their ambush, lighting up the dusky ravine with their gorgeous war-dresses, and gathered around the young girl, like a flock of tropical birds surrendering themselves to the charms of a serpent.

Mary met them fearlessly; a wild, spiritual beauty lighted up her face. The Indians lost their ferocity, and looked on her with grave tenderness; one of them reached forth his hand, she laid hers in the swarthy palm, where it rested like a snowdrop on the brown earth; he looked down upon it, and smiled; her courage charmed him.

"The white bird is brave, the Great Spirit folds his wing over her which is pure like the snow," he said, addressing his companions in their own language.

Mary knew a little of the Shawnee tongue, and looking up at the savage said, very gently:

"Why harm my father? The Great Spirit covers him, also, with a wing which is broad and white, like the clouds. Look in his face. Is he afraid?"

The Indians drew back, and looked fiercely at the missionary, gathering up their rifles with menacing gestures.

He understood their language well, and spoke to them with that calm self-possession which gives dignity to courage.

"My children," he said, "what wrong have I done that you should wish to kill me?"

The leading savage set down his gun with a clang upon the rock.

"You have sat by the white man's council-fire down yonder. The Great Father over the big water is our friend, but you hate the Indian, and will help them drive us through the wind gap into strange hunting grounds."

"I am not your enemy. See, I carry no tomahawk or musket; my bosom is open to your knives. The Great Spirit has sent me here, and He will keep me free from harm."

Unconsciously the missionary looked at the deformed girl as he spoke. The Indians followed his glance, and changed their defiant gestures.

"He speaks well. Mineto has sent his beautiful medicine spirit to guard him from our rifles. The medicine father of the Shawnees is dead, his lodge is empty. The white bird shall be our prophet. You shall be her brother, live in the great Medicine Lodge, and dream our dreams for us when we take the warpath. Do we speak well?"

The missionary pondered a moment before he spoke. He read more in these words than one not acquainted with Indian customs might have understood.

"Yes," he said at last, "I will come to your Medicine Lodge, and tell you all the dreams which the Great Spirit sends to me. She, too, will love the

Indians, and dream holy dreams for them, but not here, not in the Medicine Lodge. She must stay in Monockonok among the broken waters. The Great Spirit has built her lodge there, under the tall trees, where the Indians can seek her in their canoes. Go back to your council-fire, my children, before its smoke goes out. I will light the calumet, and smoke with you. Now the Great Spirit tells me to go with this child back to Monockonok. Farewell."

He took Mary Derwent by the hand, turned his back on the menacing rifles without fear, and walked away unmolested.

Mary had wandered miles away from home; nothing but the superior knowledge of her guardian could have found her way back through all that dense and unequal forest. It was now almost nightfall; but a full moon had risen, and by its light this man, accustomed to the woods, guided their way back towards the river. But after the wildest of her excitement had worn away, Mary began to feel the toil of her long walk. She did not complain, however, and the missionary was unconscious of this overtax of strength till she sank down on a broken fragment of rock utterly exhausted. He stopped in great distress, and bent over her. She smiled, and attempted to speak, but the pale lids drooped over her eyes, and the strength ebbing completely from her limbs left them pale and limp. She lay before him entirely senseless, with the moonbeams falling over her like a winding-sheet.

Nothing but the angels of Heaven could see or understand the look of unutterable thankfulness which came to his noble features as the missionary stooped and took the young girl in his arms. A smile luminous as the moonlight that played upon it stole over his whole face, and the words that broke from his lips were sweet and tender, such as the Madonna might have whispered to her holy child.

He took no pains to bring her back to life, but when she did come to, soothed her with hushes, and laid her head tenderly upon his shoulder till she fell asleep, smiling like himself.

As he came in sight of Monockonok a swell of regretful tenderness swept all his strength away more surely than fatigue could have done. He sat down upon a fallen tree on the bank just opposite the island and looked down into the sweet face with a gaze of heavenly affection. His head drooped slowly down, he folded her closer, and pressed his lips upon the closed eyes, the forehead, the lips, and cheeks of the sleeping child with a passion of tenderness that shook his whole frame.

"Oh, my God, my God! forgive me if this is sinful! my soul aches under this excess of love; the very fountains of my life are breaking up! Father of heaven, I am thine, all thine, but she is here on my breast, and I am but human."

Deep sobs broke away from his heart, almost lifting her from his bosom; tears rained down his face, and dropped thick and fast amid the waves of her hair.

His sobs aroused Mary from her slumber. She was not quite awake, but stirred softly and folded her arms about his neck. How the strong man trembled under the clasp of those arms! how he struggled and wrested against the weakness that had almost overpowered him, and not in vain! A canoe was moored under a clump of alders, just below him. It belonged to the island, and in that Mary must be borne to her home. He was obliged to row the canoe, and of course must awake her. Once more he pressed his lips upon her face, once more he strained her to his heart, and then with loving violence aroused her.

"Mary—come, little one, wake up, wake up! See how late it is! Grandmother will be frightened."

"Let me alone—oh! please let me alone!" murmured the weary child.

"No, Mary, arouse yourself; you and I have slept and dreamed too long. There, there! look around. See how the moonlight ripples upon the river! Look at the island; there is a light burning in the cabin. They are anxious no doubt at your long stay. Come, child, let us be strong: surely you can walk to the river's brink."

Yes, Mary could walk again; that sweet sleep had given back her strength. She sat down in the canoe, tranquilized and happier than she had ever hoped to be again. The bitterness of the morning had entirely passed away. They floated on down the river a few minutes. Then the missionary bent to his oars, and the canoe shot across the silvery rapids, and drew up in a little cove below the house.

The missionary stepped on shore. Mary followed him.

"Are you happier now? Are you content to live as God wills it?" he said, extending his hand, while his eyes beamed upon her.

"Yes, father, I am content."

"To live even without earthly love?"

Mary shrunk within herself—it takes more than a few words, a struggle, or a single prayer to uproot a desire for human love from a woman's heart.

He did not reason with her, or upbraid her then, but only said:

"God will find a way—have no fear, all human beings have some road to happiness if they will but let the Heavenly Father point it out. Good-night Mary."

"Good-night," responded the young girl, while her eyes filled with grateful tears; "good-night, my father!"

He turned around, laid his hands on her head, and blessed her, then stepped into the canoe and disappeared along the path of silver cast downward by the moon. The young girl smiled amid her tears. How dark it was when he found her at noontide; how bright when he went away!

Mary Derwent entered that log-cabin a changed being. She scarcely understood herself, or anything that had filled her life up to that day. Her own nature was inexplicable. One great shock had thrust her forward, as it were, to a maturity of suffering; her smile became mournful and sad in its expression, as if the poor creature had become weary of life and of all living things. She never again joined in the childish sports of her companions.

CHAPTER IV
THE ISLAND COVE

The two sisters stood together under the willow trees that overhung the little cove from which Mary had landed with the missionary three years before. Both had grown into girlhood since then, and both had improved in loveliness; Jane in the bloom and symmetry of her person—Mary in that exquisite loveliness of countenance which touches the soul like music in a sound, or tints in a picture. Jane Derwent was just seventeen years old that day.

"And so you *will* go, Mary, dear—though this is my birthday? I have a great mind to cut the canoe loose and set it adrift."

"And then how will your company get to the island?" said Mary Derwent, raising her eyes to the blooming face of her sister, while a quiet smile stole out from their blue depths.

"I don't care for company! I don't care for anything—you are so contrary—so hateful. You *never* stay at home when the young folks are coming—it's too bad!" And Jane flung herself on the grass which surrounded the little cove where a bark canoe lay rocking in the water, and indulged her petulance by tearing up the strawberry-vines which her sister had planted there.

"Don't spoil my strawberry-bed," said Mary, bending over the wayward girl and kissing her forehead. "Come, be good-natured and let me go; I will bring you some honeysuckle-apples, and a whole canoe full of wood-lilies. Do say yes; I can't bear to see you discontented to-day!"

"I would not care about it so much—though it is hard that you will never go to frolics, nor enjoy yourself like other folks—but Edward Clark made me promise to keep you at home to-day."

A color, like the delicate tinting of a shell, stole into Mary's cheek as it lay caressingly against the rich damask of her sister's.

"If no one but Edward were coming I should be glad to stay," she replied, in a soft voice; "but you have invited a great many, haven't you? Who will be here from the village?"

Jane began to enumerate the young men who had been invited to her birthday party; they held precedence in her heart, and consequently in her speech; for, to own the truth, Jane Derwent was a perfect specimen of the rustic coquette; a beauty, and a spoiled one; but a warm-hearted, kind girl notwithstanding.

"There are the Ward boys, and John Smith, Walter Butler from the fort, and Jason Wintermoot— —"

Jane stopped, for she felt a shiver run over the form around which her arms were flung as she pronounced the last name and saw the cheek of her sister blanch to the whiteness of snow.

"I had forgotten," she said, timidly, after a moment; "I am sorry I asked him. You are not angry with me, Mary, are you?"

"Angry? No! I never am angry with you, Jane. I don't want to refuse you anything on your birthday—but I will not meet these people. You cannot guess—you can have no idea of my sufferings when any one looks upon me except those I love very, very dearly."

"That is just what they say," replied Jane, while a flush of generous feeling spread over her forehead.

"What, who says?" inquired Mary, for her heart trembled with a dread that some allusion was threatened to her person.

After her question there was a moment's silence. They had both arisen, and the deformed girl stood before her sister with a tremulous lip and a wavering, anxious eye.

Jane was quick-witted, and, with many faults, very kind of heart. When she saw the distress visible in her unfortunate sister's face she formed her reply with more of tact and kind feeling than with strict regard to truth.

"Why, it is nothing," she said; "the girls always loved you, and petted you so much when we were little children in school together that they don't like it when you go away without seeing them. They think that you are grown proud since you have taken to reading and talking fine language. You don't have to work like the rest of us, and they feel slighted, and think you put on airs."

Tears stole into the eyes of the deformed girl, and a sudden light, the sunshine of an affectionate heart, broke over her face as she said:

"It is not that, my sister. I have loved them very much all these years that I have not seen them; but since that day— — Sister, you are very good; and, oh! how beautiful; but you cannot dream how a poor creature like myself feels when happy people are enjoying life together. Without sympathy, without companions, hunchbacked and crooked. Tell me, Jane, am I not hideous to look upon?"

This was the first time in her life that Mary had permitted a consciousness of her malformation to escape her in words. The question was put in a voice of mingled agony and bitterness, wrung from the very depths of her heart. She fell upon the grass as she spoke, and with her face to the ground lay grovelling at her sister's feet, like some wounded animal; for now that the loveliness of her face was concealed her form seemed scarcely human.

All that was generous in the nature of Jane Derwent swelled in her heart as she bent over her sister. The sudden tears fell like rain, glistening in drops upon the warm damask of her cheeks and filling her voice with affectionate sobs as she strove to lift her from the ground; but Mary shrunk away with a shudder, and kneeling down Jane raised her head with gentle violence to her bosom.

"Hideous! Oh! Mary, how can you talk so? Don't shake and tremble in this manner. You are not frightful nor homely; only think how beautiful your hair is. Edward Clark says he never saw anything so bright and silky as your curls he said so; indeed he did, Mary; and the other day when he was reading about Eve, in the little book you love so well, he told grandmother that he fancied Eve must have had a face just like yours."

"Did Edward say this?" murmured the poor deformed one as Jane half-lifted, half-persuaded her from the ground, and with one arm flung over her neck was pressing the face she had been praising to her own troubled bosom.

Poor Mary, though naturally tall, was so distorted that when she stood upright her head scarcely reached a level with the graceful bust of her sister, and Jane stooped low to plant reassuring kisses upon her forehead.

"Did he say it, Mary? Yes, he certainly did; and so did I say it. Look here." And eagerly gathering the folds of a large shawl over the shoulders of the deformed, she gently drew her to the brink of the basin, where the canoes still lay moored. "Look there!" she exclaimed, as they bent together over the edge of the green sward; "can you wish for anything handsomer than that face? Dear, good Mary, look."

An elm-tree waved its branches over them, and the sunshine came shimmering through the leaves with a wavy light. The river was tranquil as a summer sky, and the sisters were still gazing on the lovely faces speaking to theirs from its clear depths, when a canoe swept suddenly round the grassy promontory which formed one side of the cove.

With a dash of the oar the fairy skiff shot, like an arrow, into the basin, and its occupant, a young man of perhaps two-and-twenty, leaped upon the green sward. The sisters started from their embrace. A glad smile dimpled the round cheek of the younger as she stepped forward to meet the newcomer. But Mary drew her shawl more closely over her person, and shrunk timidly back, with a quickened pulse, a soft welcome beaming from her eyes, and her face deluged with a flood of soft, rosy color, which she strove to conceal with the tresses that fell about her like a golden mist.

"I have just come in time to keep you at home for once," said the youth, approaching the timid girl, after having gaily shaken hands with her sister. "I am sure we shall persuade you— —"

He was interrupted by a call from Jane, who had run off to the other side of the cove; no doubt with the hope of being speedily followed by her visitor.

"Come here, Edward, do, and break me some of this sweet-brier; it scratches my fingers so."

Clark dropped Mary's hand and went to obey this capricious summons.

"Don't try to persuade Mary to stay," said Jane, as she took a quantity of the sweet-brier from the hands of her companion. "She is as restless when we have company as the mocking-bird you gave us; and which we never could tame, besides," she added, with a little hesitation, "Wintermoot will be here, and she don't like him."

"It were strange if she did," replied the youth; and a frown passed over his fine forehead; "but, tell me, Jane, how it happened that you invited Col. Butler when you know that I dislike him almost as much as she does Wintermoot."

Jane looked confused and, like most people when they intend to persist in a wrong, began to get into a passion.

"I am sure I thought I had the right to ask any one I pleased," she said, petulantly and gathering her forehead into a frown.

"Yes, but one might expect that it would scarcely please you to encourage a man who has so often insulted your house with unwelcome visits; and Wintermoot—my blood boils when I think of the wretch! Poor Mary! I had hoped to see her enjoy herself to-day; but now she must wander off alone as usual. I have a great mind to go with her."

And turning swiftly away from the angry beauty, Clark went to Mary, spoke a few words, and they stepped into his canoe together. But he had scarcely pushed it from the shore when Jane ran forward and leaped in after them.

"If *you* go, so will *I*!" she said angrily, seating herself in the bottom of the canoe.

Mary was amazed and perplexed. She looked into the stern, displeased face of the young man, and then at the sullen brow of her sister.

"What does this mean?" she inquired, gently; "what is the matter, Jane?"

Jane began to sob, but gave no answer, and they rowed across the river in silence. The canoe landed at the foot of a broken precipice that hung over the river like a ruined battlement. Clark assisted Mary to the shore, and was about to accompany her up the footpath, which wound over the precipice, but Jane, who had angrily refused his help to leave the boat, began to fear that she had carried her resentment too far, and timidly called him back.

A few angry words from the young man—expostulation and tears from the maiden, all of which a bend in the path prevented Mary observing; and then Clark went up the hill—told the solitary girl not to wander far—to be careful and not sit on the damp ground—and that he would come for her by sundown; the young folks would have left the island by that time. They were all going down to Wilkesbarre, to have a dance in the schoolhouse. He and Jane were going, but they would wait and take her home first.

Edward was almost out of breath as he said all this, and he appeared anxious to go back to the canoe. But Mary had not expected him to join her lonely wanderings, and his solicitude about her safety, so considerate and kind, went to her heart like a breath of summer air. She turned up the mountain-path, lonely and companionless; but very happy. Her eyes were full of pleasant tears, and her heart was like a flower unfolding to the sunshine. There is pleasure in complying with the slightest request from those we love; and Mary confined her ramble to the precipice and the shore, merely because Edward Clark had asked her not to wander far. She saw him land on the island with her sister while half-sitting, half-reclining on a crag of the broken rock, at whose foot she had landed. She saw the boat sent again and again to the opposite shore, returning each time laden with her former companions.

She was aroused by the rustling of branches over her head, followed by a bounding step, as of a deer in flight; then a young girl sprang out upon a point of rock which shot over the platform on which she lay, and bending over the edge gazed eagerly down upon the river.

Mary held her breath and remained motionless, for her poetical fancy was aroused by the singular and picturesque attitude of the figure. There was a wildness and grace in it which she had never witnessed before. At the first glance she supposed the stranger to be a wandering Indian girl belonging to some of the tribes that roamed the neighboring forests. But her complexion, though darker than the darkest brunette of our own race, was still too light for any of the savage nations yet seen in the wilderness. It was of a clear, rich, brown, and the blood glowed through the round cheeks like the blush on a ripe peach.

Her hair was long, profusely braided, and of a deep black; not the dull, lustreless color common to the Indians; but with a bloom upon it like that shed by the sunlight on the wing of a flying raven. She appeared to be neither Indian nor white, but of a mixed race. The spirited and wild grace of the savage was blended with a delicacy of feature and nameless elegance more peculiar to the whites. In her dress, also, might be traced the same union of barbarism and refinement—a string of bright scarlet berries encircling her head, and interwoven with the long braids of her hair, glanced in the sunlight as she moved her head, like a chain of dim rubies.

A robe of gorgeous chintz, where crimson and deep brown were the predominating colors, was confined at the waist by a narrow belt of wampum, and terminated a little below the knee in a double row of heavy fringe, leaving the flexible and slender ankles free and uncovered. Her robe fell open at the shoulders; but the swelling outline of her neck, thus exposed, was unbroken, except by a necklace of cherry-colored cornelian, from which a small heart of the same blood-red stone fell to her bosom. The round and tapering beauty of her arms was fully revealed and unencumbered by a single ornament. Her moccasins were of dressed deer-skin, fringed and wrought with tiny beads, interwoven with a vine of silk buds and leaves done in such needlework as was, in those days, only taught to the most refined and highly educated class of whites. Mary had never seen anything so exquisitely beautiful in its workmanship as that embroidery, or so brightly picturesque as the whole appearance of the stranger.

For more than a minute the wild girl retained the position assumed by her last bounding step. There was something statue-like in the tension of those rounded and slender limbs as she stood on the shelf of rock, bending eagerly over the edge, with her weight thrown on one foot and the other strained back, as if preparing for a spring. All the grace, but not the chilliness, of marble lived in those boldly poised limbs, so full of warm, healthy life. There was spirit and fire in their very repose, for after an eager glance up and down the river she settled back, and with her arms folded remained for a moment in an attitude of dejection and disappointment.

A merry laugh which came ringing over the waters from the island drew her attention to the group of revellers glancing in and out of the shrubbery which surrounded Mother Derwent's dwelling. Flinging back her hair with a gesture of fiery impatience, she sprang upward and dragged down the branch of a young tree, which she grasped for support while throwing herself still more boldly over the very edge of the cliff.

Mary almost screamed with affright. But there was something grand in the daring of the girl, which aroused her admiration even more than her fear. She knew that the breaking of that slender branch would precipitate her down a sheer descent into the river. But she felt as if the very sound of a human voice would startle her into eternity.

Motionless with dread, she fixed her eyes, like a fascinated bird, on the strange being thus hovering over death, so fearless and so beautiful. All at once those bright, dark eyes kindled, one arm was flung eagerly outward— her red lips parted and a gush of music, like the song of a mocking-bird, but louder and richer, burst from them.

Mary started forward in amazement. Before she could lift her eyes to the cliff again, a low, shrill whistle came sharply up from the direction of the island. She caught one glance of those kindling cheeks and flashing eyes as the strange, wild girl leaped back from the cliff—a gleam of sunlight on her long hair as she darted into a thicket of wild cherry trees—and there was no sign of her remaining, save a rushing sound of the young trees, as the bent limb swayed back to its fellows. Again the notes, as of a wild, eager bird, arose from a hollow bank on the side of the mountain; and, after a moment, that shrill whistle was repeated from the water, and Mary distinctly heard the dipping of an oar.

She crept to the edge of the rock which had formed her concealment and looked down upon the river. A canoe rowed by a single oarsman was making its way swiftly to the island. She could not distinguish the face of the occupant; but there was a band of red paint around the edge of the canoe, and she remembered that Edward Clark's alone was so ornamented. It was the same that had brought her from the island. Did the signal come from him—from Edward Clark? What had he in common with the wild, strange girl who had broken upon her solitude? A thrill of pain, such as she had never dreamed of before, shot through her heart as she asked these questions. She would have watched the landing of the canoe, but all strength suddenly left her, and she sunk upon a fragment of stone, almost powerless and in extreme suffering.

In a little more than an hour she saw the same solitary rower crossing the river, but with more deliberate motion. She watched him while he moored the canoe in the little cove, and caught another glimpse of him as he turned a corner of her dwelling and mingled with the group of young persons who were drinking tea on the green sward in front.

It was a weary hour to the deformed girl before the party broke up and were transported to the opposite shore, where farm-wagons stood ready to convey them to Wilkesbarre. The sun was almost down, and the island quiet again when she saw two persons coming from the house to the cove. She arose, and folding her shawl about her prepared to descend to the shore.

Mary had walked half-way down the ledge when she stopped abruptly in the path; for sitting on the moss beneath one of these pines was the strange girl who had so excited her wonder. Mary's slow step had not disturbed her, and unconscious of a witness she was unbraiding the string of berries from her hair and supplying their place with a rope of twisted coral. The strings of scarlet ribbon with which she knotted it on her temple were bright, and had evidently never been tied before.

Mary's heart beat painfully and she hurried forward, as if some fierce animal had sprung up in her path. An uncontrollable repulsion to that wild and beautiful girl, which she neither understood nor tried to account for, seized her. When she reached the shore the canoe with Edward Clark and her sister seated in it was making leisurely towards the mouth of the ravine, and she sat down on the shadowy side of an oak, to await their coming. Their approach was so noiseless that she did not know they had reached the shore till the voice of Edward Clark apprised her of it. He was speaking earnestly to her sister, and there was both agitation and deep tenderness in his voice—a breaking forth of the heart's best feelings, which she had never witnessed in him before.

"No, Jane," he said, in a resolute voice, shaken with a sorrowful tremor; "you must now choose between that man and me; there can be nothing of rivalry between us; I heartily despise him! I am not jealous—I could not be a creature so unworthy; but it grieves me to feel that you can place him for a moment on a level with yourself. If you persist in this degrading coquetry you are unworthy of the love which I have given you. Forgive me, Jane, if I speak harshly; don't cry—it grieves me to wound your feelings, but——"

He was interrupted by a sound as of some one falling heavily to the ground. He leaped from the canoe, and there, behind the great oak, lay Mary Derwent helpless and insensible.

"She has wandered too far, and exhausted herself," said the agitated young man as he bore her to the canoe. "Sit down, Jane, and take her head in your lap—your grandmother will know what to do for her."

Jane reached forth her arms and received the insensible head on her bosom. She turned her face petulantly away from that of her lover, and repulsed him with sullen discontent when, in his attempts to restore Mary, his hand happened to touch hers.

"Set her down," she said, pushing him indignantly away. "Attend to your oars; we neither want your help or your ill-natured grumblings. I tell you, Ned Clark, you are just the Grossest creature I ever saw. Take that for your pains!"

Clark did not answer this insolent speech, but gravely took up the oars and pushed off.

They were half-way across the river when Mary began to recover animation. Edward laid down his oar, and taking her hand in his was about to speak, but she drew it away with a faint shudder, and burying her face in her sister's bosom remained still and silent as before.

CHAPTER V
THE TEMPTER AND THE TEMPEST

Tahmeroo, the Indian girl, was sitting under the pine as Mary Derwent had left her. With the coral but half twisted in her hair, she had paused in her graceful task, and sinking gently back to the bank of moss which formed her seat reclined on one elbow, with her long tresses unbraided and floating in wavy masses over her person. She was yielding to the repose of a soft and dreamy reverie—new and very sweet to her wild, young heart—when the sound of voices and the dash of an oar aroused her. She started to her feet and listened. The fire flashed back to those large dark eyes but late so pleasant and soft in their expression, and a rich crimson rushed to her cheek. The voices ceased for a moment; then were renewed, and the rapid beat of the paddle became still more audible.

Tahmeroo sprang forward and ran up to a point of the hill which commanded a view of the river. The little canoe, with its band of red paint, was making from the shore, and in it sat Jane Derwent, with the head of the deformed girl resting in her lap. The back of the oarsman was towards the shore; his head was bent, and the eyes, the beautiful eyes of Jane Derwent were fixed on him with an expression which Tahmeroo's heart, unlearned as it was, taught her to understand. A storm of surprise, anger and fear rushed through the heart of the young Indian. The oarsman turned his head, and the face was revealed. Then a smile, vivid and bright as a burst of sunshine after a tempest, broke over her features.

Tahmeroo breathed deeply and turned away. It seemed as if an arrow had been withdrawn from her heart by the sight of that face. She hurried down the hill towards a clump of black alders that overhung the river's brink and unmoored a light canoe hitherto concealed beneath the dark foliage. Placing herself in the bottom, she gave two or three vigorous strokes with the paddle, and shot like a bird up the stream.

As Tahmeroo proceeded up the river the scenery, till then half-pastoral, half-sublime, became more savage and gloomy in its aspect. Huge rocks shot up against the sky in picturesque grandeur; the foliage which clothed them grew dusky in the waning light and fell back to the ravines in dark, heavy shadows. A gloom hung about the towering precipices, and the thick masses of vegetation, like funeral drapery, swathing the pillars and wild arches of a monastic ruin. It was the darkness of a gathering tempest. There was something sublime and almost awful in the gradual and silent mustering of the elements.

Tahmeroo rested for a moment as she entered the rocky jaws of the mountain, and as her frail bark rocked to the current of wind which swept down the gorge she looked around with a feeling of hushed terror. A mountain, cleft in twain to the foundation, towered to the sky on either hand—bold, bleak and sombre. Through the rent, down hundreds of feet from the summit, crept the deep river stealthily and slow, like a huge serpent winding himself around the bulwark of a stronghold. The darkness of the forests was so dense, and the clouds so heavy, that there was nothing to distinguish the outline of the murky waters from the majestic ramparts through which they glided. All was wild, solemn and gloomy.

As the Indian girl looked upward the clouds swept back for a moment and the last rays of sunset fell with a glaring light on the bold summit of the mountain, rendering by contrast the depths of the chasm more dreary in its intense shadow

The threatened storm had seemingly passed over, and a few stars trembled in the depths of the sky when she moored her canoe in a little inlet, washed up into the mouth of a narrow ravine which opened on the river's brink.

Tahmeroo tore away the dry brambles and brushwood which clothed the entrance of the defile, and made her way through a scarcely defined footpath up the hillside. Through this ravine rushed a mountain torrent, known to the Indians as the Falling Spring, which filled the whole forest with its silvery tumult.

Tahmeroo kept close to the banks of this torrent, helping herself forward by the brushwood and trailing vines that grew thickly on its margin. Nothing less surefooted than an antelope could have forced a passage through the broken rocks and steep precipices which guarded the passage of this stream up to its source in Campbell's Ledge. A little way from the river it came, with a single leap, through a chasm in the rocks, and lost itself in a storm of white spray among the mossy boulders which choked up the ravine.

The storm had mustered again so blackly that Tahmeroo could scarcely see her course, but lost herself among the rocks and young pines below the fall. Still she climbed upward, leaping from rock to rock, till the sheer precipices that walled in the cataract on either side obstructed her passage, and she stood poised half-way up, uncertain which way to turn or how to move.

A flash of lightning revealed her position, kindled up the young trees to a lurid green; gave the slippery brown precipices to view, and shot in and out of the foaming torrent as it leaped by like flashes of fire, tearing a snowdrift into flakes again and scattering it to the wind.

The lightning revealed her peril and her path. She sprang back from the precipice, from which the next leap would have precipitated her downward with the cataract into the depths of the ravine, and tore her way into the bosom of the hills, keeping Campbell's Ledge on the right.

A less vigorous form would have fainted beneath the toil of that mountain-pass; but the young Indian scarcely thought of fatigue; for a dull, moaning sound came up from the depths of the forest, like the hollow beat of a far-off ocean; the pent-up thunder muttered and rumbled among the black clouds, floating like funeral banners above her, every other instant pierced and torn with arrowy lightning. These signs of the storm gathering so fearfully about the mountains terrified and bewildered the Indian girl. Though a wild rover of the forest, she had been gently nurtured, and for the first time in her life was alone among the hills after nightfall.

At length she stood on a high ledge of rocks, panting and in despair; she had lost the path that led to the Indian encampment, and found herself on the sweep of a mighty precipice, far above the valley. After one wild, hopeless look upon the sky, she sunk to the ground and, burying her face in her hands, muttered, in a trembling and husky voice:

"Tahmeroo has been wicked. She has acted a lie. The Great Spirit is very angry. Why should she strive to shut out his voice? Tahmeroo can die."

While she spoke there was a hush in the elements and the sound of many hoarse, guttural voices arose from the foot of the ledge. The terrified Indian lifted her head, and a wild, doubtful joy gleamed over her face as the lightning revealed it, with the damp, unbraided hair floating back from the pallid temples, the lips parted, and the eyes charged with terror, doubt and eager joy. She listened intently for a moment, then sunk cautiously to the ground as one who fears to break a pleasant delusion, and crept to the edge of the rock.

FALLING SPRING

A dozen watch-fires flashed up in a semicircle, flinging a broad light over the whole enclosure and gleaming redly on the waving vines, the weeping birches, and the budding hemlocks that intermingled along its broken ramparts. A hundred swarthy forms, half-naked and hideously painted, were moving about, and others lay crouching in the grass, apparently terrified by the tempest gathering so blackly above them.

The untrodden grass and fresh herbage told that this hollow had recently been made a place of encampment; yet, in the enclosure was one lodge, small and but rudely constructed—a sylvan hut, more picturesque than any cabin to be found in the settlements. How recently it had been constructed might be guessed by the green branches yet fresh on the half-hewn logs. A score of savage hands had been at work upon it the whole day, for the Chief of the Shawnees never rested in the open air with the lower members of his tribe when his fierce mother, his haughty wife, or beautiful daughter was of his hunting party.

Tahmeroo had wandered upward from the path which led to the encampment. She had madly clambered to the highest chain of rocks which surrounded the enclosure, when she should have made her way around its base to the opening which gave egress to the forest. She arose from the edge of the rock, where she had been lying, high above the encampment, and was about to descend to the path she had missed, when a sound like the roar and tramp of a great army came surging up from the forest. The tall trees swayed earthward, flinging their branches and green leaves to the whirlwind as it swept by. Heavy limbs were twisted off, and mighty trunks, splintered midway, mingled the sharp crash of their fall with the hoarse roar of the tempest. The thunder boomed among the rocks, peal after peal, and the quick lightning darted through the heaving trees like fiery serpents wrangling with the torn foliage.

The very mountain seemed to tremble beneath the maiden's feet. She threw herself upon the ledge, and with her face buried in its moss lay motionless, but quaking at heart, as the whirlwind rushed over her.

A still more fearful burst of the elements struck upon the heights, lifted a stout oak from its anchorage and hurled it to the earth. The splintered trunk fell with a crash, and the topmost boughs bent down the young saplings with a rushing sweep and fell like the wings of a great bird of prey, above the prostrate Indian. She sprang upward with a cry, and seizing the stem of a vine swung herself madly over the precipice. Fortunately the descent was rugged, and many a jutting angle afforded a foothold to the daring girl as she let herself fearlessly down—now clinging among the leaves of the vine—now grasping the sharp point of a rock, and dropping from one cleft to another. Twice she forced herself back, as if she would have sunk into the very rock, and dragged the heavy vines over her, when a fresh thunder-burst rolled by, or a flash of lightning blazed among the leaves; but when they had passed she again swung herself downward, and finally dropped unharmed upon the grass back of her father's lodge.

The enclosure was now perfectly dark; for the rain had extinguished the watch-fires and the lightning but occasionally revealed a group of dark forms cowering together, awed by the violence of the tempest, and rendered abject by superstitious dread.

A twinkling light broke through the crevices of the lodge; but Tahmeroo lingered in the rain, for now that the fierceness of the storm was over she began to have a new fear—the dread of her mother's stern presence. Cautiously, and with timid footsteps, she advanced to the entrance and lifted the huge bear-skin that covered it. She breathed freely; for there was no one present save her father, the great Chief of the Shawnees. He was sitting on the ground, with his arms folded on his knees, and his swarthy forehead buried in his robe of skins. The heart of the Indian King was sorely troubled, for he knew that the wing of the Great Spirit was unfolded in its wrath above his people.

Tahmeroo crept to the extremity of the lodge and sat down in silence upon the ground. She saw that preparations had been made for her comfort. A pile of fresh berries and a cake of cornbread lay on a stool nearby, and a couch of boughs woven rudely together stood in the corner heaped with the richest furs and overspread with a covering of martin-skins lined and bordered with fine scarlet cloth. A chain of gorgeous beadwork linked the deep scallops on the border, and heavy tassels fell upon the grass from the four corners. The savage magnificence of that couch was well worthy the daughter of a great chief.

Another couch, but of less costly furs, and without ornament, stood at the opposite extremity. Tahmeroo threw one timid look towards it, then bent her head, satisfied that it was untenanted, and that her mother was indeed absent. As if suddenly recollecting herself, she half-started from the ground and disentangled the string of coral from her damp hair. With her eyes fixed apprehensively on the chief, she thrust it under the fur pillows of her couch, and stole back to her former position.

Tahmeroo had scarcely seated herself when the bear-skin was flung back from the entrance of the lodge and Catharine, the wife of the Shawnee chief, presented herself in the opening. The light from a heap of pine knots fell on the woman's face as she entered; but it failed to reveal the maiden where she sat in the shadowy side of the lodge.

The chief lifted his head and uttered a few words in the Indian tongue, but received no answer; while his wife gave one quick look around the lodge, then sallied back, clasped her hands tightly and groaned aloud.

Tahmeroo scarcely breathed, for never had she seen her mother so agitated. It was, indeed, a strange sight—those small, finely cut features usually so stern and cold, working with emotion—the pallid cheek, the high forehead, swollen and knitted at the brows—the trembling mouth—the eyes heavy with anguish. This was a sight which Tahmeroo had never witnessed before. And this was the stern, haughty woman—the white Indian—who ruled the Shawnee braves with despotic rigor—whose revenge was deadly, and whose hate was a terror. This was Catharine Montour!

When Tahmeroo heard her name mingled with the lamentations of her mother, she started forward, exclaiming, with tremulous and broken earnestness: "Mother, oh! mother, I am here!"

A burst of fierce thanksgiving broke from the lips of Catharine. She caught her daughter to her heart and kissed her wildly again and again.

"Thank God, oh! thank my God! I am not quite alone!" she exclaimed; and tears started in the eyes that had not known them for twenty summers.

Without a word of question as to her strange absence, Catharine drew her child to the couch, and seeing the bread and the berries yet untasted she forced her to eat while she wrung the moisture from her hair and took away the damp robe. She smoothed the cushions of crimson cloth that served as pillows, and drawing the coverlet of martin-skins over the form of her child sat beside her till she dropped to a gentle slumber. Then she heaped fresh knots on the burning pine and changed her own saturated raiment.

The sombre chief threw himself upon the unoccupied heap of furs, and Catharine was left alone with her thoughts. Long and sad were the vigils of that stern watcher; yet they had a good influence on her heart. There was tenderness and regret—nay, almost repentance—in her bosom as she gazed on the slumbers of her child—the only being on earth whom she dared to love. More than once she pressed her lips fondly to the forehead of the sleeper, as if to assure herself of her dear presence after the frightful dangers of the storm. She remained till after midnight, pondering upon past events with the clinging tenacity of one who seldom allowed herself to dwell on aught that could soften a shade of her haughty character; at length she was about to throw herself by the side of her daughter, more from the workings of unquiet thoughts than from a desire for rest. But the attempt disturbed the slumbering girl. She turned restlessly on her couch, and oppressed by its warmth pushed away the covering.

Catharine observed that the cheek which lay against the scarlet cloth was flushed and heated. She attempted to draw the pillow away, when her fingers became entangled in the string of coral concealed beneath it. Had a serpent coiled around her hand it could not have produced a more startling effect. She shook it off, and drew hastily back, as if something loathsome had clung to her. Then she snatched up the ornament, went to the pile of smouldering embers, stirred them to a flame and examined it minutely by the light. Her face settled to its habitual expression of iron resolution as she arose from her stooping posture. Her lips were firmly closed, and her forehead became calm and cold; yet there was more of doubt and sorrow than of anger in her forced composure.

She returned to the couch and placed herself beside it, with the coral still clenched in her hand. Her face continued passionless, but her eyes grew dim as she gazed on the sleeper; thoughts of her own youth lay heavily upon her heart.

Tahmeroo again turned restlessly on her pillow, her flushed cheeks dimpled with a smile, and she murmured softly in her sleep. Catharine laid her hand on the round arm, flung out upon the martin-skins, and bent her ear close to the red and smiling lips, thus betraying with their gentle whisperings the thoughts that haunted the bosom of the sleeper.

Tahmeroo dreamed aloud. A name was whispered in her soft, broken English, coupled with words of endearment and gentle chiding. The name was spoken imperfectly, and Catharine bent her ear still lower, as if in doubt that she had heard aright. Again that name was pronounced, and now there was no doubt; the enunciation was low, but perfectly distinct. The mother started upright; her face was ashy pale, and she looked strangely corpse-like in the dusky light. She snatched a knife from its sheath in her girdle, and bent a fierce glance on the sleeper. A moment the blade quivered above the heart of her only child, then the wretched woman flung it from her with a gesture of self-abhorrence, and sinking to the ground buried her face in both hands. After one fierce shudder she remained motionless as a statue.

It was more than an hour before that stern face was lifted again; shade after shade of deep and harrowing agony had swept over it while buried in the folded arms, and now it was very pale, but with a gentler expression upon it. She laid a hand on the rounded shoulder, from which the covering had been flung, passed the other quickly over her eyes and awoke the sleeper.

"Tahmeroo," she said, but her voice was low and husky, and it died away in her throat.

The maiden started to her elbow and looked wildly about. When she saw her mother with the string of red coral in her hand she sunk back and buried her face in the pillow.

"Tahmeroo, look up!" said the mother, in a soft, low voice, from which all traces of emotion had flown. "Has Tahmeroo dreams which she does not tell her mother? The white man's gift is under her pillow—whence came it?"

A blush spread over the face, neck and bosom of the young girl, and she shrunk from the steady gaze of her mother. She was sensible of no wrong, save that of concealment; yet her confusion was painful as guilt. Catharine had compassion on her embarrassment, and turned away her eyes.

"Tahmeroo," she said, in a voice still more gentle and winning, "tell me all—am I not your mother? Do I not love you?"

The young Indian girl rose and looked timidly towards the couch of the Shawnee Chief.

"Does my father sleep?" and her eyes again fell beneath the powerful glance which she felt to be fixed upon her.

"Yes, he sleeps; speak in English, and have no fear."

Catharine went to the heap of blazing pine and flung ashes on it; then returned to her daughter, folded her to her bosom, and for half an hour the low voice of Tahmeroo alone broke the stillness of the lodge.

Scarcely had Catharine interrupted the confession of her child with a word of question. She must have been powerless from emotion, for more than once her breath came quick and gaspingly; and the heavy throbbing of her heart was almost audible at every pause in that broken narrative. Yet her voice was strangely cold and calm when she spoke.

"And you saw him again this day?"

"Yes, mother."

"Did he tell you to keep these meetings from my knowledge?"

"He said the Great Spirit would visit me with his thunder if I but whispered it to the wind."

"The name—tell me the name once more; but low, I would not hear it aloud. Whisper it in my ear—yet the hiss of a serpent were sweeter," she muttered.

Tahmeroo raised her lips to her mother's ear and whispered, as she was commanded. She felt a slight shudder creep over the frame against which she leaned, and all was still again.

"You *first* saw this—this man when we were at the encampment on the banks of Seneca Lake three moons since, and I was absent on a mission to Sir William Johnson: did I hear aright in this?" questioned the mother, after a few minutes of silence.

"It was there I first saw him, mother."

"Listen to me, Tahmeroo: were I to command you never again to see this man, could you obey me?"

The young Indian started from her mother's arms, and the fire of her dark eyes flashed even in the half-smothered light.

"Never see him? What, tear away all this light from my own heart? Obey? No, mother, no. Put me out from my father's lodge—make me a squaw of burden, the lowest woman of our tribe—give me to the tomahawk, to the hot fire—but ask me not to rend the life from my bosom. The white blood which my heart drank from yours must curdle that of the Indian when his child gives or takes love at the bidding of anything but her own will! No, mother, I could not obey—I would not."

Catharine Montour was struck dumb with astonishment. Was she, the despotic ruler of a fierce war-tribe, to be braved by her own child? The creature she had loved and cherished with an affection so deep and passionate—had *she* turned rebellious to her power? Her haughty spirit aroused itself; the gladiator broke from her eyes as they were bent on the palpitating and half-recumbent form of Tahmeroo.

The girl did not shrink from the fierce gaze, but met it with a glance of resolute daring. The young eaglet had begun to plume its wing! There was something of wild dignity in her voice and gesture, which assorted well with the curbless strength of her mother's spirit.

Catharine Montour had studied the human heart as a familiar book, and she knew that it would be in vain to contend with the spirit so suddenly aroused in the strength of its womanhood. She felt that her power over that heart must hereafter be one of love unmixed with fear—an imperfect and a divided power. The heart of the strong woman writhed under the conviction, but she stretched herself on the couch without a word of expostulation. Her own fiery spirit had sprung to rapid growth in the bosom of her child; passions akin to those buried in her experience had shot up, budded and blossomed, in a night time. The stern mother trembled when she thought of the fruit which, in her own life, had turned to ashes in the ripening.

When Tahmeroo awoke in the morning the lodge was empty. Her mother had left the encampment at early dawn.

CHAPTER VI
THE MISSIONARY'S CABIN

The history of Wyoming is interwoven with that of the Indian missionary whose paternal care had so long protected the family on Monockonok Island. Like Zinzendorf, his life was one errand of mercy, alike to the heathen and the believer. For years he had served as a link of union between the savage life of the woods and the civilization of the plains.

While a comparatively young man, he had come among the Six Nations nameless and unarmed, with his life in his hand, ready to live or die at his post. His home was in the wilderness; sometimes he passed through the white settlements, preached in their schoolhouses and slept in their cabins; but it was always as a guest; his mission lay with the forest children, and in the wilds where they dwelt was his home.

Almost the entire portion of years which had elapsed since his encounter with Mary Derwent in the hills, he had spent among the savages that kept possession of broad hunting grounds beyond the Wind Gap. But a movement of the tribes toward Wyoming, where a detachment of their own people from about Seneca Lake had been appointed to meet them in council, filled him with anxiety for his friends in the valley, and he came back also to watch over their safety. He knew what the settlers were ignorant of as yet—that the Shawnees were about to unite with the Tories, whose leader lay at Wintermoot Fort, and that great peril threatened the inhabitants of Wyoming in this union.

This man was alone in a log-cabin which Zinzendorf had once occupied on a curving bank of the Susquehanna, between Wilkesbarre and Monockonok Island. His face, always sad and merciful, now bore an anxious expression. The patient sweetness of his mouth was a little disturbed. He was pondering over the hostile attitude threatened by the Indians against the whites, and that subject could not be otherwise than a painful one.

The hut was small, and but for recent repairs would have been in ruins. It consisted only of one room. A deal-box stood in one corner, filled with books and rolls of manuscript. Two stools and a rude table, with a few cooking utensils, were the only remaining furniture. The missionary sat by the table, implements for writing were before him, and the pages of a worn Bible lay open, which, after a little while, he began to read.

It was a picture of holy thought and quiet study; but the crackling of branches and the sound of approaching footsteps interrupted its beautiful tranquillity.

The silvery flow of water from a spring close by was broken by the sound; the birds fluttered away from their green nestling places in the leaves, and a half-tamed fawn, which had been sleeping in a tuft of fern-leaves, started up, gazed a moment on the intruder with his dark, intelligent eye, and dashed up the river's bank as she crossed the threshold of the lowly dwelling.

The missionary looked up as the stranger entered, and a feeling of astonishment mingled with the graciousness which long habit had made a portion of his nature. He arose, and with a slight inclination of the head placed the stool, on which he had been sitting, for her accommodation.

The intruder bent her head in acknowledgment of the courtesy, but remained standing. She was a woman majestic in her bearing, of well-developed form, and somewhat above the middle height; her air was courtly and graceful, but dashed with haughtiness approaching to arrogance. She had probably numbered forty years; her face, though slightly sunbrowned, bore traces of great beauty, in spite of its haughty expression. The mouth had been accustomed to smiles in its youth, and though an anxious frown clouded the broad forehead, it was still beautifully fair. The missionary had spent his life amid the aristocracy of European courts, and had passed from thence to the lowly settlement, and to the still more remote Indian encampment; but there was something in the appearance of this strange woman that filled him with vague uneasiness, and he looked upon her with a sort of terror. Her air and dress were not strictly those of any class with which he had as yet become familiar. There was wildness mingled with the majesty of her presence, and her rich and picturesque attire partook at once of the court and the wigwam.

Her long, golden, and still abundant hair was wreathed in braids around her head, and surmounted by a small coronet of gorgeous feathers. A serpent of fine, scaly gold, the neck and back striped and variegated with minute gems, was wreathed about the mass of braids on one side of her head, and formed a knot of slender coils where it clasped the coronet. There was something startlingly like vitality in these writhing folds when the light struck them, and the jewelled head shot out from the feathers and quivered over the pale temple with startling abruptness. There was an asp-like glitter in the sharp, emerald eye, and the tiny jaw seemed full of subtle venom. It was a magnificent and rare ornament to be found in the solitude of an American forest; yet scarcely less remarkable than the remainder of the strange woman's apparel.

A robe of scarlet cloth, bordered with the blackest lynx fur, was girded at the waist by a cord of twisted silk, and fell back at the shoulders in lapels of rich black velvet. Above the fur border ran a wreath of embroidery, partly silk, partly wampum, but most exquisitely wrought in garlands of mountain flowers, with tiny golden serpents knotting them together and creeping downward, as it were, to hide themselves in the fur. It had loose, hanging sleeves, likewise lined with velvet, beneath which the white and still rounded arm gleamed out in strong contrast.

A serpent, mate to the one on her head, but glowing with still more costly jewels, coiled around the graceful swell of her right arm, a little below the elbow, but its brilliancy was concealed by the drapery of the sleeve, except when the arm was in motion. She wore elaborately wrought moccasins lined with crimson cloth, but the embroidery was soiled with dew, and the silken thongs with which they had been laced to the ankle had broken loose in the rough path through which she had evidently travelled.

The missionary stood by the table, while his visitor cast a hasty glance around the apartment and turned her eyes keenly on his face.

"I am not mistaken," she said, slowly withdrawing her gaze. "You are the godly man of whom our people speak—the Indian missionary?"

The man of God bent his head in reply.

"You should be, and I suppose are, an ordained minister of the church?" she resumed.

"I am, madam."

His voice was deep-toned and peculiarly sweet. The woman started as it met her ear; a gleam of unwonted expression shot over her features, and she fixed another penetrating glance on his face, as if some long-buried recollection had been aroused; then, satisfied with the scrutiny, she turned her eyes away, and drawing a deep breath spoke again.

"I ask no more than this; of what church matters little. But have you authority to perform marriages after the established law?"

"I have; but my services are seldom required. I mingle but little with the whites of the settlement, and Indians have their peculiar forms, which, to them, are alone binding,"

"True," replied the woman, with a slight wave of the hand; "these forms shall not be wanting; all the bonds of a Christian church and savage custom will scarcely yield me security."

She spoke as if unconscious of a second presence, and again abruptly addressed the missionary.

"Your services are needed in the Shawnee encampment a few miles back in the mountains. A guide shall be sent for you at the appointed time. Stay in this place during the next twenty-four hours, when you will be summoned."

The missionary, though a humble man, was by no means wanting in the dignity of a Christian gentleman. He was displeased with the arrogant and commanding tone assumed by his singular visitor, and threw a slight degree of reproof into his manner when he answered.

"Lady, if the welfare of a human being—if the safety of an immortal soul can be secured by my presence, I will not hesitate to trust myself among your people, though they come here on an errand I can never approve; but for a less important matter I cannot promise to wait your pleasure."

"Rash man! do you know who it is you are braving?" said the woman, fixing her eyes sternly on his face. "If your life is utterly valueless, delay but a moment in following the guide which I shall send, and you shall have the martyrdom you seem to brave! Catharine Montour's will has never yet been disputed within twenty miles of her husband's tent without frightful retribution."

The missionary started at the mention of that name, but he speedily regained his composure, and answered her calmly and with firmness.

"Threats are powerless with me, lady. The man who places himself unarmed and defenceless in the midst of a horde of savages can scarcely be supposed to act against his conscience from the threat of a woman, however stern may be her heart, and however fearful her power. Tell me what the service is which I am required to perform, and then you shall have my answer."

The haughty woman moved towards the door with an angry gesture, but returned again, and with more courtesy in her manner seated herself on the stool which had been placed for her.

"It is but just," she said, "that you should know the service which you are required to perform. There is in the camp now lying beneath Campbell's Ledge a maiden of mixed blood, my child—my only child; from the day that she first opened her eyes to mine in the solemn wilderness, with nothing but savage faces around me, with no heart to sympathize with mine, that child became a part of my own life. For years I had loved nothing; but the tenderness almost dead in my heart broke forth when she was born, the sweet feelings of humanity came back, and the infant became to me an idol. In the wide world I had but one object to love, and for the first time in a weary life affection brought happiness to me. You may be a father; think of the child who has lain in your bosom year after year, pure and gentle as a spring blossom, who has wound herself around your heart-strings— think of her, when dearest and loveliest, stolen from your bosom, and her innocent thoughts usurped by another."

"Forbear—in mercy forbear!" said the missionary, in a voice of agony that for an instant silenced the woman.

Catharine looked up and saw that his eyes were full of tears; her own face was fearfully agitated, and she went on with a degree of energy but little in keeping with the pathos of her last broken speech.

"A white, one of my own race, came to the forest stealthily, like a thief, and with our Indian forms, which he taught her to believe were a bond of marriage among his people, also lured the heart of my child from her mother. Now, I beseech you, for I see that you are kind and feeling—I was wrong to command—come to the camp at nine to-night, for then and there shall my child be lawfully wedded."

"I will be there at the hour," replied the missionary, in a voice of deep sympathy. "Heaven forbid that I should refuse to aid in righting the wronged, even at the peril of life."

"My own head shall not be more sacred in the Shawnee camp than yours," said Catharine, with energy.

"I do not doubt it; and were it otherwise I should not shrink from a duty. I owe an atonement for the evil opinion I had of you. A heart which feels dishonor so keenly cannot delight in carnage and blood."

"Can they repeat these things of me?" inquired Catharine, with a painful smile; "they do me deep wrong. Fear not; I appear before you with clean hands. If the heart is less pure it has sufficiently avenged itself; if it has wronged others, they have retribution; has not the love of my child gone forth to another? Am I not alone?"

"Lady," said the missionary, with deep commiseration in his look and voice, for he was moved by her energetic grief, "this is not the language of a savage. Your speech is refined, your manner noble. Lady, what are you?"

There are seasons when the heart will claim sympathy, spite of all control which a will of iron may place upon it. This power was upon the heart of Catharine Montour.

"Yes, I *will* speak," she muttered, raising her hand and pressing it heavily to her eyes. The motion flung back the drapery of the sleeve, and the light flashed full on the jewelled serpent coiled around her arm. The missionary's eyes fell upon it, and he sallied back against the logs of the hut, with a death-like agony in his face.

Catharine Montour was too deeply engrossed by her own feelings to observe the strange agitation which had so suddenly come upon the missionary. She seated herself on the stool, and with her face buried in her robe remained minute after minute in deep silence, gathering strength to unlock the tumultuous secrets of her heart once more to a mortal's knowledge.

When she raised her face there was nothing in the appearance of her auditor to excite attention. He still leaned against the rude wall, a little paler than before, but otherwise betraying no emotion, save that which a good man might be supposed to feel in the presence of a sinful and highly gifted fellow-creature.

She caught his pitying and mournful look fixed so earnestly upon her face as she raised it from the folds of her robe, and her eyes wavered and sunk beneath its sorrowful intensity. There was a yearning sympathy in his glance, which fell upon her heart like sunshine on the icy fetters of a rivulet; it awed her proud spirit, and yet encouraged confidence; but it was not till after his mild voice had repeated the question—"Lady, confide in me; who and what are you?"—that she spoke.

When she did find voice it was sharp, and thrilled painfully on the ear of the listener. The question aroused a thousand recollections that had long slumbered in the life of this wretched woman. She writhed under it, as if a knot of scorpions had suddenly begun to uncoil in her heart.

"What am I? It is a useless question. Who on earth can tell what he is, or what a moment shall make him? I am that which fate has ordained for me: Catharine Montour, the wife of Gi-en-gwa-tah, a great chief among his people. If at any time I have known another character, it matters little. Why should you arouse remembrances which may not be forced back to their lethargy again? I ask no sympathy, nor seek counsel; let me depart in peace."

With a sorrowful and deliberate motion she arose and would have left the cabin, but the missionary laid his hand gently on her arm and drew her back.

"We cannot part thus," he said. "The sinful have need of counsel, the sorrowing of sympathy. The heart which has been long astray requires an intercessor with the Most High."

"And does the God whom you serve suffer any human heart to become so depraved that it may not approach his footstool in its own behalf? Is the immaculate purity of Jehovah endangered by the petition of the sinful or the penitent that you offer to mediate between me and my Creator? No! if I have sinned, the penalty has been dearly paid. If I have sorrowed, the tears shed in solitude have fallen back on my own heart and frozen there! I ask not intercession with the being you worship; and I myself lack the faith which might avail me, were I weak enough to repine over the irredeemable past. I have no hope, no God—wherefore should I pray?"

"This hardiness and impiety is unreal. There is a God, and despite of your haughty will and daring intellect you believe in him; aye, at this moment, when there is denial on your lips!"

"Believe—aye, as the devils, perchance; but I do not tremble!" replied the daring woman, with an air and voice of defiance.

The missionary fixed his eyes with stern and reproving steadiness on the impious woman. She did not shrink from his glance, but stood up, her eyes braving his with a forced determination, her brow locked in defiance beneath its gorgeous coronet, and a smile of scornful bitterness writhing her mouth. Her arms were folded over her bosom, flushed by the reflection of her robe, and the jewelled serpent glittered just over her heart, as if to guard it from all good influences. She seemed like a beautiful and rebellious spirit thrust out forever from the sanctuary of heaven.

A man less deeply read in the human heart, or less persevering in his Christian charities, would have turned away and left her, as one utterly irreclaimable, but the missionary was both too wise and too good thus to relinquish the influence he had gained. There was something artificial in the daring front and reckless impiety of the being before him, which betrayed a strange, but not uncommon, desire to be supposed worse than she really was.

With the ready tact of a man who has made character a study, he saw that words of reproof or authority were unlikely to soften a heart so stern in its mental pride, and his own kind feelings taught him the method of reaching hers. This keen desire to learn something of her secret history would have been surprising in a man of less comprehensive benevolence, and even in him there was a restless anxiety of manner but little in accordance with his usual quiet demeanor. His voice was like the breaking up of a fountain when he spoke again.

"Catharine," he said.

She started at the name—her arms dropped—she looked wildly in his eyes:

"Oh! I mentioned the name," she muttered, refolding her arms and drawing a deep breath.

"Catharine Montour, this hardihood is unreal; you are not thus unbelieving. Has the sweet trustfulness of your childhood departed forever? Have you no thought of those hours when the young heart is made up of faith and dependence—when prayer and helpless love break out from the soul, naturally as moisture exhales when the sun touches it? Nay," he continued, with more powerful earnestness, as he saw her eyes waver and grow dim beneath the influence of his voice, "resist not the good spirit, which even now is hovering about your heart, as the ring-dove broods over its desolated nest. Hoarded thoughts of evil beget evil. Open your heart to confidence and counsel. Confide in one who never yet betrayed trust—one who is no stranger to sorrow, and who is too frail himself to lack charity for the sins of others. I beseech you to tell me, are you not of English birth?"

Tears, large and mournful tears, stood in Catharine Montour's eyes. She was once more subdued and humble as an infant. A golden chord had been touched in her memory, and every heart-string vibrated to the music of other years. She sat down and opened her history to that strange man abruptly, and as one under the influence of a dream.

"Yes, I *was* born in England," she said; "born in a place so beautiful that any human being might be happy from the mere influence of its verdant and tranquil quietness. No traveller ever passed through that village without stopping to admire its verdant and secluded tranquillity. Back from the church stood the parsonage, an irregular old building, surrounded by a grove of magnificent oaks, through which its pointed roof and tall chimneys alone could be seen from the village. A tribe of rooks dwelt in the oaks, and a whole bevy of wrens came and built their nests in the vines. With my earliest recollection comes the soft chirp of the nestlings under my window, and the carolling song which broke up from the larks when they left the long grass in the graveyard, where they nested during the summer nights.

"My father was rector of the parish, the younger son of a noble family. He had a small, independent fortune, which allowed him to distribute the income from his living among the poor of the village. My mother was a gentle creature, of refined and delicate, but not comprehensive, mind. She loved my father, and next to him, or rather as a portion of himself, me.

As a child, I was passionate and wayward, but warm of heart, forgiving and generous. My spirit brooked no control; but my indulgent father and sweet mother could see nothing more dangerous than a quick intellect and over-abundant healthfulness in the capricious tyranny of my disposition. I was passionately fond of my mother, and when she sometimes stole to my bedside and hushed me to sleep with her soft kisses and pleasant voice I would promise in my innermost heart never to grieve her again; yet the next day I experienced a kind of pleasure in bringing the tears to her gentle eyes by some wayward expression of obstinacy or dislike."

CHAPTER VII
MY FATHER'S WARD

"When I was fifteen, an old college associate died and left my father guardian to his son and heir. This young gentleman's arrival at the parsonage was an epoch in my life. A timid and feminine anxiety to please took possession of my heart. I gave up for his use my own little sitting-room, opening upon a wilderness of roses and tangled honeysuckles that had once been a garden, but which I had delighted to see run wild in unchecked luxuriance, till it had become as fragrant and rife with blossoms as an East India jungle.

"It was the first act of self-denial I had ever submitted to, and I found a pleasure in it which more than compensated for the pain I felt in removing my music and books, with the easel which I had taken such pains to place in its proper light, to a small chamber above.

"Heedless of my mother's entreaty, that I would remain quiet and receive our guest in due form, I sprang out upon the balcony, and winding my arm around one of its pillars, pushed back the clustering passionflowers, and bent eagerly over, to obtain a perfect view of our visitor. He was a slight, aristocratic youth, with an air of thoughtful manliness beyond his years. He was speaking as he advanced up the serpentine walk which led to the balcony, and seemed to be making some observation on the wild beauty of the garden. There was something in the tones of his voice, a quiet dignity in his manner, that awed me. I shrunk back into the room, where my mother was sitting, and placed myself by her side. My cheek burned and my heart beat rapidly when he entered. But my confusion passed unnoticed, or, if remarked, was attributed to the bashfulness of extreme youth. Varnham was my senior by four years, and he evidently considered me as a child, for after a courteous bow on my introduction he turned to my mother and began to speak of the village and its remarkable quietude. I returned to my room that night out of humor with myself, and somewhat in awe of our guest.

"The history of the next two years would be one of the heart alone—a narrative of unfolding intellect and feeling. It was impossible that two persons, however dissimilar in taste and disposition, should be long domesticated in the same dwelling without gradually assimilating in some degree. Perhaps two beings more decidedly unlike never met than Varnham and myself, but after the first restraint which followed our introduction wore off he became to me a preceptor and most valuable friend.

"Two years brought Varnham to his majority. His fortune, though limited, was equal to his wants; he resolved to travel, and then take orders, for he had been intended for the church. It was a sorrowful day to us when he left the parsonage. The lonely feelings which followed his departure never gave place to cheerfulness again. In four weeks from that day my father was laid in the vault of his own loved church. My gentle mother neither wept nor moaned when she saw the beloved of her youth laid beside the gorgeous coffins of his lordly ancestors. But in three weeks after, I was alone in the wide world; for she was dead also.

"Two weary, sad nights I sat beside that beautiful corpse, still and tearless, in a waking dream. I remember that kind voices were around me, and that more than once pitying faces bent over me, and strove to persuade me away from my melancholy vigils. But I neither answered nor moved; they sighed as they spoke, and passed in and out, like the actors of a tragedy in which I had no part. I was stupefied by the first great trouble of my life!

"Then the passion of grief burst over me. I fell to the floor, and my very life seemed ebbing away in tears and lamentations. Hour after hour passed by, and I remained as I had fallen, in an agony of sorrow. I know not how it was, but towards morning I sunk into a heavy slumber.

"When I again returned to consciousness Varnham was sitting beside my bed; physicians and attendants were gliding softly about the room, and everything was hushed as death around me. I was very tired and weak; but I remembered that my mother was dead, and that I had fainted; I whispered a request to see her once more—she had been buried three weeks.

"Varnham had heard of my father's death in Paris, and hastened home, to find me an orphan doubly bereaved, to become my nurse and my counsellor—my all. Most tenderly did he watch over me during my hours of convalescence. And I returned his love with a gratitude as fervent as ever warmed the heart of woman.

"I knew nothing of business, scarcely that money was necessary to secure the elegances I enjoyed. I had not even dreamed of a change of residence, and when information reached us that a rector had been appointed to supply my father's place, and that Lord Granby, the elder brother of my lamented parent, had consented to receive me as an inmate of his own house I sunk beneath the blow as if a second and terrible misfortune had befallen me.

"The thought of being dragged from my home—from the sweet haunts which contained the precious remembrances of my parents—and conveyed to the cold, lordly halls of my aristocratic uncle nearly flung me back to a state of delirium.

"There was but one being on earth to whom I could turn for protection, and to him my heart appealed with the trust and tender confidence of a sister. I pleaded with him to intercede with my uncle, that I might be permitted still to reside at the parsonage—that I might not be taken from all my love could ever cling to. Varnham spoke kindly and gently to me; he explained the impropriety, if not the impossibility of Lord Granby's granting my desire, and besought me to be resigned to a fate which many in my forlorn orphanage might justly covet. He spoke of the gaieties and distinction which my residence with Lord Granby would open to me, and used every argument to reconcile me to my destiny. But my heart clung tenaciously to its old idols, and refused to be comforted.

"It was deep in the morning—my uncle's coroneted chariot was drawn up before my quiet home. The sun flashed brightly over the richly studded harness of four superb horses, which tossed their heads and pawed the earth impatient for the road. A footman in livery lounged upon the doorsteps, and the supercilious coachman stood beside his horses, dangling his silken reins, now and then casting an expectant look into the hall-door.

"It was natural that he should be impatient, for they had been kept waiting more than an hour. I thought that I had nerved myself to depart; but when I descended from my chamber, and saw that gorgeous carriage, with its silken cushions and gilded panels, ready to convey me to the hospitality of one who was almost a stranger, my heart died within me. I turned into the little room where I had spent that night of sorrow by my mother's corpse; I flung myself on the sofa, and burying my face in the pillows sobbed aloud in the wretchedness of a heart about to be sundered from all it had ever loved. Varnham was standing over me, pale and agitated. He strove to comfort me—was prodigal in words of soothing and endearment, and at length of passionate supplication. I was led to the carriage his affianced wife.

"My year of mourning was indeed one of sorrow and loneliness of heart; I was a stranger in the home of my ancestors, and looked forward to the period of my marriage with an impatience that would have satisfied the most exacting love. It was a cheap mode of obliging the orphan niece, and Lord Granby presented the living which had been my father's to Varnham, who had taken orders, and was ready to convey me back a bride to my old home.

"Had my relative lavished his whole fortune on me I should not have been more grateful! My capacities for enjoyment were chilled by the cold, formal dullness of his dwelling. I panted for the dear solitude of my old haunts, as the prisoned bird pines for his home in the green leaves. We were married before the altar where my father had prayed, and where I had received the sacrament of baptism. The register which recorded my birth bore witness to my union with Varnham, the only true friend my solitary destiny had left to me. We entered our old home, rich in gentle affections and holy memories. I was content with the pleasant vistas of life that opened to us.

"Our united fortunes were sufficient for our wants. We determined to live a life of seclusion, study, and well-performed duties, such as had made the happiness of my parents. Filled with these innocent hopes I took possession of my old home, a cheerful and contented wife. We saw but little company, but my household duties, my music, painting, and needlework gave me constant and cheerful occupation, and three years of almost thorough contentment passed by without bringing a wish beyond my own household. At this time a daughter was born to us, and in the fulness of my content I forgot to ask if there was a degree of happiness which I had never tasted.

"The fourth year after my marriage another coffin was placed in the family vault beside my parents—that of James, Earl of Granby. My cousin, Georgiana, scarcely outlived the period of her mourning; and, at the age of twenty-two, I, who had never dreamed of worldly aggrandizement, suddenly found myself a peeress in my own right, and possessor of one of the finest estates in England, for the Granby honors descended alike to male and female heirs, and I was the last of our race.

"At first I was bewildered by the suddenness of my exaltation; then, as if one burst of sunshine were only necessary to ripen the dormant ambition of my heart, a change came over my whole being. A new and brilliant career was opened to me; visions of power, greatness, and excitement floated through my imagination. The pleasant contentment of my life was broken up forever.

"Varnham took no share in my restless delight; his nature was quiet and contemplative—his taste refined and essentially domestic. What happiness could he look for in the brilliant destiny prepared for us? From that time there was a shadow as of evil foreboding in his eye, and his manner became constrained and regretful. Perhaps with his better knowledge of the world he trembled to find me so near that vortex of artificial life into which I was eager to plunge myself.

"He made no opposition to my hasty plans—nay, admitted the necessity of a change in our mode of living; but that anxious expression never for a moment left his eyes. He seemed rather a victim than a partaker in my promised greatness. From that time our pursuits took different directions. I had thoughts and feelings with which he had no sympathy. When an estrangement of the mind commences, that of the heart soon follows.

"Again that splendid carriage stood before our home, ready to convey us to the pillared halls of my inheritance. There were few, and those few transient, regrets in my heart when, with a haughty consciousness of power and station, I sunk to the cushioned seat, swept proudly around that old church, and away from the sweet leafy bower in which I had known so much happiness.

"Everything rich and beautiful had been lavished by my predecessor in the adornment of Ashton. Paintings of priceless worth lined its galleries, and sculptured marble started up at every turn to charm me with the pure and classic loveliness of statuary. Tables of rare mosaic—ancient tapestry and articles of virtu gathered from all quarters of the globe were collected there; my taste for the arts—my love of the beautiful—made it almost a paradise, and it was long before I wearied of the almost regal magnificence which surrounded me. But after a time these things became familiar; excitement gradually wore away, and my now reckless spirit panted for change—for deeper draughts from the sparkling cup which I had found so pleasant in tasting.

"As the season advanced I proposed going up to London; Varnham consented, but reluctantly; I saw this almost without notice; the time had passed when his wishes predominated over mine.

"I am certain that Varnham doubted my strength to resist the temptations of a season in town. It was a groundless fear; there was nothing in the heartless supercilious people of fashion whom I met to captivate a heart like mine. I was young, beautiful, *new*, and soon became the fashion—the envy of women, and the worshipped idol of men. I was not for a moment deluded by the homage lavished upon me. I received the worship, but in my heart despised the worshippers.

"Varnham did not entirely relinquish his rectorship, but gave its emoluments to the curate who performed the duties, reserving the house which we both loved, to ourselves. He went down to the old place occasionally, and though I never accompanied him, it was pleasant to know that the haunts of my early love were still kept sacred. When the season broke up I invited a party to Ashton, but Varnham persuaded me to spend the month which would intervene before its arrival, at the parsonage. I was weary with the rush and bustle of my town life, and willingly consented to his plan.

"Our house was shut up, the servants went down to Ashton, and Varnham, one friend and myself settled quietly in our own former home. The repose of that beautiful valley had something heavenly in it, after the turmoil of London. Old associations came up to soften the heart, and I was happier than I had been since coming in possession of my inheritance.

"The friend whom Varnham invited to share the quiet of the parsonage with us had made himself conspicuous as a young man of great talent in the lower house; yet I knew less of him than of almost any distinguished person in society. We had met often in the whirl of town life, but a few passing words and cold compliments alone marked our intercourse. There was something of reserve and stiffness in his manner, by no means flattering to my self-love, and I was rather prejudiced against him than otherwise from his extreme popularity.

"There was something in my nature which refused to glide tamely down the current of other peopled opinions, and the sudden rise of young Murray with his political party, the adulation lavished upon him by the lion-loving women of fashion only served to excite my contempt for them, and to make me withhold from him the high opinion justly earned by talents of no ordinary character.

"When he took his seat in our travelling carriage, it was with his usual cold and almost uncourteous manner; but by degrees all restraint wore off, his conversational powers were excited, and I found myself listening with a degree of admiration seldom aroused in my bosom to his brilliant offhand eloquence. Varnham seemed pleased that my former unreasonable prejudices were yielding to the charm of his friend's genius—and our ride was one of the most agreeable of my then pleasant life.

"It was not till after we had been at the parsonage several days that the speeches which had so suddenly lifted our guest into notice came under my observation. I was astonished at their depth and soundness. There was depth and brilliancy, flashes of rich, strong poetry mingled with the argument—a vivid, quick eloquence in the style that stirred my heart like martial music. By degrees the great wealth of Murray's intellect, the manly strength and tenderness of his nature, revealed themselves. His character was a grand one; I could look up to that man with my whole being, and grow prouder from the homage.

"A love of intellectual greatness, a worship of mind, had ever been a leading trait in my character. In that man I found more than mind. He was strong in principle, rich in feeling—deep, earnest feeling—which a great soul might battle against if duty commanded, and restrain, but never wholly conquer.

"We had mistaken each other, and there lay the danger. I had believed him cold and ambitious. He had looked upon Lady Granby as a frivolous, selfish woman, who would be forever quaffing the foam of life, but never reach the pure wine; one with whom it was hardly worth while to become acquainted.

"A few days in the old parsonage house sufficed to enlighten us both. There I was natural, gentle, loving—glad to get among innocent things again. In those little rooms I forgot everything but the pleasure of being at home. Weeks passed before I knew why that home had been turned into a paradise to which all previous memories were as nothing.

"I think he recognized the evil that was creeping over us first, for he began to avoid me, and for a time, though in the same house, we scarcely spoke together. But he loved me, spite of his struggles, his sensitive honor, his iron resolves; he loved me, his friend's wife, but he was strong and honorable. The mighty spirit which had taken possession of his heart unawares could not all at once be driven forth, but it had no power to overcome his integrity. He was too brave and loyal for domestic treason.

"This nobility of character was enough to chain my soul to his forever. I did not attempt to deceive myself; well I knew that the sweet but terrible power growing up in my life was a sin to be atoned for with years of suffering, for souls like ours must avenge themselves for the wrong feelings more certainly than ordinary natures find retribution for evil deeds.

"When the first knowledge came upon me that I loved my husband's friend it overwhelmed me with consternation. The danger of a thing like this had never entered my thoughts—my heart had been asleep—its awaking frightened me. Mine was not a mad passion that defies human laws and moral ties, or that deceives itself with sophistry. Never for a moment did I attempt to justify or excuse it. I knew that such love would have changed my whole being to gentleness, holiness, humility, anything bright and good, had freedom made it innocent; but I never once thought of breaking the ties that bound me. If I was a slave, my own will had riveted the chains upon my wrist; I was not one to tear them off because the iron began to gall me.

"No, no; the love that I bore him was deep and fervent, but not weak. It might kill, but never degrade me. I believed it then; I am certain of it now. I have trampled on my heart. It has been crushed, broken, thrust aside—

but the love of that man lives there yet. I struggled against it—tortured my heart into madness—fled with this clinging love into the depths of the wilderness—to the wilderness, but it lives here yet—it lives here yet."

Catharine Montour pressed one hand upon her heart as she spoke; her face was pallid with an expression of unutterable pain. Her eyes seemed to plead with the missionary for pity.

He answered that appeal with looks of sorrowful compassion.

"There was confidence between us at last; each knew that the other suffered, and that the other loved.

"I have said that Murray was an honorable man, but his love was a tyrant, or it would never have been expressed. He was no tempter, nor was I one to be tempted. It was in his goodness that our strength lay, for we were strong, and in every act of our lives faithful to the duties that chained us.

"Murray seized upon this passion with his grasping intellect, and strove to force it into friendship, or into that deceptive, Platonic sentiment which is neither friendship nor love. My heart followed him—my mind kept pace with his—anything that did not separate us, and which was not degradation, I was strong enough to endure. We could not give up each other's society; that we did not attempt, for both felt its impossibility."

CHAPTER VIII
STRUGGLES AND PENALTIES

"Varnham was absent when our confession was first looked, then breathed, and at last desperately uttered. He had been gone more than a week, making preparations for our return to Ashton. Had every action of our lives been counted during that time, the most austere moralist could have detected no wrong. The sin with us was too subtle and deep for human eyes, even for our own. We could not believe that feelings which had no evil wish might be in themselves evil. But when my husband returned, the pang of shame and regret that fell upon us should have been proof enough of wrong. When had we ever blushed and trembled in his presence before?

"We were alone, Murray and myself, in the little boudoir which I have mentioned so often. He was sitting on the sofa, to which my husband had so tenderly lifted me on the night before my mother's funeral, reading one of my favorite Italian poets. I sat a little way off, listening to the deep melody of his voice, watching the alternate fire and shadow that played within the depths of his large eyes, the clear, bold expression of his forehead, and the smile upon his lips, which seemed imbued with the soft poetry that dropped in melody from them.

"I had forgotten everything for the time, and was lost in the first bewildering dream which follows, with its delicious quietude, the entire outpouring of the soul; when thought itself arises but as sweet exhalation from the one grand passion which pervades the whole being; when even a sense of wrong but haunts the heart as the bee slumbers within the urn of a flower, rendered inert and stingless by the wealth of honey which surrounds it.

"Murray had been bred in society, and could not so readily fling off the consciousness of our position. A shadow, darker than the words of his author warranted, settled on his brow as he read, and more than once he raised his eyes from the page in the middle of a sentence, and fixed them with a serious and almost melancholy earnestness on my face. Then I would interrupt his thoughts with some of the pleasant words which love sends up from the full heart, naturally as song gushes from the bosom of a nightingale.

He would muse a moment after this and resume his book, allowing his voice to revel in the melody of the language, then hurry on with a stern and abrupt emphasis, as one who strives by rapidity of utterance to conquer painful thoughts.

"The sudden recoil of my heart was suffocating, then its deep, heavy throbbing grew almost audible. I felt the blood ebbing away from my face and a faintness was upon me. Murray started and grasped my hand with a violence that pained me.

"'Lady Granby, be yourself; why do you tremble? Have we in wish or act wronged this man?'

"'No—no; the angels of Heaven must bear us witness—but I have a secret here; and oh, God! forgive me; I am not glad to see him.'

"'And I,' he said, turning pale, 'am I the cause of this terror?—indeed, lady, it is better that we part now—this weakness——'

"The very thought of his departure drove me wild. 'I am not weak—nor wicked either,' I said, with a proud smile; 'see if I prove so?'

"Then wringing my hand from his grasp I deliberately opened the sash-door and went out to meet my husband. He was already upon the balcony, and sprang forward to greet me with more eager affection than I had ever witnessed in him before. During one moment I was drawn to his bosom unresistingly. I was faint with agitation. He must have felt me tremble, but evidently imputed the emotion to joy at his sudden return; with his arms about my waist he drew me into the room. Oh! how thoroughly I loathed the hypocrisy which one forbidden feeling had imposed on the future! Murray nerved himself for the interview, and stood up, pale and collected, to receive his late friend. When he saw my position, a faint flush shot over his forehead, but his forced composure was in nothing else disturbed.

"I put away my husband's arm and sunk to a seat, overwhelmed with a painful consciousness of the moral degradation I had heaped upon myself.

"Murray went up to London on the next day; a few brief words of farewell were all that could be granted me. I went away by myself and wept bitterly.

"The society of my husband grew wearisome, and yet I said again and again to myself: 'We have done him no wrong; this love which fills my heart never was his—never existed before; it is pure and honorable.' As I said this, my cheek burned with the falsehood. Was not deception itself a sin? Oh! how many painful apprehensions haunted my imagination. For two days I was tormented by shadowy evils. My mornings were full of inquietude, and my sleep was not rest. Then came his first letter, so considerate and gentle, so full of manly solicitude for my peace of mind. I flung aside all doubt and self-distrust. Happiness sprung back to my heart like a glad infant to its mother's bosom. The earth seemed bursting into blossom around me. Again I surrendered my spirit to its first sweet dream of contentment, and strove to convince myself that feelings were harmless till they sprang into evil actions. When my intellect refused this sophistry I resolutely cast all thought aside.

"Murray joined us at Ashton. Among the guests who spent Christmas with us was a young lady of refined and pleasant manners, the orphan of a noble family, whose entailed property had fallen to a distant heir on the death of her father. Thus she was left almost penniless, dependent on a wealthy aunt, who seemed anxious to get rid of her trust with as little expense as possible.

"My sympathy was excited in the young lady's behalf, for her coarse relative supplied her but sparingly with the means of supporting her station in society, and in her vulgar eagerness to have the poor girl settled and off her hands was continually compromising her delicacy and wounding her pride.

"Louisa was reserved, and somewhat cold in her disposition, but my feelings had been enlisted in her behalf, and I contrived every little stratagem in my power to supply her want of wealth and to shield her from the match-making schemes of her aunt.

"Being much in my society, she was thrown into constant companionship with Murray. He did not at first seem interested in her, for she was retiring and not really beautiful, but by degrees the gentle sweetness of her character won its way to his heart, and he seemed pleased with her society, but there was nothing in the intimacy to alarm me. I was rather gratified than otherwise that he should be interested in my protégée.

"When we again took up our residence in town I occasionally acted as chaperon to Miss Jameson, but as my hope centered more trustfully around one object, my taste for general society diminished, and I surrounded myself with a small circle of distinguished individuals, and mingled but little in the dissipations of the world, where her aunt was continually forcing her to exhibit herself. I was still interested in her, but the repulsive coarseness of her relative prevented a thorough renewal of the intimacy which had existed while she was yet my guest.

"A year passed by, in which had been crowded a whole life of mingled happiness and misery, a dreamy tumultuous year that had been one long struggle to preserve the love which had become a portion of my soul, and to maintain that integrity of thought and deed, without which life would be valueless.

"The blow fell at length; Murray was about to be married. He did not allow me to be tortured by public rumor, but came and told me with his own lips.

"I had been very sad all the morning, and when I heard his familiar knock at the street-door, and the footsteps to which my heart had never yet failed to thrill approaching my boudoir, a dark presentiment fell upon me, and I trembled as if a death-watch was sounding in my ears. But I had learned to conceal my feelings, and sat quietly in my cushioned chair, occupied with a piece of fine needlework when he entered.

"He was deeply agitated, and his hand shook violently when I arose to receive him. Mine was steady. I was not about to heap misery on the heart that had clung to me. He spoke of those days at the parsonage; of the dreams, those impossible dreams, out of which we were to win happiness, innocent happiness to ourselves—a happiness that should wrong no one, and yet fill our whole lives. He spoke of it all as a dream—a sad, mocking delusion, which was like feeding the soul on husks. It was in vain, he said, to deceive ourselves longer; the love which had existed—he did not say still existed—between us must inevitably perish under the restraints which honor and conscience imposed. We were sure of nothing, not even of those brief moments of social intercourse which society allows to those who have no secret feelings to conceal.

"I neither expostulated nor reasoned, but with a calmness which startled myself I inquired the name of my rival.

"It was Louisa Jameson, the creature whom I had cherished even as a sister. No matter; I had nerved myself to bear all. If my heart trembled, no emotions stirred my face. He had not yet proposed, but he knew that she loved him, and her position was one to excite his compassion. Still he would not propose unless I consented. He had come to throw himself on my generosity.

"I did consent. Measuredly and coldly the words were spoken, but they did not satisfy him. He would have me feel willing—his happiness should not be secured at the expense of mine, if from my whole heart I could not resign him. No advantage should be taken of a freedom rendered only from the lips.

"For three whole hours I remained numb and still. At last my maid came to remind me of a ball and supper to which I was engaged.

"I arose and bade her array me in my gayest apparel. Never do I remember myself so beautiful as on that night. There was fever in my cheek, the fire of a tortured spirit—a wild, sparkling wit flashed from my lips, and among the gay and the lovely I was most gay and most recklessly brilliant.

"Murray called in the morning, for we were to be friends still. I had suffered much during the night, but I put rouge on my pallid cheeks, and with forced cheerfulness went down to receive him. He appeared ill at ease. Perhaps he feared reproaches after I recovered from the first effect of his desertion, but the anguish it had wrought was too deep for tears or weak complaints; when the death-blow comes, we cease to struggle.

"I ascertained that Miss Jameson's aunt had refused to bestow a fortune with her niece, and I knew that Murray was far, far from wealthy enough to meet the expenses of an establishment befitting his rank. I could not bear that his fine mind should be cramped by the petty annoyances of a limited income, nor his wife forever crushed beneath the humiliating consciousness of poverty. Varnham never allowed himself to exceed his own little income, and the revenues of the Granby estates far exceeded our general expenditure. It was, therefore, easy for me to raise a sum sufficient to endow my rival, and thus indirectly secure a competence to him.

"I gave orders to my agent that twenty thousand pounds should be immediately raised for me. When the sum was secured I went privately to the house of my rival, and, with little persuasion, induced her parsimonious relative to present it to Miss Jameson as the gift of her own generosity. I knew that my secret was safe, for she was a worldly woman and was not likely to deprive herself of the éclat of a generous deed by exposing my share in it.

"Then I thought of Varnham for the first time in many days, not as the husband I had been estranged from, but as the kind, good friend who had watched beside me, and loved me amid all my sorrows. I was not wholly in my right mind, and reflected imperfectly on the step that I was about to take. Mr. Varnham was at Ashton, and I resolved to go to him, but with no definite aim, for I was incapable of any fixed plan. But he was my only friend, and my poor heart turned back to him in its emergency of sorrow with the trust of former years. I forgot that it had locked up the only well-spring of sympathy left to it by the very course of its anguish.

"I flung a large cloak over my splendid attire, and while my carriage was yet at the door entered it and ordered them to proceed to Ashton. We travelled all day; I did not once leave my seat, but remained muffled in my cloak, with the hood drawn over my head, lost in the misty half-consciousness of partial insanity. I believe that the carriage stopped more than once, that food and rest were urged on me by my servants, but I took no heed, only ordering them to drive forward, for the rapid motion relieved me.

"It was deep in the night when we reached Ashton. Everything was dark and gloomy; but one steady lamp glimmered from the library window, and I knew that Varnham was up, and there. The library was in the back part of the house, and the sound of the carriage had not reached it.

"I made my way through the darkened hall and entered my husband's presence. For one moment the feverish beating of my heart was hushed by the holy tranquillity of that solitary student. There was something appalling in the sombre, gloomy magnificence of the room in which he sat. The noble, painted window seemed thick and impervious in the dim light. The rich bookcases were in shadow, and cold marble statues looked down from their pedestals with a pale, grave-like beauty as I entered.

"Varnham was reading. One small lamp alone shed its lustre on the rare Mosaic table over which he bent, and threw a broad light across the pale, calm forehead which had something heavenly in its tranquil smoothness. I was by his side, and yet he did not see me. The solemn stillness of the room had cleared away my brain, and for a moment I felt the madness of my intended confidence. I staggered, and should have fallen but for the edge of the table, which I grasped with a force that made the lamp tremble.

"Varnham started up astonished at my sudden presence; but when he saw me standing before him, with the fire of excitement burning in my eyes and crimsoning my cheeks, with jewels twinkling in my hair and blazing on my girdle, where it flashed out from the cloak which my trembling hand had become powerless to hold, he seemed intuitively to feel the evil destiny that I had wrought for myself. His face became pale, and it was a minute before he could speak. Then he came forward, drew me kindly to his bosom and kissed my forehead with a tenderness that went to my heart like the hushing of my mother's voice. I flung myself upon his bosom and wept with a burst of passionate grief. He seated himself, drew me closer to his heart, and besought me to tell him the cause of my sorrow.

"I did tell him—and then he put me from his bosom as if I had been a leper, with a cry of rage, bitter rage on the lips that had never till then known aught but blessings; not against me—no, he could never have denounced me—but on Murray. Then I bethought me of the evil that might follow. I arose from the floor and fell before him, where he stood, and tried to plead and to call back all I had said. He lifted me again in his arms, though I felt a tremor run through his whole frame as he did so; he told me to be comforted, said many soothing words, and promised never to reproach me again, but he said nothing of *him,* and when I again strove to plead in his defence he put me sternly away. Then I went wholly mad.

"I can never describe the cold, hopeless struggle of my heart to retain the delusions which haunted my insane moments when my intellect began to resume its functions. It seemed as if some cruel spirit were gradually tightening the bonds of earth about me, and ruthlessly dragging me back to reason, while my spirit clung with intense longing to its own wild ideal.

"It was a sad, sad night to me when that star arose in the sky and sent its pure beams down to the bosom of my acacia, and I knew that the clear orb would henceforth be to me only a star—that the realms which I had located in its distant bosom were but the dream of a diseased fancy that would return no more with its beautiful and vivid faith which had no power to reason or doubt.

"But we can force the fantasies of a mind no more than the affections of the heart. My disease left me; then the passions and aspirations of my old nature started up, one after another, like marble statues over which a midnight blackness had fallen. And there in the midst, more firmly established than ever, *his* image remained—his name, his being, and the sad history of my own sufferings had, for one whole year, been to me but as an indefinite and painful dream. But sorrow and insanity itself had failed to uproot the love which had led to such misery. Can I be blamed that I prayed for insensibility again?"

CHAPTER IX
THE LOST YEAR

"Varnham had watched me for one year as a mother guards her wayward child. But the sudden illness of a near relative forced him from his guardianship. In my wildest moments I had always been gentle and submissive, but I was told that he left me with much reluctance to the care of my own maid, the housekeeper, and my medical attendant. They loved me, and he knew that with them I should be safe. When I began to question them of what had passed during my confinement, they appeared surprised by the quietness and regularity of my speech, but were ready to convince themselves that it was only one of the fitful appearances of insanity which had often deceived them during my illness. They, however, answered me frankly and with the respect which Varnham had ever enjoined upon them, even when he supposed that I could neither understand nor resent indignity.

"They told me that on the night of my arrival at Ashton they were all summoned from their beds by a violent ringing of the library bell; when they entered, my husband was forcibly holding me in his arms, though he was deadly pale and trembling so violently that the effort seemed too much for his strength. At first they dared not attempt to assist him; there was something so terrible in my shrieks and wild efforts to free myself that they were appalled. It was not till I had exhausted my strength, and lay breathless and faintly struggling on his bosom that they ventured to approach.

"I must have been a fearful sight, as they described me, with the white foam swelling to my lips, my face flushed, my eyes vivid with fever, and both hands clenched wildly in the long hair which fell over my husband's arms and bosom, matted with the jewels which I had worn at Murray's wedding. At every fresh effort I made to extricate myself, some of these gems broke loose, flashed to the floor and were trampled beneath the feet of my servants, for everything was unheeded in the panic which my sudden frenzy had created.

"'Oh! it was an awful scene!' exclaimed the old housekeeper, breaking off her description and removing the glasses from her tearful eyes as she spoke. 'I was frightened when I looked at you, but when my master lifted his face, and the light lay full upon it, my heart swelled, and I began to cry like a child. There was something in his look—I cannot tell what it was—something that made me hold my breath with awe, yet sent the tears to my eyes. I forgot you when I looked at him.

"'We carried you away to this chamber and when we laid you on the bed you laughed and sung in a wild, shrill voice that made the blood grow cold in my veins. I have never heard a sound so painful and thrilling as your cries were that night. For many hours you raved about some terrible deed that was to be done, and wildly begged that there might be no murder. Then you would start up and extend your arms in a pleading, earnest way to my master, and would entreat him with wild and touching eloquence to let you die—to imprison you in some cold, drear place where you would never see him again, but not to wound you so cruelly with his eyes.

"'I knew that all this was but the effect of a brain fever—that there could be no meaning in your words. Yet it seemed to me that my master should have striven to tranquillize you more than he did. Had he promised all you required, it might have had a soothing influence; for you were strangely anxious that he should give a pledge not to hate or even condemn some person who was not named. Yet, though you would at moments plead for mercy and protection with a piteous helplessness that might have won the heart of an enemy to compassion, he stood over you unchanged in that look of stern sorrow which had struck me so forcibly in the library. He scarcely seemed to comprehend the wild pathos of your words, but his composure was stern and painful to look upon.

"'At last you appeared to become more quiet, but still kept your eyes fixed pleadingly on his face and a wild, sweet strain breathed from your lips with a rise and fall so sad and plaintive that it seemed as if half your voice must have dissolved to tears and a broken heart was flowing away in its own low melody.

"'While the music yet lingered about your lips you began to talk of your mother, of a stone church where she had first taught you to pray—of a coffin, and a large white rose-tree that grew beneath a window which you had loved because her dear hand had planted it; then you besought him to bring some of those roses—white and pure, you said—that they might be laid upon your heart and take the fever away; then none need be ashamed to weep when you died, and perhaps they might bury you beside your mother.

"'It was enough to break one's heart to hear you plead in that sad, earnest way, and I saw, through the tears which almost blinded me, that my master was losing his self-command. The veins began to swell on his forehead, and a tremulous motion became visible about his mouth, which had till then remained as firm and almost as white as marble. He made a movement as if about to go away; but just then you raised your arms and, winding them about his neck, said: "Nay, Varnham, you will not leave me to die *here*. Let us go to our own old home. I will be very quiet, and will not try to live—only promise me this: bury me beneath the balcony, and let that lone, white rose-tree blossom over me forever and ever. I cannot exactly tell why, but they will not let me rest beside my mother, so my spirit shall stay among those pure flowers in patient bondage till all shall proclaim it purified and stainless enough to go and dwell with her. Kiss me once more, and say that you will go."

"'My master could but feebly resist the effort with which his face was drawn to yours; but when your lips met his he began to tremble again, and strove to unwind your arms from his neck; but you laid your head on his bosom, and that low, sad melody again broke from your lips, and your arms still wound more clingingly about him at every effort to undo their clasp.

"'He looked down upon the face that would not be removed from its rest; his bosom heaved, he wound his arms convulsively about your form for a moment, then forced you back to the pillow, and fell upon his knees by the bedside. His face was buried in the counterpane, but the sound of his half-stifled sobs grew audible throughout the room, and the bed shook beneath the violent trembling of his form. I beckoned the maid, and we stole from his presence, for it seemed wrong to stand by and gaze upon such grief.

"'When we returned you were silent and apparently asleep. He was sitting by the bed, and his eyes were fixed on your face with the same mournful, forgiving look with which I have seen him regard you a thousand times since. He spoke in his usual gentle way, and told us to tread lightly, that we might not disturb you. It was many hours before you awoke. My master was concealed by the drapery; you started up with a wild cry, and asked if he had gone to do murder. He caught you in his arms as you were about to spring from the bed, and with gentle violence forced you back to the pillows again. Then he waved his hand for us to draw back, and spoke to you in a solemn and impressive voice; but the last words only reached me. They were:

"'"I have promised, solemnly promised, Caroline—try to comprehend me and be at rest."

"'Your fever raged many days after that, and you were constantly delirious, but never violent, and that frightful dread of some impending evil seemed to have left you entirely. Your disease at length abated, and the bloom gradually returned to your cheek, but every new mark of convalescence only seemed to deepen the melancholy which had settled on my master.

"'When the physicians decided that your mind would never regain its former strength, but that it would ever remain wandering and gentle, and full of beautiful images as the fever had left it, my master became almost cheerful. He would allow no restraint to be placed upon you, and gave orders that you should be attended with all the respect and deference that had ever been rendered to your station. He never seemed more happy than while wandering with you about the gardens, and in the park; yet there were times when he would sit and gaze on your face as you slept, with a sad, regretful look that betrayed how truly he must have sorrowed over your misfortune. There was a yearning tenderness in his eye at such times, more touching far than tears. I could see that he struggled against these feelings, as if there existed something to be ashamed of in them, but they would return again.'

"All this and much more my good housekeeper said in answer to the questions which I put to her as my reason began to connect the present with the past. She did not hesitate to inform me of anything that I might wish to know, for she had no belief in my power to understand and connect her narrative. I had often questioned her before, and invariably forgot her answers as they fell from her lips; but every word of this conversation was graven on my memory, and if I have not repeated her exact language, the spirit and detail of her information is preserved.

"There was one subject that my housekeeper had not mentioned—my child. At first my intellect was too feeble for continued thought, and I did not notice this strange omission. Besides, some painful intuition kept me silent; the very thought of my own child was painful.

"At last I questioned her.

"'Where,' I said, 'is my daughter? Surely, in my illness he has not kept her from me?'

"The old woman became deadly pale; she turned away, repulsing the subject with a gesture of her withered hands, which terrified me.

"'My child!' I said; 'why are you silent? What have you done with her?'

"Still the old woman was speechless; but I could see tears stealing down her face.

"'Bring her hither,' I said, sick with apprehension; 'I wish to see how much my daughter has grown.'

"The old woman flung herself at my feet. Her hands gathered up mine and held them fast.

"'Do not ask—do not seek to remember. Oh! my lady, forget that you ever had a child!'

"'Forget—and why? Who has dared to harm the child of my bosom, the heiress of my house?'

"She hid her face in my lap; she clung to my knees, moaning piteously.

"A vague remembrance seized upon me—that pale form shrouded in its golden hair—my heart was like ice. I bent down and whispered in the old woman's ear:

"'Who was it harmed my child?'

"She lifted her head with a wild outbreak of sorrow—my question almost drove her mad.

"'Oh! lady, my master *would* let her come to your room—we were not to blame; you had always been so sweet-tempered and loving with her that we had no fear.'

"She stopped short, frightened by my looks. I whispered hoarsely:

"'My child! my child!'

"That horrible pause was broken at last. She lifted her hands to heaven, the tears streamed down her face like rain.

"'Do not ask—oh! my lady, I beseech you, do not ask.'

"'My child—my child'

"I could feel the whispers lose themselves in my throat; but she understood them, and her own voice sunk so low that, had not my soul listened, the terrible truth could not have reached it.

"'With your own hands you destroyed her—with your own hands you dashed her from the window!'

"Slowly from heart to limb the blood froze in my veins; for two days I lay in rigid silence, praying only for death. No, not even insanity would return. As yet I had only spent the holiday of my error. God would permit my brain to slumber no longer.

"I had but one wish—to escape that house, to flee from everything and everybody that had ever known me. It was no mad desire—no remnant of insanity. I reasoned coldly and well. Why not? utter hopelessness is wise.

"I dreaded but one thing on earth—the return of my husband. We never could be united again. He would not find the helpless being he had left, but a proud woman, whose heart if not her life had wronged him. He would not find the mother of his child, but its innocent, wretched murderer. I felt how bitter must be the news of my returning reason to the man who had forgiven the errors of my real character, because they had been so painfully lost in a visionary one, which disarmed resentment only from its very helplessness. I understood all Varnham's generosity, all his extraordinary benevolence; but I knew also that he was a proud man, with an organization so exquisitely refined that the sins of an alienated affection would affect him more deeply than actual crime, with ordinary men. I felt that it was impossible for me ever to see him again.

"My plan for the future was soon formed. I resolved to leave England forever. My heart sickened when I thought of mingling in society, of meeting with people who might talk to me of things which would rend my heart continually with recollections of the past. The love which had been the great error of my life still held possession of my heart with a strength which would not be conquered. Could I go forth, then, into the world? Could I live in my own house, where everything was associated with recollections of that love—where every bush and flower would breathe a reproach to the heart which still worshipped on, when worship was double guilt and double shame? Could I look upon the spot where my child had perished, and live? No, I resolved to leave all, to break every tie which bound me to civilized man, and to fling myself into a new state of existence. I thought, and still think, that it was the only way by which I could secure any portion of tranquillity to my husband. It would be terrible for him to believe that I had died by my own hands, but much more terrible if he returned and, in place of the mindless being who had become so utterly helpless, so completely the object of his compassion, found the woman who had wronged him fully conscious of her fault, yet without the humility and penitence which should have followed his generous forgiveness. There was too much of the pride of my old nature left. I could not have lived in the same house with the man I had so injured.

"The Granby property was unentailed, with the exception of one small estate which went with the title. Immediately on coming into possession of the estates I had made a will, bequeathing the whole vast property to my child, and making my husband her trustee; but, in case of her death, all was to revert to him. He knew nothing of this; but the will was consigned to the hands of honorable men, and I was certain that it would be legally acted upon. In raising the sum which I devoted to Murray my agent had sold stocks to more than quadruple the amount. This amount had been paid to me, but in the excitement of my feelings I had neglected to place it with my banker and had left it in an escritoire at our town house, where was also deposited the most valuable portion of my jewels. I had no arrangements to make which could in any way reveal the course I had determined to pursue.

"There was one subject which I had not yet ventured to mention. My cheek burned and my heart beat quick when I at last brought myself to inquire about Murray. He was living a secluded life at a small cottage near Richmond. It was all I cared to learn.

"The second night after the conversation with my housekeeper I stole softly to the room of a sleeping housemaid and dressed myself in a suit of cast-off clothing which was not likely to be missed; then, with a few guineas which I found in my desk I went cautiously out, and left my house forever.

"Along the edge of the park ran a stream of small magnitude, but remarkable for its depth. On the brink of this stream I left a portion of the garments I had worn; then departed on foot for the nearest post-town, where I procured a passage to London. I found my house closed, but entered it with a private key and took from my escritoire the money and jewels which had been left there more than a year before.

"The third evening after leaving Ashton I stood in front of a beautiful cottage, separated from the thickly settled portions of Richmond by pleasure grounds, rather more spacious than is usual in that neighborhood, and still farther secluded by groups of ornamental trees. A light broke softly through the wreathing foliage which draped the windows of a lower room and I could distinguish the shadow of a man walking to and fro within.

"I knew that it was Murray, and that I should see him once more that night, yet my heart beat slow and regularly, without a throb to warn me of the deep feeling which still lived there in undying strength. I had no hope, and entire hopelessness is rest. I inquired for the housekeeper, and told her that I had been informed she wished to hire a housemaid; that I was without a place, and had come all the way from the city to secure one with her. I knew that she could not find it in her heart to send me back to London late at night and alone, and, as I anticipated, was invited to stay till morning.

"When the kind housekeeper was asleep I stole from her chamber and sought the apartment where I had seen the light. It was a small room, partly fitted up as a study, and partly as a parlor. Books and musical instruments lay scattered about; a few cabinet pictures hung upon the walls, and a portrait of Murray looked down upon me from over the mantelpiece as I entered. A lamp was still burning, and an open work-box seemed to have been pushed from its station on the table, directly beneath it, to make room for a small book of closely filled manuscript which lay open, as if it had just been written in. A pen lay by, and the ink was yet damp on the unfinished page. Even across the room I knew the handwriting; the impulse to read which seized upon me was unconquerable. I held my breath, for the stillness around was like a hush of a tomb, and the characters seemed to start up like living witnesses beneath my eyes as I bent over the book. Thus the page ran:

"'They tell me she is mad—that her fine mind is broken, and her warm heart unstrung forever. They say this, and comment and speculate upon causes in my presence, as if I could not feel. I sit with apparent calmness, and listen to things which would break a common heart.

"'The soft smile of my wife is ever upon me, the cheek of my boy dimples beneath my glance if I but raise my eyes to his innocent face, and yet there are times when I *cannot* look upon them. The image of that noble and ruined being is forever starting up between me and them. I did not intend this when I took upon myself the right to regulate the destiny of a fellow-being—madness—no, no, I never thought of that! I did not dream that my own nature—but why should I write this? Yet I cannot keep these feelings forever pent up in my heart.

"'It was terrible news! Why did that officious physician come here to tell me there was no hope, and this day above all others in the year? Was it any reason that he should wound me with this news, because I was known to be a friend of the family—a friend truly? How coldly the man told me that she could never recover her reason! It was like the slow stab of a poignard; my heart quivered under it. Just then my wife must come with her innocent and loving voice to give me the good-night kiss before she left me. Poor thing! she little dreamed of the melancholy tidings which caused me to return her caress so coldly. I will try and seek rest, but not with them; sometimes I wish that I might never see them again. I must be alone to-night!'

"It was but the fulfillment of my own prophecy. I knew that he could not be happy; that he never would be again; never even tranquil till he believed me in my grave. My resolution was more firmly established, I would not live a continual cause of torment to him. I had no desire that he, too, should be miserable; in my most wretched moments the feeling had never entered my heart.

"The rustle of silk caused me to start from my position as I was bending over the book. It was only the night wind sweeping through an open casement that sent the curtain, which had dropped over it, streaming out like a banner into the room. I stood upright, silent and breathless; for, on a low couch, which the window drapery had half-concealed till now, lay

Grenville Murray. The lamp shone full upon his face, and even from the distance I could see the change which a year of mental agitation had made in it.

"I went softly to the couch, knelt down, and gazed upon him with a hushed and calm feeling, like that which a mother might know while bending over the couch of a beloved, but wayward, child. Twice the clock chimed the hour, and still I knelt by that couch and gazed on that pale, sleeping face, with a cold, hopeless sorrow which had no voice for lamentation.

"A third time the clock beat. I bent forward and pressed my lips to his forehead for the first time in my life. Oh! how my heart swelled to my lips with that one soft kiss. It seemed breaking with solemn tenderness—such tenderness as we give to the dead before the beloved clay is taken from us forever. My lips were cold and tremulous, but he did not awake beneath the pressure, and I did not repeat it, nor look on him again. I knew we were parting forever, but had no power to look back.

"I passed from the house slowly, and with a solemn feeling of desolation, as one might tread through a graveyard alone, and at midnight.

"In the disguise which had served me so well I sailed for America. I had no wish to mingle with my race, but took my way from New York to the valley of the Mohawk and sought the presence of Sir William Johnson. To him I revealed myself and as much of my history as was necessary to ensure his co-operation in my plan for the future. Under a solemn promise of secrecy, which has never been broken, I entrusted my wealth to his agency and procured his promise of an escort to the tribe of Indians then located in his neighborhood. Among these savages I hoped to find perfect isolation from my race; to begin a new life and cast the old one away forever; this was more like rising from the grave into another life than anything human existence had to offer. I remained some months in the Mohawk Valley, waiting for news from England. I was anxious to hear that my efforts at concealment had been effectual and that my friends really believed me dead. News came at last that shook my soul to its centre once more. Varnham, my husband, was dead. He would not believe in my destruction, and after strict search traced me to London, and on shipboard, spite of my disguise.

"He put my property in trust, and taking the next ship that sailed followed me to America, with what purpose I never knew. The ship was lost, and every soul on board perished."

CHAPTER X
QUEEN ESTHER

"The Shawnee Indians had long been governed by a woman, whose name was both feared and respected through all the Six Nations. I need not dwell either upon her cruelty or her greatness. Had Elizabeth, of blessed memory, as sarcastic history names her, been thrown among savages, she would have been scarcely a rival to this remarkable chieftainess. The same indomitable love of power—the same ferocious affections, caressing the neck one day, which she gave to the axe on the next—the same haughty assumption of authority marked Queen Esther, the forest sovereign, and Elizabeth, the monarch of England. Both were arrogant, crafty, selfish and ruthless, proving their power to govern, only as they became harsh and unwomanly.

"Queen Esther was the widow of a great chief, whose authority she had taken up at his grave, and never laid down during twenty-five years, when Gi cngwa-lah, her eldest son, had earned a right to wear the eagle plume and fill his father's place on the warpath and at the council table. The great secret of this woman's power over her tribe lay in her superior intelligence and the remnants of an early education; for she was a white woman, brought in the bloom of girlhood from Canada, where she had been taken prisoner in the wars between the French and the Six Nations. Her father was a governor of Canada, and she had been destined to fill a high station in civilized life, but she soon learned to prefer savage rule to all the remembrances of a delicately nurtured childhood, and, wedded to a native chief, flung off the refinements of life, save where they added to her influence among the savages.

"Her name, like her history, was thrown back upon the past—the very blood in her veins seemed to have received a ferocious tint. She was, doubtless, from the first, a savage at heart. Because this woman was, like myself, cast out by her own free will from civilized life, I sought her in her wild home, and, under an escort from Sir William Johnson, claimed a place in her tribe. The lands around Seneca Lake were then in possession of the Shawnees. Queen Esther occupied a spacious lodge at the head of this lake and had put large tracts of land under cultivation around it.

"Around this dwelling she had gathered all the refinements of her previous life that could be wrested from rude nature or animal strength. Her lodge possessed many comforts that the frontier settlers might have envied. The lands were rich with corn and fruit. Her apple orchards blossomed and cast their fruit on the edge of the wilderness. The huts of her people were embowered with peach-trees, and purple plums dropped upon the forest sward at their doors. In times of peace Queen Esther was a provident and wise sovereign. In war—but I need not say how terrible she was in war. Beautiful as I have described it, was the country of the Shawnees when my escort drew up in front of Queen Esther's lodge. She came forth to meet me, arrayed in her wild, queenly garb and treading the green turf like an empress. She was then more than sixty years of age, but her stately form bore no marks of time; there was not a thread of silver in her black hair, and her eyes were like those of an eagle—clear and piercing.

"She read Sir William's letter, casting glances from that to my face, as if perusing the two with one thought; then, advancing to my horse, she lifted me to the ground and gave me her hand to kiss, as if I had been a child and she an emperor who had vouchsafed an act of gallantry. 'It is well,' she said. 'You shall have a mat in my lodge. Gi-en-gwa-tah shall spread it with his own hands, for we of the white blood bring wise thoughts and sweet words to the tribe, and must not work like squaws. When women sit in council the braves spread their mats and spear salmon for them. This is my law.'

"I answered promptly that I had brought gold, knowledge and a true heart into the wilderness; that all I asked was a corner in her lodge, and permission to rest among her people; to learn their ways and be one of them till death called me away.

"'It is well,' she answered. 'This letter says that you have fled from many tears, and brought wisdom and gold from over the big waters. Come, I have a robe embroidered with my own hand, and plumage from flame-colored birds, with which my women shall crown you before my son comes from the war-council of the Six Nations. My eyes are getting dim, and I can no longer string the wampum or work garlands on the robes my women have prepared for my needle. You shall be eyes to me; when my voice grows weak you shall talk sweet words to the warriors, and they will obey me still. When I am dead, struck down with the white frost of age, then you shall be queen in my place; I will teach the chiefs to obey you. Have I spoken well?'

"She waited for no answer, but led me into the lodge, brought forth a robe of embroidered skins such as clothed her own stately person, and clothed me in it with her own hands. If she used any other ceremony of adoption, I did not understand it, nor indeed how much this act portended. Queen

Esther was a shrewd woman, ambitious for herself and her tribe. She knew well the value of the gold which I had deposited with Sir William Johnson, and how rich a harvest my coming might secure to them.

"Queen Esther kept her promise. Her influence placed me at once in a position of power. She never asked my name, but gave me that which she had cast aside on renouncing her own race—Catharine Montour.

"I was among the children of nature, in the broad, deep forests of a new world. I had broken every tie which had bound me to my kind, and was free. For the first time in my life I felt the force of liberty and the wild, sublime pleasures of an unshackled spirit. Every new thought which awoke my heart in that deep wilderness was full of sublimity and wild poetic strength. There was something of stern, inborn greatness in the savages who had adopted me—something picturesque in their raiment, and majestic in their wild, untaught eloquence, that aroused the new and stern properties of my nature till my very being seemed changed.

"The wish to be loved and cherished forsook me forever. New energies started to life, and I almost scorned myself that I had ever bowed to the weakness of affection. What was dominion over one heart compared to the knowledge that the wild, fierce spirits of a thousand savage beings were quelled by the sound of my footsteps?—not with a physical and cowardly fear, but with an awe which was of the spirit—a superstitious dread, which was to them a religion. Without any effort of my own, I became a being of fear and wonder to the whole savage nation. They looked upon me as a spirit from the great hunting-ground, sent to them by Manitou, endowed with beauty and supernatural powers, which demanded all their rude worship, and fixed me among them as a deity.

"I encouraged this belief, for a thirst for rule and ascendency was strong upon me. I became a despot and yet a benefactress in the exercise of my power, and the distribution of my wealth. Did one of those strong, savage creatures dare to offend me, I had but to lift my finger, and he was stripped of his ornaments and scourged forth from his nation, a disgraced and abandoned alien, without home, or people, or friends. On the other hand, did they wish for trinkets, or beads, or powder for the rifles which I had presented to them, they had to bend low to their 'White Prophetess' as she passed; to weave her lodge with flowers, and line it with rich furs; to bring her a singing-bird, or to carry her litter through the rough passes of the mountains, and a piece of smooth bark, covered with signs which they knew nothing of, was sent to Sir William Johnson, and lo, their wants were supplied.

"This was power, such as my changed heart panted for. I grew stern, selfish and despotic, among these rude savages, but never cruel. Your people wrong me there; no drop of blood has ever been shed by me or through my instrumentality; but my gold has brought many poor victims from the stake, who falsely believe that my vindictive power had sent them there; my entreaties have saved many a village from the flames, and many hearths from desolation, where my name is spoken as a word of fear.

"The eldest son of Queen Esther was a noble. He came of his father's race, with something of refinement, which his mother never could entirely cast aside, blended with it. From her early recollections Queen Esther had given him fragments of a rude poetical education, and this, with the domestic refinement of her lodge, had lifted him unconsciously above the other chiefs of his tribe.

"He not only possessed that bravery which won the admiration of his people, and was essential to their respect, but in his character were combined all the elements of a warrior and a statesman. Independent of this superior knowledge, his mind was naturally too majestic and penetrating to yield me the homage which was so readily rendered by the more ignorant of his tribe.

"It is painful to dwell on this period of my life. Suffice it, again I heard the pleadings of love from the untutored lips of a savage chief. I, who had fled from the very name of affection as from a pestilence—who had given up country, home, the semblance of existence that my heart might be at rest, was forced to listen to the pleadings of love from a savage, in the heart of an American wilderness. A savage chief, proud of his prowess, haughty in his barbarous power, came with a lordly confidence to woo me as his wife. My heart recoiled at the unnatural suggestion, but I had no scorn for the brave Indian who made it. If his mode of wooing was rough, it was also eloquent, sincere, manly; and those were properties which my spirit had ever answered with respect. No; I had nothing of scorn for the red warrior, but I rebuked him for his boldness, and threatened to forsake his tribe forever should he dare to renew the subject.

"A month or two after the kingly savage declared his bold wishes a contest arose between the Shawnees and a neighboring tribe, and the chief went angry to the warpath. One day his party returned to the encampment, bringing with them three prisoners, a white man, his wife and child. My heart ached when I heard of this, for I dared not, as usual, entreat the chief for their release, nor even offer to purchase their freedom with gold. His disappointment had rendered him almost morose, and I shuddered to think of the reward he might require for the liberation of his prisoners. I had full cause for apprehension.

"From the day that I rejected her son, Queen Esther had kept proudly aloof from me. She did not deign to expostulate, but guarded her pride with stern silence, while a storm of savage passions lowered on her brow, and sounded in her fierce tread, till her presence would have been a terror to me had I been of a nature to fear anything.

"This woman seemed to rejoice at the idea of wreaking the vengeance she would not express in words on my helpless compatriots, and prepared herself to join this horrid festival of death in all the pomp of her war-plumes and most gorgeous raiment. For the first time in my life I humbled myself before this woman, on my knees, for she was one to exact the most abject homage. I besought her to save my countrymen from death.

"She met my entreaties with a cold sneer that froze me to the heart.

"'It is well,' she said, wrapping her robe around her with a violence that made its wampum fringes rattle like a storm of shot. 'The woman who refuses the great chief of the Shawnees when he would build her a lodge larger than his mother's, should be proud, and stand up with her face to the sun, not whine like a baby because her people do not know how to die.'

"Her air and voice were more cruel than her words. I saw that my intercession would only add to the tortures that I was powerless to prevent, for if the mother was so unrelenting what had I to expect from the son?

"Queen Esther tore her garments from my clasp, and plunged into the forest to join her son.

"I shudder even now, when I think of the horrible sensation which crept over me, as the warriors went forth from the camp, file after file, painted and plumed with gorgeous leathers, each with his war-club and tomahawk, to put three beings, of my blood and nation, to a death of torture.

"I dared not plead for their release in person, but sent to offer ransom, earnestly appealing to the generosity of the chief in my message. He returned me no answer. I could do nothing more, but as the hours crept by, my heart was very, very heavy; it seemed as if the sin of blood were about to be heaped upon it.

"The night came on, dark and gloomy as the grave. The whole tribe, even to the women and children, had gone into the forest, and I was alone in the great lodge—almost alone in the village. There was something more appalling than I can describe in the dense gloom that settled on the wilderness, in the whoop and fierce cries of the revelling savages, which surged up through the trees like the roar and rant of a herd of wild beasts wrangling over their prey.

"Not a star was in the sky, not a sound stirred abroad—nothing save the black night and the horrid din of those blood-thirsty savages met my senses. Suddenly, a sharp yell cut through the air like the cry of a thousand famished hyenas, then a spire of flame darted up from the murky forest, and shot into the darkness with a clear, lurid brightness, like the flaming tongue of a dragon, quivering and afire with its own venom. Again that yell rang out—again and again, till the very air seemed alive with savage tongues.

"I could bear no more; my nerves had been too madly excited. I sprang forward with a cry that rang through the darkness almost as wildly as theirs, and rushed into the forest.

"They were congregated there in the light of that lurid fire, dancing and yelling like a troop of carousing demons; their tomahawks and scalping-knives flashed before me, and their fierce eyes glared more fiercely as I rushed through them to the presence of their chief. The dance was stopped by a motion of his war-club, and he listened with grave attention to my frantic offer of beads or blankets or gold to any amount, in ransom for his prisoners. He refused all; but one ransom could purchase the lives of those three human beings, and that I could not pay. It was far better that blood should be shed than that I should force my heart to consummate a union so horrible as mine with this savage.

"I turned from the relentless chief, sorrowing and heart-stricken. The blood of his poor victims seemed clogging my feet as I made my way through the crowd of savage forms that only waited my disappearance to drag them forth to death. Even while I passed the death-fire, fresh pine was heaped upon it, and a smothered cry burst forth from the dusky crowd as a volume of smoke rolled up and revealed the victims.

"They were bound to the trunk of a large pine, which towered within the glare of the death-fire, its heavy limbs reddening and drooping in the cloud of smoke and embers that surged through them to the sky, and its slender leaves falling in scorched and burning showers to the earth, whenever a gust of wind sent the flames directly among its foliage.

"The prisoners were almost entirely stripped of clothing, and the lurid brightness shed over the pine revealed their pale forms with terrible distinctness. The frightened child crouched upon the ground, clinging to the knees of his mother, and quaking in all its tiny limbs as the flames swept their reeking breath more and more hotly upon them. The long, black hair of the mother fell over her bent face; her arms were extended downward towards the boy, and she struggled weakly against the thongs that bound her waist, at every fresh effort which the poor thing made to find shelter in her bosom. There was one other face, pale and stern as marble, yet full of a fixed agony, which spoke of human suffering frightful to behold. That face was Grenville Murray's.

"My feelings had been excited almost to the verge of renewed insanity, but now they became calm—calm from the force of astonishment, and from the strong resolve of self-sacrifice which settled upon them. I turned and forced my way through the crowd of savage forms, rushing toward that hapless group, and again stood before their chief. I pointed toward the prisoners now concealed by the smoke and eddying flames.

"'Call away those fiends,' I said. 'Give back all that has been taken from the prisoners. Send them to Canada, with a guard of fifty warriors, and I will become your wife.'

"A blaze of exultation swept over that savage face, and the fire kindled it up with wild grandeur. I saw the heaving of his chest, the fierce joy that flashed from his eyes, but in that moment of stern resolve, my heart would not have shrunk from its purpose though the fang of an adder had been fixed in it. The chief lifted his war-club and uttered a long peculiar cry. Instantly the savages that were rushing like so many demons toward their prey fell back and ranged themselves in a broad circle around their chief.

"He spoke a few sentences in the Indian tongue. Words of energetic eloquence they must have been to have torn that savage horde from their destined victim's, for like wild beasts they seemed athirst for blood. When the chief ceased speaking, the tribe arose with a morose gravity that concealed their disappointment, and dispersed among the trees; the mellow tramp of their moccasins died away, and fifty warriors alone stood around their chief, ready to escort the prisoners to a place of safety.

"I drew back beneath the concealment of a tree, and secure in my changed dress, saw them lead forth the prisoners. I heard the sobs of the happy mother as the boy clung, half in joy and half in affright, to her bosom. I saw tears stand on the pale and quivering cheek of the father, as he strove to utter his gratitude. I heard the tramp of the horses, and the measured tread of the fifty warriors come faintly from the distance; then the fire which was to have been the death-flame of Grenville Murray and his household, streamed up into the solitude, and in its red glare I stood before the savage whose slave I had become."

CHAPTER XI
THE MARRIAGE CONTRACT

Toward sunset, on the same day that witnessed Catharine Montour's interview with the missionary, Mary Derwent wandered alone into the forest, for her spirit more than ever felt the need of solitude. With a strong religious principle, which had gradually strengthened in her young heart during her daily communion with the high things in nature, she had striven to conquer the sweet impulses of love that are the heritage of womanhood, and to lend all her soul toward that heaven to which the missionary had so tenderly pointed her.

She wandered through the forest, indulging in a tranquil happiness which had never visited her before. The flowers seemed smiling with a new beauty as she turned aside, that they might not be trodden into the moss by her footsteps; the birds seemed vocal with a sweeter music, and the air came balmy to her lips; yet the day, in reality, was no finer than a hundred others had been.

Mary lingered awhile on the shelf of rocks, which we have described in a former chapter, as overhanging the Susquehanna, nearly opposite Monockonok Island, before she went down to the canoe which she had moored at its base. It seemed as if this spot was henceforth to be a scene of adventure to her, for scarcely had she been there a moment, when the copsewood above her head was agitated, as it had been on the previous day, and a young man, of two or three and twenty, stepped cautiously out upon the platform which shot above the shelf on which she stood, and where the Indian girl had previously appeared.

Mary sank back to the birch, where she could command a full view of his person without being herself seen. He was scarcely above the middle height, and of slight person, but muscular, and giving, in every firmly knitted limb, indications of strength greater than his size would have warranted. The face was one which might have been pronounced intellectual and striking. His forehead, low and broad, was shaded by hair of the deepest brown; the nose, a little too prominent for beauty, was thin and finely cut, and the large black eyes full of brilliancy, which was a part of themselves rather than a light from the soul, gave a masculine spirit to his head, which redeemed the more earthly and coarser mould of the mouth and chin.

He was expensively dressed for the period and condition of our country, but his neckcloth was loosened at the throat, as if to refresh himself with air after some severe physical exertion, and his richly laced hand-ruffles hung dripping with water over a pair of wrists which were by far too slender and white ever to have submitted to much labor. His garments throughout were dashed with waterdrops, and he had evidently been rowing hard upon the river. He wiped away the perspiration which stood in large drops on his forehead, and looked cautiously about, till his eyes settled in a long, anxious gaze up the stream.

In its side position Mary obtained a more perfect view of his face, and her heart throbbed with a painful feeling of surprise, for she recognized the matured lineaments of Walter Butler, a Tory officer, who had visited the valley some months before and was the intimate friend of young Wintermoot, the young man who had so cruelly insulted her deformity when both were school-children. In his previous visit Butler had by many a rude outrage and insolent speech shocked the moral sense of the inhabitants, and it was an evil sign when he and the Wintermoots were sheltered under the same roof. The poor girl shrunk timidly behind the birch, for she was terrified and afraid of being discovered, but she did not withdraw so far as to prevent herself watching his movements.

After waiting a few moments, he went down, so as to preclude all possibility of being observed from the island, and uttered the same sharp whistle that had answered the Indian girl's summons on the previous day. Mary almost started from her concealment with surprise, when the brushwood was again torn back, and a strange woman, singularly attired, stepped down on the platform, and stood directly before the young man as he arose from his stooping position.

Butler started back almost to the verge of the precipice, when he found himself thus unexpectedly confronted. His face became crimson to the temples, and he looked with an air of extreme embarrassment, now on the strange woman, then on the path which led from the precipice, as if meditating an escape. The strange woman kept her eyes fixed keenly upon his movements; when he stepped a pace forward, as if about to leave her presence, she made a detaining motion with her hand.

"You were expecting Tahmeroo, the Shawnee maiden. I am Catharine Montour, her mother."

The blood suddenly left the young man's face. He bit his lips impatiently, for a half-checked oath trembled upon them; but his confusion was too overwhelming for any attempt at an answer. After a moment's pause, Catharine, who kept her piercing gaze steadily fixed on his face, drew forth the string of red coral which had been given to her daughter, and said:

"Last night my daughter told me all that you bade her conceal; from your first meeting on the shores of Seneca Lake, down to the crafty falsehood of this pledge, I know everything."

The crimson flush again spread over the young man's face, his eyes sunk beneath the scrutiny fixed upon him, and he turned his head aside, muttering:

"The beautiful witch has exposed me at last," then he looked Catharine Montour in the face with an affectation of cool effrontery, and said:

"Well, madam, if Tahmeroo has chosen to confide in her mother, I do not see anything remarkable in it, except that I should be sought out as a party in the affair."

"Young man," exclaimed the unhappy mother, in a voice of stern and bitter anguish, which made even his heart recoil, "you know not what you have done—you cannot dream of the wretchedness which you have heaped on a being who never injured you. I can find no words to tell how dear that child was to me, how completely every thought and wish was centred in her pure existence. I had guarded her as the strings of my own heart—every thought of her young mind was pure—every impulse an affectionate one—I will not reproach you, man! I will try not to hate you, though, Heaven is my judge, I have just cause for hate. Listen to me—I did not come here to heap invectives on you——"

"May I be permitted to ask what you did come for?" interrupted Butler, with a cool effrontery, which was now real, for his awe of Catharine Montour abated when he saw her sternness giving way to the grief and indignation of a wronged mother. "I really am at a loss to know why you should address me in this strange manner. I have not stolen the girl from your wigwam, nor have I the least intention of doing so foolish a thing. You have your daughter, what more do you require?"

Catharine Montour drew her lips hard together, and her frame shook with a stern effort to preserve her composure.

"I would have justice done my child," said she, in a voice so low and calm, yet with such iron determination in its tone, that the young man grew pale as it fell upon his ear; and though his words continued bold, the voice in which they were uttered was that of a man determined to keep his position, though he begins to feel the ground giving way beneath his feet.

"This demand, in the parlance of our nation, would mean that I should submit to a marriage with the girl," he said; "but even her mother can hardly suppose that I, a descendant of one of England's proudest families, should marry with a Shawnee half-breed, though she were beautiful as an angel, and amiable as her respected mamma. You have evidently seen something of life, madam, and must see how impossible it is that I should marry your daughter, yet in what other form this strange demand is to be shaped, I cannot imagine."

Catharine Montour forced herself to hear him out, though a scornful cloud gathered on her forehead. Her lips writhed, her eyes flashed with the angry contempt which filled her soul against the arrogance and selfishness betrayed in the being before her.

"It is a legal marriage, nevertheless, which I require of you," she said. "Listen before you reply—I have that to offer which may reconcile you even to an union with the daughter of a Shawnee chief. You but now boasted of English birth and of noble lineage. You are young, and one's native land is very dear; you should wish to dwell in it. Make my daughter your wife—go with her to your own country, where her Indian blood will be unsuspected, or, if known, will be no reproach, and I pledge myself, within one week after your marriage, to put you in possession of fifty thousand pounds as her dowry—to relinquish her forever," here Catharine's voice trembled in spite of her effort to speak firmly, "and to hold communion with her only on such terms as you may yourself direct. Nay, do not speak, but hear me out before you answer. I make this offer because the happiness of my child is dearer to me than my own life. I cannot crush her young life by separating her from you forever; better far that I should become childless and desolate again. Take her to your own land; be a kind, generous protector to her, and there is wealth in England that will make the amount I offer of little moment. For her sake I will once more enter the world, and claim my own. But deal harshly with her—let her feel a shadow of unkindness after you take her from the shelter of my love, and my vengeance shall follow you to the uttermost ends of the earth. Give me no answer yet, but reflect on the alternative should you refuse one who has but to speak her will, and a thousand fierce savages are on your track by day and by night, till your heart is haunted to death by its own fears, or is crushed beneath the blow which sooner or later some dark hand will deal in the requital of the disgrace which you have put upon the daughter of a Shawnee."

Before Butler could recover from his astonishment at her extraordinary proposal, Catharine had disappeared among the brushwood. He stood as if lost in deep thought for several minutes after her departure, then walked the platform to and fro with an air of indecision and excitement, which was more than once denoted by a low laugh, evidently at the singular position in which he found himself placed. Once he muttered a few indistinct words, and looked towards the island with a smile which Mary was at a loss to understand. There was something of the plotting demon in it, which made her tremble as if some harm had been intended to herself.

When Catharine Montour returned, Butler was the first to speak. "Should I be inclined to accept your proposal," he said, "and to speak candidly, your daughter is beautiful enough to tempt a man to commit much greater folly; how can I be certain of your power to endow her as you promise?"

Catharine drew up her heavy sleeve and displayed the jewelled serpent coiled around her arm.

"This is some proof of my power to command wealth; at the encampment you shall be convinced beyond the possibility of a doubt."

"But how am I to be secure of personal safety, should the proof be insufficient to satisfy me, or should I see other reason to decline this strange contract. Once in the power of your savage tribe, I shall have but little chance of independent choice."

Catharine made no reply, but a smile of peculiar meaning passed over her face. She took a small whistle from her bosom, blew a shrill call and stood quietly enjoying the surprise of her companion, as some fifty or sixty red warriors started up from behind the shattered rocks and stunted trees that towered back from the precipice on which they stood, each armed with a rifle and with a tomahawk gleaming at his girdle.

"Were compulsion intended, you see I am not without power; were I but to lift this hand, you would be in eternity before it dropped to my side again; but fear nothing; go with me to the encampment, and on the honor of an Englishwoman, you shall be free should I fail to return and make good my promise."

"You give me excellent proofs of freedom," said the young man, glancing at the dusky faces lowering on him from, the shrubbery on every side.

Catharine stepped forward, and spoke a few words in the Indian tongue. Directly each swarthy form left its station, and the whole force departed in a body over the back of the precipice. Directly a fleet of canoes was unmoored from the sheltering underbrush that fringed the shore, and shot away up stream towards the Lackawanna gap. When the tramp of their receding feet died away in the forest, Catharine returned to the young man.

"You must be convinced, now, that no treachery is intended; that you are free to decide."

"I do not exactly fancy the idea of being forced to take a wife, whether I will or not; and at best, all this looks marvellously like it. But without farther words, I accept your proposal, on condition, however, that Tahmeroo is suffered to remain with her people till I may wish to retreat to England.

"There is an aristocratic old gentleman in the valley of the Mohawk, who calls himself my father; he might not fancy the arrangement, were I to introduce my Indian bride to the companionship of his wife and daughters. Arrange it that she remains with the tribe for the present, and settle the rest as you will."

Catharine gave a joyful start, which she strove in vain to suppress. The happiness of keeping her child a little longer made every nerve in her body thrill; but she grew calm in an instant, and coldly consented to that which she would have given worlds to obtain, but dared not propose.

Butler spoke again.

"Now, madam, I entreat you to return to the camp. I give my honor that I will follow in a half-hour's time, but in mercy grant me a few minutes' breathing-space. The thought of this sudden marriage affects me like a shower-bath; it is like forcing a man to be happy at the point of the bayonet. Think of having a half a dozen of those savage-looking rascals for groomsmen—rifles, scalping-knives, and all. I wish my dear, stern old father were here to give the bride away; the thought of his fury half reconciles me to the thing, independent of the thousands. Who, under heavens, would have thought of seeking an heiress among a nest of Shawnee squaws?"

The latter part of his speech was spoken in soliloquy, for Catharine had departed at his first request, without any apparent suspicion of his good faith. The concealed girl was both surprised and touched to observe that tears were streaming down the face which had appeared so stern and calm but a moment before.

"She is left to me a little longer—I could have blessed him when he said it."

Mary heard these words as the extraordinary woman passed, and her pure heart ached for the unhappy mother.

Butler remained on the rock till Catharine Montour had entirely disappeared; then he darted down the hill, and before Mary dared to venture forth from her concealment, his canoe was cutting across the river toward Monockonok Island. Mary stood almost petrified with astonishment when she saw the direction he was taking. "What had Walter Butler to do in the vicinity of her home?" Her heart throbbed painfully as she connected this question with the conversation which she had overheard between her sister and Edward Clark, on the previous day. She stood motionless till his canoe shot into the little cove where her own was always moored, and when a sharp whistle sounded from that direction, she bent breathlessly forward with her eyes fixed intently on the door of her own dwelling. It opened, and her sister, Jane, came out with her sun-bonnet in her hand, and walked swiftly toward the cove.

But the poor deformed girl pressed her hands hard upon her heart, and groaned aloud, when her suspicions were thus painfully confirmed. She sank upon the ground, and burying her face in her hands, prayed fervently and with an earnestness of purpose that brought something of relief to her fears. For half an hour she sat upon the rock with her pale face looking toward the island, watching the cove through the tears which almost blinded. Her silent, anxious sorrow was more like that of an angel grieving over the apostasy of a sister spirit, than that of a mortal suffering under the conviction of moral wrong in a beloved object. She saw her sister slowly return to the house, and remarked that she stopped more than once to look after Walter Butler, as he urged his canoe toward the precipice again. Mary buried her face in her hands, and held her breath, as his footsteps smote along the neighboring path, and were lost in the forest.

Campbell's Ledge and Scoville's Island

Catharine Montour sat in the door of her lodge at the foot of Campbell's Ledge. The encampment was almost deserted. Few women ever followed the warriors when they were called to a distant council-fire, and the men had gone into the forests on the opposite shore of the river, to meet their brethren from the Wind gap. The Tories from about Fort Wintermoot were to join the council, and from her high lodge Catharine could see a hundred council-fires gleaming out from the dense foliage which clothed the opposite hill.

The night was overcast, the moon and stars floated in soft gray vapors overhead, or were covered with black clouds sometimes sending pale ghastly gleams upon the mountains, and again whelming everything in darkness. Catharine was accustomed to the gloom of the forest, and her spirit always rose to meet the storms that swept over it; but now there was really no tempest, nothing but sombre stillness all around. The winds muttered and moaned along the mountain side. The waters rushed heavily down the valley, and those council-fires were suggestive of scenes more gloomy still. Like the black clouds overhead, they were full of brooding destruction.

But more sombre than all was the heart of Catharine Montour. On the morrow she was to resign all right over her only child to a man against whom her whole soul revolted. A bad, cruel man, whose name had even now become a terror wherever his foot had trod. She knew well that his influence among the Indians had always been pernicious; that as the war of the Revolution gathered strength, he had instigated the various savage tribes to participate in the contest and urged on cruelties that even savage warfare had not yet invented. A thousand times would that woman have died rather than given her daughter up to his wicked power, but here her supremacy was at fault. Tahmeroo loved the man, and the mother had suffered so bitterly in her own life from thwarted affection, that she dared not interpose a stern authority over the wishes of her child, otherwise the heathenish bond that already united those two persons would have been rent asunder, though she had died in the effort.

But now she had tenderness for her child, and the savage ambition of the Shawnee chief to contend against. It had long been his policy to unite his daughter with some white leader of power, for he was sufficiently educated himself to feel how unfit she would become for the savage life in which she was born; besides he wished to strengthen his political alliance with the whites and Col. John Butler, the father of this young man, was well known to the Indians as an officer of high authority among the Tories. His Tioga Rangers carried terror wherever they went, and the Shawnees had fought side by side with them in the Revolution too often for any doubt of their leader or his son. In acts of bravery, stern revenge and subtle diplomacy, such as the savages respected most, Walter Butler surpassed his father; and when Catharine looked toward the council-fires, she knew well that this young man was there, pouring his poisonous counsel into the listening ears of her people. How terribly that poison might work against herself, she did not yet know. In fact many events had transpired in the tribe during her absence from the settlement on Seneca Lake, of which she was not fully informed. Her grim mother-in-law, Queen Esther, had been busy during her late sojourn in the Mohawk Valley, and the effects of her crafty statesmanship were felt among the struggling revolutionists during the entire war. In this bold bad youth the cruel woman had found an ally, wicked and relentless as herself; in the war-councils of the Shawnees, and at the council-table of the whites he was her firm supporter.

Queen Esther had never forgiven Catharine's first refusal of her son; the indignity galled her savage pride. To this was added jealousy of the influence and power which the younger woman had soon obtained over the chief and his tribe. In the intelligence, beauty, and stern will of Catharine, Queen Esther found a rival whom she could neither overpower, despise, or intimidate. Both as a white woman and an Indian princess, she soon learned to regard her daughter-in-law with intense hate.

Like her son, Queen Esther had resolved to strengthen herself by an alliance with Tahmeroo and some partisan of her own. The chief loved his daughter with all the strength of his rude and poetic nature, and readily listened to anything that promised to give her happiness, and which should also forward these purposes.

When he learned from the crafty old queen that Tahmeroo had met the young white chief, Walter Butler, on the lake shore, while out in her canoe, and that an attachment had sprung up between them, both his ambition and his affections were aroused. Notwithstanding the great influence that Catharine had obtained over him, the pride of manhood was strong within him, and his own right of action he yielded to no one. In this Indian blood and breeding spoke out. Over his wife, his child, and his tribe, he kept dominion. Against his will even Catharine was powerless.

When he questioned Tahmeroo, and learned how completely the young white man had wound himself around her heart; when Butler himself, knowing well how lightly such ties were regarded by his own people, came and asked his daughter in marriage, according to the usages of the tribe, Gi-en-gwa-tah, regardless of the mother's absence, gave his child away, and adopted the young man as a Shawnee brave. With the Indians these ceremonies were solemn rites—with Walter Butler only one of the wild adventures he delighted in.

Directly after this heathen marriage, that section of the tribe which inhabited the head of Seneca Lake went to meet their brother Shawnees, who still remained on the Susquehanna. A swift runner was sent to inform Catharine Montour of the movement, and when she rejoined the warriors of her tribe, they were encamped in the Lackawanna gap, where a lodge had already been erected for her.

On the day of her arrival, and before she knew anything of these events, Tahmeroo had stealthily left the camp and made her way down the river in search of Butler. She knew well that some special ceremony was necessary to a marriage among the whites, and shrunk with terror from the very thought of confiding what had passed to her mother, till these forms were added to the Indian customs that already united them.

Butler had pacified her entreaties by the gift of coral, which Catharine took from under her pillow, and which led to that midnight explanation, and afterward to her interview with the missionary.

And now the unhappy woman sat waiting for the time of her sacrifice to arrive. As the shadows gathered darker and darker around her, Tahmeroo stole softly to the door and sat down on the turf at her feet; an hour back Catharine had spent some time in arraying her child for the ceremony that was to follow the breaking up of the council. With but silent indignation at the wrong that had been done her by the chief and his mother, she had performed her task. Of all her unhappy life this hour was filled with the heaviest and deepest trouble to that unhappy woman. Tahmeroo nestled close to her mother, took one hand in hers very tenderly, and laid her cheek in the palms.

"Mother, why are you so sad? Tahmeroo is very happy, but when she begins to smile this mournful look turns her joy into sighs."

Catharine turned her heavy eyes on that beautiful face. How strange it looked! The costly raiment which had displaced her savage costume seemed unnatural alike to mother and child.

"And you are truly happy, my child? say it again."

"Very happy!" answered the maiden, smiling.

"And you love this man very—very much?"

"Oh, *so* much, dear mother!"

"I am glad of this my child. I have no hope for you except in this love."

"No hope save in this love! Then your whole life may be full of hope. Without this love, Tahmeroo would die; for it fills all the world to her. Oh, mother, I did not know how beautiful the earth was till he came; the water down which his canoe passes grows pure as I look; if his hand touches a flower, it brightens to a star under my eye; the winter-berries turn to gold as he gathers them for me; I could kneel down and kiss the moss which his foot has walked over; the sound of his moccasins, away off in the forest, makes my heart leap for joy. Is not this love, mother?"

Catharine sobbed aloud; every sweet word that fell from her child brought its memory to stab her.

"Speak to me, mother; are you offended that I love him so much?"

Catharine writhed in her chair; it seemed as if she must die. Had she fled to the wilderness only to crucify her heart over again in the person of her child? Were the consequences of one error to follow her forever and ever? She lifted her clasped hands to heaven, and wildly asked these questions as if the lurid stars could answer her from the blackness that covered them. "Are you sorry that I love him so?" said Tahmeroo, weeping softly.

Catharine buried her face in both hands, while a struggle for composure shook her whole frame.

"See, see," whispered Tahmeroo, pointing toward the opposite mountains, "the council-fires have gone out. There, now that the moon gleams, I can see their canoes on the water. In a few moments he will be here."

Catharine looked suddenly up.

"Come," she said, taking Tahmeroo by the hand, "we must be ready."

As she spoke, a noise in the brushwood made her pause and listen; directly a man came forward, walking quietly toward the lodge.

Even in the darkness Tahmeroo could see that her mother turned pale.

It was the missionary who, punctual to his appointment, had found his way to the encampment. He sat down in the dim lights of the lodge. No one spoke; for he, too, seemed impressed by the solemn sadness of the hour. The next ten minutes were spent in dead silence—you could almost have heard the wild bound of Tahmeroo's heart, when sound of coming footsteps came up from the forest. Still no word was spoken. The pine knots heaped on the hearth gleamed up suddenly, and sent a ruddy glow over the lodge, revealing a strange, strange picture.

Catharine Montour sat on the couch of scarlet cloth and soft furs, robed in the same dress which she wore in the morning. Her arms were folded over her bosom, and her eyes dwelt sadly on the ground, though at every noise from without they were directed with a sharp, anxious look towards the door, that changed to a dull troubled glow, as if the approaching footsteps had something terrible in them.

Tahmeroo nestled to her mother's side, and looked wonderingly around the lodge; now upon the missionary, who sat in a rude chair opposite, with his face shaded by his hand, then on her own strange dress, with a sort of shy curiosity; she did not quite recognize herself in that rich satin and those yellow old laces. Indeed her dress would have been remarkable to any one, either savage or civilized. Her Indian costume had been replaced by a robe of gold-colored satin, of an obsolete but graceful fashion, which had prevailed twenty years before in England. A chain of massive gold was interwoven among the braids of long hair, for the first time enwreathed about her beautiful head, after the fashion of the whites; and a pair of long filagree earrings broke the exquisite outline of her throat on the other side.

There was something a little stiff and awkward in the solemn stillness of those around her, and in the strangeness of her dress, which kept her bright eyes on the ground, and sent the smile quivering from her lips as the tramp of feet came nearer and nearer to the lodge.

While the inmates of the lodge remained waiting in silent anxiety, a shadow fell across the opening, and Butler appeared before them with his clothes in much disorder, and evidently fatigued from his long walk through the forest.

Tahmeroo sprang impulsively to meet him; the wild joy of her Indian blood revelled in her cheek, and sparkled in her dark eyes, till they met her mother's reproving look, and felt the pitying gaze which the missionary fixed upon her. Then she shrunk back to her seat, blushing and trembling as if her natural joy at seeing the man she loved were something to be reproached for.

"Ha, my jewel of a red skin, have they made you afraid of me already?" said Butler, approaching her with a reckless kind of gaiety in his demeanor, and without appearing to observe the presence of any one except herself— "but why the deuce did you allow them to trick you out in this manner? You were a thousand times more piquant in the old dress. Come, don't look frightened, you are beautiful enough in anything. Pray, what are these good people waiting for?"

Then turning to Catharine Montour, who had risen at his bold approach, he said, with insolent familiarity:

"Thank you, my stately madam, for sending away your nest of Shawnee friends, though you have made me expend a great deal of fierce courage for nothing. I had prepared myself to run the gantlet bravely among the red devils. Thank you again—but I hope my solemn father-in-law is to be present, I left him camped around a burning circle of pitch and hemlock, settling all creation over his calumet."

Catharine listened with a frowning brow to his flippant speech, without deigning to answer.

"Upon my soul, this is pleasant," said the young man, turning to the missionary. "I am invited to my own wedding, but find only faces that would make tears unnecessary at a funeral. Faith, if this is considered a cordial reception into the wigwam of one's father-in-law, I'll retire."

The missionary looked gravely in his face, but did not speak; while Catharine arose with a frowning brow, and thrusting her hand under the pillows of the couch, drew forth a crimson-velvet casket, encrusted with gold, and set with three or four exquisitely painted medallions, each in itself a gem. She then drew an ebony box from under the couch, and unlocked it with some difficulty, for the spring turned heavily from disuse. This box she proceeded to open, though her hands looked cold as death, and her face was like marble as she lifted the lid.

Butler kept his eyes fixed on her movements, while he continued his unbecoming freedom of speech.

"Upon my honor," he whispered, glancing at the happy face of Tahmeroo, and drawing her towards him, "that smile is refreshing after the gloomy brow of your august mother. Pray, my dear——"

He broke off suddenly, for that instant the Shawnee chief swept aside the bear-skin from the door of his lodge and stood in the opening, with his council-robe gathered in cumbrous drapery about his imposing person, and his high, dusky brow crowned with a coronet of scarlet feathers, whence a plume shot up from the left side of his head. He was entirely unarmed, and held his calumet loosely in his right hand.

With a single stride he confronted the young man so abruptly that he drew back, catching his breath.

"Young brave," he said, in pure, stern English, "when the chief of the Shawnees bows his head to a woman, all other men speak low and look on the ground, listening for her voice. You speak fast. Your words come like the mountain brook that is shallow and breaks into foam, which is not good to drink. It is not well."

The stern grandeur of this rebuke brought the blood into Butler's face. He muttered something about a cold reception, but threw aside the flippant air which had been so offensive. It was not for his interest, or safety either, to brave the haughty Shawnee in his own encampment.

Catharine Montour came forward. She had several old documents in her hands, title deeds and letters patent, written on vellum, with broad seals, and the yellow tinge of age bespeaking their antiquity. These documents she placed in Butler's hands.

A keen, hungry greed broke into the young man's eyes as he read. Once or twice he turned his look from the parchment to Catharine's face, with increasing wonder and respect.

"And all this you consent to resign in behalf of Tahmeroo," he said, "or rather, in behalf of her husband."

"So far as the law permits, I resign it to my daughter," answered Catharine.

A flush stole over the young man's forehead; he knew by her voice that she comprehended all his meanness. But he was now more anxious than Catharine herself for the ceremony that gave so much wealth to his control; and this eager wish increased when he saw the casket open in her hand. She raised a necklace and a bracelet of magnificent diamonds from among the gems which it contained, and held them out for his inspection.

"Make yourself certain of their value," she said, in a dry, business tone, that had something of sarcasm in it, "for they are the security which I am about to offer, that my draft on Sir William Johnson shall be honorably met in a week from this date."

"I see that you intend to make a business transaction of the affair," replied Butler, carelessly receiving the jewels, which, however, he scrutinized with a closeness which betrayed a rapacious interest in their worth.

Catharine placed the casket in his hands with a smile of keen contempt.

"After you are fully satisfied of their value, this reverend man will receive them in trust. He has my sanction to deliver them to you three weeks from this day, should the draft which you hold in your hand remain at the time unpaid. Are you content with this arrangement?"

"I know little of the value of jewels," replied Butler, slowly closing the casket, "but should suppose that these might be sufficient security for the money."

"Perhaps this gentleman's opinion will satisfy your doubts," and taking the casket from Butler's hand, Catharine again touched the spring and held it before the missionary.

"No, no; I am not a judge," exclaimed the missionary, drawing back in his chair and pushing the casket away; but after a moment he looked up more composedly and said: "Excuse me, lady, I need not examine the jewels; from what I saw of them in the young gentleman's hand, I am certain that they are worth more than the sum named."

"Are you convinced?" said Catharine, again turning to Butler.

"Perfectly—let the ceremony proceed."

With a kingly gesture, the chief lifted the bear-skin again, and taking Tahmeroo by the hand, led her out upon the turf in front of her mother's lodge. Here a scene of wild grandeur presented itself. The whole encampment was surrounded by warriors in full costume, and glittering with arms. The Shawnees had risen from their council-fires, and moved in single file through the woods to the foot of Campbell's Ledge. Here they wound themselves, rank after rank, round the encampment, till the chief and his family were hedged in by a living wall. Those in the front rank held torches of pitch pine knots kindled at the dying council-brands, which flamed up in one vast girdle of fire, lighting up the savages in their gorgeous dresses, the dense forest trees in the background, and throwing smoky gleams on the bold face of the ledge itself.

The eyes of the Shawnee chief flamed up with natural triumph as he stood upon the forest sward, which those broad lights were turning to gold under his feet, and, with a wave of his hand, motioned Butler to his side.

"White brave," he said, "two moons ago I led my daughter to your wigwam, and, in the face of our tribe, she became your wife. It was well. But Catharine Montour is not content; she mourns that her child was given away, and she not there to rejoice. She says that your people have other laws, and that a wife given by the Shawnees is not a wife with our white fathers. Catharine is wise, and speaks well. The white brave shall make Tahmeroo his wife before his white brother here, who takes his law from the Great Spirit himself. Warriors, draw near and listen, while the young white brave makes his vow."

The chief placed Tahmeroo's hand in Butler's, and grasped them both in his own, while he waved one arm on high, thus commanding the warriors to draw near.

There was a stir among the savages; rank glided into rank, circle closed upon circle, till a triple ring of torches encircled the young pair, and a sea of waving plumes, wild faces, and sharp, glittering eyes, surged back into the forest. All this concourse of men stood motionless, obedient to the lifted hand of their chief.

Catharine Montour came forth from the lodge, pale and rigid, as if she were going to execution; after her walked the missionary, with a movement so still that it seemed a shadow gliding over the grass. He took his place before the young couple, opened his prayer-book, and commenced the ceremony. There was a slight delay, for Butler was unprovided with a ring. Catharine drew one from her finger, and gave it to the missionary. He touched her hand in receiving this ring. It was cold as ice.

It was a wonderful sound in the heart of that dense forest, the voice of a devout Christian giving that solemn marriage benediction, girded round by savages who had scarcely ever heard of the true God in their lives. But a strange sight it was when the haughty chief, the proud English lady, the minister, and that newly married couple sank gently to their knees, and all that tribe of savages fell to the earth also, with their swarthy foreheads in the dust, while the voice of that good man rose clear and loud, piercing the heavens with its solemn eloquence. Even the savages looked at each other with awe, and trod stealthily as they broke up in bands, and moved back toward the woods.

It was, indeed, a holy hour; for, though blood, flame, and rapine marked the course of that tribe for years after that august ceremony, the Indians sometimes grew less relentless when a cry for mercy reminded them of the marriage of their chief's daughter. When all was over, the missionary departed noiselessly as he came. The chief was disappointed when he looked round and saw that he was gone. He had munificently prepared a present of furs and wampum, which he desired to present, after the fashion of the whites. Catharine Montour saw nothing; she was still prostrate on the earth.

Butler went away soon after the missionary, scarcely deigning to make an excuse for his absence or name the time of his return. Tahmeroo gazed after him till great tears gathered in her eyes. Then a sudden thought—a quick pain; and, while her father gave orders to his warriors, and her mother bowed herself in the dust, she darted into the woods. Still dressed in those singular wedding garments, she forced her path through the forest along the mountain stream, and down the steep ramparts of Falling Spring, till she came out upon the river. Fragments of golden satin and rich lace were torn from her dress, and left clinging to brushwood and thorns in her passage, but she took no heed; the Indian blood in her veins was all on fire with jealousy. As she reached the foot of Falling Spring, a canoe shot out from the ravine through which its waters plunged to the river. She saw the waves glitter in its track, sprang downward, unmoored her own little craft, and flew along the windings of the Susquehanna like a sparrow hawk.

CHAPTER XII
THE CHERRY-TREE SPRING

Mary Derwent returned home with a mournful determination to seek the confidence of her sister—to inform her frankly of the knowledge she had obtained, and, if possible, to save her from, the consequences of her unprincipled encouragement of Walter Butler, when her faith was pledged to another.

She found Edward Clark and her sister seated by the only glazed window of the cabin, conversing cordially as usual. But, as the evening wore on, she observed that Jane grew petulant and restless. Two or three times she went to the door, looked out hurriedly, and returned without any obvious reason. She would not sit down by Clark again, but when he addressed her, answered him impatiently, as if his society had all at once become irksome.

Once Edward made some allusion to a farm which his father had promised to give him when he settled for life, and spoke of the kind of house he intended to build, asking Jane's opinion.

She answered abruptly that she was tired of farming and hard work of all kinds; indeed, she hoped the time would come when she need not be obliged to live in a log-house, and spoil her hands by washing dishes from morning till night.

Young Clark looked a little surprised at this sudden outbreak of discontent, but laughingly told the spoiled beauty that she should have a two-story frame house, with glass windows in every room when his ship came in from the moon, and the Indians were all driven from Wyoming.

Jane was about to return some saucy reply, but that instant a shrill whistle came up from the river, which brought a torrent of crimson into her face, and she looked wistfully at the door without daring to approach it.

Mary understood it all, and her pure heart ached within her. She blushed even more deeply than her sister; and when Jane attempted to speak carelessly of night birds which roosted on the island, her face grew troubled, like that of an angel who sees a beloved companion ready to fall.

Clark observed this embarrassment without suspecting its cause, while Mother Derwent droned on with her flax-wheel, and talked about the comfort of living upon an island where the wolves could only bark at you from the opposite shore, thus unconsciously aiding in her granddaughter's deception.

After a time, Clark mentioned Walter Butler, and observed that he had seen him on the river that day; something in Jane's manner seemed to excite his attention that moment, for he asked, a little suspiciously, if the young Tory had landed on the island.

Jane crimsoned to the temples again, but answered promptly, that she had not seen Mr. Butler in a week—that was, since her birthday.

This direct falsehood smote Mary to the heart; tears swelled to her eyes till she could hardly discern the beautiful face of her sister through the mist.

Filled with these unquiet thoughts, Mary went to her little bedroom, that she might weep and pray alone. As she closed the door, her sister was asking Edward Clark how far it was from Wyoming to Canada, and if all the handsome ladies there wore silk dresses and had hired people to wait on them?

Mary closed the door and went to bed, but she could not sleep; for the first time, the sweet voice of her sister, as it sounded through the thin partition, brought disquiet to her affectionate heart. She heard Edward Clark leave the house about ten o'clock, but it was more than an hour before Jane came to bed. When, at length, she felt the familiar touch of her cheek, it was heated with feverish thought. The deformed lay within her sister's arms, apparently asleep, but deliberating on the most effectual method of opening the subject which lay so heavily on her heart, when that whistle which had haunted her footsteps continually since the night before again sounded from the cove with a shrillness that cut to her heart like a dagger.

Jane caught her breath, rose suddenly to her elbow, and listened, while her frame trembled till it shook the bed. After a few minutes, during which the whistle sounded sharply again, she crept softly from the bed, put on her clothes, and stole from the house. Mary was so shocked and confounded that it was several minutes before she could collect her thoughts sufficiently to decide what course to pursue. At last she arose, and hastily dressing herself, ran down to the cove.

The trees hung in leafy quiet over the green sward, and the moonbeams shed their radiance on the waters as they rippled against the bank; no human being was in sight, but a strange canoe lay rocking at its mooring by the side of her own, and the murmur of distant voices came faintly from the direction of a spring which supplied the household with water.

The moonlight lay full on the overhanging trees as Mary approached, and, in the stillness, the voices she had heard became each moment more distinct. She paused in the shadow which fell across the footpath where it curved down into the little hollow. Her sister. Jane, was sitting on a rock just within the moonlight, which flickered through the boughs above, and by her side, with her hand in his, was Walter Butler.

He was speaking, and Mary's heart swelled with indignation as she listened to his words.

"Take your choice," he said, "remain here and become the wife, the drudge, of Edward Clark—condemn these beautiful hands to perpetual toil; milk his cows, cook for his workmen, be content with the reward of a homespun dress, now and then, to set off this form, which a king might look upon with admiration; accept this miserable life if you choose. But do not pass by the offer I make, without thought; for it is wealth, ease, luxury, in fact everything that beauty craves, against neglect and drudgery. I offer the heart of a man who knows how to estimate your beauty—who will deck it in gold and robe it in silks—who will provide servants to do your bidding, and surround you with such elegance as you never dreamed of. It is no idle promise, Jane, for I have become rich, very rich, independent of my father. What are you crying for? can I offer more than this?"

"Oh, no," replied the infatuated girl; "I was thinking of poor old grandma—dear, dear Mary; what will they do when I am gone—what will Edward Clark think of me?"

"Edward Clark again! and that old woman and selfish girl who have made you a slave. Will you never stop whimpering about them?—have I not promised that you shall send them money?"

"They would not take it; I am sure they would not touch a cent of your money. Indeed, I cannot help feeling bad when I think of leaving them in this manner. When we are married you will bring me back sometimes, won't you?"

"Yes, when we are married I will certainly bring you to see them; have no fear of that. It is now past twelve, and we must be many miles hence before daybreak. Come, dry these tears and go with me to the canoe—we are losing time—what good is there in all these tears? they only spoil your beauty; come, come."

As Butler spoke, he placed his arm round the weeping girl and drew her, with some violence, along the footpath; but they had scarcely reached the bend which led into the open moonlight when Mary Derwent stood in the way.

"The little Hunchback, by all the furies!" exclaimed Butler, girding the waist of his companion with a firm arm and attempting to drag her forward, though she struggled in his embrace, and with tears and sobs entreated him to free her.

"Jane—sister! you will not go with this wicked man; listen to me before you take this dreadful step! Ask him where he obtained the money which he but now boasted of. Jane, I have never, in the whole course of my life, told you a falsehood. Believe me now—this wicked man dares not deny what I say. He is another woman's husband! I heard him make the promise—I saw him on his way to perform that promise! Jane, it is a married man for whom you were about to forsake us. Let him deny it if he dare."

"Out of my path, lying imp! before I trample your shapeless carcass under my feet!" cried Butler, through his shut teeth.

But the undaunted girl kept her station, and her stately voice told how little effect his taunt on her deformity had made.

"I have told no lie," she exclaimed boldly, "and you dare not accuse me of it. Last evening I heard all that passed between you and the strange white woman who lives among the Shawnees. Jane, look in that face. Is there no guilt there?"

"You do not believe this," said Butler, still attempting to draw the wretched girl away.

"Yes, I do!" cried Jane, with sudden vehemence, and leaping from his grasp she flung her arms around Mary where she stood, and urged his departure with a degree of energy that he could no longer contend against. Baffled and full of rage, he loaded them both with bitter imprecations, and pushed out into the stream. Locked in each other's arms, the sisters saw him depart; one shedding tears of penitence and shame, the other full of thanksgiving.

As they stood thus, unable to speak from excess of feeling, the young vines were torn apart just above them, a pair of glittering eyes looked through, and a voice that made them cling closer to each other broke upon the night, sharp and wild as the cry of an angry bird.

"Look up, that I may see the pale face that comes between Tahmeroo and her love!"

With a wild bound that tore the vines before her into shreds, Tahmeroo leaped down among the loose rocks, and seizing Jane Derwent by the shoulder, dragged her up the path into the moonlight; for the clouds that had tented her wedding with their gloom were swept away now, leaving the sky clear, full of stars, and pearly with the glow of a full moon.

Jane Derwent shrunk and cowered under those flashing eyes. She was forced to her knees among the stones, and held there, while Tahmeroo perused her face, lineament by lineament, as if it had been a book in which her own destiny was written. A fierce, angry fire burned in those black eyes, and that mouth, so beautiful when it smiled, writhed and trembled with terror, scorn, and bitter, bitter hate. She clutched her hand on the poor girl's shoulder till its nails penetrated the skin; with the other hand she groped at her girdle, and drew a knife from its glittering sheath at her side; for this remnant of her savage dress she still retained.

Jane crouched down to the earth, shielding herself with both uplifted hands; her shrieks rang out, one upon another, till the opposite rocks echoed them back like demons.

This terror exasperated the young Indian to still keener madness. She drew back the knife with a force that lifted her clear of the form grovelling at her feet, the next instant it would have been buried in the white neck— but Mary Derwent sprang upon her, seized the uplifted arm and dragged it downward.

"Would you kill her? This is murder—she has never wronged you!"

Tahmeroo's rage broke fearfully over the gentle girl as she clung to her arm; for one instant it seemed checked by the agony of that lovely face; but another cry from Jane brought the fury back; her eyes rained fire; she tore her arm from the grasp of those poor little hands; again the knife quivered on high—again she drew back to give a sure blow.

But a stronger arm than Mary's grasped her now. The knife was torn from her with a force that sent her reeling down the bank—its blade flashed over her, struck with a sharp clink against the stones, rebounded and plunged into the spring, sending up a storm of diamonds as it fell.

"Tahmeroo—woman—squaw—how dare you touch this girl!"

Butler lifted Jane from the earth as he spoke, and holding her with one arm, thus confronted his young wife, as she rose from the stones-where he had dashed her.

She could not speak; her face was blanched; specks of foam settled on her marble lips; her eyes were lurid with smouldering fire, and all her limbs quivered like those of a dying animal.

At last her voice broke forth.

"You have struck Tahmeroo, and for her."

"Tahmeroo—woman—squaw—how dare
you touch this girl!" said Butler.

Something more than anger spoke in that voice—it had the dull hollow sound of desolation.

"Squaw—traitoress—half-breed!—go back to your wigwam before I lay you dead at the girl's feet!"

The Indian girl withered under this fiendish speech; she fell forward, grovelling, with her face to the earth, and lay there like a drift of autumn leaves, through which the wind is moaning. Her lamentations broke forth in the Indian tongue, but the tones were enough to win tears from marble.

Mary Derwent knelt down and took the drooping head upon her lap; the anguish in that face as it was turned to the moonlight went to her gentle soul.

"Oh, me! you have killed her; cruel, cruel man!" she said, lifting her eyes to the lowering face of Butler, who was striving to reassure Jane Derwent, passing by the sufferings of his wife with reckless scorn. "She cannot speak; every breath is a moan."

"Let her rest, then; no one wants her to speak, the young tigress! My poor Jane, the dagger was quivering over you when I came up. I shudder to think what might have happened but for your cries; had I been a little farther off, your cries could not have reached me, and I should have lost you eternally. Look up, dear one, now that I have saved your life it is mine, all mine."

Tahmeroo evidently heard these words; she struggled to get up, but sank back again, moaning out: "No, no, Tahmeroo is his wife!"

"You hear," said Mary Derwent, looking up at her sister, who, still trembling with terror, clung to young Butler with all her strength, and seemed soothed by his expressions of tender interest. "This poor girl is his wife, his cruel words are killing her. Leave his arms, sister; stand up alone, and look upon the woman you have both wronged, asking God to forgive you!"

"Come, come, with me now. Let the crooked little witch preach on. You are not safe here—the moment I leave you, this pretty fiend will find her knife again. She will not let you live a week. See how your sister tends her as if she, not you, had been hurt! Leave them together, sweet one; we can reach the canoe before they miss us. I shall leave Wyoming at once. Horses are ready for us down at Aunt Polly's tavern; before daylight we shall reach the Blue Mountains."

Butler whispered these words into Jane Derwent's ear, drawing her down to his side as he spoke, and enforcing his entreaties with covert caresses.

Half overcome with terror, half with these entreaties, the unhappy girl yielded herself to the power of his arm, and they both fled towards the shore.

CHAPTER XIII
THE MERITED LESSON

Tahmeroo heard the movement, sprang to her feet, and away, almost throwing Mary down the steep, with her first impetuous leap.

Recovering from the shock, Mary followed her, calling desperately after her sister.

In his hurry to reach the spring, Butler had dragged his canoe halfway up the bank, and it took a few moments to shove it into the water again. Frightened and weak, Jane had seated herself on a loose boulder, and eagerly watched him as he tugged at the little craft. By this time Tahmeroo confronted her husband, dragged the canoe desperately from his hold, and with the strength of a lioness, sent it shooting into the river.

The canoe was out of reach in a moment—for the quick current seized it, and it was soon dancing down its own silver path on the "broken waters," leaving the baffled villain and his victim helpless on the shore.

Butler ground his teeth. If he did not again load the poor Indian with rude epithets, it was from excess of rage. Tahmeroo was neither fierce nor weak now. The iron of her nature was taking its white heat; all the fiery sparks had been shot forth, but she was dangerous to trifle with just then, even without arms, and so still.

Mary was pleading with her sister.

"You are wronging her, degrading yourself—throwing away your good name forever," she said. "The poor feeling he calls love was given to her once, and you see how he outrages her now. Even though he had the power to make you his wife, her fate would be yours, Jane."

Jane turned her back upon the gentle pleader, repulsing her with both hands.

"That young Indian is not his wife, I say," she answered petulantly, and weeping, as much from annoyance as any remorseful feeling. "It takes something more than a savage pow-pow in the woods to bind an officer of the king. What does it amount to if she does call herself his wife?"

"Nothing, nothing whatever," said Butler, interposing, while Tahmeroo stood proudly silent. "Such contracts never last beyond the moon in which they are formed. If the Shawnee chief would insist on giving me his daughter, am I to blame? Such hospitality is a habit of his tribe."

"And dare you say that this is all the bond which unites you with this poor girl?" questioned Mary, with great dignity.

"Dare I say that?—of course I dare. She knows it well enough—can you think me a fool?"

"Yes," said a voice, which made the audacious young man start, "if cruelty and falsehood are folly, you are the worst of fools. How dare you stand up in the face of high Heaven and disclaim vows yet warm on your lips? Jane Derwent, for your father's sake, believe me. This very evening I, invested with sacred power by the church, married Walter Butler to this young girl. He came from the Lodge, where this ceremony was performed, directly here. I was myself coming to the island, thinking to rest in your cabin till morning, but his arm was strongest and he reached the shore first."

"You hear him—you will believe this now!" said Mary tenderly, leaning over her sister.

Jane began to sob.

"What is the difference, supposing he speaks the truth?" said Butler, also bending over her. "I love you, and have the means of performing all my promises. Who will know or care about this forest hawk in our world?"

Jane Derwent was weak and miserably vain, but not vicious. Butler had enlisted no really deep feeling in his behalf. Indeed, but for her terror of the Indian girl, it is doubtful if she would have followed him to the shore. She had been taught from childhood up to regard the missionary with reverence, and never for an instant dreamed of doubting his word. Arising with an angry gesture, she put Butler aside and submitted herself to the caressing arm of her sister.

"Go to your wife," she said, with a burst of mortification. "She is only too good for you. I am sorry for her and despise you—a pretty creature you intended to make of me."

"Not at all, my dear. It was the Lord that made you a pretty creature to begin with, or I should never have troubled my head about you. After all, I dare say the whole thing would have turned out more plague than pleasure."

"Or profit, either," said the missionary, with the nearest approach to sarcasm that his heavenly voice or features could express. "Remember, for the present, I am that poor girl's trustee; wrong her by another word, and the draft upon Sir William Johnson shall be cancelled. Before morning I will deliver it back, with the casket of jewels in my bosom, to the lady whose munificence you have abused. Gold cannot re-kindle the love that would give happiness to this unfortunate child, but it shall save her from cruelty."

"Upon my word, old gentleman, you should have been a lawyer; among that hive of red skins up yonder. I really thought praying your vocation, but you are rather hard upon my harmless enterprise. I only wanted to torment little hunchback here, who has been following me round like a wildcat the whole week; there was nothing serious in the matter, I assure you, upon the honor of a gentleman."

The missionary regarded him for a moment in dead silence; the audacity of this falsehood was something new to him. It is probable he would have rebuked this coarse attempt at deception, but Tahmeroo came proudly up at the instant, and for her sake he refrained.

During this entire conversation the Indian bride had kept aloof, standing alone on the banks of the cove; as she moved towards them Butler's last speech fell upon her ear. She drew a deep breath, and listened for more. The light shone full upon her face; it was pale, but very beautiful, with the new hope his words had aroused—her eyes shone like stars. All the spirit of her fathers lay in the movement of that slender form. With the elasticity of sudden hope she came back to her old life.

Butler was eager to retaliate upon Jane, to convince the missionary and appease his bride. With that quick transition of manner which rendered him almost irresistible at times, he met Tahmeroo half way.

"There," he said, holding out both hands, "have I punished you enough, my fiery flamingo? Did you think I could not see that you were following my canoe all the time? But for that I should have been in the fort long ago; why, child, had it not been for my seeming wrath, you would have killed that silly girl yonder, and that would have set every patriot in the valley on your track."

She stood looking at him, the haughtiness dropped away from her figure, and her lips began to tremble.

"Tahmeroo's heart is like a white flower on the rocks; it opens to the rain, but folds itself close when thunder comes," she said at last. "Speak again, that she may know how to answer."

He knew that she was trembling from head to foot; that a passionate outbreak of forgiveness lay under those figurative words.

"What shall I say, Tahmeroo?—what is there to explain, where two people love each other as we do?"

She gave him her hand then—she gathered both his against her heart, that he might feel how loudly it was beating.

Butler cast a triumphant look on Jane. It pleased him that she witnessed the passionate love, the ready forgiveness, of that spirited young creature.

"Did you think, sir," he said, leading his bride up to the missionary, "that any man could earnestly seek another while a being like this belonged to him?"

Poor Jane, she was no match for the audacity of this man, but fairly burst into tears of mortified vanity. It was a salutary lesson, which no one wished to render less impressive than it proved.

Tahmeroo stood by her husband in silence. All her sensitive modesty had returned, and she was restless, like a wild bird eager to get back to its cage.

The missionary did not reply. He seemed to have forgotten what had gone before, and stood mournfully gazing on that young face.

"God be thanked if I have saved her one pang," he murmured, in answer to some thought that arose at the sight of her beauty.

But the young man became impatient.

"Tahmeroo waits to take leave of you, reverend sir. I trust this reckless escapade has done us no harm in your good opinion. The young lady there will tell you it was but a wild freak to annoy her sister, and to punish Tahmeroo a little for the jealousy which sent her off like a wild hawk upon the night. I trust you will not think it worth while to mention the affair to my august mother-in-law before we meet again in the valley of the Mohawk!"

"I understand," answered the missionary briefly, "and inform you that the power to enforce the conditions of your marriage contract rests with me, so let the fact of your visiting this island remain among ourselves."

"You are generous, sir," answered Butler, covering the bitterness of his defeat under an appearance of grateful feeling. "Come, Tahmeroo, show me your craft, and I will take you back to the Ledge. My poor canoe is half-way to Wilkesbarre by this time, I dare say."

He wound his arm around the young Indian exactly as he had supported Jane Derwent a few minutes before, passed by that astonished girl with a careless nod of the head, and in this fashion was about to leave the cove; but Tahmeroo disengaged herself from his arm, and came back with a wild grace that touched the missionary to the heart. She knelt down before him, and bent her head for a blessing, as she had bowed at his feet once before that night.

He did not touch her head; some unaccountable feeling kept him from that; but he lifted both hands to heaven and blessed her fervently. Tahmeroo arose, passed Jane quickly, and, taking Mary's hand, with a look of ineffable gratitude laid it against her heart.

"When the war storm comes, Tahmeroo will remember the white bird."

With a throb of affection, for which she could not account even to herself, Mary wound her arms around that bending neck, and drew the Indian girl close to her bosom. For an instant those two hearts beat against each other with full heavy throbs. When Mary unlocked her arms, it seemed as if a portion of her own life had been carried away, leaving her richer than ever.

Before she had time to wonder at this, Tahmeroo and her husband had disappeared.

Jane Derwent might well have trembled, had she known the vindictive feelings that man took away with him.

Mary Derwent arose early in the morning. She had not slept over night, but strove with many a gentle wile to soothe the indignant grief of her sister, and win for her the sleep that forsook her own eyelids. All night long she heard the missionary walking up and down the outer-room, with a sad, heavy step, as if some painful subject kept him from rest. At daybreak the front door closed, and his tread rose softly up from the green sward as he passed down to the water.

Mary stole out of bed and followed him. Jane had dropped asleep at last, and lay with the tears still trembling on her closed lashes and hot cheeks. Both anger and penitence for the time were hushed in slumber. Thus the deformed girl left the cabin unmolested, and overtook the missionary just as he was getting into his canoe.

"May I go with you?" she said, bending her sweet, troubled face upon him as he took up the oars.

"Why did you follow me, child?" he answered. "It is very early."

"I do not know—I was awake all night—something told me to follow you. They are all asleep and will not miss me—please take me in. I want to feel the wind from the river—our room has been so close all night that I can't breathe."

The missionary grew thoughtful while she was speaking; but at last he smiled, and bade her step into the canoe. She placed herself at his feet, sighing gently, as if some pain had left her heart.

"Is it far?" she asked, looking up stream toward Campbell's Ledge.

The missionary had told her nothing of his object; but he answered as if there had been some previous appointment between them.

"Last night they were encamped under the Ledge."

"And you will tell this white queen what happened—you will keep that bad man away from Monockonok?"

"It is for this I seek the camp; but why did you follow me?—how did you guess where I was going?"

"I don't know. That strange lady never spoke to me—never saw me in all her life; but I want to look at her again. She seemed standing by the bed all last night, asking me not to sleep. Sometimes I could almost see her crimson feathers wave and hear the wampum fringes rattle on her moccasins. I think that no shadow was ever so real before."

"And it was this strange fancy that sent you out so early?"

"Yes, for it was a fancy. I could see, as the day broke, that grandmother's crimson cardinal, which hung again the wall, had flung its shadow downward; but the idea of that strange lady had sunk into my heart before the light told me what it was. I longed to hear her voice again, to see her with the sunlight quivering about her head. Indeed, sir, she was like a queen standing there upon the rock. I caught my breath every time she spoke."

"And yet she did not speak to you?"

"No; I was out of sight, behind the brushwood. She did not know that a poor creature like me existed—how should she?"

The missionary bent heavily to his oars; drops of perspiration rose to his forehead; he beat the water with heavy, desperate pulls; but it was long before he answered.

They landed at Falling Spring, and made their way into the hills. A trail was broken through the undergrowth, where the Indians had passed up to the ledge the night before. Here and there a blackened pine-torch lay in the path, and fragments of rude finery clung to the thorn bushes.

The missionary moved on, buried in thought. Mary followed after, panting for breath, but unwilling to lag behind. At last he noticed that she mounted the hill with pain, and began to reproach himself, tenderly helping her forward. She saw that he grew pale with each advancing step, and that his hand hung nervously as he took hers, in the ascent. Why, she could not think. Surely he did not fear the savages then, after having stood in their midst the night before.

At last they came out upon a pile of rocks that overlooked the encampment. The whole basin, so full of savage life ten hours before, lay empty at their feet; not a human being was in sight; trampled grass, extinguished torches, and torn vines betrayed a scene of silent devastation. In the midst of it all stood Catharine Montour's lodge, drearily empty. The bear-skin was torn down from the entrance; the rich furs that had lined it were all removed; it was a heap of bare logs, through which the morning winds went whispering—nothing more.

The missionary and Mary Derwent looked wistfully in each other's faces; a dead feeling of disappointment settled upon them both.

"They are gone," he said, looking vaguely around; "gone without a sign; we are too late, Mary."

"It is dreary," said the deformed, seating herself on the threshold of Catharine's lodge; "I had so hoped to find the white lady here."

All at once she shaded her eyes with one hand, looking steadily westward.

"See! see!"

"What, my child?"

Far off, up the banks of the Susquehanna, she saw glimpses of moving crimson and warm russet breaking the green of the forest. The missionary searched the distance, and saw those living masses also.

"It is the whole tribe in motion—another dream vanishing away," he said, following the train with a look of indescribable sadness. "Let us descend, Mary; this is not God's time, but it will come."

Mary sat upon a fragment of rock, gazing up the river, with a feeling of keen disappointment; she had hoped to see that stately white woman again, and to have said one more kindly word to the young Indian bride; but there was no chance of that left. Even as she gazed, those living waves swept over a curve of the hills, and were lost in the green west. The girl sighed heavily, and stood up to go.

They went silently down the mountain together, and then as silently floated with the current of the river till their little shallop once more shot into the cove at Monockonok Island.

Jane was still asleep when her sister entered their little room; but an angry frown gathered on her face, and she muttered discontentedly as Mary strove to arouse her. When they came forth, Mother Derwent had the breakfast ready, waiting before the kitchen fire. The spider was turned up before a bed of coals, and the johnnycake within rose round and golden to the heat; a platter of venison steaks stood ready on the hearth, and the potatoes she was slicing into the hot gravy which they had left in the long-handled frying-pan hissed and browned over the fire, while the old lady stood, with the handle in one hand and a dripping knife in the other, waiting for the family to assemble around the little pine table set out so daintily in the centre of the kitchen.

Jane came from her room sullen and angry. The old lady was a little cross because no one had volunteered to help her get breakfast, and, as the best of women in those olden times would, scolded generally as she proceeded with her work.

"It was very strange," she said, "what had come over the young people of that day—the smartness had all gone out of them. When she was a girl, things were different—children were brought up to be useful then. They never thought of having parties, and dressing in chintz dresses—not they. An apple-cut or a log-rolling once a year, was amusement enough. True, some families did get up an extra husking, or quilting frolic, but when such excessive dissipation crept into a neighborhood, the minister took it up in his pulpit, and the sin was handled without mittens."

Jane sat down by the window, moody and restless. At another time the old granddame might have croned on with her complaints, and the girl would scarcely have heard them, she was so used to this eternal exaltation of the past over the present, which always has been, and always will be, a pleasant recreation for old ladies; but now Jane was fractious, and disposed to take offense at everything; so she broke into these running complaints with a violent burst of weeping, which startled the old dame till she almost dropped the frying-pan. The dear soul was quite unconscious that she had been scolding all the morning, and Jane's injured looks startled her.

"Are you sick, Janey dear?" she inquired kindly.

"No, Janey was not sick—but she wished she was dead—that she had never been born—in short, she didn't know what people were born for at all, especially girls that couldn't help being good-looking, and that nobody would let alone. If she had only been laid by her dear, dear father under the cedar trees the whole world wouldn't have been bent on persecuting her, especially her grandmother!"

This touched the old lady's heart to the centre. She forgot to stir the potatoes, and let them brown to a crisp in the pan. Indeed, she went so far as to rest that long handle on the back of a chair, and forsook her post altogether.

"Why, Janey, what is all this about, dear? Grandma wasn't scolding you, only talking to herself in a promiscuous way about things in general. Don't cry so—that's a darling. Come, now, grandma will get you something nice for breakfast—some preserved plums."

"No, Jane had no desire for preserved plums; she only wanted to die; it was a cruel world, and she didn't care, for her part, how soon she was out of it. Everybody was set against her. Mary did nothing but find fault, and as for Edward Clark—well, of course, some one would be slandering her to him next. The missionary himself might do it—ministers always must be meddling with other people's business. She shouldn't be surprised if Clark were even to believe that she didn't care for him, but was disappointed that Captain Butler had demeaned himself into marrying that little good-for-nothing squaw, who had been chasing after him so long. In fact, such was her own opinion of human nature—she shouldn't be astonished at anything, not even if the missionary, who had more silver on his head than he would ever get into his pocket, should fall in love with Mary."

At this, Grandma was horrified. How could Jane think of anything so dreadful?—but then, poor child, she was out of temper, and said whatever came uppermost—of course, it meant nothing, and Jane must not think she was scolding again—nothing of the sort.

But Jane did think grandma was scolding. Perhaps it was right that she, a poor orphan, who had only one dear grandmother in the wide, wide world should have that grandmother set against her. This was her destiny, she supposed, and submission was her duty; she only hoped nobody would be sorry for it after she was dead and gone, that was all.

How long Jane Derwent might have kept up this state of martyrdom it is difficult to say, but just as she was indulging in another outbreak of sorrowful self-compassion, Mary came up from the cove, looking pale and concerned. She had been to call the missionary to breakfast, and found him bailing out his canoe, ready to start from the island. He had spoken few words in leaving, but the hands which touched her forehead, as he blessed her, were cold as ice. She felt the chill of that benediction, holy as it was, at her heart yet; the sorrow upon her face startled Jane into a little natural feeling. She forgot to torment that kind old woman, and condescended to approach the breakfast table without more tears.

"Where is the minister?—why don't he come to breakfast?" inquired Mrs. Derwent, looking ruefully at the crisp little pile of potatoes left in the frying-pan. "I've had the table sot out a hull hour, and now everything is done to death. I wonder what on earth has come over you all!"

"The minister has gone away," answered Mary, and the tears welled into her eyes as she spoke.

"Gone away! marcy on us! and without a mouthful of breakfast. Why, gals! what have you been a-doing to him? He ain't mad nor nothing, is he?"

Mary smiled through her tears. The very idea of petty anger connected with the missionary seemed strange to her.

"Oh, grandma, he is never angry," she said; "but he seems anxious and troubled about something."

"Worried to death by them Injuns, I dare say," muttered the granddame, with a shake of the head that made her cap-borders tremble around the withered face. "They'll scalp him one of these days, for all the pains he takes."

"No, no; they love him too well—you don't really think this, grandma," cried Mary, turning pale with sudden terror.

"Well, no; I suppose he stands as good a chance as the rest of us; but that isn't saying over-much, for I tell you what, gals! there'll be squally times in the valley afore another year goes over our heads, or I lose my guess. All these 'ere forts and stockades ain't being built for nothing."

Jane started up in affright. "You don't think they mean to attack us at once?—that they are camping under the ledge in order to pounce upon us unawares, do you, grandma? Oh, I wish I was away! I wish I'd gone while there was a chance! They'll scalp me the very first one—I can almost feel that horrid Indian girl's knife in my hair!"

"Don't fear," said Mary; "they have left Campbell's Ledge. I was up there at daylight, and found the camp empty."

"You up there at daylight, Mary? What for?" cried Jane, flushing with angry surprise. "Who did you go to see?"

"I went with the missionary."

"And who was he after, I should like to know?"

"I believe, Jane he wished to speak with the young girl whom he married to Walter Butler last night, and perhaps to her mother, the strange white lady, also."

"And what about?—what business has that man with Walter Butler's affairs? I should think he'd meddled enough already," cried the angry beauty.

"It was not Butler, but his wife whom the minister went in search of."

"His wife!" cried Jane, with a magnificent curve of the lip, and a lift of the head that Juno might have envied. "What does an Indian wife amount to in the law?"

"A great deal, if she has been married by the law."

"But I don't believe one word of that; Butler isn't such a fool; he only said it to torment me, to—to—"

Jane lost herself here, for the keen look which Grandmother Derwent turned upon her brought caution with it.

"Well, gals, what on earth are you talking about? I don't want the name of that Tory captain mentioned under my cabin roof. His place is with the Wintermools, the Van Garders, and Van Alstyns—birds of a feather flock together. While I live, the man that makes himself friends with the off-scouring from York State had better keep clear of Monockonok Island."

Jane bit her lips with vexation, but she said nothing; for when the old woman waxed patriotic there was no opposing her, and even the beautiful favorite feared to urge the conversation farther.

Mother Derwent stepped to the door, and shading her eyes with one hand, looked up and down the river. Her kind old heart was distressed at the idea of the missionary going away without his breakfast. She saw his canoe at last gliding along the opposite shore and turned briskly around.

"There he is, neither out of sight nor hearing yet. Mary, run upstairs and shake a white cloth out of the garret window. You, Jane, bring me the tin dinner-horn. I'll give him a blast that shall bring him back, depend on't."

Mary ran to make the signal, and Jane took down a long tin dinner-horn from behind the door, which Mother Derwin blew vigorously, rising on tiptoe, and sending blast after blast upon the water, as if she had been summoning an army. The missionary heard the sound, and saw Mary with her white signal at the window. He waved his hand two or three times, sat down again, and directly disappeared in a bend of the shore.

Mary watched him with a heavy heart. It seemed as his canoe was lost to her sight that half her life had departed forever, and he, looking mournfully back, saw the snowy signal floating from the window, with a gush of tender sorrow. It was like the wing of an angel unfurling itself with vain efforts to follow him.

CHAPTER XIV
AUNT POLLY CARTER

But old Mother Derwent was not altogether disappointed. As if answering the blast of her horn a female appeared on the opposite shore, signalizing for a boat with great vigor. Mary could only see that the woman wore a short scarlet cloak, and that the brilliant cotton handkerchief flaunting so impatiently was large enough for a sail to any craft on the river.

Jane had withdrawn sulkily into the bedroom. She was by no means pleased with the efforts her grandmother was making to bring the missionary back; in her heart she was beginning to detest the good man.

When Mary came down and saw there was no one else to answer the stranger's signal, she went at once to unmoor her pretty canoe, and was soon across the river.

"Oh, is it you, my pet?" cried a cordial voice, as she neared the shore. "I thought mebby Jane would be on hand to row me across. Is grandmarm to hum, and how's your sister? Purty well, I hope?"

Mary's face brightened. The visitor was Aunt Polly from the Elm-tree tavern on the Kingston shore, a welcome guest at any house from Wilkesbarre to the Lackawanna gap, but a woman who seldom, left the shelter of her own roof, and her presence so far from her home might well be a matter of wonder.

"Why, Aunt Polly, is it you? How glad grandma will be," said Mary, looking up from her seat in the canoe with pleasure in her eyes.

"Yes, it's me sure enough, safe and sound. I'll just take the bits out of Gineral Washington's mouth, and let him crop a bite of grass while I go over and say how-do-you-do to grandma. See how the old feller eyes that thick grass with the vilets in it! There, old chap, go at it."

As she spoke, the old maid went up to a huge farm horse, cumbered with a saddle much too narrow for his back, which bore unmistakable evidence of its Connecticut origin; for the horns curved in like those of a vicious cow, and the stirrups were so short that a tall rider, like Aunt Polly, was compelled to double her limbs up till they formed a letter A under her calico skirt whenever General Washington had the honor of carrying her in state upon the wonderful mechanism of that side-saddle, which was the pride and glory of her house.

"There, now," she said, unbuckling the throat-latch, and slipping the bridle, bits and all, around General Washington's stumpy neck, which she patted with great affection. "Go in for a feed, and no mistake, Gineral; only keep to the bank, and, mind you, don't roll on that saddle—it couldn't be matched on this side the Green Mountains, I tell you, now."

General Washington seemed to understand all this perfectly, for he gave his great lumbering head a toss which signified plainer than words that he understood the value of that saddle quite as well as his mistress, and knew how to keep his peace, if it came to that, without being lectured about it. He whinnied out his satisfaction, in answer to Aunt Polly's caresses, and trotted off with great dignity toward a little rivulet on the bank, where the grass was green as emeralds, and the violets blue as a baby's eyes.

"There," said Aunt Polly, looking after him as he rolled heavily along, with the flesh quivering like a jelly under his sleek hide, "isn't he a picterful sight? Why, Mary dear, that hoss knows more than two-thirds of the men in Wyoming. Now, that saddle is jest as safe on his back as if it was hung up by the stirrup in my kitchen—he's a wonderful critter, is Gineral Washington."

With her head half turned back, in proud admiration of her steed, Aunt Polly let herself down the bank, talking all the time, and at last sat down in the bottom of the canoe, gathering her scarlet cloak around her, and covering her ankles decorously with the skirt of her striped dress. Then, with a gentle dip of the oars, Mary headed her little craft for the island.

Mother Derwent was both pleased at and annoyed by the sight of her visitor—pleased, because Aunt Polly Carter was born in the same old Connecticut town with herself; and annoyed, that she, the very best cook and housekeeper in Wyoming, should find a spoiled breakfast on the hearth—potatoes browned into chips, venison steaks with all the gravy dried up, and the johnnycake overdone. It was a terrible humiliation, and Mother Derwent felt as if she had been detected in some shameful act of negligence by her old friend of the Elm-tree tavern.

"Just in time," exclaimed Aunt Polly, taking off her cloak and untying her bonnet; "I was afraid breakfast 'ed be over afore I got here. Gracious goodness! Miss Derwent, don't you see that johnnycake's burnt to a crisp?—here, give it to me—half cold too, dear, dear—never mind, good soul! it might a-been worse—there, take it this way, and beat it between both hands a trifle—oh, that tea smells something like, oh, ha—you haven't forgot to cook a meal of victuals yet; you and I can give these Pennsylvanians a lesson any day, Miss Derwent."

Grandma explained how the breakfast had been kept waiting till it was quite spoiled; but Aunt Polly would listen to nothing of the kind—everything was excellent, the tea drawn beautifully, and the butter perfection. As for the preserved plums and crab-apples, she had tasted nothing equal to them in years; they had the real Connecticut flavor—quite put her in mind of old times.

They had all been seated at the table some minutes before Jane made her appearance. She was still moody, and received Aunt Polly with distrustful reserve, which the good lady did not seem to regard in the least, but went on with her breakfast, tranquil as a summer's day.

After they arose from the table there was a world of questions to ask, and experiments to try. Aunt Polly took pride in exhibiting all her accomplishments before the young girls. She sat down at the flax-wheel, arranged the threads in the flyers, and directly the whole cabin was filled with their hum.

"Look here, girls, and see how an old housekeeper can spin. Why, long before I was your age I had yards and yards of homespun linen out in father's spring meadow, whitening for my setting out. I've got a great chest full of that 'ere identical linen in my house this minute, that's never been used, and never will be till I'm settled for life."

Now, as Aunt Polly was a middle-aged woman when she left Connecticut, and had lived at the Elm-tree tavern twenty-five years, this idea of settling for life-which, of course, comprised a husband, who might also be landlord to that establishment—struck the young girls at once as so improbable that they both smiled.

Aunt Polly knew nothing of this, but kept spinning on—tread, tread, tread—now dipping her fingers in the dried shell of a mock-orange, that hung full of water to the distaff, and daintily moistening the flax as it ran through them—now stopping to change the thread on her flyer, and off again—hum—hum—with a smile of self-satisfaction that was pleasant to behold.

After this little display, the good landlady tried her hand at the loom, where a linen web was in progress of completion; but finding the quill-box empty, she called out with her cheerful voice for Jane to come and wind some quills, for she was dying to try her hand at the shuttle, if it was only to show them how things were done when she was a girl.

Jane could not altogether resist this good humor; still she came forward, half pouting, dragged the lumbering old swifts out from under the loom, banded her quill wheel, and soon supplied the empty shuttle, which Aunt Polly was so impatient to use.

Now there was a clatter indeed; the treadles rose and fell with grating moans beneath those resolute feet; the rude gearing shrieked on its pulleys; the shuttle flew in and out, now darting into the weaver's right hand—now into the left, while the lathe banged away, and the old loom trembled in all its timbers.

"That's right—look on, girls," cried the old maid with enthusiasm. "It'll be a good while, I reckon, before either of you can come up to this; but 'live and learn' is a good saying. Your grandmother and I've seen the time when we broke more threads with awkward throws than we knew how to mend with two thumbs and eight fingers. Just see this shuttle fly—isn't it beautiful? Oh, girls, there's nothing like work—it keeps the body healthy, and the soul out of mischief. Wind away, Janey, it'll do you lots of good; we'll keep at it till Miss Derwent has washed up the morning dishes; an extra yard'll help her along wonderfully—that's the music—keep the old wheel a-going—more quills—more quills!"

Jane took a double handful of quills from her lap and brought them to the loom. While Aunt Polly was putting one in her shuttle, she looked keenly in the young girl's face, shook her head, and went to work again more vigorously than before. Mary saw this, and was satisfied that the old maid had some deeper object in her visit than these experiments with her grandmother's wheel and loom.

But Aunt Polly went on with her work, becoming more and more excited with every fling of the shuttle. She let out her web and rolled her cloth-beam eight or nine times before her enthusiasm began to flag.

"There," she said at last, laying the empty shuttle daintily upon the cloth she had woven, and forcing herself out from the slanting seat, "if anybody wants an evener yard of cloth than that, let them weave it, I say. Now, Janey, come and show me your garden, and let's see if it's as forward as mine. I've had lettuce and peppergrass up this week."

Aunt Polly strode toward the door as she spoke, and Jane followed her.

"Now," said the old maid, facing round as they reached the garden, "you needn't suppose that I took Gineral Washington from the plough, and come up to Monockonok just to see you all. I should have waited till after planting-time for that; but I heard something last night that worried me more than a little, and I want to know what it means, for we marriageable females ought to stand by each other. How comes it, Jane Derwent, that the young men in my bar-room talk about you with their loose tongues, and dare to drink your health in glasses of corn whiskey which they sometimes forget to pay for?"

"Who has done this?" questioned Jane, firing up, "and if they have how can I help it?"

"I'll tell you how it was, Jane Derwent. Last night, nigh on to morning, Walter Butler and young Wintermoot, with three or four other rank Tories from the fort, came to my house, banging away at the door for us to get up and give them something to drink. Now, I hate these young fellers worse than pison, but one can't keep tavern and private house at the same time when a sign swings agin your door; any loafer has a right to call you out of bed when he pleases. Well, they knocked and hammered till I woke up the bar-keeper, and sent him down with orders to make their sling weak, and get rid of them the minute he could; but, mercy on us, gal, they had come down the river like a flock of wolves, and was just as easy to pacify. The amount of whiskey they drank among them in less than an hour no one would believe that hadn't seen it. There was nothing but a board partition between me and the bar-room; so I heard every word they said, and considering that I was a respectable female that might be called upon to accept an offer of marriage any day, their conversation was not exactly what it should have been."

"And they mentioned me—you said that?"

"Mentioned you? I should say they did—Butler, Wintermoot, and all the rest of em. I declare it made my blood bile to hear the language they used."

"Will you tell me what it was, Aunt Polly—me, and no one else, for I would not have grandma and Mary know it for the world?"

"Yes—that is what I came for. Young Wintermoot began first—teasing Butler because he'd tried to run away with you, and had to give it up after you'd both started, when a little hunchback and a sneak of a minister said he mustn't. These were his exact words. Then another set in and wanted to drink success to the next time in bumpers of hot toddy. Directly there was a crash of glasses and a shout, and in all the noise I heard your name over and over. Some were laughing; some said you were a beauty and no mistake, while Butler talked loudest, and said he was sure to get you away from the hunchback yet, spite of all your pride and ridiculous nonsense."

"He said that, did he?" cried Jane, biting her lips with silent rage.

"Yes, he said that, and more, yet. When one of the fellows asked what the pretty squaw would do, he laughed, and answered, as well as he could for hiccuping, that after he'd got some money that he expected from Sir John Johnson, she might go to Amsterdam, or where she could find more fire and less water, for all he cared. Then he went on telling how he had left her in the woods above Falling Spring, only a few hours before, crying like a baby because he would not stay and tramp back to Seneca Lake with her tribe.

"The young Tories received all this with bursts of laughter, joking about his squaw wife, and telling him what a fool he was to let you go when once a'most off. They said it was clear enough you didn't want to go with him, that he'd got the mitten straight out, because you liked Edward Clark better than him, and so he had married the squaw out of spite.

"That set him to swearing like a trooper; he said there wasn't a word of truth in it, that you were crazy in love with him, and would follow him like a dog to the ends of the earth, wife or no wife, if you could only escape from the island, and no one the wiser—more, he said that he left you crying your eyes out that very night because he went off with the Indian girl instead of you."

"It was false—there was not a word of truth in it, Aunt Polly. I hope I may drop down dead in my tracks if there was," cried Jane, trembling with rage and shame. "I was glad to see him go; Mary can tell you as much."

"Then you have seen him?" questioned Aunt Polly—"then he was on the island last night, as he said?"

"I can't help his coming to the island, Aunt Polly; every one comes here who has a boat, if he pleases; but I can say nobody wanted Walter Butler. He's been a-visiting the Wintermoots off and on for three or four months. I invited him and the Wintermoots to my birthday party, and was a fool for my pains; but as for liking him, the Tory, the young outcast, I—I——"

Here Jane burst into a torrent of angry tears. Aunt Polly began to dry up this sorrow tenderly with her great cotton handkerchief, which seemed large enough to block up a mill-sluice.

"Don't cry, Janey, don't cry, that's a dear. There, there, I shan't tell anybody but yourself about the scamp's boasting, not even Edward, though his father is my cousin."

"No, don't, Aunt Polly, don't tell him, of all people in the world."

"Why—why, Janey dear? How red you are! Tell me, you and Edward ain't keeping company, nor nothing, are you?"

"Yes, we are, Aunt Polly, and have been this ever so long. He would kill that hateful villain if he knew half that he said at your house last night."

"But he shan't know it, child; you, and I, and Mary will settle that affair amongst ourselves, to say nothing of grandma, who would be worth us all if it came to a running scold."

"Don't—don't say a word to Mary or grandma," cried Jane, in breathless fear; "but you have not told me all yet."

"No, Jane; what is to come makes the old Connecticut blood bile in my veins. I swan to man! it was all I could do to keep from jumping out of bed, and going in amongst them, when they sot down, and made up a plot to carry you off—them young Wintermoots was to do it, and meet Butler in the Blue Mountains after he'd got a heap of money that he expected from Sir John Johnson. I suppose that's the son of Sir William Johnson, the old reprobate who had so many Injun wives in the Mohawk Valley, as if one wife wasn't enough for any man in a new country where women folks are scarce. Well, as I was a-saying, Butler told 'em to go over to the island some night, and whistle like that—here he sent a long whistle through the partition that made me e'en a'most start up in bed, and the young Wintermoots practised on it like schoolboys learning their a-b-abs till they filled the hull house like a nest of blackbirds and brown thrashers.

"Butler told 'em that you'd spring out of bed like a hawk from its nest the moment you heard that, and if they only flattered you a little, and told you for earnest that he didn't care a king's farthing for the Indian girl, and wasn't married to her, only Indian fashion, you'd be off with them, and glad enough to go."

"He did, ha? he thinks I'll follow him. Never mind, Aunt Polly. Let him come—let them whistle. Oh, how I wish I was a man."

"Yes," said Aunt Polly, thoughtfully, "men have their privileges. It's something to be able to knock a chap down when he deserves it, and then, agin, when a man's heart is full he can speak out, and not let his feelings curdle like sour milk in a pan. Yes, Janey, I think it would be pleasant if some of us could be men once in a while; but human nature is human nature, and it ain't to be expected."

"And this was all these wicked men said?" questioned Jane, who had lost half this speech in her own bitter thoughts.

"Yes, for when their plot was laid, they left the house. I peeped through the window, holding the valance close, that they could not see my nightcap, you know, and watched them shake hands before Butler mounted his horse. He rode off down stream, and the other fellers turned up the road towards Wintermoot's Fort."

"And this was all?"

"All that belongs to you; but now I've a word to say to Mary; by that time Gineral Washington will be tired of cropping vilets, I reckon, and we'll be jogging down stream again."

"Mary! what can you want with Mary?—not to tell her——"

"By no manner of means, Janey. If you want anybody else to help you, arter what I've told about these chaps, the truth is, you ain't worth helping anyhow. A gal that can't take care of herself when once warned, wouldn't be kept back from ruin if a hull meeting-houseful of jest sich angels as our precious Mary was standing in the way. No, I don't mean to torment that heavenly critter with any sich wickedness; but yet I've got a few words to say to her, and you'll oblige me by going to the cabin and sending her out here at onst."

Jane was glad to obey. This interview with the old maid had not been so pleasant that she wished to prolong it; so she went and summoned Mary.

That gentle girl went into the garden a little anxious, for the excitement of the last night had found its reaction, and she was ready to tremble at the fall of a leaf.

The change that had come over Aunt Polly was a beautiful proof of the influence of a character like that of Mary Derwent. With Jane the old maid had been peremptory and dictatorial, feeling very little respect for the wayward girl—she expressed none; but for Mary her heart was filled with a world of tender reverence. She touched her daintily, as she would have plucked a snowdrop, and spoke to her in a low, earnest voice, such as she would have used in prayer, had she been much inclined to devotion.

"Mary," she said, laying one hard hand lightly on the maiden's shoulder, "a strange thing happened to me this morning. As Gineral Washington and I was on our way up stream, a woman came out from the beach-woods on the flats, and stopped right in the road, afore that knowing animal and me, as if she wanted to say something; but she didn't speak, and the Gineral sort o' shied at fust, for the red dress, all glittering with wampum, was enough to scare any hoss."

"Had she a scarlet dress on, a crown of feathers around her head, and a glittering snake twisted in her hair?" inquired Mary, quickly.

"That's her to a T. I shall never forget the sharp, red eyes of that sarpent; a live rattlesnake couldn't have eyed the Gineral and I more fiercely. I waited a minute, to give the woman a chance, if she wanted to speak, but she was searching my face with her eyes, as if she wanted to look me through afore she opened her lips. I was a'most tempted to up whip and ride straight over her; but the Gineral seemed to have his own idee—not a huff would he lift.

I shook the bridle like all-possessed, and chirruped him along, as if he'd been a nussing baby; but there he stood stock-still in the road, a-eyeing the strange woman jest as independent as she was eyeing him and me."

"And did she say nothing?"

"By-an'-by she spoke, and though it was afore sunrise, it seemed as if a bust of light broke over her face, it lit up so.

"'Can you tell me,' she said, 'where I can find a small island that lies in the river about here? I have passed one or two, but there are no houses on 'em, and the one I want has a cabin somewhere near the shore.'

"'Maybe you want Monockonok,' says I, 'where old Miss Derwent lives?'

"'Yes,' says she, 'that is the island and Derwent is the name. She has two daughters, I believe.'

"'Two granddaughters,' says I.

"'Granddaughters, are they? And de you know these girls?' says she.

"'Well, yes, I reckon so,' says I, 'and mighty smart gals they are. Jane's a beauty, without paint or whitewash, I can tell you; and as for Mary——' But no matter what I said about you, my dear; it wasn't all you deserved, but——"

"No matter—oh, there was no need of saying anything about me," murmured the deformed, shrinking within herself, as she always did when her person was alluded to.

Aunt Polly paused abruptly, and began to whip a sweet-briar bush near her with great vigor. She had but a vague idea of all the keen sensitiveness her words had disturbed, but that was sufficient; her rough, kind heart was troubled at the very idea of giving pain to that gentle girl.

"Well, I only said if ever there was an angel on earth, you was one; but I'm sorry as can be, now; I wouldn't 'a' said so for the world if I'd thought you didn't like it," pleaded the old maid with deprecating meekness. "You know, Mary Derwent, I always thought you was the salt of the 'arth—that's the worst I will say of you any how, like it or not."

"But the woman, Aunt Polly—the strange lady with that living serpent around her head—what did she want of Jane and me?" inquired Mary, keenly interested in the subject. "What could she mean by inquiring about grandmother?"

"Not knowing, can't tell, Miss Mary. She fell to thinking, with her hand up to her forehead—a purty hand it was, too—afore I'd done talking; at last says she:

"'That is the one I wish to speak with.'

"'Which,' says I, 'Miss Jane?'

"'No,' says she, 'the golden-haired one that you've been telling me about.'

"'Well,' says I, 'what of her, marm;? I'm just a-going over to Monockonok, and can show you the way, if you want to see her.'

"'No, not just now,' says she, 'I've something else to attend to first; but if you see this girl, tell her to meet me, near sunset, at the spring where she went so late last night—she will understand you.'

"'Well,' says I, 'if I may be so bold, what do you want with Mary Derwent?'

"'I wish to speak with her,' says she, with a wave of her hand that made Gineral Washington back off sideways; 'only give my message, good woman, and here's a guinea for you.'

"Here she took a piece of gold from her pocket, and held it out."

"But you did not take it, Aunt Polly?"

"Didn't take it! trust me for letting a bright golden guinea slip through these fingers when it can be honestly come by—of course I took it."

Here Aunt Polly drew forth a shot-bag from her enormous pocket, untied the towstring, and exhibited a quantity of silver and huge copper pennies, and from among them, daintily folded in a dry maple-leaf, she took a bright piece of gold.

"There it is, harnsome as a yaller bird," she cried exultingly. "Look at it, Mary—I don't mind your holding it a minute or so in your hand. I'd like to see any woman in Wyoming match that!"

"I never saw a golden guinea before," said Mary, scanning the coin with innocent curiosity. "It is very beautiful; but somehow, Aunt Polly, I can't help wishing you hadn't taken it."

"Well, if you think so," said the old maid, eyeing the gold with a rueful look, "if you really think so, Mary Derwent, jest give it back to the lady when she comes. I don't want to be mean, nor nothing, but—but—no, give it here—I can stand a good deal, but as for giving up money when it's once been in my puss, that's too much for human nature to put up with."

She snatched eagerly at the gold, and, with a grim smile upon her mouth, and a flush about her eyes, hustled it back into her shot-bag, tied the strings with a jerk, and crowded the treasure down into the depths of her pocket, uttering only a few grim words in the energetic operation.

"There now—I'd like to see anybody strong enough to get that 'ere money-puss out of this 'ere pocket, that's all!"

Mary felt how impossible it was for the old maid to release her hold on money, when she once got it in her grasp; so with a faint smile, which made the stingy old soul flush about the eyes once more, she turned the subject.

"At sunset, did you say, Aunt Polly?"

"Yes, at sunset to-night, and you wasn't to fail—I promised that much."

"Can I tell Jane or grandmother?" inquired Mary, thoughtfully.

"Not on no account. The lady—for anybody that dressed up like that, with a pocket full of gold, must be a lady, anyhow you fix it—the lady—says she: 'Tell Mary Derwent to come alone,' and, says I, 'she shall, if my name's Polly Carter.' When my word is giv, it's giv—so you must go down to the spring all alone, jest at sundown, Mary Derwent."

"Yes, I'll go," said Mary, looking wistfully into the distance; "of course, I'll go."

"That's a good gal—I was sure you would. Now, I'll jest say good-by to Miss Derwent, and Gineral Washington and I will make tracks for home."

Aunt Polly strode away up the garden, muttering to herself:

"Wal, I've killed two birds with one stone, and catch'd a goldfinch to boot. That 'ere side-saddle wasn't mounted for nothing. If vartue al'es gets rewarded in this way, I'll keep Gineral Washington a-going."

These muttered thoughts brought the old maid up to the cabin, and she called out from the threshold:

"Jane, remember what I was a-saying, now do. When will you all come and take tea with me? Shall be proper glad to see you any time—the sooner the better. Good-bye, Miss Derwent; good-bye all."

Here Aunt Polly gave a comprehensive sweep of the hand, including grandma in the house, Mary in the garden, and Jane, who stood by her on the door-stone.

"Good-bye all. Come, Janey, set me on the other side, and I'll speak a good word for you to the beaus when they come to my tavern."

Jane tied a handkerchief over her head, followed the old maid to the cove, unmoored her canoe, and soon reached the western shore.

Aunt Polly shook her by the hand, repeated a word of grim advice, then mounted the bank and threw out her handkerchief as a signal to Gineral Washington.

That inestimable beast had made the best of his time, and would willingly have stayed longer; but seeing his mistress's gorgeous signal fluttering in the air, like the mainsail of a schooner, he made one more desperate crop at the rich herbage, and came trotting decorously forward, with the foam and short grass dropping from his mouth at every step.

Aunt Polly replaced the bit, let out an inch of the girth, to accommodate the animal's digestive organs, mounted a hemlock stump, littered all round with fresh chips, and, after coaxing Gineral Washington into the right position, seated herself grimly on the side-saddle and rode away.

CHAPTER XV
THE SERPENT BRACELET

Mary Derwent was restless and dreamy all day after Aunt Polly left the island. Spite of herself, she was sad—no cause existed now—Jane was safe at home, sorry for her indiscretion, at heart, no doubt; Butler, she hoped and believed, had left the valley—certainly there was nothing to apprehend nor much to regret—yet tears lay close to those beautiful eyes all the day long. She pined to hide herself in some quiet place, and cry all her fancied trouble away. The strange woman was before her every moment; she could not, with any force of will, put that picturesque image aside; it came, like the shadow from some wild dream, and took full possession of her.

She went to the spring early, just as the first golden waves of sunset began to ripple up the west. The blossoming crab-apples flung a rosy tint above her, and the soft whispers of the spring, as it ran off among the stones, sounded sad and tearful as the breath in her bosom.

There was no sound, for the Indian moccasin treads lightly as a leaf falls, and Catharine Montour stood close by the young girl before she was aware of any human approach.

Mary lifted her face suddenly, and there, revealed by golden gleams of light that penetrated the boughs, she saw that strange face, surmounted by the serpent whose blood-red eyes glittered on her like a venomous asp about to bite.

Mary was the first to speak.

"You are the lady who wished me to be here?"

Her voice scarcely rose above the whispering waters, but Catherine heard it distinctly. Still she did not speak at once—some unaccountable emotion checked the breath on her lips.

"Yes; I asked a woman who said she was coming here to give my message. You are very kind to answer it so promptly."

These were not the words Catherine had intended to say; but the gentle, almost holy presence of that young girl changed the whole current of her feelings. She came haughtily, as an inquisitor who had suffered wrong, but remained overpowered by the meek dignity of her reception.

"I had seen you once before, lady, and was glad to come."

"Seen me, child, and where?"

"At the ledge, on the opposite shore, when you met Walter Butler."

"And you heard that conversation?"

"Yes. I could not help it. Before it was possible to get away you had said everything."

"Then you know that he is married to my daughter?"

"I know that he is married to a young Indian girl, who may be your daughter. The missionary told me of the marriage, but nothing more."

"And your sister—for it is of her I wish to speak, it is her I warn—did she know this?"

"She knows it now."

"Yet last night Tahmeroo, my daughter, the bride of Walter Butler, found your sister here under these very branches, planning to elope with him."

"I know it," answered Mary, shrinking together, and turning pale as if she, not Jane, had been in fault—"I know it; but that is all over now."

"Do not be so sure of that, my poor child; there is no security against treachery and weakness; but if you are already informed that Walter Butler is married by every law that can bind two persons for life, my errand here is half done. Last night my unhappy child came to the camp wild with the torture that wicked man had inflicted. I will not speak harshly of your sister: if her folly works sharper than wickedness, it is not your fault; but my business here was to warn her of the danger she is braving. I did not wish to see a person whose folly has already irritated a temper not particularly placable, but sent for you, because my child told me of your kindness—your true, generous courage. I wished to thank you—to impress you with the danger that hangs over your family if Tahmeroo receives farther wrong or insult here."

"I would rather die than think it could happen again," answered Mary Derwent, with gentle earnestness. "My sister is so young—so very, very beautiful, that she is not content with the love of a single heart, as one who has nothing pleasant about her might be. It is only a fancy—a wild dream with her. I'm sure you would believe it could you see how dearly she is loved by—by one, oh! so much superior to this Captain Butler."

"Then your sister is beloved—she is engaged, perhaps?"

"Beloved—oh, yes!" answered Mary, in a voice so sweetly mournful that the haughty soul of Catharine Montour thrilled within her. "They are engaged, too, I believe. You know it would be impossible for him to live near Jane and not wish to marry her. As for him, of course she cannot help loving him—who could?"

The last two words were uttered in a sigh so deep and heart-broken that Catharine felt it thrilling through her own frame. Her forest life had never possessed the power to dull or break that one string in her heart; it was sensitive and tremulous as ever. She understood all that Mary was suffering, and back upon her soul rushed a tide of sympathy so earnest and delicate that for a time those two beings, so opposite in all things else, felt painfully together—the one sad from memory, the other suffering under the weight of a cruel reality eternally present in her own person.

Unconsciously Catharine's right hand fell upon the beautiful head, which bent under it like a flower on its stalk.

"Poor, poor child!" she murmured, and tears kept resolutely from her eyes, broke forth in her voice: "I know well how to feel for you."

"No, no," answered Mary. "One so grand—so like a queen, could not feel as I do; I never expect it. In the wide world there is not another girl like me. I sometimes feel as if the angels would only give me pity-love after I am dead, and then there would be no heaven for me either."

"And are you so lonely of heart?" inquired Catharine, seating herself on the stone before Mary, and taking both her pale little hands with a kindly clasp. "You and I should feel for each other; for the same rugged path lies before you that I have trod."

"The same—oh no, lady! You are straight and proud as a poplar. You don't know what it is to go through life with your face bent to the ground, and the heart in your bosom warm and full of love, like other people's."

"Poor soul, and does this thought trouble you so? Are you indeed worse off than I have been, and so patient, too? Has the wilderness no hiding-place for human suffering?"

"I don't know," said Mary, filled with her own thoughts. "It seems as if I never could hide away; people are sure to find me out and stare at me. I think there is no place but the grave where one would be sure."

Catharine could not speak; tears overmastered her and fell down her face like rain.

"Poor soul," she said, "how can I comfort you?"

"I don't know," said Mary. "The minister sometimes tries to comfort me, but I'm afraid he has gone away for a long time; when he tells me that I can be useful, and make others happy just as I am, this trouble goes off a little. Oh! ma'am, I wish you could know the minister; or if you really care about making a poor girl like me feel better, talk as he does."

"Alas!" said Catharine, "I am not humble and good, like him; but I can pity these feelings, and be your friend—a more powerful friend, perhaps, than he is, for I can protect you and yours from the hatred of the Indians."

"Oh, but the Indians are my friends now; they love me a little, I am sure, for they smile when I speak to them, and call me pet names, as if I were a bird; perhaps it is because the minister likes me so much."

"No; it is because—because of your——"

"Of this," said Mary, interrupting her with a frightened look, and touching her shoulder with one hand. "Is it only pity with them, too?"

Catharine looked upon that pale spiritual face with ineffable compassion. She understood all the sorrow that rendered it so painfully beautiful.

"No, my child, it is not pity with them, but homage, adoration. That which you feel as a deformity, they hold to be a sacred seal of holiness which the Great Spirit sets upon his own. With them you, and such as you, are held only as little lower than the angels. This superstition may yet be your salvation, but a time is coming when even that will not be enough to protect you from harm."

"What! would the Indians kill me—is that it?"

"They are savages, and hard of restraint; but I think that nothing human could be found to harm a creature so good and so helpless."

"Then you think they could not be brought to kill me?" said Mary, with a look almost of disappointment.

"Why, you speak sadly, like one who wishes death." Mary shook her head.

"No, I dare not wish death; but if the Indians wanted any one, and must have a life, they couldn't find any person so ready to go, I'm sure."

"This is very mournful," said Catharine, drawing Mary's head, with all its loose golden hair, to her bosom. "I wish the missionary, or any one else were here to console you. I am struck mute. Yet Heaven knows, if my own life could remove the cause of your sorrow, I would lay it down this moment. Do you believe me, child?"

"Oh, yes; but is this love or pity?"

"Pity is a gentle feeling, but it would not urge one to a sacrifice like that. Love, compassion, sentiment—I do not know what it is; but I solemnly say to you, Mary Derwent, in twenty years I have not felt my heart swell with feelings like these—not even when my own child was first laid in my bosom."

"It is love!—this is love!" cried Mary, joyfully winding her arms around Catharine Montour's neck, and laying her cheek close to the proud woman's face. "I think—I am sure this is love!"

"God knows it is some holy feeling that has overtaken me unawares."

"Yes, yes; love is a holy feeling!"

"But this is the first time you and I have ever met."

"Is it? I don't remember this moment—my thoughts will not take the thing in; but I am sure we shall never be strangers again—that we never were strangers in all our lives. At first I was afraid of you; now I should like to follow after you like a wild bird, that you would feed sometimes with crumbs from your hands, and call me by pretty pet names. I should like, of all things, to watch over you in the night, and keep everything still, that you might dream sweet dreams. That beautiful girl, your daughter, should not care for you more than I. Is not this love, dear lady?"

"It is something very heavenly," said Catharine Montour. "I dread to have it pass away, and yet it must!"

"Must! And why?"

"Because all things beautiful do pass away—love with the rest, nothing is immortal here."

"But yonder," said Mary, pointing upward, where a young moon rode the sky like a golden shallop laden with pearls.

"I know nothing of that," answered Catharine, with momentary impatience. "It is at best a land of dreams and conjectures to us all, but we will not talk of that deep mystery—the future—my child. I would not willingly disturb any belief that can make you happier. I can dream no longer, hope no more—mine will be a life of wild action, and then——"

"And then——" repeated Mary, turning her pure eyes upward, "and then, there is a God above, and rest, eternal rest—yet eternal action too, with his angels."

"Who taught you these things; surely this is not the language of a frontier settlement?"

"I don't know," said Mary, with sweet thoughtfulness, "such ideas spring up most naturally, I should think, in the woods which God alone has touched; men teach us words, but thought comes to us, I am sure, as flowers spring from the grass; we scarcely know when they shoot, bud, or blossom, till their breath is all around us. I cannot remember, lady, that any one ever taught me to think."

"Not the missionary?"

"Perhaps it might have been unawares—but no, he told me once, I remember, that God himself sent me many thoughts that other children never have, in order to be company for me when I sit alone in the woods. So, after all, dear lady, the missionary understands what they mean, and tells me; that is all. The thoughts come from God himself."

Catharine Montour was weeping, for that gentle girl had found the well-spring of her nature; laying her cheek down upon those golden tresses, which remained on her bosom, silent from tender reverence.

"Are these thoughts so strange that you wonder at them?" asked Mary.

"Yes, they are very strange to me now."

"Don't let them be strangers after this, dear lady; when you send them away, as I did once, it is like turning angels out of doors." Catharine sobbed for the first time in years and years.

"When they come swarming around your heart," continued Mary, "let them in, for they are pleasant company, and, better than all, crowd so much trouble out."

"Alas!" said Catharine, covering her face with both hands in a burst of sorrow, "it is long since these thoughts have visited me."

"That is because you keep the door shut against them, I dare say; but it is open now, or you would not cry so; gentle thoughts always follow tears, just as violets start after a brook overflows."

Catharine stooped forward with one hand to her brow; she could not realize that tears were dropping so fast from her eyes, or that any human voice possessed the power of unlocking such feelings of tenderness in her soul. She who had become iron, scarcely recognized her own identity when the old nature came back. Mary grew anxious at her long silence.

"Have I offended you, lady?" she said, pressing her timid little hand on that which lay in Catharine's lap.

"Offended me! Oh, no, no."

"Please look up then; while you stoop, the shadows fall around you like a mourning cloak, and I grow chilly; hark! what is that?"

Catharine Montour started up, for a low cry like that of some wild animal in pain sounded from the water. "It is my Indians," she said, hurriedly; "they are restive at this long stay—I must go now or they will come in search of me."

"But not far—not forever, lady; I have only seen you twice in all my life; but it seems as if a stone had fallen on my heart when I think that you may never come back."

"I will come back, trust me I will. How and when it is impossible for me to say; but, rest certain, we shall meet again, and that for good to us both."

"But soon—oh, tell me that it will be soon."

"I cannot say; these are wild times on the frontier, and worse may be expected; but if danger comes I shall not be far from you; rest sure of that."

Mary looked—oh, so wistfully—into the lady's face.

"And will there be danger for you?"

"None, child! but you and the inhabitants of this valley will be forever in peril. Stay, put back the sleeve from your arm, undo this bracelet, a gleam of moonlight strikes the spring just here—so!"

As she spoke, Mary touched the clasp pointed out, and directly one of the serpent bracelets uncoiled from Catharine's wrist, as if it had been a living thing, and she wound it on Mary's arm, above the elbow, shutting the spring with a noise that sounded like a hiss.

"It will guard you," she said, eagerly. "There is not a Shawnee savage who does not hold that sign sacred, nor one among the Six Tribes who will not protect its wearer—keep it on your arm night and day, till we meet again.

"I came here to learn all that relates to your sister's acquaintance with Walter Butler, to warn her of the peril which will surely follow her reckless daring, if she even sees him or speaks with him again; but somehow you have led my thoughts far from the subject, and there is no time for much that I intended to say. But I have no fear that, under your influence, this girl can wrong my daughter."

Before Mary could speak, a long kiss was pressed on her forehead—a rustling of the branches as they swayed to their places, and she was alone—more alone than she had ever been in her life.

CHAPTER XVI
THE OLD JOHNSON HOUSE

In the Mohawk Valley, about four miles north of Fonda, stands to this day the first baronial mansion ever erected in the state of New York. Its present proprietor, Mr. Eleazer Wells, has, with unusual good taste, preserved the old mansion with all its historical associations undisturbed, and even in this age of republican palaces, the old Johnson House would be considered a noble mansion. Its broad front, flanked at each end by massive block-houses of stone, perforated near the roof with holes for musketry, has an imposing appearance. The broad entrance hall, with heavy balustrades winding up the stairs, all hacked by savage tomahawks; its high ceilings; its rooms wainscoted with panel work, and ornamented with elaborate carving—all speak of former wealth and power.

In 1775–6 this mansion was occupied by Sir John Johnson, the heir of Sir William, its first proprietor, whose loyalty to the crown, and cruelty to the patriots of the Revolution, are on record forever in the history of the great period of our national struggles. Then the hall was surrounded with forests, deep, broad, and seemingly boundless as the ocean. Sir William had hewed an estate out of this wilderness, which lay upon a gentle slope, like a beautiful glimpse of Arcadia, surrounded and framed in by the woods.

The season had deepened since the Indians were encamped in the Wyoming Valley. The cultivated trees, then in blossom all over the country, had set their fruit; Indian corn was half a foot high; and the wheat fields looked like meadows ready for the scythe. The thickets around Johnson Hall had cast off their flowers, and were now heavy with leaves and swelling nuts. The whole region was beautiful, as if no war existed in the world.

It was just after dusk on one of these late spring days, when a horseman, with two or three Indians in his train, rode up to the front of this mansion, inquired for Sir John Johnson, and dismounted, like a person well acquainted with the premises, and certain of a cordial reception. The Indians followed him to the front portico, and sat down on the steps, waiting in solemn patience for his return.

Walter Butler entered the hall unannounced, and opening a side door, stood some moments on the threshold before its inmates became aware of his presence. It was after dusk; but Sir William Johnson had carried all the aristocratic arrangements of his European life into the wilderness, and those habits were strictly followed up by his son. Thus, late as the hour was, Sir John remained at table with a guest who shared his hospitality, and as the wine passed sluggishly between them, the two men conversed together with more earnestness than is usual at the dinner table.

Butler was well acquainted with Sir John—a handsome youngish-looking man, who sat at the head of the table, a little flushed either with wine or some excitement of suppressed temper, and apparently doing the honors of his own house with unusual constraint. The other person, who sat quietly picking over the nuts on his plate—for the meal was evidently at its conclusion—was a tall man, a little past middle age, and of a calm, lofty presence, difficult to describe, except by its contrast with the restless and somewhat coarse manner of the frontier baronet. The repose of his appearance was perfect; yet there was a faint red on his cheek, and a scarcely perceptible curve of the lip, that betrayed deep though well curbed emotions, which had received some shock.

Butler had never seen this man before, and his presence was by no means agreeable; the interview which he desired with Sir John was of a kind which rendered witnesses unpleasant, and for an instant he paused in the door, hesitating to enter. Sir John supposed it was a servant, and went on with his conversation.

"No," he said, a little roughly, "you on the other side can hardly be expected to understand the necessity of these measures. It is easy enough making speeches in the House of Lords or Commons—humanity serves well to round off an eloquent period with, I dare say—but we live in the midst of dangers; the war is a real thing to us; we do not study it out on a parchment map, while lolling in a cushioned easy-chair, but tramp after the rebels through swamps and over mountains. If we burn their cabins, they retaliate on our halls—nothing is safe from them. Why, the very plate off which you are dining will be stowed away in the block-house, under a guard of muskets, for safe keeping, the moment it leaves the table."

"The loss of your plate, Sir John, costly as it is, would be a trifle, compared to one burning cabin, where the bones of women and children are found in the ashes," said the stranger, casting a careless glance at the gold and silver plate glittering on every part of the board. "I would consent to dine upon a wooden trencher, all the days of my life, if that could save one of these innocent families from destruction. I repeat it, Sir John, the savage warfare commenced in this neighborhood is shocking to humanity. If the rights of our king can only be maintained by hordes of savages, let them go; the loyalty of an enlightened people will never be secured by barbarisms, at which even the better educated savage revolts. This league with the Six Nations is inhuman, nay, a statesman would say, worse—it is bad policy."

"It holds the traitors in fear, at any rate. They dare not be insolent when the war reddens their hearths."

"As a Commissioner of the King, Sir John, I protest against the introduction of savage tribes into His Majesty's army. It may be carried out in violence to this opinion, for in war men become ruthless; but so far as I have influence with the Ministry this odious policy shall not prevail."

Butler, regardless of the low breeding exhibited by the act, stood in the door, and listened to this conversation; but as the stranger ceased speaking, Sir John looked up, and called out cheerfully, like one who gets a much-needed ally:

"Ha, Butler, is it you? Come in—come in; we are just discussing a subject with which you are more familiar than I am. Mr. Murray, this gentleman belongs to the king's army—Capt. Walter Butler, of the Tryon Rangers. As half his father's forces are Indians, he will be able to speak advisedly on the question we were discussing, or, I am afraid, almost disputing."

The two gentlemen saluted each other rather distantly. Then Butler turned to his host and said, with a dash of offhand impudence:

"No war or politics for me, Sir John. I came on a very different errand; so cut the field and give me some dinner, unless your negroes in the kitchen are hacking away at the venison and roast-beef as usual, before the master is through with his dessert."

Sir John laughed, knocked on the table with the handle of his knife, and ordered the black slave, who obeyed the summons, to see that something was sent up from the kitchen fit for a gentleman to eat.

The slave grinned till his white teeth glittered again, and went lazily towards the kitchen. Meantime Butler went into the hall, threw his hat and whip on a table, and strode back with his spurs ringing on the sanded floor, and his fine hair half escaping from the crimson ribbon that gathered it in a queue behind.

"I beg ten thousand pardons," he said, throwing himself on a seat, and leaning his elbow on the table, with his back half turned upon the stately guest. "Pray, congratulate me, Sir John. I forgot to tell you that it is a married man you have the honor of entertaining."

"Hallo, Butler, what is this? Married—what—you? Nonsense!"

"True as the Gospel, upon my honor."

"But the bride—where on earth did you find the bride?"

"Among the wigwams. Like your honored father, Sir John, I have a fancy for picturesque women. My wife is a half-breed—no, I am too deep— she is a white on her mother's side, and half Indian in the paternal line, but bright as a hawk, sharp as steel, and moves like a panther."

"And you have married an Indian girl—absolutely and lawfully married her?"

"Absolutely and lawfully married her," answered Butler, taking a knife from the table, tapping the cloth with its silver handle, and nodding his head, as if he were beating time to music. "Handcuffed for life. No jumping the broomstick in this affair; none of that Indian hospitality which your father installed, but a downright, honest marriage, done to a turn, by an ordained minister of the church, and served up with this order, which you will please countersign or cash without delay."

Sir John took the document extended to him, and read it with evident surprise.

"Catharine Montour; it is her signature and secret mark. In Heaven's name, where did you get this document, Butler?"

"From the lady's own fair hand. You recognize her writing, it seems, and I hope hold possession of the needful mentioned. Rather a good speculation for a clasp of the hands, locked by a dozen words of nonsense, ha!"

"I do not comprehend."

"You understand the draft, and that is the most important thing just now, Sir John; as for the rest, it is a pill which I can swallow without the help of friends."

Sir John laid the draft down upon the table, and began to smooth the paper with both his hands, regarding it with a puzzled, doubtful look, like one who cannot make up his mind how to act.

"There is no doubt regarding the funds, I hope," said Butler, growing meanly anxious at this hesitation.

"No," was the hesitating reply; "but have you any knowledge of the position in which a marriage with Catharine Montour's daughter places you?"

Now, Butler had no information on this subject, nor had he ever heard it mentioned; but he saw by Sir John's manner that some mystery was kept from him, and, with characteristic cunning, hinted at a knowledge which he did not possess.

"Have I any knowledge of my position? Now, that is too good, Sir John; can you possibly suppose me fool enough to marry the girl with anything unexplained?"

"Then you know who Catharine Montour really was, and to what her daughter is heiress?"

"Know? of course. Do I look like buying a pig in a poke?"

"Complimentary to your bride, at any rate; but I am glad Lady Granby has been frank at last."

Butler started, but his surprise was nothing to the effect the announcement of that name made upon the king's commissioner. He started from his chair with the sharp spasmodic movement of a man shot through the heart. His forehead contracted, his lips grew white as marble. Sir John shrunk from the terrible expression of that face.

"Lady Granby—Lady Granby!"

The words dropped from his lips like hail-stones when a storm is spent. He began to shake and quiver in all his limbs, then fell into his chair, with one elbow on the table shrouding his face. Sir John and Butler looked at each other in dumb astonishment; the sudden passion of that man was like the burst of a volcano which gives forth no warning smoke. The silence became oppressive.

"Did you ever know the lady?" inquired Butler, who respected no man's feelings, and never allowed laws of etiquette to interfere with his curiosity.

Murray withdrew the hand slowly from his face, and looked at his questioner with dull, dreamy eyes for some moments. The eager curiosity in that face brought back his thoughts; he was not a man to expose his heart long under a gaze like that.

"Yes," he said, leaning back in his chair, "The Granby title is among the most ancient in our country, and the more remarkable because the entail extends to females of the blood as well as males."

"Ha!—is that so, Johnson?" inquired Butler, quickly.

"Yes. This fact was among the secrets entrusted to my father, and transmitted to me."

"And the estates must be very large to allow of accumulations like the deposits in your custody," said Butler, keenly alive to his own interests.

"I believe they are among the finest in England," said Sir John, drily.

Butler started up, and walked the room, urged into action by selfish excitement. Murray again shaded his face with one hand, while Sir John examined the draft once more.

"Are you sure," inquired Butler, at last, "are you sure, Sir John, that this lady was legally married to Queen Esther's son? for, after all, everything depends on that."

Sir John smiled a little sarcastically. Butler was too coarse in his selfishness not to be understood. Murray again looked up. He evidently felt a keen interest in the question.

"She was legally married, I fancy. Whatever might have been the cause which drove her to the wilderness, Lady Granby was not a person to degrade herself knowingly."

"You fancy, Sir John! I should like to have some security besides a man's fancy where an inheritance like this is concerned. You are certain, sir, that the property is entailed—that female heirs come in, in short——"

"In short," interrupted Sir John, with cutting sarcasm, "I have no fear that your interests are in peril, unless there is some informality in her mother's marriage; your wife is the legal heiress of the Granby estates."

Butler sat down again, struck breathless by this unexpected good fortune, so far beyond his wildest hopes.

"You mistook my meaning," he said, even his coarse nature becoming conscious of the revolting light in which his conduct must appear to any observer; "I was thinking of Tahmeroo—she is too lovely a flower to waste her bloom in the wilderness."

"You grow poetical, sir," said Sir John, laughing; "your wife's perfections are dawning upon you with new force."

Butler did not appear to notice this remark, but went on with his own train of reflection.

"Then were Catharine Montour dead, no power could deprive Tahmeroo of the Granby estates and titles?"

"None, sir; the daughter of Gi-en-gwa-tah, the Shawnee chief, will be Countess of Granby."

Murray started anew at that name so rudely uttered, his hand clenched itself on the arm of his chair, and a spasm of wounded pride contracted his forehead. With a powerful effort he mastered himself once more, and leaned back in his seat, with his face turned from the light, and listening with apparent calmness to their conversation.

"And the rents," said Butler, "the income—you have an idea of its amount?"

"Have you never ascertained?" asked Sir John.

"Not exactly—you see, Catharine Montour dislikes to speak of anything connected with her past life, and it is difficult to get a clear answer from her concerning the actual amount of the property."

"Then, sir, I, of course, am not at liberty to betray anything which she sees fit to keep secret."

"But there can be no treason in asking a question concerning a fortune which will one day be my own?"

"There may be none in your asking, if you think it proper," returned Sir John; "but it certainly would be treachery in me to expose anything which the lady desires to remain untold."

"You inherit all of your father's chivalry," retorted Butler, insolently. "Doubtless he had good reason for keeping the lady's secrets."

A flush shot up to Sir John's forehead, and his lips compressed themselves suddenly; but, restraining his anger, he replied, with unmoved courtesy:

"I trust that I possess the chivalry which should be the birthright of every true gentleman. As for my father, no man trifles with his name or memory here."

"Well, that is vastly fine; but plain speech in these days helps a man along faster than the chivalry of all the old crusaders could do," said Butler, carelessly. "Out in the woods here, fine speeches and poetic sentiments are thrown away."

"That depends entirely upon the person with whom one chances to come in contact. I have seen as true gentlemen in the wilds of this new world as I ever met at the court of a European sovereign."

"Of course," returned Butler, laughing; "you and I live here, you know, following your grand old father's example."

Sir John's lip curled, for this attempt at playfulness was even more distasteful to him than the man's previous conversation had been, and without reply he resumed the scrutiny of the document which Butler had placed in his hands.

"What the deuce could have put it into Catharine Montour's head to come out here and marry my dusky father-in-law?" continued the young man. "She must have been mad—or worse——"

"Doubtless she is a better judge of her own actions than either you or I," replied Sir John, losing all patience with his guest.

"Oh, I'll wager that she had some good reason," sneered Butler, irritated by the other's haughtiness, and his own failure at discovering the amount of fortune which he hoped one day to claim. "Women don't do those out-of-the-way things unless they are forced. Now, be honest, Sir John, and tell me why this woman left a high position and great wealth in her own country, and came here to act the part of a Shawnee squaw in the valley of the Mohawk."

"There are many good motives which might have prompted an act like that," said Sir John, gravely; "the good which she could do among those ignorant savages—the forbearance and cessation from cruelty which she is able to teach them——"

"Stuff and nonsense! Catch an old bird with chaff, if you can! No, no, I'm not fool enough to believe that Catharine Montour came over here for any such reason! There's some confounded mystery somewhere, and sooner or later I'll get to the bottom of it. Take my head for a target, if you don't find that my Lady Granby had played out her game in England, and found it convenient to disappear from among the haughty dames of England."

"Stop, sir!" exclaimed a low voice, that made both listeners start, as if a thunder-clap had burst over their heads. "Couple the Lady Granby's name with insult again, and it is to me that you must answer for it!"

Murray had risen from his seat, and stood before the astonished man with burning eyes and a brow of iron.

"What the deuce have I said?" muttered Butler.

"You have said that which I cannot allow to remain unanswered, Captain Butler," answered Sir John, with more dignity than he had yet assumed. "One portion of your question I can answer without betraying confidence which was sacred with Sir William, and rests so with me. You ask why a high-born English lady forsook her own land to become the wife of an Indian chief? Why she left England, I am not at liberty to say; but, upon the honor of a gentleman, it was from no unworthy act or motive— her career had been a proud and blameless one, as this gentleman can, doubtless, testify; but the deeper reasons which influenced this expatriation no human being except herself has ever possessed the power to explain."

"Nor why she took up with a swarthy Indian, when she got here— that is one of her delicate mysteries also, I dare say," retorted Butler, growing insolent under the stern glances turned upon him by the English Commissioner. "Come, come, Johnson, it's hardly worth while exhausting eloquence on the subject; the whole affair has given me a picturesque little wildcat of a wife, who loves me like a tempest. Better than this, she promises to make me a potentate one of these days, unless the lady-mother outlives her, which may happen after all, for she has the vigor and health of a tigress. As for disinheriting her child, or anything of that sort, she hasn't the power, thank my stars! But the main question is left out, after all: how and where was Catharine Montour married to the Shawnee chief? Was it a ceremony which our English laws hold valid? If not, my wild bird has nothing but her pretty plumage after all."

"Do you consider this nothing?" said Sir John, holding up the draft.

"Faith, I don't know. It seemed a good deal when I presented it; but now that I have learned how much remains behind, it seems as if my queenly mamma had treated me rather shabbily."

"Sir John, forgive me, but you have not answered Captain Butler's question: by what train of circumstances was a lady so delicate in all her tastes as Lady Granby led into a union with a savage? Surely it could not have been of her own free will," said the commissioner.

"If a martyr ever went to the stake of his own will—if self-abnegation of any kind is free—this lady did voluntarily marry the Indian chief. It was a sublime sacrifice, which every true man must regard with homage—an act of chivalric humanity of which few women, and scarcely a man on earth, would have been capable."

"I can well believe it," exclaimed Murray, with kindling eyes.

"Then she was decidedly married," cried Butler, faithful to his mercenary instincts, and hunting that one fact down like a hound.

"I saw her married myself, on the steps of this very mansion, where she stood like a priestess between two races—for the hall was crowded with whites, of which my father, Sir William, was the head; while on the lawn, in the thickets, and all around, belting the forest, three thousand warriors were gathered. The whole Six Nations were represented by their bravest chiefs. It was a sight to remember one's lifetime. The red sunset streamed through the forest trees, only a little more gorgeous than the savage groups that camped under them. The windows of the Hall blazed with gold; the whole interior was illuminated. In the flower-beds and thickets the Indians grouped themselves like flocks of orioles, flamingos, and restless ravens. It was the most picturesque sight I ever beheld."

"But Caroline—Catharine Montour—what of her?" exclaimed the commissioner, losing his self-control; "was all this savage pomp assembled to witness the sacrifice of that noble creature?"

"Yes; in the midst of it all she stood, white as death and firm as stone, her hand in that of the chief—a fine, noble-looking fellow he was, too, with just enough of white blood in his veins to save the whole thing from being repulsive. Indeed, in my whole life, I have seldom seen a man of nobler presence. On the mother's side, you are already informed, he was nearly white; from her he had learned many of the gentler graces, both of manner and costume, which made his appearance rather picturesque than savage. Instead of a blanket or skin robe he wore a hunting-shirt of some rich color, heavy with fringes and embroidery; his hair was long to the shoulders, black and glossy as a crow's wing. After all, a woman of good taste might have been excused for admiring the fellow for his own sake."

The commissioner writhed in silence under this description; his eyes burned with deep fire; his very fingers quivered with suppressed excitement.

"And she was married thus?" he questioned, in a hoarse whisper.

"Yes, it was done bravely before the whites assembled in my father's hall; before the Six Nation, swarming upon the grounds. Her lips were white as snow when the vow passed them; her eyes burned like a she-eagle's when her young is threatened; she clenched the chief's hand till even he must have felt the pain. Yes, it was bravely done; she had promised, and no entreaty could move her to reconsider the matter. Sir William, who was not much given to sentiment, besought her with tears in his eyes to desist; the women who crowded the hall wept like children; but she stood firm; I can almost hear her deep, ringing voice now, as she answered the priest."

"Then it was a marriage by the priest!" almost shouted Butler, dashing the handle of his knife down on the table, till the plate rang again.

"She had pledged herself to become the chief's wife, and was a Christian—how could she keep her vow, except by Christian rites. He had honorably fulfilled her conditions—she as honorably redeemed her promise."

"What were those conditions?" inquired the commissioner, and his voice became lower and hoarser each moment.

"The redemption of three white prisoners from torture."

"Three prisoners—three?"

"Yes, a gentleman, his wife, and child, taken on the Canada frontier."

"And when was this?"

Sir John mentioned the date rather carelessly; he was pouring out a glass of wine, and did not observe the wild anxiety with which his guest awaited this answer.

"Oh, my God—my God!"

His arms spread themselves on the table, his face fell between them, while a terrible burst of passion shook him from limb to centre.

"Oh, my God—my God!"

It was all he could say; the words were suffocating him as they rose.

The host and Butler looked at each other in silent amazement. An earthquake could not have surprised them more. Even Butler was awed by an outbreak of feeling, the more impressive because of the apparent composure that had preceded it.

At last Murray lifted his head; every feature was quivering with emotion—joy, regret, sharp pain, and wild triumph struggled there.

"Gentlemen," he said, "it was I—it was my wife and child whose lives Lady Granby bought by the horrible sacrifice. Till to-night I was ignorant of all this—ignorant that she yet lived. You will not wonder that I am unmanned."

"But she never mentioned your name, Mr. Murray," said Sir John.

"Perhaps she did not know. She might have done as much for strangers even; upon the broad earth there does not exist a woman so capable of great sacrifices."

Butler laughed, and looked meaningly at his host.

"I dare say it was no great sacrifice, after all," he said. "By Sir John's account, the Indian was as handsome as a young Apollo——"

"Stop!"

The word flew from Murray's lips like a hot bolt, his eyes flashed fire.

"Another word against that lady, here or elsewhere, and I will hold you to a sharp account, young man!"

Murray passed around the table as he spoke, laid his hand with a heavy pressure on Butler's shoulder, and bowing to Sir John, passed from the room and the house. Before either of the gentlemen left behind had recovered from their surprise, the sound of a horse's hoofs galloping down the hard carriage road warned them of Murray's abrupt departure from the Hall.

"Well, upon my word, this is high tragedy!" exclaimed Butler, recovering from his stupor of cowardly astonishment. "What the deuce did I say that need have aroused a tempest like that?"

"Common decency, sir," said Sir John, for a moment yielding to his better feelings, "should have prevented your expressing such doubt of any woman; least of all, of one who is the mother of your wife."

"Well, well, let it rest—we won't quarrel. I have no reason to think hardly of the Countess of Granby. Relations should agree," he continued, uttering the name with pompous pride, as if feeling that the title reflected honor upon him. "Come, Sir John, let's talk seriously."

"Concerning what, sir?"

"This fortune, of course—these estates."

"I can give you no farther information, Mr. Butler; any future knowledge that you may desire must be obtained from Catharine Montour herself."

Butler pushed back his chair with a muttered oath, then remembering how impolitic a quarrel with Sir John might prove, he drew towards the table again and smoothed his forehead, endeavoring to fall into a more friendly and familiar style of conversation, an effort in which he was not at first seconded by his companion.

"Well, let the wigwam rest for once; we have talked about these things long enough," he said, with a great effort, wrenching his thoughts from the Granby estates. "What does this crusty Don want at Johnson Hall, when he leaves it with so little ceremony?"

"Oh," answered Sir John, firing up, and draining glass after glass of wine while he was speaking; "he is a sort of commissioner from the king, sent to keep us all in order—our mode of warfare does not suit his taste, he was just making an eloquent protest against bringing Indians into the service, as you came in."

"And be hanged to him!" cried Butler, filling his glass. "Why, we might as well strike our tents at once; the savages work beautifully—besides they make capital scapegoats when we wish to indulge in a little of their amusements; upon my word, Johnson, there's a sort of relish in their way of scalping and roasting a traitor when he comes in, that has its charm; do away with the savages! why, that would be throwing aside buckler and cloak, too."

"I told him so plainly enough," said Sir John, whom the wine was making more and more social. "Why, Schuyler himself could not have preached mercy with more eloquence; he a king's commissioner. I wish the Indians had roasted him when they had the chance—to come here lecturing me, a Johnson, of Johnson Hall; as if I had not been outraged and insulted enough by General Schuyler and his minions at Guy Park."

"Is it true, Sir John, that Schuyler forced you into giving up the stores and ammunition which had been gathered here at the Hall?"

"Forced is a strong word, captain," answered Sir John, turning red with the humiliating remembrances brought up by the rough question; "he required my word of honor not to act against Congress, and demanded the arms, stores, and accoutrements held by our friends, and the Indians. I refused to comply, and he marched upon the Hall; I sent for our Indian allies, and for you. My messenger found Queen Esther almost alone in the Seneca Lake encampment. The whole tribe were gone to hold a council-fire in Wyoming. You were away, no one could guess where. After this fashion, Captain Butler, was I sustained by my friends."

"Faith, I had no idea of Schuyler's movement till the escort came in with Catharine Montour, who would force me to stay and get my hands tied; but the very day after our wild wedding I was on the road," said Butler.

Sir John grew more and more excited.

"I could have driven the traitors back with my brave Highlanders, without going beyond the estate, for he started with only seven hundred men, but the Tryon county militia turned out like wasps, and increased his force to three thousand; with no hopes of reinforcement from you or your father, my Indian allies absent, and no time for preparation, I was compelled to negotiate, and to a certain extent succumb, but it was only for a time; to-morrow you must ride over to Fonda and collect our forces. Brant is hard at work among the Senecas. Where have you left Gi-en-gwa-tah with his warriors?"

"They are on the lake by this time."

"That is good news, we will soon have them at work; my tenants are all under arms; I expect Brant to join us in a few days, with an account of his organization. We will give the rebels a hot reception the next time they venture into this county, or——"

Sir John broke off with a quick exclamation; the loud gallop of a horse approaching the house brought both the baronet and his guest to their feet.

"What is that?" said Sir John, listening; "surely not the Hon. Mr. Murray returning—no, no, he would keep the road; but this fellow rides over everything. Now that hoof strikes the turf, now the gravel; it can be no good tidings that bring any one here in such hot haste at this hour. I must learn at once what it means."

He rose hurriedly from his seat, and Butler followed, but before they reached the door it opened, and one of Sir John's slaves, a faithful and confidential old servant, entered the room, evidently in great agitation and fear.

"What is it, Pompey?" Sir John asked.

"There is a man wants to speak to massar right off; something very 'portant: them consarned Whigs is up again."

"Call him in—be quick, Pomp!" exclaimed Sir John. "What can these traitors be at now?" he continued, as the servant left the room to execute his order.

"I thought you would get into difficulty with them about this time," replied Butler; "they begin to suspect that you haven't kept that extorted promise very faithfully—your Highlanders have come out too boldly, and begun to worry the enemy—they are sure of re-enforcements."

"A promise made to a set of traitors!" said Sir John, scornfully; "only wait till the time comes that I can crush them like so many vipers; miserable rebels!"

Before Butler could answer, the door was opened again, and Pompey ushered into the room a man whose disordered garments betrayed the haste in which he had arrived.

"Your errand?" cried Sir John, imperiously—"don't waste words, but speak out!"

"The rebel Congress has taken measures against you," returned the man, bluntly, "and a company of soldiers are on their way here to take you prisoner."

"This does look like earnest," said Butler, with a prolonged whistle; "what is the cue now, Sir John?"

"How near are they?" inquired the baronet.

"They will reach here in an hour, at the farthest—you have no time to spare."

"An hour—so, so! We shall see—they haven't caught the fox yet! Where is Mr. Murray, Pomp?"

"Gone, massar; the commissioner rode off half an hour ago; said he wasn't gwine to come back."

"Confound him!" muttered Butler; "he'd be little help, I fancy. What shall you do, Sir John—no chance to stand a fight."

"Fight—no! Curse them, they have left me neither arms nor ammunition; there's nothing for it but to decamp in double-quick time, and take our revenge after."

"Who has command?" asked Butler.

"Congress ordered General Schuyler to take measures, and he commissioned Colonel Dayton with the command of the expedition."

"Which will prove a fruitless one, unless my lucky star has deserted me," said the baronet. "Here, Pomp, I can trust you. Collect all the plate, and put it in the iron chest that stands in my office."

"What are you going to do with it?" inquired Butler.

"Bury it deep, as I wish these infernal rebels were. You don't think I intend to leave it for them, do you? Be alive Pomp; I'll bring you the papers and valuables out of my chamber, and do the work yourself quietly, without saying a word to any one."

"Yes, massar—trust old Pomp for that."

"I know I can, you sooty villain; you are one of the few men, black or white, in whom one can place confidence."

"Tank yer, massar," and the old slave grasped his hand with fervor. "Now, do yer get off, and leave me to manage eberyting; dem rebels ain't cute enough for dis yer chile, I'se willin' to bet; ha, ha!"

"Take care of yourself, Pomp—I must leave you behind. What's that, now?" he cried, breaking off hurriedly.

"Another swift rider," said Butler. "Can it be the rebels?"

"Quick, massar—don't lose a minute!"

"It isn't them," interrupted the messenger; "I rode like the wind—they cannot have so nearly overtaken me."

"See who it is, Pomp—some friend, perhaps—if it only proves so, I should like to give them a hot welcome."

Before the negro could obey, the door was flung open, and a muscular, powerful man strode into the room.

"Brant!" exclaimed both gentlemen at once.

"Yes, Brant," returned the man, in a deep, stern voice. "Like a fool, I left the Indians to follow me, or we would give the rascals down yonder hot work."

"Then you have brought me no help, Colonel?"

"Not fifty men; you must run for it this time."

The savage uttered the words in a tone of sullen wrath which betrayed his deep hatred of the Whigs. His hand clutched unconsciously over the hilt of his knife, and a terrible frown settled upon the heavy darkness of his forehead. He was a picturesque object in spite of the evil expression of his features. Like his manner, the dress that he wore was a singular mingling of the Indian costume and the attire of the whites. Under his frock of deer-skin was buttoned a military vest, doubtless the spoil taken from some one of his numerous victims, and over his shoulders was flung an Indian blanket, worn with the grace of a regal mantle. His long, black hair fell in dull masses about his neck, and from under his shaggy brows blazed his unquiet eyes with a deadly fire from which the bravest might well have recoiled.

"Do you go with me, Brant?" asked Sir John.

"Yes, Brant will be your guide. Queen Esther is not many miles away with a portion of her tribe; you will find protection among them."

"Is Catharine Montour there?" interrupted Butler.

"No, she rests at Seneca Lake; the young woman whom you have made your wife is with her. Sir John, you have no time to lose in useless questions—is all ready?"

"In one moment. Here, Pomp, come to my chamber."

They went out; and in a few moments Sir John returned, prepared for flight.

"Choose your best horse," said Brant; "we must take to the forest at once, for there we have friends."

They followed him into the hall, through the open door of which were visible their horses, ready for a start.

"Stop!" exclaimed Brant, "I must leave a sign behind."

He mounted the stairs, and brandishing his tomahawk, began making deep gashes in the balustrade at a distance of about a foot apart.

"What the deuce are you doing?" exclaimed the men, in astonishment.

The renegade made no reply, but continued his work to the top of the staircase.

"The house is safe now," he said, as he came down again. "Should it be attacked by the Indians during your absence, they will leave it uninjured."

"You leave a stern mark, Colonel," said Butler, glancing up at the hacked wood.

"That Brant always does—he will leave a more lasting one, though, on these rebels before long."

The party hurried into the open air and mounted their horses, but before they could gallop away, Pompey rushed out and grasped his master's bridle.

"It's all safe, Massar John," he whispered; "let 'em come now as soon as they like; this chile has matched 'em."

"That's a fine fellow—hold them at bay, Pompey—I shall see you again—keep a good heart."

"Good-by, massar—come back 'fore long—old Pompey'll keep dem 'ere silver platters, and milk-jugs, and all de cetras safe as de dead folks in 'em graves—you can 'pend on dat, massar."

"Good-by, Pomp—good-by!"

They put their horses into a gallop, and rode away through the forest. For many moments no one spoke, and the only sound that arose was the smothered beat of their horses' hoofs on the turf, and the mournful shiver of the leaves, as the wind sighed through them. Brant took the lead, tracking the narrow path as unerringly as if it had been a highway. Suddenly he checked his horse, and made a signal to his companions to halt.

"The rebels are coming," he said; "they have got on our traces."

They listened; the heavy tramp of steeds came up from the distance.

"They will overtake us!" exclaimed Sir John; "what are we to do, Brant?"

"Let them pass—we will baffle them yet—follow me—we know the woods, at any rate."

He turned aside from the path, and urged his horse through the underbrush, followed by his companions, until he reached a little dell, through which a brook crept with a pleasant gurgle.

"They will go on, and so miss us," he said, reining in his horse. "If we had only our guns now!"

Nearer and nearer came the tramp of the horses—rushing past the dell in hot pursuit, and growing fainter in the distance.

"They have gone by," said Butler. "Oh, for a good rifle—I'd have one shot!"

"We must take another path," said Brant; "keep a tight rein, gentlemen."

While he was glancing around in the starlit gloom for some trace to guide his course, there came up a sudden cry from the depths of the forest; the trees were illuminated by torches, and in an instant they were surrounded by their pursuers.

"This way," shouted Brant; "they are upon us!"

He urged his horse through the woods, closely followed by his companions. Butler was last; his horse slipped in ascending the bank, rolled over, carrying his rider with him. The rest fled, ignorant of his misfortune, and before he could free himself from his saddle the pursuers had surrounded him.

"Is it the baronet?" asked one.

They flashed a torch in his face, and at the sight of those features a simultaneous cry went up:

"The Tory Butler! Tie him fast!"

Butler struggled and attempted to draw back; he was speedily overpowered by numbers; his hands tied, and himself bound upon a horse. After a brief consultation, they resigned the pursuit of Sir John, and turned to retrace their steps, with the prisoner in their midst.

When the fugitives drew rein, to breathe their horses, they perceived for the first time that Walter Butler was missing.

"They have caught him!" exclaimed Sir John.

"Fool!" said Brant, contemptuously. "He deserves hanging, but I am sorry it happened; Queen Esther likes him, and I would rather encounter a troop of fiends than her tongue, when she learns what has happened."

"But we are not to blame—we were powerless to assist him, and——"

"As if that would change her mind! No, no; I can promise you a hot welcome. But it is not for her interest to risk a serious quarrel with us, and her majesty looks to that, I can tell you."

They rode on for another hour in security, and on reaching a break in the forest, the camp-fires of the Indians became visible in the valley below.

"Here we are," said Brant; "now for Queen Esther."

They rode into the camp, and Brant was received by the savages with demonstrations of joy.

"Where is the queen?" he asked, in the Shawnee dialect.

"Yonder is her tent—she is still watching."

"Follow me, Johnson," said Brant; "we must pacify the old tigress before she shows her teeth."

"But I am not in fault."

"Make her believe it then!"

"But she will not dare——"

"She would dare everything! But you are in no danger—only be ready to receive every sort of invective that a woman's tongue can invent, or the fury of a she-panther give birth to."

They moved towards the tent; Brant seized his companion by the arm and drew back, for that moment the heavy matting which fell before the tent was flung suddenly aside, and Queen Esther stood before them—not fierce and wild, as Sir John had expected to find her, but with the sharp, cool look of a person so used to adventure that nothing could surprise her. Though a tall woman, she was scarcely imposing in her person, for a life of sharp action had made her nerves steel, and her muscles iron; of flesh she had only enough to bind these tough threads of vitality together. The rest was all intellect and stern passion.

As if in scorn of all those wild or gentle vanities, which are beautiful weaknesses in the sex, both in the wigwam and drawing-room, Esther allowed no bright color or glittering ornament to soften the grey of a stern old age, which hung about her like a garment; her doe-skin robe, soft, pliant, and of a dull buff color, had neither embroidery of wampum or silk; her leggings were fringed with chipped leather; and over her shoulders was flung a blanket of fine silver-grey cloth, gathered at the bosom by a small stiletto, with a handle of embossed platina, and a short, keen blade that glittered like the tongue of a viper, and worn as a Roman woman arranged her garments in the time of the Cæsars. Her hair was white as snow, silvery as moonlight, and so abundant, even at eighty years of age, that it folded around her head in a single coil, like a turban. The high, narrow forehead, the aquiline nose, curved with time, like the beak of an eagle, and the sharp, restless eyes, stood out from beneath this woof of hair stern and clear, as if chiselled from stone. The very presence of old age rendered this woman majestic.

She paused a moment in the entrance of her tent; a torch burnt within, sending its resinous smoke around her, as she appeared clearly revealed, with a background of dull crimson—for the tent was lined with cloth of this warm tint, and she stood against it, like a grey ghost breaking out from the depths of a dusky sunset.

"Are you friends or enemies?" she inquired, shading her eyes from the smoky torch-light with a hand that looked like a dead oak-leaf.

"Who but friends would dare to enter Queen Esther's camp at night?" answered Brant, stepping forward. "You and I are on the same hunt; our warpaths cross each other here, that is all."

"Ha, Colonel Brant, this is well! I had dispatched a swift runner in search of you. Schuyler has sent a force of armed men into Tryon County, and the settlements are astir. Gi-en-gwa-tah was away when the news came, but I have brought his warriors forward. Our spies send word that they threaten the master of Johnson Hall."

"He is here," said Brant, pointing to Sir John; "we got news of Dayton's approach just in time to fly."

"In time to fly! Were there no armed men upon the estate, that you should sneak away from your ancestral hall, like a dog which fears the lash? This was not the way that your father defended himself, young man."

"There were but three of us, besides the servants," said Brant, laying his hand heavily on Sir John's arm, to prevent the sharp reply which sprang to the baronet's lips; "there was no time to summon the tenants; even your new grandson, Walter Butler, counselled escape to the forest, where we can organize at leisure and sweep down upon the rebels when they least expect us."

"Walter Butler—the husband of my granddaughter—and is he with you?"

Esther spoke without emphasis, and with an intonation sharp as the ring of steel; there was neither softness, anger nor surprise in that voice. She turned her keen glance from Brant to Johnson, questioning them both.

"He was with us a few minutes ago," answered Sir John, whose indignation was aroused by this cutting composure, "but an ambush scattered us in the woods, and he has not come in yet."

A cold glitter shot into Queen Esther's eyes; her lips sunk with a quick pressure, and almost lost themselves between the contracted nostrils and the protruding chin. She beckoned to the Indian who had stood sentinel before her tent, uttered a few words of his own language in a whisper, that sounded like the suppressed hiss of a snake, and, with a slow sweep of the hand, passed from before her guests suddenly and softly, as a cloud precedes the tempest.

"A cold reception this," said Sir John, when his hostess was swallowed up in the night. "Is her serene highness about to grill us for the loss of her cub?"

"From her quietness I should think it likely," said Brant. "When her majesty grows polite and silky, it is a sure proof that she intends to strike. Like a leopard, she never shows her nails in earnest till the paw falls. She is a wonderful woman—the only person in all the Six Nations whose influence can oppose mine!"

"But you cannot really think she intends us any harm," said Sir John, whose bravery was not always bullet-proof.

"Don't trust her! If she finds out, or fancies that we have got Butler into this scrape she will make smooth work of it. I have seen her shave off a head, as if it had been an over-ripe thistle, with her own hand. Her tomahawk is sharp, and quick as lightning. It is the only thing she is dainty about: the head is burnished with gold, and the ebony handle worn smooth as glass is richly veined with coral and mother-of-pearl. That which other women lavish on their persons she exhausts upon her arms. But for your comfort, Sir John, if Queen Esther ornaments them like a woman, she wields them like a man. No warrior of her tribe strikes so sure a blow."

"But she will not dare!"

"I should not wonder if the Earl of Essex said as much when he lay in the Tower; but his faith did not prevent Elizabeth, whom I can't help thinking a good deal like our savage queen here, chopping off his head."

"But you are powerful—more powerful among the savages than she can be—and I——"

"Yes, with three thousand warriors at my back; but just now my body-guard is scattered, and if this lady-tiger chooses to tie us up to the next tree, and give her people a human barbecue, I could only fight single-handed like yourself."

"Hark! they are gathering now," said Johnson, turning pale. "How quietly she does her work!"

Brant listened, and cast a sharp glance around the encampment. A low, humming noise came from its outer margin, like that of a hive of bees swarming; he began to be really alarmed.

"Surely she is not so mad!" he muttered, grasping the handle of his tomahawk. "A man would not dare—but this creature has enough of her sex to be uncertain, if nothing more."

The noise that had startled him, instead of increasing, died away. He looked keenly forward; a train of human beings swept out from the heart of the camp, headed by a single horse, whose tramp echoed harshly back from the mellow sound of a hundred pair of retreating moccasins.

"By the great Medicine, she has left the camp!" almost shouted Brant. "I tell you, Sir John, that woman would shame the bravest officer in your king's army."

As he spoke a savage came forward and addressed Brant. A tent had been pitched near that of Queen Esther, and she had politely left an invitation that he and the baronet would take possession of it, and rest after their journey.

"This does not look like *auto-da-fe*," said Sir John, preparing to accept the invitation.

"The more for this politeness," was the answer, "as I told you. Queen Esther carries the etiquette of her father's court even into her son's camp. The daughter of a French governor, the widow and mother of savages, is always courteously cruel. We shall see what all this means when she returns."

"Why wait for that? Supposing we take to the woods again. My cousin Guy must be in force somewhere in the district; I have no fancy for hospitality like this."

"Take to the woods!" cried Brant, with a scornful laugh—"what, run from a woman? Not I; besides, Sir John, just look at this fellow—with all his sullen civility, he is nothing more nor less than a guard set to watch us. So make the best on't; till the fate of that scoundrel Butler is ascertained, we are nothing more nor less than prisoners."

"But what if the rebels have killed him?"

"No danger," cried Brant, with a scornful lift of the shoulder, which made all the fringes on his hunting-shirt rattle again; "the fellow wasn't born to be killed in honest battle! he'll turn up somewhere, depend on't. So as the tent is ready, and our guard of honor set, let's take a little rest while the old silver headed dame settles our fate."

Brant strode off to the tent as he spoke, followed by Sir John, who was not a little crestfallen and apprehensive. Up to this time he had met the Indians as a monarch musters his vassals, on the steps of his father's hall, with wealth, power, and a vast tenantry to back him. Now he was a fugitive, separated from his followers, in the hands of a woman exasperated by the loss of her favorite, and evidently filled with scorn of his cowardly desertion both of the home of his ancestors, and the companion of his flight. It was an unpleasant position, and one which Brant maliciously rendered more distressing by his cool review of the dangers that surrounded them. The crafty and brave Indian gloated over the cowardly fears of his companion, for in the depths of his heart he both hated and despised his white allies. It was his happiness to torment them whenever the opportunity arose. Though a willing tool in their hands, he was not a blind one.

Meantime Queen Esther swept on with her train of warriors into the forest. A savage ran before her horse, searching out the trail with his keen eyes. He was one of the Indians that had followed Brant from the Hall. As she rode along, Queen Esther questioned this man in a cautious voice till she had gathered all the information he possessed.

"So you took shelter in the deep cut, and he was lost? Wheel to the left; there is a shorter cut—they will return to the Hall. On!"

Quick and sinuous as a serpent might alter his course, the train of savages swept on one side, and darted off in a run, following their stern leader. For a full hour they kept forward, steady, silent, and swift, threading the wilderness as a flash of lightning cuts through a storm cloud.

"Hist!"

It was the Indian scout who came running back with one hand uplifted.

"Hist—hist!" The word ran like a serpent's hiss through the whole train, and every moccasin rested in its track.

Queen Esther dismounted, and a savage tied her horse to a tree. Again that low hiss ran through the line, and it swept forward. Scarcely a branch swayed, scarcely a stick of brushwood crackled: the wind sighing in the tree-tops made a louder noise than all that band of fierce human beings.

Crash, tramp, crash—the sound which the scout had detected came sharp and clear now. Hoofs beat the turf, oaths rang on the air. The rush of a quick progress swept back louder and louder. In the oath, Queen Esther detected the voice of Butler.

"Ha!" she said, sharply, "he is alive. Faster, faster; but more silently. Are your rifles ready?"

She was answered by the sharp click of flints. Again that silent sweep of human beings. They moved more boldly now for the close beat of hoofs bore down the faint noise of their moccasins.

Again Esther whispered the word of command. The cavalcade were in sight. One horseman, carrying a lantern on his saddle-bow, revealed the rest. With a sudden manœuvre a detachment of savages, headed by Queen Esther, threw themselves in front of the party. Quick as thought, the rest fell into place, surrounding the enemy with a triple hedge of men—a wall of rifles bristled around the doomed group.

The leader was taken by surprise and reined back his horse. The motion exposed his left side; crack! a bullet passed through him. The horse reared, plunged, and fell dead, striking against his nearest companion. Before the revolutionists could reach their holsters, it was too late. Some turned to fly, but the flash of muskets, shedding lurid fire among the green leaves, met them everywhere. A few broke the lines, and rushed away, wounded and bleeding. Three or four escaped unhurt, and fled like madmen into the deep forest. Queen Esther took no prisoners, but shot down her enemies in their track. Shrieks of pain and sharp cries of defiance answered to the storm of her bullets. Her blood rose, the fiery serpent in that woman's heart crested itself. She shrieked to her followers, urging them on, and flinging her scalping-knife into the melée, called aloud for trophies.

Stern and terrible was that conflict, the more terrible because it occupied but a few minutes. The candle that burned in that lantern where it had dropped, was not the fraction of an inch shorter, and yet more than twenty souls had been torn out of life in that brief time.

"Now," cried Queen Esther, cutting the thongs that bound Butler's wrists, and sheathing her red scalping-knife, "catch their horses, mount and follow me to the camp. Some few stay behind, and kill those who are not quite dead. Remember, every rebel's scalp is worth a piece of silver and a bottle of firewater—on!"

She took the stiletto from her bosom, pricked her black steed on the shoulder, and was carried away, with Butler by her side, sweeping that train of red warriors like a whirlwind through the darkness.

A few hours after, they came thundering into the camp; Queen Esther dismounted, without a flush on her cheek or a quickened breath to tell of the dreadful work she had done. Just as gravely and coldly as she had left the camp, she preceded Butler to the tent provided for her guests. Brant stood in the entrance with exultation in his eyes.

"I expected as much," he said. "In the whole Six Tribes there is no warrior like Queen Esther. You see, Sir John, our heads are safe; the victorious are always generous. Well, Butler, I did not expect to see you again to-night."

"And so left me to be rescued by a woman. I thank you," said Butler sullenly.

Brant's massive features broke into a smile.

"Tush," he said; "a man who suffers himself to be taken prisoner by a handful of rebels deserves no better. I am not leagued with your white troopers to pick up the fools that drop off in a skirmish; men who surrender without even a blow of the fist should be left to the women."

"Take care!" answered Butler, fiercely; "you have indulged in these taunts more than is wholesome for you. At any rate, you are not hired to insult the king's officers."

"Hired!" said Brant; "hired!"

"Yes, hired; do your people bring in a scalp which is not paid for in so much gold or silver? It is a better business than trapping mink, and so you take it."

Not another word passed between those two men, but their fierce eyes met as Butler turned upon his heel and left the tent, and that glance told of the mortal enmity which must henceforth exist between them. Still they slept under the same blanket for an hour or two before the day broke that morning.

CHAPTER XVII
THE LAKE BY STARLIGHT

A thousand stars shone upon Seneca Lake; clear stars that smiled goldenly alike on scenes of strife, such as we have left, and pictures of thrifty peace, to which we now turn.

On the shore lay Catharinestown, the Shawnee village, one of the most lovely spots in the world. All the land between the shore and that charming cluster of lodges was richly cultivated; fruit trees stood thick where the hemlocks and oaks had fallen. If a grove or thicket was left here and there, it was the result of Catharine Montour's fine taste, for her gold had served to turn the wilderness on that lone shore into a paradise, and her own poetic spirit had shed beauty on everything she touched. Thus grape-arbors screened the humbler lodges, and bowers of peach-trees drooped over the unseemly wigwams. What Sir William Johnson had done for his estate in the Mohawk Valley, Catharine Montour, in less time, and with better taste, had accomplished at the head of Seneca Lake.

If she had achieved nothing more than this advance in civilization, the life of that unhappy woman had not been utterly thrown away since she came to the wilderness. With her benevolence, her gold, and those wonderful powers of persuasion, with which no woman was ever more richly endowed, she had softened many a savage heart, and won many a rough acre of forest into smiling culture. The large stone mansion which Queen Esther haughtily denominated her palace was by far the most imposing building in the settlement. But nearer the brink of the lake, and sheltered by a grove of sugar-maples, was a smaller lodge of hewn logs, on a foundation of stone, with a peaked roof and deep windows, neatly shingled and glazed. The walls were covered on one end by a massive trumpet vine, that crept half over the roof, where its burning flowers lay in great clusters through all the late summer weeks. Wild honeysuckles, sweet-brier, and forest-ivy crept over the front, and a majestic tulip-tree sheltered it with a wealth of great golden blossoms when these were out of flower. Thus, with the rude logs clothed with foliage, the windows brilliant with pure glass, and no uncouth feature visible, Catharine Montour's residence was far more beautiful than that of her fiercer mother-in-law, and a stranger might well have marvelled to see anything so tasteful in the neighborhood of an Indian settlement.

From this dwelling, Catharine Montour and her daughter looked out upon the lake on that starlit night. Queen Esther and the chief had each gone forth with a detachment of warriors to their separate warpaths. Thus, but a few of the tribe remained at home, and these were under Catharine's direct control, for the younger brother of Gi-en-gwa-tah had accompanied the chief, and no meaner authority was acknowledged in the tribe.

It was a pleasant scene upon which Catharine gazed. A hundred canoes, each with a burning torch at its prow, lay, as it were, sleeping upon the waters. At her command, the warriors left behind by her mother-in-law and husband had gone out to spear salmon, and she was watching the picturesque effect of the canoes on the water, with a gentle thrill of admiration of which her heart had been incapable a few months before. Tahmeroo was at her feet, resting against her lap, and looking—oh, how wistfully!—far beyond the group of canoes with their flaming lights, that fell like meteors on the waters. Her heart, poor girl, was full of wild longings and those vague fears which always follow want of trust in a beloved object.

They had been silent a long time; one watching the fishers, the other looking far beyond them into the still night.

"Mother!"

Catherine Montour started, and withdrawing her eyes from the lake, looked with a kindly glance into the earnest face lifted to hers.

"Well, my child?"

"Is it possible—oh, tell me, mother—mightn't he come to-night?"

"My poor child!"

"Why do you call me poor child, mother, and with that voice, too? Is it because you fear that he will not come?"

"Not that, Tahmeroo. I dare say he will be here before long; for your sake, I hope so."

"And only for my sake, mother; is there no love in your heart for my husband?"

"I love you, child," said Catharine, with a tender caress.

"And not him! Oh, mother, try and love him a little, if it is only for my sake."

"Be content; I shall give him all the love he merits, and more for your dear sake."

"It is a long, long time, since he went away from Wyoming. We have been here one entire week; indeed, it seems like years. Johnson Hall is not so far away that he cannot come back any time now—is it, mother?"

"No, my child; he might have been here to-night. But your father left us soon after he did, and has not yet been heard of."

"Has he been gone so long? I did not know it," said Tahmeroo, innocently.

Catharine sighed; had she, too, become of so little account with her child?

"The chief has gone through a part of the country thick with enemies," she said, probing that young heart with jealous affection.

"But he is wise and brave", answered Tahmeroo, proudly. "The very glance of our chief's eyes would send an enemy from his path."

"But there is war on every side now. It may be a long, long time before he comes back to the lake." "Oh, no; when Walter comes he will send all our warriors to help the great chief."

Again Catharine sighed. It was hard to see the very soul of her child carried off by that bad man. Tahmeroo did not heed the sigh, but started up suddenly, catching her breath with a throb of keen delight.

"Look, mother, look away, away off where the shadows are thick. The stars cannot strike there, and yet I see light—one, two, three, a hundred—the black waters are paved with them—oh, mother, he is coming."

"You forget," said Catharine, straining her eyes to discover the lights which Tahmeroo saw at once with the quick intelligence of love. "It may only be Queen Esther returning with her detachment of warriors—Heaven forbid that she has found an enemy."

"No, mother, no. I am sure those torches are lighting him home. Let us meet him. The stars are out, and all the lake is light with our salmon fishers. It is warm and close here—my canoe lies among the rushes—come mother, come, I will carry you across the lake like a bird."

Catharine arose with a faint smile and followed her daughter to the shore.

With eager haste, Tahmeroo unmoored her little craft, and rowing round a sedgy point, took her mother in. The salmon fishers lay in a little fleet a few rods off, reddening the waves with their torches. At another time Catharine would have paused to rock awhile on the waters, and watch the Indians at their picturesque work, as she had done a hundred times before; but Tahmeroo was full of loving impetuosity; she cut through the crimson waters—saw spear after spear plunged into their depths, and the beautiful fish flash upward and descend into the canoes without notice. How could such scenes interest her when the distant shores were lighted by his presence? Away she sped, turning neither to the right nor left, but on and on, cleaving the silver waters like an arrow, and wondering why the distance seemed so much greater than it ever was before.

At last a fleet of canoes came rounding a point—cast a ruddy light over the forest trees that fringed it in passing, and floated out on the broad bosom of the lake. In the foremost canoe sat a young man with his hat off, and the night winds softly lifting his hair.

"It is he! oh, mother, it is he!" said Tahmeroo. All at once her strength forsook her—the oars hung idly in her hands, and her face fell forward upon her bosom. She remembered how coldly Butler had parted from her, and became shy as a fawn. Like a bird checked upon the wing, her canoe paused an instant on the waves, then turned upon its track, and fled away from the very man its mistress had sought in such breathless haste.

But she had been recognized. A shout followed her retreat; two canoes shot from the rest, and pursued her like a brace of arrows.

"Tahmeroo! Tahmeroo!"

It was his voice—he was glad to see her; never had so much cordial joy greeted her before. She dropped the oars, crept to her mother's bosom, and burst into a passion of tears—oh, such happy, happy tears! That moment was worth a lifetime to her. A canoe darted up. The Indian girl felt herself lifted from the arms of her mother and pressed to her husband's bosom.

As Catharine relinquished her child, a hand clutched the other side of her canoe, and turning quickly she saw Gi-en-gwa-tah stooping toward her, while the cold grey face of Queen Esther peered up on her from behind. Catharine was chilled through by that face, and cowered down in the boat, afraid almost for the first time in her life—and why? The Indian chief was grave and kind as ever; as for the old queen, she was smiling.

Butler and Sir John Johnson went to Catharine's lodge, while Esther marched up to the settlement at the head of her warriors.

In the interior of her house Catharine had gathered so many beautiful objects which appertained to her civilized life, that it appeared more like the boudoir of some European palace than a lodge in the backwoods of America; books, pictures, and even some small specimens of statuary stood around; draperies of rich silk flowed over the windows; and while his tribe maintained most of their savage customs, no prince ever dined on more costly plate and china than did the Shawnee chief when he made Catharine's lodge his home.

With her face all aglow with happiness, Tahmeroo hurried back and forth in the room where her mother sat with her guests, preparing the evening meal with her own hands, for Catharine seldom allowed any personal service that was not rendered by her daughter; it was the one thing in which her affection had ever been exacting.

Tahmeroo loved the gentle task which affection imposed on her. With lips smiling and red as the strawberries heaped in the crystal vase she carried, the young girl brought in the luscious fruits and cream, glancing timidly from under her black lashes to see if Butler was regarding her. He looked on, well pleased. How could he help it? Bad as he was, the wild grace of that young creature would make itself felt even in his hard heart. And Tahmeroo was happy. She did not dream, poor child, that a new power had been added to her attractions since Butler had learned that she was heiress to a title and the vast wealth he could never hope to touch, except through her. Three weeks before, the selfish man would have laughed at the idea of a wild, bright girl like that breaking her heart from his indifference; now her life was very precious to him, and there was no degree of affectionate regard which he would not have feigned, rather than see her cheek grow a shade paler.

Catharine saw this, and her heart rose against the man whom she was forced to acknowledge as her son; but Tahmeroo was satisfied. Of the inheritance that might sometime be hers, she knew nothing, and cared less; her husband's love was all the treasure she coveted on earth.

Butler saw Catharine's eyes following him, and struck with a malicious desire to retaliate on her, broke out, just as they were all seated at the table, with a rude allusion to the English commissioner who had visited Johnson Hall on the evening before its master was driven away.

"Oh, dear lady, I forgot to tell you," he said; "Sir John had the honor of entertaining an old friend of yours the day before he left the Hall; a person who knew you well in England, he said; and who professes that it was to purchase his life you married the chief here."

"Captain Butler," exclaimed Sir John, with sharp indignation; "by what right do you repeat conversation heard at my table?"

"Hallo, have I been blundering, and told tales in the wrong presence? I am sure Murray spoke of the whole thing openly enough."

A low cry broke from Catharine; but one, for she seemed frozen into stone by that name. Every feature was hushed and cold; her very hands looked hard and chiselled, like marble.

The chief glanced at her, a slow fire rose and burned in his eyes. His savage heart was stung with memories to which those few cruel words had given a bitter interpretation. No king upon his throne was ever prouder than that stern chief.

"Surely, that stately old potentate was not a former lover," said Butler, glorying in her anguish; and urged on, both by malice and self-interest, to wound that proud spirit in every possible way; but his coarseness overshot its mark—Catharine arose, bent her head in calm courtesy, and saying, in a low, sad voice:

"I cannot forget that you are my daughter's husband," moved quietly out of the room.

The chief arose also and left the house. He wandered in the woods all night, while she lay fainting and still as marble on her chamber floor; but the bolt was shot, and no one ever knew how terrible was the anguish of that night.

The next day Catharine and the chief recognized each other as ever. But alas! in their souls they never met again.

For weeks and months after this, Butler made his home in the Shawnee camp, till at last the war raged too hotly, and he went once more to his murderous work.

CHAPTER XVIII
WALTER BUTLER'S CAPTURE

In a lonely, deserted spot, on the outskirts of the little village called the German Flats, stood a dreary-looking board house, inhabited by a man named Shoemaker, who enjoyed the unenviable reputation of being a Tory in disguise.

One evening in the early part of the month of August, in 1777, this man and his family were gathered about their supper-table, in one of the lower rooms of the house. The heat of the weather precluded the idea of fire, but after the fashion of many farmers of that period, the hearth was filled with blazing knots of pitch pine, which served to illuminate the apartment in place of candles. The evening meal of samp and milk was just concluded, and they were moving back from the table, when a cautious knock sounded at a door in the rear of the house.

Seated at the table with the family was a workman, a staunch Whig, who had for some time watched his employer with vigilance, and the slightest occurrence of an unusual nature was enough to rouse his suspicions.

He saw Shoemaker start when the knock was repeated, and, rising hastily, offered to open the door.

"Keep your seat," exclaimed the farmer; "I open my own doors, and don't thank any man to be putting on airs, as if he was the owner."

"Some neighbor, I dare say," suggested the wife, as her husband walked towards the door in answer to a third signal.

"They're mighty afeard of coming in," muttered the Whig, moving restlessly in his chair.

"Manners is manners," retorted the old lady, sententiously. "You don't expect strangers to pull the string without knocking; if you do, I don't."

As she spoke, the farmer opened the door; a few whispered words passed between him and some one outside; but instead of ushering the visitor into the house, he stepped out and closed the door behind him. Before those within could express their surprise, except by looks, Shoemaker returned, slamming the door, and saying, with a rough laugh:

"Who do you think it was, but that tarnal Jim Davis, come up here, thinking to find Betsy Willets that he was sparking last winter. That are was the rap he used to give by way of sign, to call her out. I told him she wasn't here now, and sent him off about his business."

If Shoemaker thought by this to quiet his suspicious friend—he had only awakened a new uneasiness, for during several months back, Master Sim had regarded the aforesaid Betsy with wistful appreciation.

"Consarn the fellow's impudence!" he exclaimed, springing to his feet; "if I don't larn him better manners than to be knocking after gals that like his room better'n his company, my name isn't Sim White."

He made a stride towards the door, with the look of a man quite ready to extinguish the claims of half a dozen rivals; but the farmer caught his arm.

"Jest set down and mind your business—I'll have no muss about my house—set down, I say."

"Wal," muttered Sim, sinking slowly into his chair again, and ejecting his tobacco with great violence among the blazing pine knots, "only wait till I meet him with that new Sunday coat of his on—ef I don't embroider it off for him in fine style, I miss my calculation—that's all I've got to say."

"Don't be a fool," expostulated Shoemaker; "never quarrel about a gal—you don't know where you'll find yourself. I wish you'd go down to the tavern for me, and ask Jacob Harney to come up here to-morrow; if he wants that grey mare of mine, he's got to take her now."

"It's getting late," suggested Sim.

"You can stay all night, and come back in the morning. Consarn me, if I don't believe the fellow's afeard of meeting Jim Davis."

Sim disdained to reply either to this taunt or the housewife's laughter; but, planting his old straw hat firmly on his head, was going out of the back door.

"That's a new fit of yourn," called out the farmer; "don't you know that t'other door leads to the road, you blockhead you!"

Sim turned back without a word, and passed out of the door Shoemaker had named; but once in the road he stopped and looked back at the house.

"There's something wrong," he muttered. "Old Ike Shoemaker, you ain't cute enough yet for this chap, by a long shot. I'm bound to see what's going on here; that wan't Jim Davis, no how; the darned old Tory has got some mischief afloat, and I'm a-goin' to find it out."

He turned and hastened down the road, for at that moment the door opened, and the farmer's wife appeared, looking eagerly around, evidently to discover if he were lingering about the house. Sim walked quickly on, and waited till everything should once more be restored to tranquillity before he ventured to return and verify his suspicions.

As soon as they believed him gone, Shoemaker opened the back door and gave a low whistle. Instantly a number of men started up in the gloom and filed into the stoop, moving very cautiously. Shoemaker grasped the hand of their leader, and drew him into the room. When the flame of the pine knots fell upon his face, it exposed the features of Walter Butler.

"What on earth, captain!" exclaimed Shoemaker, looking out in astonishment at the group of men.

"I will explain all to you," returned Butler; "but first you must find some place for my men—we are too many to stay in this open room—we want some supper, too."

"Up this way," said Shoemaker, opening a door that exhibited a stairway leading to an upper story. "Light a dip, Sally—I'll take 'em up; they'll be safe there; and the old woman will find 'em some supper, I guess."

Butler made a signal, and a band of twenty-eight men, fourteen whites and fourteen savages, with arms concealed under their blankets and outer garments, entered the room, and passed almost noiselessly up the staircase.

As they mounted the stairs, unremarked by any of the occupants of the room a human face appeared at the window and looked cautiously through a gap in the curtain, watching every movement with keen vigilance.

When the farmer had seen the men safely stored in the loft, he closed the door behind them and returned to the room, where Walter Butler had thrown himself into a chair, like one wearied by a long march.

"Why, captain, who'd a-thought of seeing you here?" said Shoemaker, taking a seat near him, and lighting his pipe, with all the phlegm of his Dutch ancestors. "You oughtn't to come on a fellow so sudden; you might have been ketched as easy as not, if I hadn't had the gumption to get rid of a fellow who was here."

"Well, we're safe now, at all events," said Butler, carelessly; "there's nothing to be gained, if we don't dare all; my men and I have been in greater peril than this during the last few days, I can tell you, Shoemaker."

"Why, where do you come from?"

"From Seneca Lake, where the Shawnees have made their headquarters most of the time for the past year. The old queen don't lead off as she used to, but she's out again now."

"But what brings you to this place—what on earth do you expect to do here?"

"Give us some supper before you ask me to open my mouth; I am fairly worn out."

"Hurry up, old woman!" said Shoemaker. "While she's about it, captain, here's what'll set you all right," he continued, producing from a cupboard a bottle of rum and a couple of tin cups.

Butler poured out a quantity of the spirits, and drank it off at a swallow.

"That has the right flavor," he said, wiping his lips; "we haven't had a drop since yesterday."

In the meantime the farmer's wife had been busy frying a large platter of ham and pork, and, assisted by her daughter, began spreading a homespun cloth upon the table, to prepare Butler's meal. A liberal portion of this savory food was carried to the men above stairs; and when all was ready, Butler seated himself before the table, with the keen appetite of a man who had not tasted food for twelve hours.

"Fall to, captain," said Shoemaker, pushing the bread and butter within his reach; "the victuals arn't handsome much, but I guess you'll find 'em good, especially after a long fast."

Butler's appetite proved that hunger had given a keen relish to the humble fare, and the farmer smoked his pipe in silence, until his guest pushed back his plate, and filled his glass again from the bottle of spirits.

All this while the face at the window was intently regarding them. Picking loose the putty from one of the window-panes with his fingers, Sim took the glass softly out, as the old woman and girl prepared to leave the room, and the two men drew close together, and began their conversation. Thus, with his ear close to the opening, he listened to all that passed.

"So you can't understand what brings me here," Butler said, sipping his rum. "You see, I've doffed my regimentals," he added, pointing to the hunter's frock which he wore, "and am ready for any kind of work."

"I wouldn't 'a' known you, I do believe, cap'n. Wal, fine feathers do make fine birds, and no mistake. You look like one of us now."

"Wesson is in command of Fort Dayton, isn't he?" Butler asked.

"Yes, and keeping a sharp look-out. You don't mean to attack him, do you?"

"No; but before morning I intend to sack old Davis's house—he's got some papers of Sir John Johnson's that we must have, and we may as well take his useless life along with them."

"Wal, I guess the neighborhood can spare him," said the farmer, indifferently. "He's one of the worst rebels in the district. Jest set fire to his haystacks while you're about it—I'd like to see 'em burn."

"His house isn't near the fort, is it?"

"No; it's on the other road, and stands as much alone as mine does; you won't have any difficulty about settling his hash."

"I'll have the papers, if I murder and burn the whole settlement!" exclaimed Butler, with an oath.

"Wal, they'd do the same by you if they ketched you. It isn't a week since I heard old Davis himself say he'd hang you if ever he laid hands on you."

"Let him look to himself!" muttered Butler, all the ferocity of his nature breaking forth in his glance. "My men shall tie him hand and foot, and burn him in his own house."

"When will you start?"

"About midnight. By that time the whole neighborhood will be quiet, and my men refreshed—we've had a long march, and they are tired enough, but always ready for this kind of work."

"There's no trouble about it," said Shoemaker; "we'll make it as merry as a wedding."

The face which had long watched them disappeared from the window, and the fugitive fled lightly down the road towards the fort.

"Will you, indeed?" muttered Sim White, as his long legs measured off the ground at a tremendous pace. "We'll see about that! I've got you this time, you old Tory; I haven't watched you two months for nothing! Old Davis, indeed! and to think I wanted to lick Jim—only jest wait a little!"

The two men continued their conversation in fancied security. At length Butler flung himself upon a rude settle, with his Indian blanket under his head for a pillow, and fell into a heavy slumber. The farmer remained in his chair, but after a time his head fell forward, the pipe dropped from his fingers, and he also sank into a quiet sleep.

Sim White made no pause for breath until he reached the little block-house which was dignified by the name of fort. His violent knocking speedily aroused the sentinels, and the door was cautiously opened.

"A pooty set of fellers," exclaimed Sim, as he rushed in panting and exhausted, "to be snoozing here, while all our lives are in danger! Call up Colonel Wesson!"

"What is it, Sim?" echoed a dozen voices.

"The Tories and Injuns are at us, that's all!" returned Sim. "Call the colonel, you darned blunder-heads!"

"Here I am!" exclaimed a manly voice, and the commander appeared from the inner room. "What has happened?"

Sim explained in a few energetic words the scene that he had witnessed, and the projected attack upon Davis's house.

"You hain't got no time to lose," continued Sim. "There's twenty-eight of 'em, Injuns and Tories, and that Walter Butler at their head, and old Ike Shoemaker is as bad as any, cuss him! Only let me get my grip on him! Only to think that I've lived in his house a'most a year, and he a flat-footed Tory all the time!"

Colonel Wesson quickly arranged the plan of action, and in a few moments the men he selected were in marching order.

"All you've got to do is to surround the house," said Sim. "The men are up in the loft, and there's no winder for 'em to fire out of. We'll have them like so many rats in a haystack."

"Come on, men," said the colonel. "Sim, do you go with us?"

"Go with you? Wal, now, that's a pooty question, ain't it? When did you ever know Sim White to shrink out of a fight with the bloody Tories? Give me a pitchfork, or a scythe, or anything that comes handy. I'll stick 'em, or mow off their heads to the tune of Yankee Doodle. Go with you? I wonder what you mean by that!"

"We'll look you up a gun, Sim," said the colonel, laughing; "you'll find that more useful."

"I ain't no ways perticler about the weapon," replied Sim; "all I ask is a shy at old Ike. Ef I don't stuff his pipe down his piratical old throat, I hope I may have to sarve crazy George to sthe end of my days, that's all!"

"Shed as little blood as possible, men," said Colonel Wesson; "and, by all means, take Walter Butler alive."

"Yes, sir," said Sim; "there's an old rope in Shoemaker's barn, that they tie the kicking heifer with—the noose in it'll fit that feller's neck to a T."

"We are all ready," said the colonel. "File out, men—steady and quiet. Forward, march!"

Walter Butler still slept upon the wooden settle, moving restlessly in his slumbers, and uttering broken exclamations which betrayed how even his dreams took a share in the cruel and bloody projects he had formed. The farmer dozed quietly upon the hearth, the pine knots had burned almost to ashes, and the kitchen was wrapped in gloom, save when the dying embers crackled and sent up a lurid flame for an instant, only to die out and leave the gloom and stillness deeper than before.

Up the road came that little band of faithful Whigs, in stern and silent indignation against the men who had so often laid waste their peaceful homes, and scattered ruin and desolation wherever they passed.

The troops surrounded the house with noiseless caution, but still there was no sound within. The door had been left unfastened in their secure carelessness, and yielded without an effort to the assailants' touch.

Suddenly there was a tread of heavy feet—the room was bright with the glare of torches, and Walter Butler sprang to his feet from a troubled dream, to find himself in the sure grasp of the men he had so often persecuted.

"The rebels are on us!" he shouted. "Here, men, men!"

This cry was echoed by a war-whoop from the Indians above, but as the foremost of his men burst upon them, he fell dead, pierced by a bullet from one of the Whigs. Another and another shared the same fate, and the savages and Tories retreated in confusion to their place of concealment.

Walter Butler struggled with the desperate energy of a man fighting for his life; striking aimlessly with his hunting-knife, but he was speedily overpowered and thrown upon the floor.

Shoemaker, as soon as he could collect his wits, had sought refuge in the pantry, but Sim White speedily discovered his hiding-place, and dragged him back into the kitchen, where he fell upon his knees, writhing and supplicating in abject fear.

"I'm not to blame—I'm an innocent man!" he cried. "Don't kill me, don't kill me, Sim White; it's agin nature that you should kill a man you've sat at table with."

"Shut up!" said Sim, giving him a vigorous shake; "nobody wants yer cussed old life, you ain't worth killin'!"

Butler shouted again to his men with loud curses; once more they essayed to force a passage into the room, but the foremost fell under the unerring aim of the Whigs, and they retreated again. Before the Whigs discovered it, they had found means of egress through the only window the loft contained, and escaped, leaving their leader behind.

"Cowards!" cried Butler, writhing himself free from the grasp of his captors and seeking to draw his pistols, "I'll sell my life dearly, any way!"

Again he was overpowered, flung upon the settle, and tied securely hand and foot, so that he could only vent his rage in impotent blasphemies.

Sim stood guard over the farmer, who besought him in vain to be released.

"Only let me go, Sim; I'll tell you the whole. I will, sartin as you live."

"As if I didn't know the hull—didn't I hear every word you said? Jim Davis, indeed, you pesky varmint. Shut up, not a word out of yer Tory head!"

"Just let Jim Davis lay his hands on you, that's all!" added another; "he'll settle your affair sudden, now I tell you."

Walter Butler lay writhing in ineffectual efforts to free himself; his struggles attracted Sim's attention.

"Somebody hold the old chap a minute," he said; "while I get the halter for the captain, the noose 'ill fit his neck as well as any other wild colt's."

Colonel Wesson checked them in their project.

"He is here taken on our ground—a spy, and worse than a spy. Mr. Butler must be brought before a court-martial," he said; "we will give him a fair trial. You have no right to commit murder."

"Who wants to commit murder?" said Sim. "I only meant to noose him, that's all. Here, old shaking bones, stand up and have your hands tied—come along." "Oh, don't, don't!" shrieked the trembling coward. "Let me go—I've got a wife and child!"

At this moment the mother and daughter rushed into the room, where they had remained concealed, quaking with fear, and besought Colonel Wesson to spare his life.

"We shall not harm him," replied the soldier; "but he must go with us; his fate is in the hands of others."

"They'll hang me! They'll hang me!" groaned the farmer.

"Of course they will," said Sim, consolingly; "but it's quick over! Set fire to old Davis's haystacks, will you? you pesky old weasel!"

Conducting their prisoners, the party returned to the block-house, where a court-martial was speedily formed, to decide upon the fate of Walter Butler.

He listened in sullen silence to the arguments, smiling ferociously when different acts of his cruelty were cited, and exhibiting a callous unconcern, which was the effect of desperation rather than manly courage.

He was sentenced to be hung as a spy at daylight, and when the court-martial broke up, was placed in rigid confinement during the few hours which must elapse before his death. After his removal, Colonel Wesson debated the validity of their sentence, and deemed it more prudent to grant the prisoner a reprieve, and have him removed to Albany, where the Commander-in-chief might control his fate. This was received with disfavor by the Whigs, but Wesson's arguments finally prevailed, and it was decided that instead of meeting his sentence at daybreak he should be conveyed at once, under a strong guard, to Albany.

The old Tory, Shoemaker, was condemned to receive a score of lashes, and left to return home. Sim listened to the sentence with the utmost glee, and made strange confusion amid the solemnity of the scene, by offering to apply the lashes with his own hand.

When morning dawned, Walter Butler was sent forth from the settlement a prisoner. For once his cruel schemes had failed; and as he possessed only the courage of a weak, wicked man, he looked forward, with inward trembling, to the doom that awaited him.

For a year he pined in the close confinement of a jail; at the expiration of that time he was reported ill, and through the intercession of his father's friends among the patriots, he was still closely watched, but allowed more liberty of action, and surrounded by the comforts and luxuries which his sensuous nature found so essential, in spite of the training and capability for enduring hardships, which a long residence in the backwoods had given him.

CHAPTER XIX
THE WIFE'S STRUGGLE

Many months had elapsed since Walter Butler's capture, and no tidings of him had reached his young Indian wife, left mourning in her home on the borders of Seneca Lake.

Catharine Montour believed that he had deserted her child, for she knew him to be a man capable of any deed, however despicable, and though her heart was wrung with anguish by the sight of Tahmeroo's suffering, she could not regret his absence, feeling that the misery of desertion was nothing compared to that which the poor girl might have been forced to endure from his indifference and cruelty.

Queen Esther had exhibited no astonishment at Butler's absence, but in truth her lion-like heart was stirred by many conflicting emotions, all overpowered by a strong desire to avenge the slight which he had dared to put upon her grandchild. So, amid them all, Tahmeroo found little comfort, and wore away the time as best she might, concealing her sorrow with all the fortitude of her savage nature, though her altered face and wasted form betrayed the grief preying within.

At length her father returned from the warpath, and, after much persuasion, consented to go forth and seek for tidings of the absent husband. Even his stern nature was moved by his daughter's suffering, and, collecting a band of his warriors, he set forth, promising ere long to return with tidings which should relieve the girl's wretchedness.

On the fourth day of his absence Tahmeroo went up to the great stone house where Queen Esther dwelt in almost regal state. The old woman was absent, and Tahmeroo sat down in a deserted apartment, to await her return. She crouched upon a low stool in a darkened corner, not weeping, but hiding her face in her hands, and bearing her suffering with the silent endurance natural to her Indian blood. She could not believe that Butler had deserted her, and, still confident of his love, could she but discover his residence, would gladly have crept to him with the affection which nothing could shake, and besought him to return. That strong love had completely subdued the passionate pride of her nature, and, rather than be parted from him, she would have sold herself a slave in his behalf, asking only the sunshine of his presence and the glory of his love. That wild devotion had so mingled itself with the religious creed her mother had taught the girl that it became a part of her religion, and only death could have torn it from her heart.

There she sat in the gloomy chamber, motionless as a figure carved from stone, her garments falling over her bosom in stirless folds, as if no pulse beat beneath. A touch roused her, she sprang to her feet and glared around with her feverish eyes, thinking it might be her father who had returned, but when she met her granddame's steely glance she fell back to her seat in the apathy of deeper despair.

Queen Esther had entered the room with her usual panther-like movement and approached her unheeded. She stood for a moment regarding her in silence, her withered hand still resting upon the girl's shoulder. If any feeling of sympathy stirred in that stony bosom her hardened features were incapable of expressing it, and her cold eyes looked down upon the unhappy girl in unmoved sternness.

"Arise, Tahmeroo," she said at length, in her clear, metallic voice; "a chief's daughter should not crouch down and weep like a puny pale face. Wrestle with your sorrow, and if you cannot cure it, tear the heart from your bosom."

"I am not weeping," replied the girl, sullenly; "Tahmeroo has no tears, and she is not afraid to meet her grief—is not Queen Esther's blood in her veins?"

"Brave girl! Wait—wait—we will lie in ambush for our prey, and when we catch him, Esther's knife shall avenge her grandchild's wrongs."

"No, no!" shrieked the affrighted creature, grasping the old woman's uplifted arm; "you will not harm him, promise me that you will not—have mercy!"

"Did Esther ever fail to avenge a wrong? Does Tahmeroo think the old queen in her dotage that she talks to her of mercy? To an insult there is but one answer—a bullet, flames, or the knife!"

"Then I swear by the Great Spirit that you shall kill me, too; the knife that drinks his blood shall be sheathed in mine; then let Queen Esther carry it next her bosom, if she will."

Her form was thrown back in wild energy, all the fire and beauty returned to her face, before so pale and spiritless. The woman looked at her with exultation which she seldom exhibited.

"The blood of the Shawnee chief is hot in his daughter's bosom," she said, proudly. "Let Tahmeroo have patience, the white brave may yet return; he is no traitor, and he loves our wandering life; he hates the rebels, too, and in his cabin hang many war-scalps, with pale hair streaming from them." Tahmeroo heard only a portion of these words and her heart clung to that cold assurance as if it had been a prophecy.

"He will return!" she exclaimed; "I know he will return—perhaps he may come back with the chief; he has been delayed by sickness, or——"

"Death!" said Esther.

The word fell like a blow on the heart of her listener.

"No, he is not dead," she sobbed. "Tahmeroo would have known it; the dream-spirit would have revealed it to her—say that he is not dead."

A wild animal would have been softened by the anguish of her tone, but Esther only waved her off, saying, coldly:

"We shall know; let Tahmeroo be patient."

The tramp of horses sounded from without, and through the casement Tahmeroo saw her father dismounting before the door, in the midst of his warriors.

She rushed into the broad hall, but Queen Esther drew her back with a fierce grasp.

"Shame!" she hissed; "will the chief's daughter expose herself to her father's braves, like the burden-women of her tribe?"

She flung Tahmeroo aside, as she might have thrown down one of the young panther cubs, which she fed daily from her own hands.

The chief Gi-en-gwa-tah entered the room with his usual stately tread, and in spite of her grandmother's warning frown Tahmeroo sprang towards him, extending her hands in mute supplication.

"What news does the chief bring to his daughter?" Queen Esther asked in the Shawnee dialect, for she seldom spoke her own language, carrying her hatred of the race even to an aversion of their tongue.

"The white brave is alive," Gi-en-gwa-tah replied.

"Then, why does he not come?" asked Esther, sternly.

"Speak, father," pleaded Tahmeroo; "is he sick? where is he? let me go to him!"

"Tahmeroo questions like a foolish maiden," he said, reprovingly, "and gives the chief no time to answer."

"The girl is anxious," Esther said, sternly, with a woman's true spirit of contradiction, rebuking the chief for severity which she herself would have shown had he remained silent. "Where is the young pale face? speak."

"A prisoner among the rebels," returned Gi-en-gwa-tah.

Tahmeroo fell forward with a low moan, and lay upon the floor writhing in silent anguish. Even the chief's dark face softened, and though nothing enraged Queen Esther so violently as any display of weakness, she spoke no word of chiding, but raised the girl and placed her on a seat.

"Where—where?" gasped Tahmeroo, as soon as she could speak.

"In Albany—there he has been for months, confined in jail under sentence of death."

"Save him, oh, save him!" pleaded Tahmeroo. "You are a great warrior, my father; you will save him! Grand-dame—queen—bring back Tahmeroo's husband or let her die, now."

"If he is killed, we will avenge him!" hissed Esther, clutching the hilt of the hunting-knife which she wore in her girdle. "Look up, Tahmeroo, we will have blood for blood!"

"That will not give him back to me," said Tahmeroo, shuddering; "blood, always blood—I am sick of vengeance—I want my husband."

"We can do nothing," Esther replied; "nothing yet—Tahmeroo must be patient; she knows that the young chief is true to her."

"Who dared think otherwise?" exclaimed Tahmeroo, with passionate defiance. "Let all beware—Tahmeroo can revenge also, not herself, but her husband. I must find him," she continued, shrinking again into her womanly weakness; "he shall be set at liberty. Father, father, is there no way?"

"Let Tahmeroo leave us for a while," said Esther; "the chief cannot counsel with children."

"But you will free him—you are very powerful?"

"We can do nothing yet, but we can revenge his death!"

Tahmeroo hurried away, horror-stricken by the oft-repeated word, and flew down the road towards the lake. Her mother's house was upon the border of the water, and full three miles distant; but Tahmeroo never paused for breath, speeding along with the grace and swiftness of a young doe. There was a terrible pressure at her heart, but hope had once more begun to revive in it; she knew where her husband was, and could not believe that those so-all-powerful as she deemed her own family, could be without ability to save him.

Catharine Montour was seated in her lonely house, brooding over the sad thoughts which for months had returned to torture her with greater force from the few vague words which Butler had dropped that night, half in wantonness, half in revenge. Her conversation with the missionary had opened her long-silent heart, and amid the solitude of her life she was forced to listen to its troubled beatings. She had lost much of the indomitable will which had so long supported her, and the barbarous cruelty by which she was surrounded became every day more painful and revolting; as her own noble nature resumed its sway, she grew kind and gentle as a child but very sad.

Those cruel words which Butler had flung like a dagger at her heart were harder to bear than all beside. Murray was still alive—the evil chances of their destiny might bring them once more together, and that meeting would be as painful as if all the long weary past had been obliterated and the early vitality of their suffering brought back upon them. Catherine was worn out with struggles; her former pride and courage had forsaken her, and she longed to creep away to some quiet haunt where she might die alone.

The hard spirit of infidelity which she had forced upon her soul was shaken off; she could no longer delude herself with the false belief with which she had long endeavored to silence the pleadings of her conscience, and the familiar truths taught her in childhood, which were coming back to her soul, like a flock of doves to their desolated nests, had not yet acquired strength enough to afford her comfort.

When the door opened, and Tahmeroo rushed into the room, pale and agitated, she looked dreamily up, like one whose thoughts come back, with an effort, from afar, unfolded her hands from the loose sleeves of her robe, and smiled a sad welcome.

"Mother—oh, mother!" exclaimed the girl, "the chief has news—my brave is a prisoner among the rebels."

Catharine Montour felt almost a pang of disappointment; she knew that his desertion or death would be nothing to what must come. Tahmeroo's pride would, in a measure, have aided her to bear the former; but there was no refuge from his coldness or neglect. His safety seemed to her a misfortune.

"Speak, mother—comfort Tahmeroo, she is very wretched! Will you not help her—will you not save her husband? The granddame talks of vengeance, but your child pines for her mate—you are merciful and good—oh, help me!"

"Alas, my poor bird!" Catharine said, folding her to her heart, "I am powerless; the rebels are our enemies, and I cannot go into their camps."

"But he is in their city—in Albany."

"There, least of all—they would only imprison me also."

"What is imprisonment or death!" cried Tahmeroo.

"I would dare everything to be near him! Go with me, mother—go with me!"

"It is impossible—the chief would never consent; besides, we should rather do harm than good. I will write to Sir John Johnson, who is in Canada; he may have captives that he can exchange for your—for Butler."

"But weeks and months will be wasted, and I must find him at once."

"But there is no way; be calm, child—you cannot."

"Mother, I will! The blood of great warriors beats in Tahmeroo's heart; she will dare everything—danger, death—to free her husband!"

"Listen to me, Tahmeroo, and try to understand; don't tremble and look so wild! The means that you propose could be of no avail. You must wait until we hear from Canada; then we shall be able to decide what is best."

"I cannot—oh, I cannot!" cried Tahmeroo, with a sudden burst of grief. "Nobody has any pity on me—none of you ever loved, or you would not treat Tahmeroo so coldly."

Catharine's arms released their hold and fell to her side; a sickly pallor gathered about her mouth, and her sad eyes grew dim.

"Everywhere the same!" she murmured, "everywhere! Life, life, if we could only escape it—cast it forth!"

"What do you say, mother? How white your lips are. Oh, you do pity Tahmeroo—hold me to your heart again, and tell me that you pity me!"

Catharine took the unhappy girl to her bosom in a long embrace, and Tahmeroo wept for a time in silence. But soon her impatience came back, and again she began pleading for aid to send after her husband.

"Let a band of warriors go to their city," she said; "we will burn it to ashes, if they refuse to give him up!"

"Oh, Tahmeroo!" shuddered Catharine; "do not become a fiend like the rest—let not my own child be an added curse to me! Think of the bloodshed, the innocent lives that would suffer; the loving hearts—hearts like your own—that would be tortured!"

"Forgive me, mother; but ah, I suffer so! I seem going mad! Then the whole tribe will pity me, for when the Great Spirit tortures a brain with fire, they can pity."

She fell at her mother's feet, with renewed prayers and supplications; but Catharine was powerless, and though she pitied her child, she was so worn out by the struggles of the past months that she had no energy left. She arose at length, and pushing Tahmeroo gently away, walked slowly out of the room.

The girl stood for some moments in despairing silence; then a gleam of hope brightened over her face.

"I will go," she exclaimed aloud, "I will go myself to Albany—at least, I shall be near him. And the young pale face of Wyoming—the Great Spirit has given her strange power—I will go to her, she will help me."

Before her mother returned to the apartment, Tahmeroo had disappeared—whither, no one knew. Half a dozen of her father's warriors quitted the settlement with her; but they left no trail in the forest by which her route could be traced.

CHAPTER XX
HOUSEHOLD TALK

The brightness of a sunset in early May settled on Monockonok Island. It was now the spring of 1778—that year so eventful in the annals of Wyoming—but as yet there was no warning of the fell tragedy which afterwards desolated that beautiful spot.

In the tidy kitchen of their little cabin Mother Derwent was seated at her work, while her two granddaughters sat by. The old lady's wheel was flying round with a pleasant hum, and the placid expression of her wrinkled face betrayed thoughts that had gone back to pleasant memories of the past. Mary Derwent sat by the window, a Bible lay open on her lap, from which she had been reading loud; and the spring breeze fluttered through the casement, making restless lights on her golden hair, and rustling with a musical sound among the worn leaves of the sacred volume. The past year had somewhat changed Mary; her look of patient sorrow had given place to one of undisturbed resignation; those soft blue eyes had cleared themselves from every mist, and if there was no joyousness in their depths, neither was there a trace of human grief—they were pure and serene as violets that have caught their hue by looking up to heaven.

On a low stool at her feet sat her sister Jane, occupied with some feminine needlework; but her skill seemed often at fault, and she would put her work on Mary's lap, with pretty childish petulance, asking for help. Mary would look up from her reading, take the work, and by a few dexterous touches of her nimble fingers, set it once more in order; then restore it with a kind smile to the beautiful girl, whose mind seemed diverted by pleasant fancies from her task oftener than was at all compatible with its progress.

Jane, too, looked happier and more quiet, the loveliness of her face was no longer disfigured by the discontent which had formerly brooded over it. The holy influence of Mary's life had wrought its effect on her wavering character. The pure soul of one sister had buoyed up the weak girlishness of the other; from the calm strength of her sister's mind Jane caught rays of light, full of serenity and trustfulness. With no tempter by, and good influences all around her, Jane had thrown off much that had been reprehensible in her character, and was now more reasonable and considerate than she had ever been in her life.

The afternoon wore on, and Jane hovered restlessly over her work, like a bird longing to forsake its nest for the free air, ever and again glancing towards the winding road of the Kingston shore, which was visible from the window.

"There, Mary," she said, at length, unable longer to control her impatience, "I have almost finished it. Don't you think I might as well leave off till to-morrow—my fingers do ache so?"

"You have been very industrious this afternoon," Mary said smiling. "I really think you have earned your liberty."

"Besides," said Jane, "it is almost sundown."

"And then?"

The color spread over Jane's forehead, and she laid her head on Mary's knee, twisting her apron-strings with girlish modesty, born of real love, which she now really felt for her affianced husband, though she replied as if her sister had spoken plainly.

"Yes; Edward Clark is coming. Oh, Mary——" She broke off abruptly, and turned her face still more away, while the color deepened on her cheek.

"What is it, Janey?"

"He is coming, because—that is, I promised——"

"Well—tell me what you promised."

Grandmother Derwent's wheel hummed on, and she heard nothing of their conversation.

"When he was here Sunday," continued Jane, with that desperate haste with which one rushes into a difficult revelation, "he made me promise to name the day the very next time he came, and he will be here in an hour."

The pulses of Mary Derwent's heart grew faint and tremulous, but she forced back the rising emotion, her face grew clear as moonlight, and when she answered, her voice was soft, but with a touch of sadness in it.

"And is that so difficult?" she asked. "Have you not learned by this time what will make your chief happiness?"

"Yes, yes, and I have to thank you for it, Mary. You have taught me to be a better girl; I never will be wayward again—indeed I won't. But I can't make up my mind to set the time—I know I can't."

Mary laid her hand caressingly upon her white forehead, and brushed back the long tresses from it.

"When can you be ready—how long will it take?"

"Oh, I can be all ready by July," returned Jane, eagerly; then checking herself, she added, "at least I think so. I want to whiten another web of cloth, and Aunt Polly Carter has promised me a rag carpet, though, when it comes to the point, I don't believe she can find it in her heart to give one away."

"Then you must tell Edward that you will be ready in July," Mary said, seriously, not heeding the petty details to which her sister's mind had wandered. "And oh, remember, Jane, this is one of the most serious moments in your life. Do not leave a single consideration unweighed before you make this decision. It is an important thing to do, my sister."

"Don't look so sober and talk so gravely—please don't! I have thought about it a great deal—I know I shall be happy as—as——"

She paused again, but this time Mary made no effort to urge her completion of the sentence. She sat in dreamy silence, with her eyes bent upon the rushing waters. Jane went on with an effort, and a great seriousness came over her, when she added:

"As Edward Clark's wife."

Even her volatile nature was moved by the enunciation of those solemn words which fell—oh, with such desolation—on Mary's ear. For many moments Jane sat in silence, hiding her face in the folds of her sister's dress.

Suddenly the sound of oars broke up through the stillness, and Jane started to her feet with a bustle that roused Grandmother Derwent from her reverie.

"I know who's coming," she said; "there's only one pair of oars on the river that can make Janey jump so."

Jane was hastening out of the room, but she upset her basket, and was forced to pause and collect its scattered contents, so that, blushing crimson, she had the full benefit of the old lady's speech.

"It was rather different when Walter Butler used to come. Jane ain't the same creetur she was in them days."

"Oh, Grandmother, you are too bad!" exclaimed the poor girl, letting her basket fall, fairly running out of her room, though not quick enough to escape the audible tone in which the good woman continued her reflections.

"Well, it's the truth; she's worth a hundred times what she was then, and does double the work. I like Edward Clark; nobody need be any more industrious than he is, and if his wife ain't as happy as the day is long, it'll be her own fault, I am sure of that."

Jane had escaped, and Mary, after quietly putting aside the disordered work, threw a light shawl over her head, and went out. She was in no mood to witness the oppressive happiness of those two young beings, so full of life, and strength, and hope. She felt the need of solitude, and stole quietly out to the humble grave beneath the cedar-tree, which had been from childhood her favorite haunt for thought and prayer when these melancholy feelings came over her.

The gorgeousness of the sunset fell around her, and sitting down by her father's grave, Mary's heart went up in a silent prayer for strength and resignation. When she lifted her head again, she saw the missionary standing a little way off, regarding her with the beaming affection which his face always wore when he looked upon her.

Mary went towards him without the slightest surprise or embarrassment, and laid her hand in his, which closed over it with a mute caress.

"I thought you would come yesterday," she said, leading him to their accustomed seat under the shadow of the trees, "but I was disappointed."

"I was occupied, my child, and had not a moment to spare, but I thought of you a great deal, and felt that you would be expecting me. Have you been well—is all at rest within? You were praying, I think, child, when I came up."

"But not in grief," Mary replied, with heavenly sadness; "only I am a weak creature and need to pray more than other people; if I don't, strange thoughts are sure to crowd into my heart and I get quite frightened at myself."

"Poor child!" returned the missionary; "poor chosen lamb, how little you know of yourself! And is all well at home—Janey?"

"She is well—oh, sir, she is going to be married very soon." Mary uttered the words untremulously, and if the missionary noted the flutter at her heart he made no comment.

"I am glad," he said; "I never felt that she was really safe; young Butler may return at any time, but, once married to Edward, we need have no fear."

"She will be happy," said Mary, "very happy; he loves her and she loves him, you do not know how much! She is not so childish now—she grows quite womanly in her ways, and works till grandma does nothing but boast of her industry. This is all very pleasant and our home is so quiet now, one can rest in it."

"And you, Mary, what are you going to do?"

Mary looked startled—what was she to do? The thought had so seldom presented itself that she was astonished by its strangeness.

"Do?" she repeated. "Live with grandma; what else can I do?"

"But the time will come when she will no longer need your care, or feel your affection."

"Then I shall stay with Jane—no, I think that could never be, at any rate, for a long time; but I have you; perhaps, if grandmother left me, you would not mind it if I came to live with you."

"What! in the wilderness?"

"Yes, I love the woods best."

"An angel might love you for a companion," murmured the missionary; then he added, aloud, "but have you never thought of a more extended field of usefulness? Is there nothing higher for which your mind and acquirements fit you?"

"No, never; but it was wrong of me," she said, reproachfully. "I am afraid I have been very idle—what must I do? Is there anything I can do?"

"You have left nothing undone, my child; you have been everything to your grandmother, a guardian angel to your sister. But the time may come when they will not need you."

"Then I shall come and ask what I am to do—you will teach me and help me, I know that well enough."

"Always, child, darling, always!"

Mary clasped her hand over his again, and they stood, side by side, looking across the waters into the fading glory of the sunset. The crimson and gold died slowly away, the sombre tints of twilight struggled with the clear blue of the evening sky, a few stars came out and trembled on the horizon, as if eager to wing their flight towards the pale moon that had been riding the heavens a full hour, looking like a faded cloud amid the brightness of the setting sun.

The plash of oars disturbed them as they stood there. Mary looked quickly around.

"It cannot be Edward going so soon," she said; "I did not know that any one else was on the island."

There was the soft tread of moccasins on the grass, and before either could move, Tahmeroo, the Shawnee chief's daughter, was standing before them.

Mary uttered an exclamation of joy and surprise; the Indian girl threw herself forward, as if to kneel at Mary's feet, but the gentle girl stretched forth her arms and drew the young Indian to her bosom with a fervent embrace. The missionary stood silent and pale during that prolonged caress, his hand extended almost as if he would have repulsed the savage and forced Mary from her clinging arms.

"I began to think you would never return," murmured the deformed, when the Indian girl raised her head; "I am so glad to see you once more!"

"Yes, it is many, many moons; but Tahmeroo has never forgotten the young pale face. Tahmeroo has great trouble, and she comes to you for help, to you and this good prophet," she continued, turning toward the missionary.

"What can we do for you?" Mary asked.

"Much—the white medicine is very powerful; he will help me, and you, too, you will not send Tahmeroo away miserable, and without some hope of seeing her lord again."

The missionary looked at her earnestly, and the stern pallor of his face softened. That short year had wrought a great change in the poor girl. The habitual brown of her cheek had given place to a sickly pallor, her temples were hollow and sunken, and her black eyes blazed with a strange brilliancy, which betrayed the consuming fever within. Her dress looked travel-stained, and there was a carelessness about her attire widely at variance with the picturesque neatness which had formerly characterized her.

The unrest of the heart was in her face, painful always to remark in the young, doubly painful when breaking through the wild beauty of that youthful savage. She understood the impression which her altered lineaments made upon her observers, and said, with a forced smile:

"Tahmeroo is a girl no longer; sorrow has forced the freshness out of her heart, as the thunder tempest beats the breath out of the wild rose."

"What has happened to you?" questioned Mary. "Your mother, your noble mother?"

The missionary started, and echoed the words "Your mother?"

"Catharine Montour is well, though she may be pining for her child; but he, my husband, they have taken him prisoner; Tahmeroo has not seen him for months; they will kill him, perhaps, before she can reach the spot. No one would help save him, not even my mother, so I fled hither."

"I had heard of this," whispered the missionary; "he was taken nearly a year since, and put in prison as a spy."

"A spy!" repeated Tahmeroo, overhearing the last word; "he serves his king. Those that have captured him are miserable rebels. But let them beware—it is Gi-en-gwa-tah's son that they have imprisoned; the children of Queen Esther never forget nor forgive."

Her face darkened with passion, and would have been absolutely forbidding, had not womanly tenderness for her husband softened its hardness.

"Shame, Tahmeroo!" exclaimed the missionary. "You must know that such thoughts are wrong; your mother has taught you that they offend the Great Spirit."

"Forgive me, oh forgive Tahmeroo!" she cried, throwing herself on the ground at his feet, and clasping his knees with her wasted arms. The missionary struggled for an instant, as if her touch were unpleasant to him, but she held him firmly. "Tahmeroo is very wretched, oh speak some comfort to her—a good prophet finds consolation for every one, Catharine Montour says—oh, take pity on her child."

The missionary raised her gently, and for the first time held her hand firmly in his clasp, though his form shook with emotion. Mary's tears were falling like gentle rain as she bent over the suffering girl, and the missionary placed Tahmeroo's head upon her bosom, saying, softly:

"Ay, comfort her, little one; it is but right!"

Tahmeroo remained motionless for many moments; at length she raised her head, and wiping away the teardrops with her long black hair, strove to relate her story more connectedly.

"I came all the way from Seneca Lake to find you," she said. "No one could help me—our great medicine men could only pity me when asked for counsel. My father had power to revenge his loss, but that did not bring him back. Catharine, my mother, who was once brave as a lion when Tahmeroo was wronged, even in a little thing, now looked on with heavy eyes, and when I pleaded with her, said—oh, with such cruel stillness: 'It is better thus, my child; his presence here must ever be a curse to me and mine.' Such words stung me like wasps—my heart burned—I remembered you, a sweet medicine spirit, whom even our enemies love. I left my grandmother's lodge in the night, caught a horse, and fled."

"And you will," she said in conclusion, while the tears of her spent gust of passion rolled slowly down her cheeks; "you will help the Indian girl, for you are good and powerful. When you ask, his enemies will give him up."

"My poor child!" returned the missionary; "I can see no way to help you."

"If they will only let her see her husband once more, Tahmeroo would be a slave to his enemies."

"But he is in prison; you cannot get near him."

"But the white prophet will ask, and the prison door will be left open, that Tahmeroo may steal in."

"Yes, I will write to General Schuyler; he will hardly refuse to let a wife see her husband."

Tahmeroo fell to kissing his hands, while the tears in her eyes flashed like diamonds.

"You will write. They will take pity on me, and let me hear him speak."

"But they will not let you remain with him."

"But I will stay in sight of his prison; I will sell myself as a slave—do anything, if they will only let me stay near him."

The missionary sat down upon the ground, and taking from his coat the little case of writing materials which he always carried about him wrote a few lines and gave them to Tahmeroo.

"Read them," he said; "I can do nothing more."

"It is enough, enough! Bless you, bless you!" exclaimed Tahmeroo, seizing his hand and pressing it to her lips. The missionary withdrew it gently and rose to his feet.

"And when do you start?" Mary asked.

"Before the evening stars look into the water Tahmeroo will be far away."

"Come home with me first, and get some food and rest," Mary urged, taking her hand.

"Tahmeroo has no need of food and rest." She laid one hand on her heart, and finished the sentence with a mournful bend of the head.

"Do not go to-night—stay with me."

"The pale medicine is very kind, and Tahmeroo loves her, but she must go; some of her father's warriors wait near the old camping-ground, and will show her the way."

"But you must not seek your husband in that dress. The Shawnees are enemies to the people you seek; to go in their costume would be dangerous. Mary, see to this; one of your sister Jane's dresses will answer. Take the poor stranger into the cabin and prepare her for the journey."

With gentle hospitality Mary led the young Indian away. Fortunately, the old lady had gone down to the spring to dampen some cloth she was whitening there, and, as we have seen, Jane was rambling upon the opposite shore with her lover.

The missionary was right, Jane's dresses fitted Tahmeroo very neatly, and fifteen minutes after she entered the little bedroom, arrayed in her own gorgeous raiment, she came forth as pretty a country girl as one would wish to see; carrying her own clothes tied up in a little bundle, for she could not be persuaded to leave them behind.

"But you will come back again," said Mary, with tears in her eyes, as they once more stood by the missionary under the cedars.

"Or sleep," said Tahmeroo, pointing to the earth with a significant gesture; "for when the corn shoots green you will call for help, and Tahmeroo will keep her ears open."

"But the distance is great—you will perish on the way."

"Farewell! Tahmeroo must follow her heart. She has her rifle, and knows how to shoot. Son of the Great Spirit, lay your hand once more upon her head; it will give me courage."

She bowed her head before the missionary, and he lifted his eyes to heaven, full of devout pity for that poor creature, who had been so hardly tried.

"Farewell!"

Without a word more, Tahmeroo turned from the spot, sprang into her canoe, and pushed it out of the cove, a few vigorous strokes of her lithe arms sending it far up the river.

Once she looked back and waved her hand; Mary saw the signal through her blinding tears, and waved her shawl in return. The Indian girl did not cast another glance towards them; but bending all her energies to the task kept her little craft on its course up the stream.

Mary and the missionary stood watching her until a bend in the shore shut the canoe from sight; then they turned and walked slowly towards the house, inexpressibly moved by the sight of that poor girl's wretchedness and fortitude.

CHAPTER XXI
THE JAIL AT ALBANY

An Indian girl—no uncommon thing in the streets of Albany in the days of the Revolution—stood patiently waiting before the entrance to the jail at Albany. She had remained in the same spot at least six hours, without moving from the stone abutment against which she leaned, or turning her eyes from the door, with its iron knobs and enormous lock, which was sunk deep into the gable-end of that old building. The hot noonday sun had beat upon her head; she drew the crimson shawl a little more over her face, but gave no signs of moving. The quaint gables threw their lacework shadows down where the sun had been; but she took no heed. It was only when some step approached near the jail, or a sound came from within, that she gave signs of the quick life burning in her bosom.

Three or four times during that day had Tahmeroo beat her hands against that cruel door, hoping madly that some one might come and let her in. But prison portals do not yield readily to human impatience, either from within or without, and the poor girl had nothing left but that long watch, where she stood motionless, though on the alert, full of fiery impatience, but of stubborn resolution too.

As she stood upon this steady watch, a horseman rode up the street, followed by a servant. Instead of galloping on, as so many had done during the day, he drew up before the jail, flung his bridle to the attendant, and going up to the door which Tahmeroo was eyeing so wistfully struck it a blow with the loaded handle of his riding-whip.

Tahmeroo sprang forward when she heard the bolts begin to move, but she was an instant too late. A dark passage within engulfed the visitor, and the door swung back to its lock again with a loud jar, which made the poor girl almost cry out, so great was the shock of her disappointment.

The servant saw the anguish in her face, and being a good-natured fellow, with nothing else to employ him at the moment, moved towards the jail, and kindly inquired what she wanted.

"I only want that door to open and let me in," she said, casting a pitiful look at the entrance, from which she had been so cruelly excluded.

"And who is it you want to see, my purty red bird? Now, I tell you what, it's easier getting into that door than getting out again, as many a poor feller can tell you. Who is it you are after?"

"I want to see my husband."

"Your husband?"

"Yes, Captain Walter Butler."

"Hallo! and you are his wife? Why, the general has just gone in to see with his own eyes if the Tory spy is as sick as he pretends."

"Sick—is he sick, did you say?" cried Tahmeroo, turning of an ashen paleness.

"Don't turn so pale—don't fret about it—I've an idea its all sham; but the general will soon find out—it isn't easy cheating him."

"But he is sick—I must see him this moment—do you hear? this moment—tell me where I can carry this letter; they told me the gentleman was not here, but I will go where he is—I'll follow on, and on, forever to find the man that has power to pass me through that door!"

"Let me look at the letter."

Tahmeroo gave it to him, trembling with impatience to be off.

"Why this is to General Schuyler himself! All right—just wait here and give it to him as he comes out—don't be afraid; for all his grand looks, he's tenderhearted as a baby. Come, come; don't get so down in the mouth; it'll all turn out right somehow—things always do."

"And was that the man who holds my husband in prison?" said Tahmeroo, flushing with indignation. "By what right—how dares he?"

"Hush—hush!—that talk'll never do; soft words are better than bullets here; just let them bright tears creep into your eyes again, if you can just as easy as not; they'll do more for you than a hull artillery of curses."

Tahmeroo scarcely heard his advice, but stood with the letter in her hand, keenly watching the door. She placed herself directly between the restive war-horse and the entrance to the jail. At last there was a clang of bolts, a sudden swing of the ponderous door, and Tahmeroo saw in the darkness beyond two men who paused together in that gloomy arch for a moment's conversation.

One of these men the Indian girl recognized at once, by the glitter of his uniform and the singular dignity of his countenance, which in breadth of forehead and the grave composure, which marks a well-regulated character, was not unlike that of General Washington himself.

After a moment Schuyler stepped out of the darkness. He was then forty-four years of age; a period when the impulses of youth are mellowed, but not hardened, in the bosoms of truly great men.

"Now—now!" whispered the attendant. .

Tahmeroo held her breath, and went slowly forward, her bright, steady glance fastened on the general's face, till their very intensity drew his glance that way.

"What is this?" he said, stopping short with the missionary's letter in his hand, but perusing that young face with a penetrating glance before he opened it. "A letter from— —, ha! I understand it now—and have you come all this distance to see your husband? so young, too!"

Tahmeroo could only point to the door with her trembling finger.

"My husband—he is there—oh, make them open the door. Tahmeroo has no breath to speak with till they let her in yonder."

Schuyler smiled, turned upon his heel, and knocked again at the prison door. It was promptly opened.

"Conduct this young woman to Captain Butler's room; she is his wife," he said, addressing the jailer.

"See that no one treats her rudely—but this one interview must be enough; to-morrow the young man will be removed to the custody of a private family, where his health can be cared for; he frets like a caged panther here."

Turning to Tahmeroo, before he mounted his horse, the general said in a kindly, paternal way: "Now make the best of your time, my poor girl; it is well you caught me here, for I should have been off to the camp again in less than an hour."

Tahmeroo could not speak; she saw the door open, and casting back one brilliant glance of gratitude darted through.

Schuyler smiled quietly, muttered, "Poor thing, poor thing!" once or twice, and mounting his horse, rode away.

"My husband—Walter!"

Butler sprang to his feet, with an exclamation of delight. He was prostrate on a low camp-bed when she entered, as General Schuyler had left him, apparently exhausted by illness.

"Tahmeroo, my hawk—my pretty rattlesnake."

"Oh, you are sick; you are dying!" cried the heart-stricken wife, losing all strength and dropping on her knees by the bed he had just left.

"Hush, hush! child—don't make all this outcry. It isn't sickness at all; see, I am strong enough to lift you." And taking the young Indian in his arms, he bore her across the small room and returning again, sat down on the bed, still holding her in his embrace.

She did not speak, she did not weep; to breathe then and there was happiness enough for her.

"Ah, but you cheat Tahmeroo. Your face is white as snow; you, you——"

"I tell you I am well, never better in my life," he whispered, hurriedly; "but my only chance of escape lay in seeming ill. I have petitioned again and again to see General Schuyler, but until to-day he never came. I have made my face white and my voice weak for him. It has done its work, Tahmeroo; to-morrow I shall be taken from this gloomy place, and confined in a private family, from which there is some chance of escape. Now, are you satisfied that I am not dying?"

Tahmeroo laughed, and clasped her hands hard to keep from clapping them, in her joy. Her eyes shone like diamonds. The whole thing fired her Indian blood, which delighted in craft almost as much as in courage.

"And I shall go with you—I shall see you every day. Oh, I remember now—that proud man said that I must only come this once—only once."

"Don't cry; don't begin to tremble after this fashion. An Indian wife should be brave," said Butler, terrified by her agitation.

She lifted her head, and shook back the hair from her temples with a gesture of queenly pride.

"Tahmeroo is brave. See, if you can find tears in her eyes."

"That's right; now listen. Since you have come in I have thought of something. If you only had an old dress with you, such as white people wear; but these things are too fanciful; they will never do."

As the door opened Tahmeroo darted forward
exclaiming, "My husband—Walter."

"How! you want a poor dress, stained by water and faded by the sun;
is that it?"

"Exactly; but this toggery can never be brought into the right condition."

"Look; will this do?"

Tahmeroo untied a little bundle which she had carried under her shawl,
and displayed the dress Mary Derwent had given her, worn and faded by
a long journey on horseback; and which, notwithstanding the missionary's
advice to the contrary, she had exchanged for her own more brilliant
costume, before visiting her husband.

"Do! it is just the thing. Put it up—put it up, before the jailer comes in.
Now listen—thank Heaven, you can read. In this paper you will find the
name of a family with which they intend to confine me. The people excused
themselves from taking me to-day from want of help. Servants are not easily
got in Albany these times—do you comprehend?"

"Yes," answered Tahmeroo, taking up his thoughts quick as lightning.
"I am to put on this dress, comb back my hair, look like a white girl used to

work, and be a servant to these people. Then, then—some night, after all are asleep, I must watch the sentinel, give him firewater, or take the flint from his gun, and then away for the forest."

"My brave, bright girl!"

Tahmeroo went on:

"My warriors are in the neighborhood, waiting with their horses—I have gold in my dress—I am strong, proud—it seems as if all our warriors were fighting for you, and I leading them on, this moment!"

She fell into his arms, trembling for very joy.

He held her to his heart—it was not all base when that noble creature lay against it. He kissed her warmly. There was a world of selfishness in that kiss, but Tahmeroo guessed nothing of that.

"Now go, my lark, go—search out the house they intend for my prison. To-morrow I shall find you there."

Tahmeroo arose; she was in haste to be at work; the idea of saving her husband made her forget that he was eager to send her away. No one but the jailer saw her when she departed; but he wondered at the splendor of her beauty, which seemed to have heightened tenfold since she entered the building.

A middle-aged gentleman and lady sat in one of those quaint parlors, which occupied the gable-front of an old Dutch house, such as may be seen in Albany, as relics of a past age, even to this day. The room was neat, almost to chilliness; blue tiles ornamented the chimney-piece; blue tiles ran in a border round the oaken floor; the gentleman's coat was of blue; his stockings were seamed with blue and his dame's linen dress was striped with the same color. Thus they sat in this coldly-tinted apartment, after dinner, conversing together about the strange guest they had consented to receive into their house, at the urgent request of General Schuyler, who believed that close confinement had really endangered Butler's life, and wished to be humane; while he was not willing to set a man so dangerous at perfect liberty.

While the good Dutchman and his wife were talking over the difficulties of this arrangement, which became more important from the fact that their only maid-servant had left her place, on hearing of the new claim likely to be made on her labors, a staid old man, who had been detailed to guard the prisoner when he came, entered the room and announced a country girl from across the river who wished to hire herself out.

This was a piece of good fortune which neither of the occupants of the parlor had expected—for servants were not to be had for the asking, when so much wild land lay ready for tillage, and labor was mostly applied in building up homes for the working classes.

While they were quietly congratulating themselves, the applicant came into the room. She was a plain, and rather shabbily dressed girl—singularly handsome, notwithstanding the poverty of her raiment—who entered the parlor with the free grace of a fawn, and spoke in accents which would have appeared far too pure for her humble appearance with any one to whom the English language was a native tongue.

The Dutchman, fortunately, understood very little English, and the country girl was profoundly ignorant of Dutch; so as the conversation was necessarily carried on between the soldier and the girl, the matter of reference was easily settled. In half an hour after her entrance, the maid was busy at her work in the kitchen.

The next day Butler was brought to his new prison, seeming very feeble, and scarcely strong enough to walk to the chamber, far up in the peaked roof, which had been assigned for his safe keeping. The soldier observed that he looked earnestly at the new maid-servant in passing upstairs, and that a smile quivered on his lip when he saw her. But this was not strange; older eyes than his might have kindled at the sight of that beautiful face; it almost made a fool of the tenderhearted soldier himself.

After the prisoner had been installed in his chamber, the new servant would linger there a little, after serving his meals, and once the sentinel fancied that he saw the two whispering together as she sat down the dishes; but when the rustic beauty came out she was sure to drive all suspicion from his head with an arch smile that intoxicated him more deliciously than the best corn whisky he ever drank.

On the third day what little heart the poor fellow had left after his first interview was completely gone; and when she came up at nine o'clock, and asked him, with a charming smile, to step down into the kitchen and taste a mug of hot punch with lemon in it, which she had just been brewing, it required all his patriotism to refuse; and he apologized for doing his duty, with humility, as if it had been a sin.

The new servant pouted at first, but took better thought and suffered herself to be appeased; so, as a pledge of perfect reconciliation, after the little quarrel, she proposed to run to the kitchen and bring the jug of punch up to his post, where he might drink and smoke at his leisure, while she filled the glass.

This was a charming arrangement, and the sentinel enjoyed it amazingly; he drank of the punch, and tried the Dutchman's best pipe, which the maid brought surreptitiously from the parlor, after the master had retired to bed. Thus he drank and smoked till everything became foggy around him, and he seemed to be encompassed by half a dozen pretty girls, all serving out punch for him, to say nothing of any number of grotesque pipes that danced under his nose, and a whole stock of muskets that crowded round his own trusty shooting-iron, which rested against the door.

After this singular phenomenon, the trusty sentinel kept his post with great pertinacity—but he was sound asleep, and breathing like an engine under a double head of steam.

Then the chamber-door was softly unlocked, and the pretty maid-servant gave a signal to some one within. Directly Butler appeared, ready dressed, and, treading softly over the sentinel, followed his Indian wife down stairs, out of the house, and along the narrow streets of Albany.

A quick walk to the outskirts of the town, a low whistle, and out from a piece of woods came half a dozen mounted savages, leading two horses, forest bred, and swift as deer.

Tahmeroo leaped upon one, Butler mounted the other, and away for the Valley of Wyoming, where Butler knew that his father would soon meet him with an avenging army.

CHAPTER XXII
THE GATHERING STORM

The year of 1778 marked a terrible epoch in the annals of our Revolution. Sir John and Guy Johnson, with the Butlers and other native Tories of New York State, had vigorously co-operated with Brant, Queen Esther and Gien-gwa-tah, whose united influence gave almost the entire strength of the Six Nations to the British. With all these unnatural combinations at work on the frontier—with Brant perpetrating his barbarities on one hand, Sir John Johnson sweeping down from his refuge in Canada, devastating wherever he went, and the regular army too busily occupied on the seaboard for any hope of succor from that source, the isolated towns and villages of what was then the "far west" became the scenes of the most ruthless system of warfare ever perpetrated among civilized nations.

But all the cruelties that had commenced in 1777 were nothing compared to those now in preparation, when the savages were ready to take up arms in masses, after their own ruthless fashion, and the exiled Royalists, driven out from their homes, had become more vindictive, if possible, than their savage allies.

The Valley of Wyoming was that year peculiarly exposed. Its strongest men were serving in the general army, but those who were left not only foresaw the peril which lay before them, but prepared against it to the extent of their ability. Wintermoot's Fort was nothing less than a stronghold of the enemy, and the resort of Tories who had fled or wandered from the interior of New York, for the real natives of the valley were true patriots, almost to a man.

With prompt energy these men went to work, strengthening their defences. Block-houses, already made, were put in repair; stockades were planted, new forts were built, till the river above and below Wintermoot's Fort was, to every possible extent, fortified against the common enemy.

But this military work was done in connection with the usual agricultural labor. While forts were building, seed was put into the earth, and on the first of July, 1778, every acre of land as yet redeemed from the wilderness was rich with a springing harvest.

Each farmer, as he worked, held himself ready for military duty. Ready to seize his axe or scythe at the blast of a horn, or the summon of a conch-shell, in the hand of an old woman or child, if peril threatened either, and lay down life, if need was, in their defence. In those days men carried their muskets to the meadow, or plough-field, regularly as they went to work.

The women of Wyoming rose and took their places bravely upon the hearthstone, ready to defend the children who clung to their garments, when the son or father fell upon the door-step. They worked like their husbands; impending danger gave them quick knowledge, and women whose ideas of chemistry had never gone beyond the ash-leech and cheese-press fell to manufacturing saltpetre. They tore up the floors of their cabins, dug up the earth, put it in casks, and, mingling the water, drained through with ash-lye, boiled it above their fires, and when the compound grew cold in their wash-tubs, saltpetre rose to the top, and thus a supply of gunpowder was obtained. Nor did the women of Wyoming stop here. While the young men were carried off to the Continental army, and old silver headed men were left to till the earth and muster in companies for defence, delicate women and fair young girls took to the field and worked, side by side, with the old men, whose strength was scarcely greater than their own. It was a brave, beautiful sight, which the American woman of our twentieth century will do wisely to remember.

That doomed valley might well be on the alert. The Six Nations had receded entirely from the solemn pledges of neutrality and, in connection with Brant, the Johnsons, and Colonel John Butler, were fighting upon the upper waters of the Susquehanna. Many of the Tories from about Wintermoot's Fort had fled to them with complaints of harsh treatment from the patriot Whigs. In vain these doomed people had petitioned Congress for help. Then, as now, Congress was slow to act, while the enemy was prompt and terrible.

Thus lay the Valley of Wyoming when our story returns to it.

The first signal of the mustering storm came suddenly one afternoon, about the first of July, when Walter Butler, whom every one had thought a close prisoner at Albany, appeared at the head of eight or ten mounted savages, and, with his young Indian wife galloping by his side, swept up the valley towards Wintermoot's Fort.

The very hardihood of this appearance among his bitterest enemies probably secured his safety, for, before the astonished inhabitants could realize the amount of his audacity, and while the glitter of her rich Indian dress was before their eyes, his cavalcade thundered into the fort, and a clamorous shout from those within attested the satisfaction with which he was received.

A long wooden bridge at this time connects Wilkesbarre with the Kingston side of the Susquehanna; a spacious and most excellent hotel stands on the sweep of the road where it winds over from the former place, and engine-whistles may be heard shrieking almost every hour as some train rushes fiercely up the valley, dashing over coal beds, sweeping across the broad river, at its juncture, and away where the Indian war-trail was first laid along the Lackawanna; but, in 1778, there was neither bridge nor hotel, unless a low log-house, fronted by a magnificent elm, and made of consequence by a log-stable, a huge haystack and a shingle roof, might be called such. A public house it certainly was intended to be, for a rudely painted sign hung groaning and creaking among the thick leaves of the elm, and the chickens which congregated about the haystack were always seen to flutter and creep away into hiding-places whenever a traveller was seen to emerge from the shaded road which leads across the Wilkesbarre mountains, a kind of timidity seldom observed at private houses, except at the approach of a travelling minister or a schoolmaster who boards about.

There was little of refinement, but everything essential to comfort, in the interior of Aunt Polly's tavern, for to that respected female the log-building with its sign belonged. Two small square rooms, separated by a board partition, were divided off from the kitchen; one was the dormitory of Aunt Polly herself, while the other, which served the chance wayfarer as bed-chamber, dining and sitting-room, had the usual furniture of splint chairs, a small looking-glass, surmounted by a tuft of fresh asparagus—a fireplace filled with white-pine tops, a bed decked with sheets of the whitest homespun, and a coverlid of blue and white yarn, woven in what Aunt Polly called orange quarters, and doors and windows.

Later in the evening which witnessed Walter Butler's return, a gentleman was impatiently pacing this little room, and more than once he opened the door which led to the kitchen, to hurry Aunt Polly in her preparations for supper. This restless impatience in her guest put Aunt Polly somewhat out of patience.

"She was doing as fast as she could," she said, "and she did hate to be driv."

Still, at each interruption, the good lady dipped an unfortunate chicken, with more desperate energy, into the kettle of hot water that stood on the hearth before her, and tore away the dripping plumage, handful after handful, with a zeal which might have satisfied the most hungry traveller that ever claimed hospitality at her door. An iron pot, filled with potatoes, and a tea-kettle hung, like a brace of martyrs, in the blazing fire, and everything was in fair progress for a comfortable meal when the young man entered the kitchen, as if weary of remaining alone, and began to chat with Aunt Polly while she dissected the unfortunate fowl after it came out, clean and featherless, from the hot bath in which she had plunged it.

"I see you keep everything clean and snug as usual, Aunt Polly," he said, looking about the apartment where, however, might be observed greater marks of confusion than was common with the thrifty old maid.

"Nothing to brag of," replied Polly, shaking her head and looking at the loom which stood in one corner with a web of rag carpeting rolled on the cloth beam. A quill wheel and a rickety pair of swifts were crowded against the heavy posts, the one unhanded, and the other with a few threads of tow-yarn tangled among the sticks, and a skein of cut rags falling heavily around them. "I don't know how it is, Captain Butler, but you al'es make me fling everything to sixes and sevens when you come. Now, I meant to have wove a yard on that are carpet afore night—anybody else would have took up with a cold bite; but you're awful dainty about victuals, captain, and al'es was."

"Well, never mind that, Polly; you know I am always willing to pay for what I have. But, tell me, is there no news stirring in the valley? I see you have got a new fort over the river—who commands there?"

"Who but Edward Clark, your old schoolmate; though I rather think that there won't be much watch kept up there this week—the captain's got better fish to fry. You hain't forgot how reg'lar he went a-sparking to old Mother Derwent's, have you?"

As Aunt Polly received no answer she busied herself stirring the simmering members of the fowl with a large wooden spoon, while her auditor began to pace the floor with a brow that grew darker and a step that became heavier each instant.

The landlady wiped the perspiration from her face and looked rather inquisitively at him.

"Why, what has come over you?" she said; "you look as black as a thunder-cloud all tu once."

"This week. Did you say that Edward Clark and Jane Derwent were to be married so soon?"

"Yes—they'll have a wedding on the island afore Sunday, or I'll lose my guess."

"What day and hour—do you know the hour?"

"Why, no—I don't s'pose they're particular to a minute."

"So the rebel dog thinks to have Jane Derwent at last, does he!" exclaimed Butler, pausing angrily in his walk, and bending his flushed brow on the landlady; then turning away he muttered between his teeth:

"By the Lord that made me, I will spoil his fun this once!"

"Lard a-marcy! how mad you look," said Aunt Polly. "You a'most make my hair stand on end—but the first sight of you was enough for that; why, we all thought you were dead and hung long ago."

"And were rejoiced at it, I dare say?"

"Can't pretend to answer for the men folks, not al'es knowing exactly where to find 'em, but for my part, men's too scarce in this region for us women folks to want 'em hung."

"But I dare say your precious patriots, as they call themselves, would hang me high as Haman if they had the chance, which I don't intend to give 'em, though I was fool enough to come here."

"Why, they haven't any right to touch you, captain. York State laws ain't good for nothing here, are they?"

"None, that I would not answer back with a shower of bullets," answered Butler, fiercely; "so, once for all, keep quiet about my being here, or anything I have said; it will prove the worse for you if you don't."

"Why, how you talk—there ain't no mischief a-brewing agin the valley, is there, captain? Edward Clark would not be persuaded to leave the fort, if it was to get married, if he thought so."

Butler paid no attention to her question, but made a rapid succession of inquiries about the family on Monockonok Island, and craftily gathered from the old maid a pretty accurate account of the military force now in the valley. At last a noise from without, which Aunt Polly evidently did not hear, made him start and listen. He took out his watch, and hastily replacing it, muttered something in an undertone, and left the house, regardless of the supper which he had been so impatient for a few minutes before.

"I wish to gracious Sim White was here; I rather guess my hay will suffer if the captain feeds his own hoss," said the old maid, as the door closed; "the feller thinks no more of a peck of oats than if it was cut-straw. I wish he'd make haste tho', the victuals is purty near done, and I begin to feel kinder hungry myself. Oh, I'd a'most forgot—these Tory fellers al'es want tea—just to spite us, I reckon; but a tavern is a tavern, and while my sign swings on that are elm-tree, travellers shall have just what they ask for when I've got it."

With these words Aunt Polly opened a rude closet, took out a small tin canister containing the unpopular herb, and filling the little round top, smoothed it off with her finger, and "put the tea to drawing." Then spreading a snowy tablecloth in the best room, she placed thereon the nicely cooked fowl, the smoking potatoes, a plate of bread and a ball of golden butter, and gave the finishing touch to her table by saucers of preserved crab-apples and wild plums placed on each corner. After all was ready, she seated herself by a little waiter, scarcely larger than a good-sized snuffer-tray, and as she placed and replaced the milk-cup and sugar-bowl, muttered her impatience for the return of her guest.

"I wonder what on 'arth keeps him so—I could 'a' foddered my whole stock afore this. Walter Butler didn't use to be so long tending his horse afore he eat, himself. Dear me, the gravy is gitting thick about the chickens—the fried cabbage is stun cold, and the tea'll be drawn to death! I do wish—oh, here he comes!"

The old maid brightened as she heard footsteps coming through the kitchen, and snatching up the tea-pot, she began pouring out the half-cold beverage into the little earthenware cups which were only produced to regale the Tory guests who graced her house.

"Do come along, and set to, captain—your supper is gitting stun cold," she said, without raising her eyes from the tea-cups. "I've been awaiting this ever so long."

"I hope that I have made no mistake, my good woman," replied a strange voice from the door, in answer to her hospitable invitation; "I supposed this to be a public house."

Aunt Polly set down the tea-pot, her hands dropped to her lap, and her eyes grew large with astonishment; a tall, stately gentleman stood in the doorway, where she had last seen her younger guest; he was evidently of higher rank, and of far more dignified and lofty carriage than any person who had ever before sought the shelter of her roof. His hat was in his hand, and a few grey hairs silvered the dark locks about his high forehead. The expression of his face was that of stern decision, yet there was a softness in his smile as he observed the astonished landlady, which made it almost winning. He advanced into the room with a courteous ease, which Aunt Polly could feel much better than understand.

"I hope I am not mistaken—at least, you will not refuse me a portion of this tempting dish?" he said, laying his hat and riding-whip on the bed.

By this time Aunt Polly had recovered her speech. "There is no mistake, this is a tavern that advertises feed for man and hoss, and does all it promises," she said, with an accession of pompous hospitality; "so set by, and help yourself to such as there is. I've kept public house here these ten years. Don't stand to be axed, if you want supper—it's all ready, I began to think that I had cooked it for nothing. You take tea I s'pose from the looks of your coat."

The stranger seated himself at the table, and took the proffered cup.

"You have prepared for other guests?" he observed as she arose to get another cup and saucer from the closet.

"Yes—Captain Butler will be in purty soon, I reckon; but there's no calculating when."

The stranger looked up with a degree of interest when the name was pronounced. "Is it of Captain Walter Butler you speak?" he inquired.

"Yes, his name's Walter, and an awful smart feller he is, too—but the worst sort of a Tory. Do you know him? if I may be so bold."

"Can you tell me how he escaped from confinement, and by what means he reached the valley?" inquired the stranger, without seeming to heed her question.

Aunt Polly broke into a crackling laugh, one of those sharp cachinnations which sometimes frightened her poultry from the roost.

"How did he escape? I only wondered how anybody managed to keep him. Why, he's a fox, an eel, a weasel. Of all them Hudson and Mohawk Valley chaps that hive at Wintermoot's Fort he's the cutest. They says he's made lots of money lately in making believe he married one of the handsomest little squaws that you ever sot eyes on; some say that he is married in rale downright 'arnest; but I don't believe all I hear—it's been a kind of Indian scrape—a jumping over the broomstick, I s'pose. He rode through the valley with her this afternoon as bold as a lion, followed by a lot of wild Injuns. The hull biling on 'em may be a-coming down on us, for all I know."

"But the mother of this Indian girl—is she in the valley?"

"Catharine Montour? is that the person you want to ask about? 'cause if it is, I saw that identical woman once, and a rale, downright lady she is. I've got the gold guinea she gave me in my puss yet."

"And you saw her?"

"Yes, with these two eyes, and that's more than most folks can say. She came out on Gineral Washington and I—that's my hoss, sir, not the commander-in-chief—jest as the angel stood before Balaam. At first I thought that I was struck dumb, and the gineral'd have to speak for me, whether or no."

"But the lady—how did she look? changed, older—was she beautiful?" cried the man, while a quiver of agitation ran through his voice—up to this time so calm and measured.

"Harnsome? I suppose you mean by all that. Wal, yes, I should carculate that a'most any one would 'a' called that lady harnsome enough for anything. She wasn't so young, mebby, as she had been; but, marcy on us! no queen on her throne ever looked grander."

"And did she seem happy—content?"

"Wal, that's difficult saying; wimmen don't tell out all that's in their bosom at once. She looked sort of anxious, but there's no telling what it was about; but if you stay in these parts long, and my out-room is empty if you want it—you'll likely as not see her yourself; when the young Injun gal is here, Catharine Montour can't be far off. The hull tribe camped under Campbell's Ledge a year or two ago, and held a grand council with the Injuns about the Wind Gap. I hope they won't come for anything wuss the next time."

"And did you converse with this lady?"

"Yes; I reckon what was said atween us might 'a' been considered convarsing. She sent a message to Mary Derwent, and I carried it. The talk was purty much all about that."

"And this is all you can tell me of her?" said the stranger, in a tone of bitter disappointment, which interested the old maid more and more in his behalf.

"It is all I know, sartainly; but if you want to hear more about her, the Injun missionary'll tell you all about her. He was up to the camp when they held that council-fire, and talked with her face to face——"

"And where can this missionary be found?"

"Well, jest now, that would be hard to say; he's been in the valley, off and on, all last year; but a month or two ago he went away to Philadelphia to tell the Congress and Gineral Washington to send our own sojers back to take care of us, if they can't afford nothing more. But he ought to be back about this time, and I shouldn't wonder if you found him at his old place, in Toby's Eddy. He's got a cabin down there, in the very spot where the rattlesnake scared off the Injuns when they went to kill Mr. Zin—Zin—Zin——"

"Zinzendorf, probably that is the name," said the traveller, smiling gravely. "I remember the circumstance. So, you think it possible that I might find the minister at Toby's Eddy? Can you tell me what direction to take?"

"Keep on down stream till you come to a spot where the river gives a bend like this." Here Aunt Polly bent her elbow into an angle, which she endeavored in vain to torture into a curve which should describe that magnificent crescent formed in the banks of the Susquehanna, and known as Toby's Eddy.

"When you reach the spot, you'll know it by the great sycamore trees with their white balls; ask somebody to show you the missionary's cabin. You couldn't miss it if you tried."

The stranger thanked her gravely, and laying a piece of gold on the table went out quietly as he had entered.

Aunt Polly started up, and going to the back door, cried vigorously across the bed of young cabbages for Sim White, the hired man, who had lived with her all winter, to hurry up and bring out the gentleman's critter. But while the words were on her lips she heard the tramp of a horse, and running to the front window saw her guest riding at a brisk pace down the river.

"Well, if this don't beat all creation," said the old maid, laying the guinea in her palm, and examining it on both sides with delight. "I wonder who on 'arth he can be!"

Muttering these words, the landlady drew forth her shot-bag from a corner cupboard, and after examining the gold pieces already there, with loving curiosity, laid her new treasure beside it.

"Now, there's luck in that," she said, tying the shot-bag up with a grim smile. "I wonder what'll come next. It never rains but it storms. The gold has come, and now I must take a run on something else. I wonder where Sim White has hid himself. If Captain Butler don't want this 'ere chicken, I don't know any one that has a better right to it than Sim."

As she was covering the dish, to set it down by the fire, Aunt Polly happened to glance towards the back window, and there, much to her surprise, she saw the face of her hired man, Sim White, peering curiously in.

"There now, if that ain't too much," she said, flushing to the eyes with the force of a new discovery that had just dawned upon her. "If the critter ain't getting jealous arter all; well, now, I never did! He thought that grand-looking gentleman a beau of mine. Just as likely as not—well, I won't let him know that I ketched him peeking, anyhow."

Aunt Polly busied herself about the fire—acting upon this generous resolution, till the door softly opened, and Sim thrust his head cautiously in, and gave a sharp look around the room. Aunt Polly smiled with grim satisfaction, and began to punch the fire vigorously, though she could not resist the temptation to cast side glances towards the door all the time.

"Where is he?—hush! speak in a whisper—where is the eternal rascal gone to? I've got a dozen stout fellows out in the yard, armed to the teeth with scythes and pitchforks, and a beautiful halter hitched to a beam in the barn, all ready. I shan't trust to the law this time; it ain't worth a towstring, or his hash'd 'a' been settled long ago—come, speak out, where is he?"

Now, Aunt Polly was rather pleased with the idea of Sim's jealousy; but when it took this ferocious form, and she thought of her guests being strung up one by one to a beam in her own barn, the whole thing began to take a form that she did not quite relish.

"Mr. White," said she, with great dignity, "what do you mean? Can't I speak to a traveller in my own kitchen, but you must talk of scythes and pitchforks, and halters, too?"

Sim did not answer, but went peering about the kitchen, opening closets and looking under tables, until he landed in the out-room, where his search was continued still more vigilantly. At last he opened the door of Aunt Polly's bedroom and stepped in. The white valance in front of the bed was in motion; his eyes began to glisten. He had no doubt that the object of his search was there. Daintily lifting the edge of the valance between his thumb and forefinger, he stooped and looked under. It was only to meet the glaring green eyes of Aunt Polly's cat, who had inadvertently disturbed the valance, and thus led Sim White into a dilemma; for as he dropped the muslin, and was about to rise from his stooping position, Aunt Polly stood before him, towering in wrathful indignation.

"Mr. Simon White, what do you mean?"

"I mean to find out if that eternal scamp is hid away in this 'ere house or not," answered Sim, looking desperately around the little apartment. "He's my prisoner. I took him myself at German Flats just afore I come here to live. If them fools in Albany have let him loose, I'll tighten him up again in short order."

"Who on 'arth are you talking about?"

"Why, that Butler, to be sure; only let me lay my hands on him, that's all."

"Why, Captain Butler went off an hour ago," said Polly, in accents of deep mortification.

"Which way?"

"I don't know; he slid off without saying good-bye! I was just saving his supper for you."

"And I've had all this trouble for nothing, consarn the fellow!"

"Come now, ain't you a'most ready to go out?" said Aunt Polly, sliding up to the bed, where her nightcap crowned one of the posts. Snatching it off and dexterously concealing it behind her, she muttered to herself: "I wouldn't 'a' cared so much if it had only had a ruffled border." Then she added, rather tartly: "Come, the chicken'll be stun cold."

Sim turned and followed her to the kitchen. He was terribly disappointed at the failure of his attempt to regain his prisoner, and sent away the farmers, who had gladly rallied to his aid, with a crestfallen look, which was more than equalled by Aunt Polly's downcast countenance. She was unusually cross all the evening, poured any quantity of water into the tea-pot, set away the preserves before Sim had tasted them, and altogether acted in a very unaccountable manner indeed.

CHAPTER XXIII
THE FIRST SKIRMISH

The vague rumors that had reached the inhabitants of Wyoming, no one could exactly tell how, filling each household with alarm, were not without foundation. A force of eleven hundred strong, under the command of Colonel John Butler, consisting of Tory Rangers, a detachment of Johnson's Royal Greens, and six hundred savages, picked warriors from the Shawnee and Seneca tribes, had already crossed Genesee county. They had embarked from Tioga Point in canoes, which were abandoned at the mouth of Bowman's Creek, where the whole body was encamped on the second of July.

Queen Esther, Gi-en-gwa-tah, and two or three Seneca chiefs commanded the savage forces. Catharine Montour was in the army, for she had been warned by one of the Indians who had aided in Walter Butler's escape from Albany that he had proceeded at once to Wyoming with his wife, and would await the appearance of his father at Wintermoot's Fort.

The hopes of seeing her child, and a harassing terror lest that angel girl on Monockonok Island might come to harm in the savage warfare impending over the valley, had forced her into scenes from which her very soul revolted, and she opened her eyes with terror as each day carried the fearful war-whoop of her tribe nearer and nearer that peaceful region.

From the encampment at Bowman's Creek scouts were sent forward, and a small detachment of warriors swept down the river in the night, headed by Queen Esther's youngest son, a handsome brave, who, eager to earn the first eagle's plume in the coming fight—having won this privilege from the grim queen and his lofty brother—set forth on his errand of blood.

Like a flock of redbirds on the water, the chief and his warriors floated down the Susquehanna, each with a rifle at his feet, and a tomahawk or a sharp knife glittering in his girdle.

Their persons glowed with war-paint; their sinewy arms bent to the oars. Now and then, as they passed through the sloping mountains, a faint whoop broke on the waters, betraying their impatience for contest.

But as they reached the rocky jaws of the Susquehanna all was still as death; no flock of birds ever flitted over that stream more silently. About a mile above Fort Jenkins they took to the shore. This fort was in the hands of the patriots, and the chief thirsted to strike a leading blow in the contest. Instead of proceeding to Wintermoot's Fort, he drew his warriors from the river, and clearing the stockades like a pack of wolves, took the fort by surprise.

But brave men lay waiting behind those rough logs—old men of cool courage and nerves of iron. Three of their number fell dead in front of the fort, where, unconscious of danger, they had been conversing in the starlight. The savages rushed on to complete their work, but they were met with a blaze of musketry, so sudden and furious that half a dozen stalwart forms fell upon the men they had murdered. Then the crack of a single rifle—a shrill cry—the youngest son of Queen Esther leaped into the air, and fell dead upon the sward he had been so eager to bathe with blood.

The skirmish had not lasted half an hour when that band of savages retreated, under shelter of the night, and laying the body of their chief in a canoe, floated down the river with a low, monotonous death-chant, which was lost in the deep solitude of the woods. When they came opposite Wintermoot's they again lifted their chief and bore him among them into the fort, still wailing out that mournful death-song.

The garrison was aroused; armed men came out and bore the body of the dead brave into the inclosure.

Tahmeroo, who lay awake, waiting the return of her husband, heard the death-wail of her tribe, and followed the sound, pale with apprehension. A group of warriors sat upon the earth, with their faces buried in their robes; the death-song was hushed, but the silence of those stout hearts was more solemn even than the mournful voices had been.

In the centre of this group she saw the prostrate form of a chief, with his gorgeous war-robes lying in heavy masses around him. The Indian girl held her breath and crept forward, looking fearfully down into the face of the dead. It was her father's brother! She asked no questions, but crouched down on the earth among those silent warriors, and was still as the dead she mourned.

After a little, a young warrior rose from the circle and went out; no one spoke, no one looked up; but they all knew that he was departing to bear to Queen Esther tidings of her son's death.

Slowly and with mournful steadiness the lone savage crept up the river; he broke the profound stillness of the mountains with the death-cry as he passed along; the lonely whip-poor-will answered him from the woods; and between the pauses of its melancholy wail the sleepless owl hooted him for not dying instead of his chief. It was daybreak when he reached the encampment at Bowman's Creek. Queen Esther was lying awake in her tent; indeed no one could tell if the old woman ever slept; come upon her at any time in the night—no matter with what tidings—and she was sure to meet you with those vigilant glances that seemed never to relax an instant. When the warrior lifted the mat from her tent, and stood so solemnly in the light of her dying fire, she prolonged that look, till it seemed to cut into him like steel. All at once a gleam of cruel trouble shot into the glance; those stony features moved, and a spasm of agony locked them closer than before. The smoky light could not alone have left those shadows on her face; they were the color of ashes.

He laid the tomahawk, red at the edge, the keen scalping-knife, and the rifle that had belonged to her son down at the old queen's feet. There was a rustle under her robes, as of dry boughs in winter, and her head drooped slowly forward on her bosom, while her fierce eyes gleamed down on the implements of death colder and sharper than they.

The following morning Aunt Polly rose at an early hour and went vigorously about her multifarious duties, preparing breakfast for herself and Sim, helping to milk the cows, and setting the house in order generally.

Thoughts of much importance were evidently weighing with great force upon Aunt Polly's mind, for all through breakfast she was very absent-minded, though her manner to Sim was unusually gentle—even bordering on tenderness.

"Now, Sim," she said, when he rose from the table, "have Gineral Washington saddled by the time I get the dishes washed, for I'm going right over to the island."

"So Jane Derwent and Clark are really goin' to be married?"

"And it's the best thing for 'em! When a man has made up his mind to ask a woman to have him, what's the use of putting it off till the Day of Judgment? He may as well speak up at once."

Sim assented with a dubious shake of the head; and with his thoughts reverting to the fickle Betsy, remarked sententiously that women were onsartin creeturs.

"Some on 'em," replied Aunt Polly, "but not all! I like a woman that can make up her own mind; but, just mind this, Mr. White, if a man wants a wife that's good for anything he mustn't marry a little fool of fifteen or sixteen—no gal is fit to get married under thirty-five."

Sim nodded his head.

"Did you ever see my settin' out, Sim? If it hasn't been used long afore this, it wasn't for want of offers."

Sim never had seen this wonderful setting out, and Aunt Polly promised to show it to him at some future time. Finally he sauntered away about his work, and Aunt Polly began clearing up the table. When everything was in order, she sat down before the loom, in which was the unfinished rag carpet that she had promised to Jane Derwent as a wedding present. She unrolled from the ponderous beam the yards which were completed and looked at them admiringly.

"There never was a neater carpet," she said, "never; that orange in the warp is as bright as a guinea, and I never see a purtier blue. I don't believe, arter all, it would fit any room in Edward Clark's new house, and I don't see what Jane wants of it; young folks shouldn't begin life by being extravagant."

She folded the carpet slowly up, regarding it with covetous eyes.

"I guess," she continued, slowly, "I'll look out a counterpane for her; she'll like it just as well, and it's a better wedding present; folks can get along without a carpet, but they must have bed kiverin'."

She went up to a spare chamber, and opened the chest of drawers in which were safely packed the various articles appertaining to her own much-lauded "setting out." There were piles of linen and bed-clothes, all getting yellow from disuse; from the latter she selected a blue and white yarn counterpane and spread it over the bed.

"Wal, that is dreadful purty! I kinder hate to part with it; mother helped me make it, and I don't feel as if 'twould be exactly right to give it away. I'll give Janey a pair of sheets and ruffled pillow-cases instead."

She took out the sheets and pillow-cases, smoothing down the ruffles and admiring their fineness. They looked more elegant than ever, and Aunt Polly decided that the sheets alone would be present enough, so she refolded the pillow-cases and put them back in the drawer, where they had formerly reposed. Still she was not satisfied, and wavered a long time between a woolen blanket and the sheets; but Jane's bridal stock was doomed to want both. Aunt Polly's eye fell upon a roll of articles which seemed intended for the decoration of a baby's cradle; even in her chaste solitude the old maid fingered them with decorous hesitation.

She unrolled the bundle and took up two patch-work quilts exactly alike, and pieced from gorgeous scraps of calico by her own fair hands. She compared and measured them, to see that there was no difference, and finally chose the one that proved a fraction of an inch narrower than the other.

"It's big enough," she murmured, absently; "it'll cover a child a year old, and that's as much as any one could reasonably ask for."

Having made her decision, she seemed more at ease in her mind, laid the other things carefully away, sprinkled fresh lavender over them, and turned the key once more upon her treasures, taking up the quilt with a jerk and hastening down stairs, as if she feared to remain longer, lest she should lock that up too.

Before Sim brought General Washington out of the barn, Aunt Polly was in readiness. She had heroically picked her finest bell-necked squash, and stood on the stoop in front of her house, her monstrous poke bonnet sitting up on her head, with a defiant air, and grasping in her hand that enormous vegetable, which might have been scooped out as a drinking-cup for one of the giants of the olden time.

At length Sim appeared, leading the old white horse up to the stump which served as a mounting-block, on which Aunt Polly established herself, with her skirts held closely about her, as if she were preparing for a dive.

"Gineral Washington looks like a picter," she said, regarding the old horse admiringly. "Wal, I always did say, Sim White, that you could curry a horse better than any other man in Wyoming; why, the old feller shines like a looking-glass; I can't bear a man that is careless with a horse; I wouldn't marry him if he had ten bags of golden guineas, for if he can't treat a dumb creetur well, what would he do to a wife?"

"Are you going to Mother Derwent's right off?" Sim asked, somewhat heedless of Aunt Polly's remark.

"Yes, I am; I want to see that they've got everything all right. Now, make the Gineral side up, and help me on."

The old maid rested one hand on the horn of the saddle and the other upon Sim's shoulder, who put his stalwart arm about her waist, and before she could make any resistance, if she had felt so inclined, lifted her to her seat.

"Wal, if I ever!" she exclaimed, indignantly, though the corners of her mouth worked with suppressed pleasure. "I never did see such a man—ain't you ashamed?—get away now—suppose anybody had come by and seen you!"

"You see I couldn't help it, Aunt Polly."

"Aunt Polly!" shrieked the old maid, in anger and defiance. "Miss Carter, ef *you* please—that's my name! You're a mannerly feller, ain't you? Pretty age you are, to be calling me such a name! Get away with you, and if that garden ain't all weeded afore I get back you needn't expect many good words from me."

"Now don't get into a passion," said Sim, either really anxious to mollify her, or impelled by a desire to escape his task; "I didn't mean no harm; the boys and gals call you so."

"Wal, you ain't a boy, nor a gal neither; there's grey in your hair, plain enough to be seen!"

"Now, don't be mad," said Sim, catching hold of her bridle, as she manifested some intention of riding away; "I'll never let my tongue slip again; come, Miss Carter!"

The old maid put her hand on his shoulder, and said, with her blandest smile:

"Put the squash in my lap, Sim, and hang the bundle on the horn; you may call me Polly—I don't mind that, though I don't know," she added, with virtuous reflection, "whether it's just the thing afore people are married."

"It can't do no hurt," returned Sim, sagely turning his tobacco over in his mouth, "even if they don't intend to get married."

"Yes, it can!" retorted the spinster. "No man shall ever call me Polly that don't want to marry me right out, now, I tell you!"

Sim retreated a little, and did not exhibit that eagerness to pronounce the euphonious syllable which Aunt Polly seemed to expect, and she chirruped to General Washington with renewed displeasure.

"Are you a-coming up to the wedding?" she asked, sharply.

"I s'pose so; Edward Clark wanted me to play the fiddle for them to dance a little."

"Wal, I jest wish you wouldn't go—it makes it very unpleasant for me."

"Why on 'arth shouldn't I go, Miss Carter?"

"They all laugh at me so," said Aunt Polly, with interesting confusion.

"What do they laugh at you for—'cause I choose to fiddle?"

"Your actions, I suppose," she replied, indignantly; "'tain't likely I've told 'em all the things you've said to me. If I had, I know my friends would insist on my settling things right off—but I'm hard to coax, very hard, Sim."

Her hand went down on his arm again, and this time Sim rather took it of his own accord.

"Are you?" he said, doubtfully; "I guess not very hard—be you, Aun—Polly?"

"Oh, Sim, you shouldn't have spoken out so sudden—women is sensitive creeturs. Wal, I don't know; I wouldn't say yes to any other man, as plenty of 'em could tell you from experience; but since it's you, Sim, there, just let out that stirrup-leather a trifle."

She gathered the skirts decorously around her feet while Sim performed this duty, and rested her hand on his shoulder in settling herself again. Sim looked a little puzzled, and somewhat unappreciative of the honor Aunt Polly had bestowed upon him; but he passed it off with better grace than could have been expected, and even called her outright by her baptismal appellation.

"I'm goin' now," said the old maid, crimsoning with delight. "I shall have to get some of the gals to come and stay a while with me. It wouldn't be proper for us to be alone in the house, you know. I guess we'll have to hurry things, too, on their account; for they can't none of 'em stay away from home long. Good-bye, Sim; never mind the garding—good-bye. Get up, Gineral Washington. Come over early, Sim—and oh, you'll find some new gingerbread in the stone crock. I've put out a nice dinner for you. Good-bye, Sim."

She rode off, and left Sim standing in the road, buried in deep thought.

"Wal," he said at length, putting a fresh morsel of tobacco in his mouth, and speaking aloud, "she seems to think it's all settled; and I don't know as I much mind, either way. I'd kind o' like to show Betsy Willets, too, that I don't care a rush for her marryin' Jim Davis—consarn her! The old maid's worth having, any way; this is just as good a farm as there is in all Wyoming, and the tavern stand ain't so bad as it might be. A feller might go farther and fare worse. Besides, 'tain't manners, dad used to say, to look a gift horse in the mouth—so, if she's suited, let it go."

Sim gave his head a philosophical shake and turned towards the barn, whistling Yankee Doodle as he went. There were a few tremulous variations now and then, which threatened to subside into Old Hundred, as an image of the faithless Betsy would present itself; but Sim solaced his mind by glancing about the neat, thrifty-looking premises, and fell to whistling harder than before, conscientiously repeating the parts which he had slurred over with a firmness that would have satisfied Aunt Polly herself.

The old maid rode on up towards the river, and as she reached the turn of the highway, leading to Forty Fort she spied, in advance of her, a troop of soldiers on horseback and on foot, proceeding towards the fort.

"What on airth!" exclaimed Aunt Polly, urging General Washington on; "what are they about?"

She rode without hesitation towards the little band, and discovering an acquaintance in the leader, called out:

"Why, Captain Slocum, what's up now?"

"Nothing very important, Miss Carter," he replied. "There were some men shot at Fort Jenkins last night, and Walter Butler, with a troop of Injuns, is in the valley. We must be on our guard."

"Aint a-going to have a fight to-day, are we?"

"I can't tell; it may come any minute."

"Wal, do your duty, Captain Slocum; do your duty!" said Aunt Polly, assuming the tone in which she had heard revolutionary speeches delivered. "Wyoming expects every man of ye to stand up to the mark—take care of the widows, the orphans, and perticlarly of such young females as haven't yet secured their natral protectors."

"We will do our best, Miss Carter," returned the captain, concealing a smile, and glancing reprovingly towards his men, who looked more amused than moved by Aunt Polly's eloquence.

"I know you will; I can trust you, captain," replied the old maid, approvingly, as if she felt that a great responsibility rested upon her shoulders. "If you want a hoss, captain, send for Gin'ral Washington, you're welcome to him; the old feller has stood fire too many training days to be afraid of Tories or Injuns ither."

"Thank you; if we have occasion, I'll send for him," said the captain, trying to move on, a manœuvre difficult to execute, for Aunt Polly had stationed herself directly in front of the troop.

"Do; and oh, captain," checking the general, as he seemed inclined to give way to the soldiers, "if you want a treat for your men, I've got a keg of Jamaica spirits in my cellar that's a leetle ahead of anything you've tasted lately—you're welcome to it."

"That is very kind of you," replied Slocum, while his men listened with lively interest; but he had rashly interrupted Aunt Polly.

"Let 'em drink all they want," she said. "I know you're too much of a man to cheat me out of a gill, captain. I can trust you—Sim White'll show you where it is."

"Forward, men!" exclaimed the commander; "we're losing time here."

"Law bless me, don't run over a body!" cried Aunt Polly; "the Gin'ral and I ain't Tories, captain."

But the men pushed on, heedless of her expostulations, and the old maid was forced to give way.

"Don't forget the rum!" she shrieked after them. "You and I'll settle for it to-morrow, captain."

She rode on without farther interruption until she came opposite the island. She dismounted with the bell-necked squash under her arm, took a small bundle carefully off the saddle, loosened the girth a little, and sent the general up the bank with a pat of her hand. A vigorous and prolonged call speedily brought Mary Derwent out of the house, and in a few moments her little canoe had reached the shore where Aunt Polly stood.

"You see, Mary, I've come over early," she said; "I thought you'd have lots to do. Here, ketch this bundle; handle it carefully, it's something for Janey. I guess I wish I'd taken the saddle across, too, for it might be stolen by some of them rascally Tories."

"Are they around again?" Mary asked, anxiously.

"Yes, so Captain Slocum told me. I met him and his men a-goin' to Forty Fort. I told 'em their duty, and they looked quite sober about it."

"I fear that terrible times are coming," said Mary, sadly; "the Valley has never been in such confusion as it is now. Edward Clark could only stay with us a few moments last night, and won't be back till evening."

"That's right!" exclaimed Aunt Polly. "'Tisn't proper for him to come till the minister does. I never was married myself, but I know what ought to be done as well as anybody—there's nothing like being prepared, one never knows when an offer may pop up."

She looked very meaningly at Mary, but the poor girl was too anxious and troubled to take notice of the peculiarity of the old maid's manner.

"Don't say a word to trouble grandma and Jane," she said, when they reached the island; "it will do no good."

"Of course not; when did you ever know me to speak the wrong word at the wrong minute? Give me that squash, Mary; handle it keerful—that's it."

She walked towards the house, and Mary, having secured the canoe, followed at a slower pace. Within the little kitchen there was a savor of chickens roasting, and various other eatables preparing for the evening. Mother Derwent was frying doughnuts when Aunt Polly entered, and she wiped her floury hands on her checked apron, in order to return her friendly greeting with due cordiality.

"Wal, Jane," said the old maid, turning to Jane, who was rolling out pie-crust with great diligence; "how do you do? You see, we all have to come to it, first or last—but, law! the thought takes away my breath. I never can bear it as you do."

"Why, Aunt Polly, do you think of getting married, too?" said Jane, laughing.

"Stranger things than that have happened," returned the spinster. "Men are sich determined critters, there ain't no getting rid of them when once they get sot on a thing—a body has to say yes, whether or no."

"Who is the man that torments you so much?" Jane inquired, laughing merrily.

"No, you don't—you can't surprise no secrets out of me!" Aunt Polly turned away her face in pretended confusion, to Jane's great amusement; at length she recovered, and taking the squash from the table, where she had placed it, she held it towards the old lady.

"How are you off for pies, Miss Derwent?"

"Wal, pretty well; we've got lots of strawberries and raspberries, and some dried pumpkin."

"Dried punken!" repeated the old maid, with awful disdain; "jest try that are squash; dried punken, indeed! This'll just finish you up—now get me a knife, and I'll have it sliced in short order."

The day wore on in busy employment for all, though Mary's heart was full of evil forebodings, which she did not breathe aloud, and she heard little of the running stream of talk which Aunt Polly kept up all the while her hands were so actively employed.

At length the old maid drew Jane mysteriously into the inner room, and pointed to a bundle laying on the bed.

"There's a present for you, Janey," she whispered; "don't say nothing about it. You're just as welcome as can be."

Before Jane could express her thanks, Aunt Polly had untied the package, and held up before the astonished girl a small patch-work baby quilt, valuable as a curiosity, and with a rising sun in gay colors forming the centre.

"I knew I couldn't give you nothing more useful, nor purtier," she continued, complacently, while Jane stood looking at her in confused surprise. "'Tain't no common quilt—that was a part of my own settin' out; I pieced it with these two hands. I've got another jest like it, only the middle is pink and blue; but I had to keep that," sinking her voice to a whisper, "for 'tain't best to leave oneself quite destitute."

Jane tried to murmur something, but between suppressed mirth and confusion she was dumb.

"You see, it's so much better for you than that carpet we talked about, that ain't near done, and I'm so slow; besides, young folks oughtn't to cosset themselves up with such things. Scrubbing floors is the wholesomest work you can have, and I really think carpets are unhealthy; they make you ketch cold every time you go into the air."

Jane expressed her perfect satisfaction with the gift, and Aunt Polly fell into a confidential conversation with her, and before they returned to the kitchen had revealed her intended marriage with Sim White, under promise of proposed secrecy. Jane was faithful to her pledge, but as Aunt Polly, in the course of the afternoon, was closeted with Mary and the old grandmother, each in her turn, and confided the interesting news to both, under the same vow of solemn silence, Jane's fidelity did not meet with its due reward.

Before four o'clock everything was prepared, and the whole house set in order.

"Wal," said Aunt Polly, glancing with pride at the rows of pies and huge piles of doughnuts and cakes; "if anybody wants nicer fixin's than these, let them get 'em up, that's all. If ever I get married—not that I say I'm goin' to—but if I ever should, I won't have no stingy doin's—good eatin' and plenty of it'll be had, now I tell you."

At last Mary escaped, to obtain a few quiet moments for reflection; and Jane retired to the other room, to give the finishing touches to the simple bridal attire spread out upon the coverlet. Aunt Polly and Grandmother Derwent sat down in front of the door, to indulge in a quiet chat, and when the girls were fairly out of sight, Aunt Polly took sundry surreptitious pinches of snuff from the old lady's box, by no means with the air of a novice, but like a woman refreshing herself after a season of rigid self-denial.

CHAPTER XXIV
THE CHIEF'S BURIAL

For a full half-hour Queen Esther sat motionless in the chill of that appalling silence, her eyes fixed upon the weapons of death at her feet with a dull glare, more terrible than the fiercest rage of passion.

She rose slowly, at length, laid the rifle and scalping-knife carefully aside, and clutching the tomahawk of her dead son in her hand, passed noiselessly out of the tent. At the entrance she met the chief, Gi-en-gwa-tah, motioned him to follow with a stern gesture of command, and moved on towards the roused encampment, issuing her brief orders in a voice hard as iron.

From the seclusion of her own tent, Catharine Montour watched the hasty preparations for departure, and her heart sank at the sight of those rigid faces, as the old queen and her son went out, for she understood only too well what their calmness portended.

She dared utter no word of remonstrance; the bravest heart would have shrunk from offering consolation to that grim woman. It was still dark as midnight, and the smouldering fires cast a lurid glare around, lighting up the stern visages flitting like shadows among the tents, while the waning moon trembled like a crescent of blood on the verge of the western horizon, a sign of approaching carnage and warfare.

At length a detachment of warriors, armed with rifles and tomahawks, and hideous with war-paint, broke out from the great mass, and mounting their horses, remained stationary on the outskirts of the camp. Queen Esther's horse was led out, flowing with gems torn from the persons of former victims; her tomahawk glittered at the saddle-bow, and the head of her steed was decorated with raven's plumes, that waved slowly to and fro with every motion of his proud neck. Catharine saw the old Queen come forth again from her tent, grasping in her hand the weapon which her son had wielded in his last battle. Passing with stern composure through the group of Indians, she planted one hand upon the saddle, and with a single effort of her sinewy arm lifted herself to the seat. With no sound but the muffled tread of their horses on the short turf, the band swept on, with that silent woman leading them on, and were lost in the darkness beyond.

The great body of Indians and the army of whites encamped at a little distance still kept their position, though preparations for departure were evident among them—carried on by the Indians in sullen quiet, far more terrible than the shouts and oaths which came up from the Tory tents.

Catharine Montour watched all, heard all, but still she did not move. The chief did not at once approach her tent, and though a sickness like that of death was on her, she knew that the slightest remonstrance would only increase the Shawnee's thirst for vengeance. She did not stir from the spot until everything was ready for their departure and her horse was led up to the entrance of her tent.

Swiftly the detachment, with Queen Esther for their leader, swept down the rocky path which led towards the Susquehanna. After a ride of about twenty miles, they came out upon the river, opposite the foot of Campbell's Ledge, and, crossing the stream there, continued their course into the valley, only pausing while Esther dispatched a scout in advance, to see that their way to the fort would be unobstructed.

She had halted just where the Falling Spring came leaping down the steep precipice, white and spectral in the gathering day. Beyond loomed up the giant masses of the Ledge, and at her feet the river flowed in its pleasant quietness, bearing no warning of ill to the doomed inhabitants of the valley.

During the absence of their scout the silence was unbroken; the warriors were banded together in portentous impassibility; and Queen Esther, with her horse drawn a little distance apart, the reins falling loosely upon his neck, sat with her eyes fixed upon the tomahawk still grasped in her hand. The Indian returned, and at his signal the party swept down the war-trail, which ran in nearly the same course that the roadway of the present day takes, following the river in its sinuous windings.

Just above Pittston the Susquehanna and Lackawanna meet, and at their point of union a little island, picturesque even now, rests on the bosom of the waters. The band paused on the shore of the Susquehanna, in sight of this island. A scow, used by the inhabitants of the region as a common means of transportation across the stream, was unmoored, and the whole band were rowed over to the opposite shore. Again they paused, and waited until the main force of Tories and savages came up, with Gi-en-gwa-tah at their head, and Catharine Montour in their midst.

At the chief's command, the body of Indians swam their horses over to the little island, their leader guiding the steed on which Catharine rode, and commenced immediate preparations for the rearing of her tent.

On swept the Tories, headed by Queen Esther and her band, over the smooth plains, then green with rustling forests, and keeping within sight of the river. When the dawn broke, grey and chill, Wintermoot's Fort, the stronghold of the Tories, loomed before them, surrounded by bristling stockades and fortified outworks.

At their approach the gates were thrown open, and the whole army swept into the inclosure. Those within the fort crowded around, in eager curiosity, to gaze upon the old queen, but she seemed unconscious of their glances, dismounting at once from her horse, and following the commander of the fort into the room where the body of her son had been carried.

Tahmeroo was sitting on the floor by the corpse, but she did not raise her head when the door opened, and Queen Esther moved towards the bench where the body lay, without paying any heed to the presence of her grandchild. She stood over the dead chief without any sign of emotion; her frame never once relaxed—not a muscle moved, not an eyelash quivered; her motionless right hand fell at her side, with the gleaming tomahawk still clutched between her clasped fingers.

The Indians entered the room, took up the body and bore it forth, with a low death-wail that sounded ominously drear in the solemn stillness which came over all within the fort.

Among that group of awe-struck gazers stood Grenville Murray. He had come into the fort a few hours before, and had vainly attempted to instill some idea of mercy into the ferocity of the Indians and Tories, but the pacific measures which he pleaded were as much unheeded as if they had been made to wolves in the forest.

The train bearing the dead chief passed through the inclosure, and Queen Esther followed, erect and still, looking neither to the right nor the left, while Tahmeroo crouched behind—horror-stricken and pale.

"Will she take him away?" Murray whispered to the commander.

"Yes; for burial."

"But she is partly a white woman; surely she will not allow him to be buried in this heathenish fashion."

"Do you think Queen Esther a saint?" sneered the leader; "the scalping-knife is her religion!"

Murray stepped forward and stood before the queen. She looked up, neither in anger nor surprise, when he ventured thus to confront her:

"Madam," he said, in a low tone, "I am informed that there is a clergyman in the neighborhood—will you not wait here until he can be summoned? At least, let your son be buried with the rites of your country's faith."

"The wilderness is my country," she replied, in a voice the more startling from its iciness; "my son was an Indian brave; no mummeries of the pale faces shall desecrate his grave."

She passed on without giving him an opportunity to reply, and the procession moved out of the fort, down to the bank of the river, where several canoes had been procured for the removal of the corpse.

Into the bark with the dead man stepped Tahmeroo and the old queen. The rowers bent to their task, and the canoe swept up the current. The Indian girl sat down by the body of her relative, but the old queen stood upright in the stern of the boat, the rising sun gilding the faded dun of her robes, and gleaming balefully over the murderous weapon in her hand.

A tent had been erected on the lower part of the beautiful island, and in the doorway stood Catharine Montour, watching the approach of the three canoes. The Indians, with their chief, were grouped about the shore, and as the canoes came in sight they struck up a death-song, in answer to the chant from the boats, prolonged by the women into a mournful wail which, accustomed as she was to such scenes, made Catharine's blood run cold.

The boats came up, the old queen remained standing on the shore, while Tahmeroo sprang forward and was silently clasped to her mother's bosom. It was the first time they had met since the girl's flight in search of her husband, but there was no time given for joy, and, without a word, they stood side by side while the mournful ceremonies proceeded.

At the lower extremity of the island may be seen, to this day, a group of four willow trees, with their trunks distorted and bent, and when the wind is low the long branches sway to the ground with a sorrowful music, which sounds like a requiem prolonged from that funeral wail.

Under the shadow of those trees they dug the young chief's grave and laid him therein, his face covered with war-paint and his most precious possessions by his side. Rifle and scalping-knife were placed reverently down, but when they searched for the tomahawk Queen Esther took her own decorated weapon from an Indian near by and flung it beside the body, standing erect as ever while the earth was thrown in and the grave filled quickly up.

When all was over, obeying her imperious motion, the tribe withdrew to a little distance, and she stood alone by the head of the grave, with her right hand stretched over it—once her lips moved faintly, then shut and locked themselves closer than before; but in that moment of fearful self-communion Queen Esther had registered a terrible vow.

As the groups broke up, Butler landed in his canoe and came towards them. Passing Catharine and Tahmeroo with a hasty nod, he approached Queen Esther and whispered in her ear:

"The man I told you of is at the fort; they tell me he spoke with you—the missionary also is near. Queen Esther need not go beyond her own camp-fires to discover the instigator of this deed."

The queen returned no answer, but a slight shiver of the tomahawk proved that his fiendish whisper had produced its effect, and Butler moved away. Though their conference lasted scarce a second, and their glances never once wandered towards the place where she stood, Catharine Montour felt that the first threads of some plot against her safety and life had been formed above the grave of the young warrior.

She laid her hand on Tahmaroo's arm and entered the lodge, trembling so violently from weakness and nervous agitation that she was unable to stand. The girl sat down, chilled by her husband's coldness, and awaiting his entrance with impatience, the more harassing from a mournful consciousness that she occupied no place in that reckless man's heart.

After a little, Queen Esther collected her own band of warriors and left the island, retracing the path towards Wintermoot's Fort. Butler and the chief, Gi-en-gwa-tah, held a conversation together upon the shore, during which the gloomy brow of the Indian grew constantly darker, and the fire in his eyes kindled into new ferocity. At length he turned away from the young man, and entering his wife's tent sat down in sullen quiet.

Catharine Montour sat apart, with her eyes fixed in painful apprehension on the wrathful face of the chief. There was nothing of the fierce courage in her demeanor that had formerly characterized it; a most astonishing change had been gradually wrought in her mind and person since the day which witnessed her interview with the missionary, and more visibly after Butler's return from Johnson Hall, with intelligence of Murray's presence in America. The healthful roundness of her person had fallen away, and her features had sharpened and grown of a cold paleness, till they seemed as if chiselled from marble. Her cheeks were hollow, her high forehead was changed in its lofty and daring expression, a calm sadness had settled upon it, and her eyes, formerly fierce and keen almost as a wild eagle's, were full of gentle endurance, at that moment disturbed by apprehension and fear, but by no sterner emotion.

Never in the days of her loftiest pride had Catharine Montour appeared so touchingly lovely, so gentle and so woman-like, as on that evening. She had been pleading for her people with the fierce chief—pleading that vengeance should not fall on the inhabitants of the neighboring valley in retribution for the death of a single brave. But the Shawnee had taken other counsellors to his bosom within the year. Since the fierce pride of Catharine's character had passed away, her influence over him had decreased; while that of Butler was more thoroughly established, and Queen Esther had regained all the supremacy which for a season had yielded to the influence of his wife.

When almost as stern and unyielding as himself, Catharine might command—now she could but supplicate. The higher and better portion of her nature was, like her history, a sealed book to him; he could understand and respect strong physical courage, but the hidden springs which form the fearful machinery of a highly cultivated woman, making weakness in some things a virtue, and even fear itself lovely, he could not comprehend. A terrible suspicion had been instilled in his proud nature, and he mistook her utterly; his nobility of character, which was lifted above either savage or civilized cunning, had made him the dupe of a bad man. When moral goodness began to predominate in Catharine's character, he mistook its meek and gentle manifestations for cowardice, and she became to him almost an object of contempt. There was no longer any power in her patient perseverance and persuasive voice to win his nature to mercy; the daring spirit which had formerly awed and controlled his had departed forever beneath the gradual deepening of repentance in her heart.

Tahmeroo joined earnestly with her mother's pleading; but he answered only with abrupt monosyllables, and even with their voices in his ear his sinewy fingers worked eagerly about the haft of his knife, conveying an answer more appalling than the fiercest words could have given. There had been silence for some time. Catharine Montour sat with one hand shading her troubled brow, pondering on some means of preventing the bloodshed which she had so much cause to apprehend, and sorely repenting that she had ever instigated the Indians to take up arms in the dispute waged between England and her colonies. Tahmeroo stole away to a corner of the tent, and resting her cheek on the palm of her hand, listened for the footstep of her husband, hoping with all the faith of affection that he would second her mother's plea for mercy; and nestling closer and closer down, as she thought of the mother and infants whom her father's warriors had already murdered, and whose scalps hung with their long and sunny hair streaming over the door of the lodge.

"Oh, if Butler would but come in!" she murmured, while tears started to her eyes, brought there by her mother's sorrow and the pain which his absence during the whole night had produced, increased by the lonely vigil which she had kept over the body of her relative—"He can do anything with the tribe."

As she spoke, the mat was flung aside, and her husband stood before her. Tahmeroo sprang joyfully to his bosom, and kissed his cheek, and lips, and brow, in all the abandonment of a happy and most affectionate heart; nor did she mark the stern and malignant expression of the face she had been covering with kisses, till he hastily released himself from her arms, and without returning her greeting, advanced to the chief, to whom he whispered again.

A fiendish light broke to the Shawnee's eye; he arose, thrust a tomahawk into his belt, and taking up his rifle, went out. Butler was about to follow, but Tahmeroo again stood before him, extending her arms with an imploring gesture.

"You will not go away yet," she said. "You have scarcely spoken to me since we reached Wyoming—don't go yet!"

"Stand out of the way, foolish child!" he exclaimed, rudely pushing her aside. "I have other matters to think of!"

The Indian blood flashed up to Tahmeroo's cheek, her eye kindled, her form was drawn to its proudest height as she stood aside and allowed her husband to pass out.

Catharine had started to her feet when the Shawnee went out, and now stood pale as death; so much agitated by her apprehensions that the rudeness offered to her daughter escaped her notice. But as Butler was hurrying through the doorway she stepped forward and grasped his arm with an energy that caused him to turn with something like an oath at what he supposed the importunity of his wife. Catharine took no heed of his impatience.

"Butler," she said, "I fear there will be more bloodshed; for sweet mercy's sake, appease the chief. You have the power; oh, do not lose the opportunity. I think it would kill us all were another scalp to be brought in——"

She broke off suddenly, and shrunk back with a sick shudder, for a gust of wind swept the long hair which streamed from a female scalp over the entrance, directly across her face. Butler took advantage of her emotion to make his escape.

"Have no fear, madam," he said, freeing his arm from her grasp, and brushing the scalp carelessly back with his hand, as he went out; "you shall have no cause. I must hasten to the council at the fort."

Catharine Montour comprehended him; but, too sick for reply, drew back to her daughter's couch, and sat down, faint and quite overcome. There had been something horrible in the feeling of that long, fair hair as it swept over her face; her nerves still quivered with the thought of it.

"Mother," said Tahmeroo, rising from the ground, where she had cast herself, and winding her arms around Catharine, "oh, mother, comfort me—do comfort me, or my heart will break!"

Catharine pressed her lips upon the forehead of the young wife, and murmured:

"What troubles you, my child?"

She looked fondly and affectionately on the grieved face which lay upon her bosom as she spoke, and her heart ached when she saw how disappointments, regrets, and checked tenderness had worn upon its former rich beauty. The wrung heart had spread a sadness over those features, as the worm in the bosom of a flower withers all its surrounding leaves.

Tahmeroo burst into a passion of tears at her mother's question.

"Did you not see him, mother?—how he pushed his own wife aside, as if she had been a wild animal—did you not see him thrust her away without a kiss, or one kind word? Oh, mother, my heart is growing hard. I shall hate him, mother."

Catharine laid her hand on the throbbing forehead of her daughter, and remained in a solemn and serious thought. At length she spoke in a deep and impressive voice.

"No, my child, I did not see this rudeness, for my thoughts were on other things—but listen to me, Tahmeroo. Since the day that you were first laid in my bosom, like a young bird in the nest of its mother, my heart has hovered over yours, as that mother-bird guards its youngling. I have watched every new faculty as it has sprung up and blossomed in your mind. I have striven to guide each strong passion as it dawned in your heart; your nature has been to me as a garden, which I could enter and cultivate and beautify, when disgusted with the weedy and poisonous growth of human nature as

I have found it in the world; as I have found it in my own heart; but there is one thing which I have not done. I have laid no foundation of religion and principle in this young soul; I had become an unbeliever in the faith of my fathers. I acknowledged no God, and resolutely turned my thoughts from a future. My spirit had erected to itself one idol—an idol which it was sin to love, and double sin to worship as I worshipped.

"I will not show to you, my child, the progress of a life—a wretched destiny which was regulated by one sin; a foible most men would call it, for human judgment fixes on acts, not on that more subtle sin, a train of unlawful thoughts; I will not show to you the working of that sin; it is the curse of evil that its consequences never cease; that thought is interlinked with thought, event with event, and that the effects of one wrong creep like serpents through the whole chain of a human life, following the perpetrator even in the grave.

"My own destiny would be a painful illustration of this truth—might be the salvation of many in its moral, but when did example save? When did the fall of one human being prevent the fall of another? Why should I expose my own errors, in hopes to preserve you, my child, from similar wrong? What you have just said startles and pains me; I know your nature, and know that you will never cease to love the man whom you have married; indifferent you will never be—a sense of wrong indignation, if indulged in, may make the love of your heart a pain—may sap away the good within you, engender all those regrets that poison the joy of affection.

"Tahmeroo, struggle against this feeling; you little dream of the terrible misery which it will bring to you. Bear everything, abuse, insult, neglect—everything, but cast not yourself loose from your only hope. Your safety lies in the very love which, though it make the bitterness of your life, is its safeguard, too. In your own heart is the strength you must look for, not in his. If he wrongs you, forget it, if you can—excuse it, if you cannot forget it. Think not of your own rights too much; where struggling is sure to bring misery, it is better to forbear. I could say much more, for my heart is full of anxiety and sorrow. I know not why, but my spirit droops, as if your head were on my bosom, and your arms about me for the last time forever."

Catharine stooped down and kissed the tremulous lips of her child. She was answered back with a gush of gentle tears.

"Weep on, my daughter; I love to see you shed such tears, for there is no passion in them. I cannot tell you how dearly I love and have ever loved you, for deep feeling has no words; but we shall part soon; there is something in my heart which tells me so—the grave will come between us, and you will be left with no stronger guide than your own warm impulses.

"Kiss me once more, and listen. Should we be parted by death, or should Butler claim my promise to send you to England, go first to the missionary, and convey to him the little ebony box at the head of your couch; tell him all that I have said to you, and ask him to become a protector and a friend to Catharine Granby's child. Tell him that since the night of her daughter's marriage she has been a changed woman—that the voice of his prayer that night awoke memories which will never sleep again—awoke answering prayer in a bosom which had almost forgotten its faith. He will listen to you, my child, and when I am gone you will find a safe and wise protector in him. He will teach you how to regulate your too enthusiastic feelings. Promise that you will seek this good man when I am taken away—do you promise, Tahmeroo?"

"I will promise anything—everything, mother; but do not talk so sadly—your voice sounds mournful as the night wind among the pines."

Tahmeroo said no more, for her heart was full; but she laid her cheek against her mother's, and remained in her embrace silent and sorrowful.

CHAPTER XXV
THE WHITE QUEEN'S GIFT

While these events were transpiring, the morning wore on at Mother Derwent's cottage in the quiet which we have before described. But while Aunt Polly and the old lady held their cheerful conversation by the door, the sound of drums and shrill fifes came from the distance, and confused sounds rose from about Wintermoot's Fort. The two women started up in affright. Jane Derwent rushed, half-dressed, from the inner room, trembling with terror. Mary was aroused from her solitude, and came forth very pale, but self-possessed and calm.

"Do not be alarmed," she said, "it will probably only lead to a skirmish."

"Oh, if Edward should be out!" exclaimed Jane.

"If he is," returned Mary, solemnly, "God takes care of those who perform their duty—trust to him, sister."

"If anything should happen to him!" said Jane, weeping; "I have treated him so bad, teased him so dreadfully!"

"Law, Janey, don't fret!" urged Aunt Polly; "it does the men good to tease 'em afore you're married, soon enough to give up after the knot is tied."

"Hark!" exclaimed Mother Derwent. "Hear that shout."

"I wish we knew," said Mary; "if I were only on the shore."

"Don't go, Mary!" pleaded Jane; "I shall die if you leave me. Besides, I ain't dressed—oh Mary, do help me; it'll all turn out well enough, I dare say—come."

"Yes, go," said Aunt Polly, smoothing out her dress; "I'll stay with grandma." Mary followed the agitated girl into the little bedroom which they had occupied since their childhood. The room was neatly arranged. Mother Derwent's best blue worsted quilt, with the corners neatly tucked in at the foot posts, covered the high bed, and the white linen pillows lay like snow-heaps upon it. The old lady's best patch-work cushion was placed in the arm-chair which stood in a corner, and a garland of Princes' pine hung around the little looking-glass, before which Jane Derwent stood "with a blush on her cheek and a smile in her eye," arranging the folds of her white muslin bridal dress over a form that would not have seemed out of place in a palace.

"Mary, shall I tie this on the side or behind?" inquired the blooming girl, holding up a sash of the most delicate blossom color, with the usual volatility of her nature, forgetting her alarm in the pleasant excitement of the moment. Mary lifted her face from the wreath of wild roses which she was forming for her sister's hair, and smiled as she answered; but it was a smile of soft and gentle sadness, patient and sweet as the breath of a flower, though her cheek was pale with anxiety, for she felt that something terrible was close upon them.

"Let me tie it for you," she said, laying the wreath on the pillow, and removing a handful of roses from her lap to a basket which stood on the rude window seat. "There, now sit down, while I twist the roses among your curls."

Jane sunk gracefully to her sister's feet, while she performed her task. When the last blossom was entwined on her temple, the bride raised her beautiful face to her sister's with an expression of touching love.

"Oh, Mary, should I have been so happy, if it had not been for you? How glad I am that you persuaded me to tell Edward about that bad man!"

Mary did not answer in words, but her eyes filled with pleasant tears, she bent down and laid her cheek against that of the bride, and they clung together in an embrace full of love and sisterly affection.

While they were talking, a boat put off from the opposite shore, and, as Jane looked out, she saw Edward Clark and the missionary land on the island. Edward ran towards the house in breathless haste.

"Oh, Mary, that's him and the minister. Please go out first, sister, while I get my breath."

But while she was speaking, Edward Clark ran through the kitchen, and dashing into the bedroom flung his arms around Jane, who stood with her lips apart, lost in astonishment.

"Jane, dear Jane, forgive me! Oh, how beautiful you look! But it cannot be. Mary, Mary, the wedding is all broken up. Wintermoot's Fort is swarming with Tory troops. The woods are full of Indians! Get ready, I beg of you—get into my boat, and make the best of your way to Forty Fort. The Tories have already taken Fort Jenkins; but we shall give them hot work before they get hold of another block-house. Jane, dear Jane, look up—don't tremble so! come, be a brave girl, like Mary. Grandmother—Grandmother Derwent, do you know what I am saying? Aunt Polly Carter, you ought to have some courage; do come and help them off! Keep close to the east bank of the river till you get opposite the Fort, then land, and run for your lives. Jane, Jane, in the name of Heaven, do not faint!"

"Edward, Edward, what is it—how can we go—what must we do?" exclaimed Jane, throwing her arms around his neck, wild with terror.

"Our marriage, it cannot take place to-day. The valley is full of enemies. Our people are half-way to Wintermoot's; I must go back at once—every man is needed," he repeated, breathlessly.

"They will kill you—they will kill you, and us!" shrieked the bride.

"Hush, Jane!" and Mary drew her sister away; "this is no time for tears; Edward has need of all his strength."

At that moment the missionary came in.

"Away!" he cried, addressing Clark; "why do you loiter here? your friends are on the move by this time. Away, I tell you! Leave the family to me."

A scene of confusion followed. Jane Derwent sank fainting in the arms of her sister, and all Mary's energies were tasked to recover her from that death-like swoon.

"God save her!" cried Edward Clark, pressing a kiss on the forehead of his betrothed, and hastening away.

"Oh!" exclaimed Aunt Polly; "if I only knew where Sim White was!"

"I saw him last at Forty Fort," replied Clark, rushing past her.

"Then I'm a-goin' there, too!" she exclaimed. "Here, Grandma Derwent, give me a sun-bonnet, a handkerchief, or somethin'. 'Tain't no use to spile my best Sunday bonnet."

"We'll all go!" cried Mrs. Derwent; "we shall be safe there. Mary, Mary Derwent!"

"What shall we do?" cried Mary, who heard this call from the next room, turning to the missionary—"how must I act? She is quite senseless, and I cannot carry her."

"Give her to me," answered the minister. "Go and get something to wrap around her."

A mantle hung on the wall. Mary left her sister to the minister, and reached up to take the garment down. Her sleeves broke loose in the effort, and fell back from her arms, exposing the jewelled serpent that Catherine Montour had clasped around it. The missionary saw the jewel, and gave a start that almost dislodged Jane from his hold.

"Where—tell me, child—where did you get that?" he said with a sort of terror, as if he had seen a living snake coiled on the snow of her arm.

"She gave it to me—the white queen whom they call Catharine Montour."

"Where and when?"

"One night—the very next, I remember now, after Walter Butler tried to persuade her. You know all I would say. This strange lady sent for me to meet her at the spring."

"And you went—you saw her?" cried the minister, forgetting the danger of the insensible girl in his arms—everything in the question.

"Yes, I saw her. She talked to me—ah, how kindly!—and at the end, clasped this on my arm. Now I remember, she told me if danger threatened me or mine from the Indians, to show them this, and it would save us."

"Trust to it—yes, trust to it, and remain here in safety. This strange lady is in the valley; her tents are pitched on the little island in the mouth of the Lackawanna. Her jewel must have power among the savages."

"I feel certain of it," answered Mary, dropping her arm, and leaving the mantle on the wall. "I would risk more than my life on that noble lady's word."

The missionary looked on her earnestly, and evidently without knowing it, for his eyes filled with tears, which he made no effort to hide.

"You saw her, and she saw you? Was she kind—was she gentle?"

"Oh, very kind—very gentle. If I dared, perhaps I might say more than kind, for she held me against her heart almost all the time we were talking, and once I am sure she kissed my hair."

"Stay here; trust to her promise till I come again," said the minister, laying Jane on the bed, and preparing to leave the room.

"I will stay," answered Mary, bending over her sister, and kissing her lips, which were just beginning to crimson with new life.

As the missionary passed through the kitchen Aunt Polly ran after him.

"If you're going over just set me across. Gineral Washington is on t'other side, and I can't leave him among the Tories anyhow. We'll set Mother Derwent and the gals afloat, and then every one for his self, says I. There,

Miss Derwent, don't patter round, looking for sun-bonnets any longer. I'll risk the other rather than wait. Mary—Mary Derwent, I say!"

The missionary did not appear to understand her, but passed through the room as if she had not spoken. Mary left her sister for an instant, and entered the kitchen.

"Come, get ready and go with me," cried the old maid. "Mrs. Derwent and Janey can pull down in the canoe, and I'll take you behind me on the Gineral."

"No," replied Mary; "we are safe here—the Indians have always liked me. Be calm, grandmother; you are in no danger—we will stay here. I may be able to assist those on the shore if the battle goes against us."

"I'm gone!" cried Aunt Polly, dashing forward after the missionary. "The Tories ain't a-goin' to scare me! I hope to goodness Captain Slocum'll fight in the rear; I shall never git my pay for that 'ere rum if he don't turn up safe."

She followed the missionary, and placed herself in his boat just as it was putting off, leaving old Mother Derwent weeping helplessly on the hearth, and Mary encouraging her sister, full of serene fortitude, and praying silently for the safety of the neighbors and friends who were marching to the fight.

And now the cry of mustering battle rose like wildfire through the valley. The farmers forsook the fields, mechanics left their workshops, and armed with such weapons as presented themselves, gathered in companies, eager to drive out their invaders. Women left their cabins, and with their children sought the shelter of various forts, or armed themselves like the men, and stood at bay on their own thresholds. It was one of these companies, filing off towards Forty Fort, the most extensive fortification on the river, which Aunt Polly had met on her way to Monockonok Island. Col. Zebulon Butler, a staunch patriot and an officer of the Continental army, had chanced to return home on a visit to his family at this awful period, and was, by unanimous consent, made commander-in-chief. Colonels Denison and Dorrance volunteered their aid, and that day came five commissions from the army, accompanied by the missionary, who having attained intelligence of the invasion, went to urge their presence. Thus the raw recruits were officered by experienced men, and there was hope from delay, for Captain Spralding was already on his march to the valley with a well-drilled company.

With these advantages and hopes there arose a division of opinion in the council at Forty Fort; but the impetuous and inexperienced carried the day, and the opinion of the brave commander was overruled. Alas! for that council and the men who controlled it! The fatal order was given. In a body the patriots were about to storm Wintermoot's Fort, hoping to surprise its garrison.

Having decided their own fearful destiny, this band of martyrs marched out of the fort and mustered under the clear sun, which they would never see rise again.

FORTY FORT

It was a mournful sight—those old Connecticut women standing in front of the block-house ready to say farewell and call God's mercy down upon the heads their bosoms had pillowed, in some cases, for fifty years; heads too grey for the general service for which their sons had gone, but not too grey for defence of those grand old wives and mothers, who, fired with patriotism and yet pale with terror, stood to see them go.

Seldom have troops like those gone forth to battle. No fathers and sons marched side by side there, but grandfathers and grandsons, the two extremes of life, stood breast to breast on that fateful day. Congress had drawn the strength and pith of the valley into its own army and left it cruelly defenceless. Thus each household gave up its old men and boys, while the mothers, already half-bereaved, looked on with trembling lips ready to cry out with anguish, but making mournful efforts to cheer them with their quivering voices. Lads, too young for battle, saw their elder brothers file off with reckless envy, while the little grandchildren, who looked upon the whole muster as a pleasant show, clapped their hands in glee, more painful still, and followed the grey-headed battalion with sparkling eyes.

Younger women, with husbands in the wars, strove to console their mothers, but dropped into silence with the vague words upon their lips, while the children tugged at their garments and clamored for one more sight of the soldiers.

When all were gone—when the hollow tramp of those moving masses could no longer be heard, the women looked at each other with a vague feeling of desolation. The bravest heart gave way then; one woman threw an apron over her head, that no one might see her crying; another looked upon the earth with her withered hands locked, and tears finding mournful channels in the wrinkles of her quivering face; another sat down on the ground; gathered her children around her, and wept in their midst, while two or three strove to dash their fears away with wild attempts at boastfulness and defiance, and the rest fell to work preparing to receive the fugitives who were every moment applying for admission to the fort.

Thus the day wore on. For some hours everything outside the fort was still as death, but a little after noon that dull tramp of feet came back, measured and stern, and a little girl who had climbed to a loop-hole in the fort called out that she saw the "sogers going through the trees, with their guns and bayonets a-shining like everything"; and again, that she saw "Colonel Zeb. Butler on his great brown horse, with his cocked hat on, and a grand feather dancing up and down—oh, beautifully!"

"What next, what next—who goes next?" cried the granddame; "look, Hetty, do look if you can see grandpa anywhere."

"No, grandma," cried out the child, in great glee, "but there's Colonel Denison, and Leftenant Dorrance, and Leftenant Ransom, all with their swords out. Oh, Aunt Eunice, Aunt Eunice! here comes Captain Durkee."

"My son—my son!" cried an old woman in the crowd, while the tears coursed down her face, "look again, Hetty dear, and tell me just how he seems."

"I can't, Aunt Eunice, 'tain't no use; here comes Captain Bidlack ahead of his company. Oh, here's a lot of folks I know—Mr. Pensil and Mr. Holenback, and there goes Mr. Dana, and, oh dear! oh dear! there's Uncle Whitton looking this way."

"My husband—my husband!" cried a fair young girl, only three weeks a bride; "here, Hetty, catch my handkerchief and shake it out of the port-hole; he'll know it and fight the harder."

"Do, Hetty darling; that's a purty gal; do look once more for Captain Durkee. There," continued the old woman, appealing to the crowd around her with touching deprecation, "I hain't hardly had a chance to speak to him yet. Mebby you don't know that when the Continentals wouldn't give him leave to come hum and take care of his old marm, he just threw up his commission, and there he is a volunteer among the rest on 'em; so du give me one more chance—du you see him yet, Hetty?"

"Yes, Aunt Eunice, I kinder think I see his feather a-dancing over the brush."

"And not his face? Oh, dear! if I could only climb; will some on ye help me? Du now, I beg on ye."

The poor old woman made a struggle to climb up the rude logs, but fell back, tearing away a handful of bark and bringing it down in her grasp.

"They've all gone now," cried out the child; "I can't see nothing but some cows agin the sky, follering arter 'em."

"Following arter 'em—Lord 'a' massy upon us then!" whispered the old woman, drawing a heavy breath, and she turned with a deadly paleness on her face, without addressing the child again.

"There they all go on the run now—hurrah—hurrah! Won't the Injuns catch it—hurrah!"

All the little voices in the fort set up an answering shout as the child clambered down from her post. The younger women received this infant battle-cry as an omen. Their faces, hitherto so anxious, flushed with enthusiasm; those who had wept before, started up and went to work at random, tearing up old sheets and scraping lint, while a group of little boys built a fire within the stockade, and went to work vigorously, moulding bullets from hot lead they melted in the iron skillets, which were yet warm from cooking the last household breakfast.

The women knew that the troops had moved up stream, and would go on till they met the enemy; so, with their hearts leaping at every noise, they waited in terrible suspense for the first shot. Thus two hours crept by—two long, terrible hours, that no human being in that fort ever forgot. Two or three times little Hetty climbed up to her look-out—the loop-hole, but came down in silence, for nothing but the still plain met her search. The third time, however, she called out, but with less enthusiasm than before:

"Here comes somebody down the cart-road, full trot, on a great white horse; oh, it's Aunt Polly Carter, with her go-to-meeting bonnet on, a-riding like split; I guess somebody 'ed better let her in; for she's turning right up to the fort."

"She comes from up stream; she must 'a' seen the army; some one run and tell the guard to let her in," cried a score of voices; "she's got news—she'll bring news."

With a clamor of eager expectation, the women rushed up to meet Aunt Polly, who, in defiance of all military laws, rode General Washington within the stockade, and close up to the fort. She was greatly excited; her huge bonnet had taken a military twist, and loomed out from one side of her head, giving her grim features to full view; a large cotton shawl, flaming with gorgeous colors, was crossed over her bosom and tied in a fierce knot behind; she carried a long walnut switch in her right hand, worn to a tiny brush at the end, for in the excitement of that ride she had beaten General Washington into a hard gallop every other minute.

"Have I seen 'em?—of course I have, and a wonderful sight it was—hull battalions of sogers a-moving majestically."

"Did you see my son—was the enemy near—can they surprise Wintermoot's Fort?"

"Don't ask me, neighbors—don't say a word!" cried Aunt Polly, dismounting from General Washington, and turning from one eager inquirer to another, "for I don't know much more than you do; but this is sartin, them Tory Butlers know what they're about; they're outside the fort, and drawn up in battle array; I never could 'a' got through the sogers if it hadn't been for Captain Walter Butler; he knew me at the first sight, and made some of his men ride by Gineral Washington till we got this side his army."

"How many are there—did you see any Indians?"

"I couldn't begin to calkerate; yes, I did see a lot of Injuns skulking in the swamp; but, seeing the Tories with me, they didn't shute."

"But our side, our side—where did you meet them?"

"About half-way, marching right straight on—Sim White and all—every man of 'em ready to die for his country. Mr. White couldn't do more than slip out of the ranks, to tell me how he come to be there, instead of waiting on me hum from Miss Derwent's to-night, when Captain Durkee called arter him."

"Then you saw my son?" whispered Mrs. Durkee, drawing close to the old maid; "how did he look? Du tell me!"

"Brave as a lion, Miss Durkee; except Sim White there wasn't a man to match him in the hull company. 'Fellow citizens, do your duty,' says I, stopping Gineral Washington as they come in sight."

"'We will—God help us, and we will! Tell our women folks at Forty Fort to keep a good heart; every man here'll die in his tracks afore the enemy reaches them.'"

Aunt Polly drew the back of her hand across her eyes as she said this; her words were answered by a simultaneous sob; even the children began to look wistfully at each other through their tears.

"By-and-by," said Aunt Polly, "you'll hear 'em beginning. Lord 'a' massy on us! that's a shot."

A low cry ran through the crowd; then a drawing in of the breath, and a deep hush. Faces, tearful before, became suddenly pale now; the old women locked their withered hands, and sent dumb prayers to Heaven; the children huddled together and began to cry.

"That's an awful sound," said Aunt Polly, looking over the crowd. "Let every mother as has got a son up yonder, and every woman as has got a husband tu lose, kneel down with me and say the Lord's Prayer; we women folks can't fight, and I don't know nothing else that we can do. Lord 'a' massy on us!"

They fell upon their knees—old women, young wives, and little children—uttering broken fragments of prayer, and quaking to the sound of each volley that swept down the forest. At first the shots fell steadily and at intervals; then volley succeeded volley; hoarse cries, the more terrible from their faintness; then the awful war-whoop rose loud and fierce, sweeping all lesser sounds before it.

The words of prayer froze on those ashen lips; wild eyes looked into each other for one awful moment; the horror of that sound struck even anguish dumb; the shots died away, fainter and fainter; a moment's hush, and then louder, shriller, and approaching the fort, came another whoop, prolonged into a sharp yell.

Old Mrs. Durkee rose from her knees; her voice rang out with tearful clearness over the crowd:

"Mothers, orphans, and widows, lift your faces to Heaven, for nothing but Almighty God can help us now."

CHAPTER XXVI
THE BATTLE-FIELD

Fired with stern enthusiasm, three hundred men—a large proportion of them grey-haired and beyond their prime, the rest brave boys—had filed out from the fort and organized on the banks of a small stream, which winds its way from the mountains and falls into the Susquehanna, above Kingston. Six companies marched from the fort, and here the civil officers and justices of the court from Wilkesbarre joined them. After a brief consultation, Captain Durkee, Ransom and Lieutenants Ross and Wells, were sent forward to reconnoitre. As their horses thundered off, the Wyoming companies approached separately, and filed into columns; there was the pallor of stern courage in every face; a gleam of desperate energy in every eye.

The march commenced; steadily and eagerly that little body of patriots moved forward; the hot sun poured down upon them; the unequal plain broke the regularity of their march; but the steady tramp of their approach never faltered; the youngest boy in the ranks grew braver as he passed the fort where his mother watched, and turned his face to the enemy; old, grey-headed men lifted their bent frames and grew eagle-eyed as they looked back towards the shelter of their dames, and onward for the foe.

Late in the afternoon they came in sight of Wintermoot's Fort. The enemy was prepared to receive them: Colonel John Butler and his Rangers occupied the banks of the river between them and the fort, and all the black, marshy plain, stretching to the mountains, was alive with savages, led on by Gi-en-gwa-tah and Queen Esther. Indian marksmen stood at intervals along the line, and Johnson's Royal Greens formed on Colonel's Butler's right.

The Butlers had chosen their own battleground—a level plain, covered with shrub oaks and yellow pines, with patches of cultivation between.

The Americans halted. For one moment there was a dead, solemn pause. Col. Zebulon Butler spurred his horse, and rode in front of his lines; he lifted his hand—his voice rang like a trumpet from man to man.

"Men, yonder is the enemy. We came out to fight, not for liberty, but for life itself, and, what is dearer, to preserve our homes from conflagration, and women and children from the tomahawk. Stand firm the first shock, and the Indians will give way. Every man to his duty!"

There was no shout, no outcry of enthusiasm, but a stern fire burned in those old men's eyes, and the warrior boys grew white with intense desire for action. The brave leader wheeled his horse, and fronted the enemy. His sword flashed upward—three hundred uncouth weapons answered it, and the battle commenced, for against all that fearful odds the Americans fired first, obeying their orders steadily, and advancing a step at each volley.

The Tory leader met the shock, and thundered it back again. His plumes and military trappings were all cast aside; a crimson handkerchief girded his forehead, and he fought like any common soldier, covered with dust and blackened with smoke, while his son, who held no other command, galloped from rank to rank, carrying his orders.

But notwithstanding the fierce valor of their leader and the discipline of those troops, the charge made by men fighting for their wives and little ones was too impetuous for resistance. The British lines fell back after the third charge. He threw himself before them like a madman, rallied them, and gained his own again. Then the fight grew terrible on both sides; the Americans, brave as they were, began to feel the power of numbers.

A flanking party of Indians, concealed in the shrub oaks, poured death into their ranks. In the midst of this iron rain Captain Durkee was shot down, leading on his men. The Indian sharp-shooters saw him fall, and set up a fiendish yell that pierced the walls of Forty Fort and made every soul within quake with horror.

The strife was almost equal. On the left wing the force under Colonel Denison fought desperately against the Indians, but they outflanked him at last, and, pouring from the swamp, fell like bloodhounds on his rear—a raking fire swept his men.

Thus beset by the savages behind and the Tories in front, he thought to escape the iron tempest by a change of position. In the heavy turmoil, his order was mistaken, and the word "retreat" went hissing through his ranks. It flew like fire from lip to lip, striking a panic as it fell. The British lines already wavered, another moment and they would have yielded. But that terrible mistake gave them the victory. As Denison's division fell into confusion they rallied, pressed forward, and the battle became a rout.

In vain Zebulon Butler plunged into their midst, and riding like a madman through a storm of bullets, entreated them to rally.

"Don't leave me, my children!" he cried; "one blow more—a bold front, and the victory is ours!"

It was all in vain. The ranks were already scattered, the Indians leapt in among them, like ravenous wild beasts. The captains were cut down while striving to rally their companies. Tomahawks and bullets rained and flew after them as they fled. Some were pierced with stone-headed lances; some fell with their heads cleft; some broke away towards Forty Fort, or, making for the river, plunged in, and struggled against the rushing stream for their lives.

No beasts of prey were ever hunted down like those unhappy men. They were shot down everywhere—in the grain fields, in the swamp. Regardless of all cries for mercy, they were chased to the river bank, dragged out from the bushes in which they sought to hide themselves, even back from the waves, or beaten and slaughtered among the stones which smoked with the warm blood poured over them. Thus the pursuit raged opposite Monockonok Island. Towards Forty Fort scenes of equal horror were perpetrated. The Indians rushed, leaping and howling, like hungry wolves, over the plain, cutting off retreat to the fort, and those poor fellows who turned that way were shot and hewed down in scores, or dragged back prisoners, and hurled among the savages for future torture.

For a long time Catharine Montour and her daughter remained absorbed in painful reflection amid the silence of the tent; then, as their thoughts began to revert to surrounding objects, the stillness reigning upon the island roused them at the same moment.

"Mother, how is this? I hear no sound abroad!" exclaimed Tahmeroo, starting from her mother's arms, and looking apprehensively in her face.

Catharine rose to her feet, and went out into the camp. The island was wholly deserted, save by a few squaws and the usual guard around her tent. In a moment she returned with something of former energy in her manner.

"There is treachery intended here," she said; "not an Indian is on the island. This bloodshed must be prevented. Hark! there are shots. I hear distant drums—that yell! God help the poor souls that must perish this day!"

"But what can we do, mother? The fight rages now!"

"Give me time to think," returned Catharine, clasping her hands over her forehead, and striving to force back her old fortitude.

"Oh, may God help me! that angel girl on the island! Tahmeroo, we must save her. I have promised—but the warriors leave me—that bracelet may not be enough!"

"Mother, I will preserve her life with my own—let us go, for this will be a terrible day. Come, mother, come!"

"Listen!" exclaimed Catharine; "I hear the sound of oars."

"It may be Butler—oh, if it is!" cried Tahmeroo, the thought of her husband always uppermost in her mind.

Catharine hastened towards the entrance of the tent, but at that moment the hangings were put aside, and the missionary stood before them.

"Woman—Lady Granby!" he exclaimed, "what do you here?—death and blood are all around—beware that it does not rest on your soul. Stop the progress of your savages—save the innocent."

"My God! I am helpless!" broke from Catharine's lips. "Go, Tahmeroo, go at once and find the queen or the chief—hasten, if you would not have this murder on our heads. Oh, sir, I am almost powerless here; but what a weak woman can do, I will."

Tahmeroo bounded away like a wild animal, while Catharine sank into a seat, unnerved as she had not been for years.

"This is no time for weakness," exclaimed the missionary, almost sternly; "you have grown too familiar with scenes of blood to shrink here, 'lady.'"

"But I am unusually helpless now," she said, despondingly; "my power is gone."

"Is not Gi-en-gwa-tah your wedded slave?—is not your will a law among his people?"

"It was while I was reckless and strong to maintain it; but now, alas! I am only a poor weak woman! Since we first met on the banks of this river, thoughts have awakened in my bosom which had slept for years. This terrible life shocks me to the soul, and the chief despises what he deems cowardice. Queen Esther has regained her old power, and Walter Butler, my child's husband, urges them on like a demon. They have left me here without a word; Heaven only knows what the end will be."

"You must do something—do not give way; there is not a moment to spare; human life is at stake!"

"It is like a dream," said Catharine, vaguely; "the present is gone from me—your voice carries me back—back to my early youth. Where did I hear it then?"

"This is no time for dreams, lady," cried the missionary. "Only rouse yourself—come away. Do you hear those shots—that yell?"

But Catharine yielded more completely to the power which dulled her senses—she could realize nothing: years rolled back their troubled tempest from her brain; she was once more in her English home. Even the war-whoop of her tribe could not arouse her.

"Will you not move?" groaned the missionary. "The whole valley will be slaughtered—that innocent child on the island will be killed. A second time, Caroline, as you value your soul, save her!"

"That child—the girl with an angel's face, and that form," said Catharine, dreamily, but with a look of affright, as if she were just awakening. "Bless her, Heaven bless that angel girl!"

"Can you realize nothing? Then I must say that which will waken, or drive you wholly mad! Woman—Lady Granby—fly—save that girl—for, as there is a God to judge between us two, she is your own daughter."

Catharine sat motionless, staring at him vaguely with her heavy eyes.

"I have no daughter but Tahmeroo," she said; "and she is only half my child now."

"I tell you, Mary Derwent is your daughter—the child whom you nearly killed in your insanity! and believed dead."

Catharine started up with a cry, so long and wild that it made the missionary start almost with terror.

"And you," she gasped; "you——"

"I am Varnham, your husband!"

She fell back with the dull heavy fall of a corpse, burying her face in her robe. The missionary raised her, trembling, and shrinking both from her and himself.

"Caroline—my—wife—look up. Or has God been merciful, and is this death?"

"My husband—my husband—is dead; he is dead—drowned, in the deep, deep unfathomable sea, years and years ago."

"Caroline, do not longer deceive yourself. Look at this picture, this ring; do you recognize me now?"

"And Heaven has not blasted me!" she moaned. "I live still!"

"Your daughter—our child—Caroline! They will murder her!"

"My daughter!" She rose to her feet again and repeated the words with a gasp, as if she were shaking a great weight from her heart. "My daughter!"

"Save her. The battle rages close by the island where she lives. Go with me; your presence alone will protect her."

The anguish of his tone might have roused marble to consciousness; it brought back Catharine's tottering reason.

"Child—Mary—daughter—I will go, I will go. At least, we can die together! I and that child whom the angels loved, but would not take."

She rushed from the tent, followed by Varnham. They met Tahmeroo, who had just landed.

"They are near the fort," she cried, "fighting like wolves. The chief and Queen Esther are in the thickest of the battle, and Butler, too, my husband— oh, my husband!"

"Fly to her, and say her mother is coming, Varnham. Man, or ghost, help me," cried Catharine. "I cannot speak—I cannot even have your forgiveness; but we will save her, and then God may be good, and let us die."

He rushed to his canoe without a word, and sped down the waters like an arrow from a bow. All of Catharine's strength came back. With resolute command she put off the madness which had begun to creep over her, and turned to Tahmeroo.

"Follow me to the island near the fort. There is a young girl there. Oh, my God, my God! let me see her once more! Let me call her my child, and die."

They pushed off in their canoe, and kept steadily down the stream until within a mile of the island.

The sun was setting, and the crimson of the sunset deluged the western sky, but the whole horizon was dark with smoke. The report of firearms— the echo of bullets—the shrieks of the dying filled the air with clamor and surged heavily over the waters.

"My husband, my husband!" moaned Tahmeroo.

Catharine never spoke, but watched eagerly for a sight of the island. She scarcely breathed, and her eyes were terrible in their strained gaze.

At that moment a party of Indians appeared on the western shore. They pointed to the canoe with angry gestures. Suddenly they sprang into the water like wild beasts and swam towards the canoe.

"Mother," cried Tahmeroo, "they are coming here. Queen Esther has sent them to murder us!"

A dozen hands grasped the frail bark, and dusky faces, terrible with war-paint, glared on the two women.

"Back!" exclaimed Catharine, rising up in her canoe and drawing her knife; "dare to disobey me, and you shall be sent from the tribe. Catharine Montour has spoken."

"The chief commands; Catharine Montour must go on shore."

"Yes, on the island yonder, but nowhere else. Tell Butler, your white chief, that he will find me there."

They wrested the knife from her grasp, and sprang into the canoe, offering no harm to either of the two women, but urging the boat to the shore, heedless of cries and expostulations.

"God, oh God, my child!" groaned Catharine from between her clenched teeth; "lost, lost!"

When they reached the shore, the savages forced them out of the boat, and with their tomahawks stove it to atoms. Then they rushed off with a whoop that apprised their employer of his triumph.

"This is Butler's work!" cried Catharine. "They are lost!"

"No, mother; come, we will go on foot—it is not far—there may be a boat near the island."

They hastened along the shore with frantic speed through the gloom of the coming night, pausing neither for words nor breath, clasping each other's hands closer as the breeze bore nearer and nearer the sounds of conflict.

The storm of battle was over, but the scenes that followed were more terrible by far than the first shock of arms had been; for now murder ran red-handed over the plains, and the demons of victory were, like wild beasts, ravenous for more blood.

Along that vast plain there was but one hope of escape; a broad swamp, teeming with Indians, lay between them and the mountains, who covered the ground above Forty Fort, and cut off the wretched men who turned that way; but Monockonok Island was almost in a line with the battlefield, and, though the river was swollen from a late freshet, to a good swimmer a passage was not impossible; from thence they escaped up a gully in the hills on the other side; and to this point the patriots made, in the frenzy of desperation.

As Catharine Montour and Tahmeroo came down the river, urged to breathless speed by the shrieks of dying men and the fiendish yells of their captors, fugitive after fugitive fled to the water; some were shot down before their eyes; some making superhuman efforts, swam for the island, and, dashing across, either escaped or perished on the other side; the savages followed them like demons; but their human game was too thick in the bushes of the shore for individual pursuit upon the river and when a man escaped that way the painted hounds sent a derisive yell after him, and turned to other bloody work.

The Tories were more relentless still; to them kindred blood gave zest to murder, and many a brother fell on that awful shore by the hands that had helped rock his cradle.

To this spot Grenville Murray came, while Catharine was toiling towards it in the gathering twilight. He had appealed to the Butlers, and expostulated with the savages, but all in vain; he might as well have attempted to force bloodhounds from their scent as persuade these monsters from their horrid work. So desperately were they urged by insatiate passion that torches were applied to their own fort, that the red glare of conflagration might give them light for more murder when the sun refused to look down upon their sickening cruelties.

Hopeless of doing good, and shocked to the soul by scenes into which he had been inadvertently thrown Murray turned to the island, hoping to find the missionary there, and unite with him in some project to save the prisoners yet left alive.

As he stood upon the shore, looking vaguely for some means of conveyance, a figure rushed by him, plunged into the water, and swam for life towards the nearest point of land; a half dozen Indians bounded after the man, shrieking and yelling out their disappointment. Directly a young man, black with powder and fierce as a tiger, sprang in among the savages, crying out:

"Have you got him? Give me the scalp—twenty-five guineas to the man who holds his scalp!"

The Indians pointed to the struggling man, now but dimly seen in the smoky twilight; Butler uttered a fierce oath, snatched a rifle from the nearest savage, and, levelling it with deliberate aim, fired—sending an oath forward with the bullet.

The fugitive sank, and his disappearance was greeted with another yell from the savages; but a moment after the head reappeared, and Edward Clark struggled up the banks of the willow cove and went towards the cabin, staggering either from exhaustion or some wound.

"I've missed him!" cried Butler, tossing the rifle back to its owner; "but we'll save that island, and all that's on it, for our night carouse. There is a little hunchbacked imp that you may have for your own humors, but as for that young rascal, and a girl that we shall find there, I don't give them up to any one. Now off again; here are more rats creeping to the river."

Murray had stopped behind a tree as the party came up and rushed away again, yelling and whooping as they went. He was about to throw off his coat, and attempt to spring into the river, and make for the island, when he was startled by footsteps and the quick, heavy breathing of persons in his neighborhood. He peered among the thick trees that towered around him, but could discern no one, though the sound of murmuring voices came distinctly to his ear.

"Thank God!" said a clear, female voice, in accents of deep feeling, "thank God! the horrid work has not commenced here; let us hasten to the fort—we may yet be in time!"

"No, mother, no," replied a voice of sadder melody; "if there is more bloodshed, it will be done on that little island. If my husband has a part in this, the fair girl whom I have seen gliding among the trees yonder, day by day, waiting his coming, that girl will be his victim; she must have angered him in some way. That beautiful girl was to have been married to-night, mother. Can you think why Butler should seek vengeance on her? Oh, you do not know all! You have not heard him whisper her name in his sleep, sometimes mingling it with endearments, and again with curses. You have not felt his heart beating beneath your arm, and know that it was burning with love, or hate born of love, for another. But why do we stand here? I do not wish her to die, and he shall not take her alive. Let us go and give them warning; is there no boat—nothing that will take us over?"

"Alas, no! what can we do?"

"Mother, help me pull off my robe; I can swim."

"Father of heaven! No; the distance is beyond your strength—the water is very deep!" exclaimed the first voice, in alarm.

"Mother, he shall not kill that angel girl—he shall not have the other. I am very strong; I *can* swim to that island; see, now the lights stream upon the water; it does not look so dangerous. Let me try!"

"Is there no other way?" exclaimed the answering voice. "I cannot consent to this risk; it may be death to you, my child!"

But while the words were on her mother's lips Tahmeroo flung off her robe, and with a wild leap, plunged far out into the waves, calling back:

"Stay there—do not move—I will come back with a canoe."

"My child—oh, Father of mercies! she is lost!"

"Not so, madam; she is light and self-possessed—have no fear," said Murray stepping out from the shadow in which he had stood.

Before Catharine could turn, or had distinctly heard his voice, a man rushed by her, with the bound of a wild animal, and plunged into the river. Catharine caught one glimpse at the wild face, but before she could catch her breath he was struggling with the current and his pursuers stood upon the bank. The men were both white, though the ferocity of fifty savages broke from the eyes which glared down upon the water, where that old friend was struggling.

"Come back, Lieutenant Shoemaker—come back!" cried the man upon the bank; "the current is too swift—you'll be lost; come on shore and I'll protect you."

The fugitive turned. That man had fed at his table; partaken of his wealth and his kindness; he belonged to the Tory army, and a word from him was safety. He was almost sinking, but these words of sweet charity brought him to life again; and swimming back to the shore, he held up his trembling hand to be dragged from the water. Windecker, for that was the demon's name, grasped the hand, whirled his tomahawk aloof, and buried it in that noble forehead, uplifted in gratitude towards him!

Catharine Montour uttered a shriek of horror; the fiend turned his face towards her with a sickening laugh, and, lifting the body of his benefactor half from the water, dashed him back, reddening the waves with his blood, and shouting:

"That's the way to serve traitors!"

All this happened so suddenly that the horror was perpetrated and the assassin had fled while Murray and Catharine were stunned by the shock.

When the atrocity came upon her in its force, Catharine sat down on the earth, sick and trembling, while Murray drew his sword, to cut the murderer down; but he plunged into the bushes and rushed off towards the fort, which was now one vast cloud of lurid smoke.

Murray returned to the bank just as Tahmeroo shot across the river in Mary Derwent's little craft, which she found in the cove.

"It was bravely thought of!" exclaimed Murray, stepping into the boat and drawing Catharine after him; "they must search for other boats, and this will give us time. Hah! they have completed their work at the fort. See!"

As he spoke, a volume of dusky light surged heavily across the river, and a spire of flame shot upwards, quivering and flashing, and flinging off smoke and embers, till the forest trees and the still waters gleamed red and dusky for miles about the burning fort. The poetry of Catharine Montour's nature was aroused by the fierce solemnity of this scene.

"See!" she cried, starting to her feet in the canoe, and pointing down the river, where the fire reflected itself like a vast banner of scarlet, torn, and mangled, and weltering in the waters. "See! the very river seems aflame—the woods and the mountains, all are kindling with light. Can a day of judgment be more terrible than that?"

She stood upright as she spoke, with one hand pointing down the stream. Her crimson robe floated out on the wind, and the jewelled serpent about her brow gleamed like a living thing in the red light which lay full upon her. As she stood there, the very priestess of the scene, her extended arm was grasped until the gemmed bracelet sunk into the flesh, and a face, pale and convulsed, was bent to hers.

"Woman—Caroline—Lady Granby! speak to me." The words died on Murray's lips; he remained with his grasp still fixed on her arm, and his eyes bent on her face, speechless as marble.

A wild, beautiful expression of joy shot over Catharine Montour's face; her heart leaped to the sound of her own name, and she started as if to fling herself upon his bosom. The impulse was but for an instant; her hand had quivered down to her side, but while his eyes were fixed on her face, it became calm and tranquil as a child's. She released herself gently from his grasp and sat down.

"Grenville Murray," she said, in a clear, steady voice; "for more than twenty years we have been dead to each other; do not disturb the ashes of the past. My child—my first-born child is in danger on that island. Help me to save her, and then let us part again forever and ever!"

The words were yet on her lips when a bullet whistled from the shore, and cut away the ruby crest of the serpent which lay upon her temple.

She fell forward at Murray's feet, stunned, but not otherwise injured. A moment, and she lifted her head.

"Who was shot? Was he killed?" she muttered, drawing her hand over her eyes, and striving to sit upright.

"The gentleman is safe, mother," said Tahmeroo, "and I—you hear me speak?—and I am well."

"Bless you, my brave girl! Grenville Murray, why are we here? There is death all around us! On, on!"

Murray had regained his self-command; he took up the oar which Tahmeroo had dropped, and urged the canoe forward with a steadiness that belied his pale face and trembling hands. Bullet after bullet cut along their track before they reached the island; but the distance became greater, and the aim of their pursuers was more uncertain.

They reached the little cove and sprung on shore. But they had scarcely touched the green sward, when the flames rushed up from the burning pile in a bright, lurid sheet of fire, revealing the opposite shore, and the forest far beyond, as if a volcano had burst among the mountains.

"Mother, look yonder!" said Tahmeroo, in a voice full of terror, which arose to little above a husky whisper, and she pointed to the opposite shore, where it lay in the full glare of the burning fort. A swarm of red warriors were gathered upon the steep banks, and lay crouching along the brink of the river, like a nest of demons, basking in the fire-light; and there, on the spot which they had just left, she saw her husband, standing with arms in his hands, stamping with rage as he saw them from the distance.

"We have landed on the wrong side of the island," said Catharine Montour, after a hasty glance at the demons swarming on the shore, and securing the cable of another boat that lay moored in the cove. "Tahmeroo, remain with this gentleman and warn the people at the house while I take the boat to the opposite side—there will be no escape within the range of their rifles."

"Caroline—Lady Granby, this must not be," said Murray, evidently forgetting their relative positions in the deep interest of the moment. "How are you to escape the rifle-balls which those fiends may level at you? for they are mad with blood, and fire on friends and foes alike. I will take the boats round while you and this young woman warn the people up yonder."

The familiar name which Murray had unconsciously used melted like dew over the heart that listened; but Catharine struggled against the feeling which almost made a child of her, even in that hour of danger. The thoughts of other years were swelling in her bosom, but there was calmness and decision in her voice as she answered him.

"The danger would be alike to either," she said; "nor could one person row the canoe and secure the others at the same time. I will go with you. My child, hasten to the house and warn them of their danger—keep within the bushes as you pass; send them down to the shore in small numbers; and, mark me, avoid bustle or appearance of alarm. Do you understand, and have you courage to go alone?"

The unhappy young woman stood with her face turned towards the shore; tears rolled down her cheek and dropped on her clasped hands while her mother was speaking.

"Yes, mother, I understand, and will save that poor girl—though he kill me, I will save her. I know the path; I have trodden it before," she replied, in a sorrowful and abstracted voice.

A low howl, like the prolonged cry of a pack of hungry wolves, fired her to action once more. She looked on her mother. "They have found some means of crossing," she said; "they will murder us when they see us warning their prey; but I will do it. Kiss me, mother—farewell!"

One wild kiss, a quick embrace, and Tahmeroo dashed up the path with the bound of a wild deer.

Catharine Montour turned wildly to her companion. "That cry! In—in!" she cried, vehemently, springing into the canoe. "They are upon the water; let them fire upon us if they will. Give me an oar; I can use one hand. Father of heaven! Did you hear that shout?"

Murray saw that no time was to be lost. He sprang to her side and steered round the island as rapidly as her impatient spirit could demand, though his superior coolness kept them from danger which she would have braved. By rowing close within the shadows of the island he escaped observation from the Indians; and those two persons who had been a destiny each to the other, sat alone, side by side, without speaking a word, and with scarcely a thought of each other. The lives of more than fifty persons were in peril, and among them Catharine had two children—the Indian girl, already on her path of mercy, and the gentle deformed, whom she was to call child for the first time.

They landed on the eastern shore of the island. Murray was drawing the canoes half on land, while Catharine dashed forward, expecting every instant to meet Tahmeroo with the family she had come to save. But instead of the females she sought, a half dozen men, white as death, with bloodshot eyes and hair erect with terror, dashed by, aiming for the gully on the eastern shore. They were fugitives from the battle, and reeled with the terrible exhaustion of swimming the river as they passed her with wild, staggering bounds.

They saw her Indian dress, swerved with a despairing cry, and fell upon their faces.

"On, on!" cried Catharine, waving her hand as she ran towards the house; "I am no enemy. In the name of heaven, save yourselves!"

They started up again, and rushed to the river—saw the canoes half in the water, half upon the land—pushed them into the stream, dashed Murray aside, and sent him reeling back against the trunk of a tree, when he attempted to interfere, and, tumbling over each other in desperate haste, pushed off, leaving the family on the island, and those who had come to save them, in a more desperate situation than ever.

CHAPTER XXVII
THE WARNING AND FLIGHT

All that day Mary Derwent, her grandmother, and sister remained alone in the house. They heard the mustering battle, the sharp strife, and the scattering horrors of the rout that followed. Towards nightfall the plain grew foggy from the smoke which began to rise and spread from the smouldering fort. The yells and sharp rifle-shots came close to the shore and rang with horrible distinctness over the island.

The two girls were on their knees by the window, looking out between the fragments of prayer which fell from their pale lips, and quaking from soul to limb, as the savage yells came nearer and nearer the shore.

Mother Derwent was affected differently, and, bringing down an old rusty rifle that had belonged to her son, set to work and scoured out the lock, and wiped the muzzle with a piece of oiled deer-skin, which she afterwards wrapped around her bullets when she was ready to load; and such a charge it was—what with powder, wadding, buck-shot, and bullets, the old rifle was as good as a cannon, only it was a great deal more likely to beat the old woman's brains out by vicious recoil than pour all that amount of lead upon the enemy. Still, Mother Derwent waxed valiant as the danger grew near, and, with every war-whoop, put in a new charge, pushing it down with a stick from her swifts, which was the best ramrod to be found, and waited for another whoop to load again.

"Come, gals, don't be sitting there, scared to death; that ain't no way to act in wartime. Don't you see my ammunition's give out a'ready? Bring out the pewter tea-pot, and I'll melt it down. Oh, marcy on us! here they are!"

The girls started up, looking wildly out of the window. A man came up the footpath, bounding towards the house, his clothes dripping wet, and water streaming from his hair.

"It is Edward Clark!" shrieked Jane Derwent, rushing towards the door.

"It is Edward," whispered Mary, with a throb of exquisite thankfulness.

Mother Derwent only heard footsteps rushing towards her cabin. Planting herself on the hearth, she lifted the rifle to her shoulder, and stood with her face to the door, ready to fire whenever the enemy appeared.

But the door burst open, and while she was tugging at the obstinate trigger, Edward Clark rushed by her, calling out:

"Flee to the east shore, one and all. A horde of savages are making for the river!"

While he spoke, half a dozen more fugitives came rushing up, followed by others, till fifteen or twenty men, too exhausted for swimming, and without other hope, turned at bay, and proceeded to barricade themselves in the cabin.

"You will not let them murder us?" gasped Jane Derwent, clinging to her lover with all the desperation of fear.

The young man strained her to his bosom, pressed a kiss upon her cold lips, and strove to tear himself from her arms; but she clung the more wildly to him in her terror, and he could not free himself.

"Jane," said a low, calm voice from the inner room, "come and let us stay together. The great God of heaven and earth is above us—He is powerful to save!"

Jane unwound her arms from her lover's neck, and tottered away to the foot of the bed where her sister was kneeling. There she buried her face in her hands and remained motionless; and none would have believed her alive, save that a shudder ran through her frame whenever a rifle-shot was heard from the river. A few moments of intense stillness—then a loud, fierce howl, appallingly near, and several rifles were discharged in quick succession. A paler hue fell on every stern face in that little phalanx; but they were desperate men, and stood ready for the death—pale and resolute.

The door was barricaded, and Edward Clark stationed himself at the window with his musket, and kept his eye steadily fixed on the path which led to the cove. But with all their precaution, one means of entrance had been forgotten. The window of Mary Derwent's bedroom remained open; and the basket of roses lay in it, shedding perfume abroad, sweetly as if human blood were not about to drench them.

The hush of expectation holding the pulsations of so many brave hearts caused Jane, paralyzed as she was with fear, to raise her face. Her eyes fell on the window—a scream broke from her, she grasped her sister's shoulder convulsively, and pointed with her right hand to a young Indian woman who stood looking upon them, with one hand on the window-sill. When she saw those two pale faces looking into hers, Tahmeroo beckoned with her fingers; but Jane only shrieked the more wildly, and again buried her face in the bed-clothes.

Mary arose from her knees, and walked firmly to the window, for she recognized Tahmeroo. A few eager whispers passed between them, and Mary went into the next room. There was a stir, the clang of a rifle striking the hearth, then the valorous woman rushed into the bedroom.

Tahmeroo had torn away the sash, and had leapt in—forcing the bewildered girl through the opening. When her charge was on the outer side, the young Indian cleared the window with the bound of an antelope, and dragged her on, calling on the rest to follow.

"Let the fair girl keep a good heart," whispered the Indian, urging her companion to swifter speed; "if we have a few moments more, all will be saved."

The words were scarcely uttered, when a blood-thirsty yell broke up from the cove: the war-whoop, the war-whoop!

"The boats are waiting—be quick! more can be done yet," cried Catharine Montour, as she rushed up from the river towards the house.

Oh, it was a horrid fight—that which raged around Mother Derwent's dwelling the next moment. A swarm of fiends seemed to have encompassed it, with shouts and yells, and fierce, blood-thirsty howling. The whizz of arrows, the crash of descending tomahawks, and the sharp rifle-shot, mingled horribly with the groans, the cries, and oaths of the murderers and the murdered. The floor of that log-house was heaped with the dying and the dead, yet the fight raged on with a fiercer and more blood-thirsty violence, till the savages prowled among the slain like a host of incarnate fiends, slaking their vengeance on the wounded and the dead, for want of other victims.

Through all this carnage the Moravian missionary passed unscathed, searching for his child. Many a fiery eye glared upon him; many a hatchet flashed over his head; but none descended. Another tall and lordly man there was, who rushed in the midst of the savages and strove in vain to put an end to the massacre. They turned in fury upon him. He snatched arms from a dead Indian, and defended himself bravely. Savage after savage rushed upon him, and he was nearly borne to the ground, when Catharine Montour sprung in the midst, with a bound of a wounded lioness, and flinging her arms about him, shouted:

"Back, fiends! back, I say. He is our brother."

The descending knife recoiled with the fierce hand that grasped it, and the savage darted away, searching for a new victim. That instant Queen Esther sprang upon them, the bloodless grey of her face looking more horrible from a glare of smouldering fire that broke up from the kitchen behind her.

She had just flung her tomahawk, but wrenched the stiletto from her torn robe. It flashed upward, quivered, and fell noiselessly as a blasted leaf descends. Catharine gasped heavily—again the knife descended. Murray felt a sharp pang, but so keen was the agony of feeling that woman on his bosom, so close, and yet so far away, that he was ignorant when the poniard entered his side.

He cleared the door with one spasmodic leap; and, as the dwelling burst into flames behind him, rushed toward the spring with his bleeding burden, nor slackened his speed till her arms relaxed their clasp, and her face fell forward on his breast. He felt the warm blood-drops falling upon his bosom, and pressed her closer to him, but with a shudder, as if they had been dropping upon his bare heart.

Down the tortuous path he staggered growing deathly sick as he sat down, folding her madly in his arms. He thought that it was the beat of her heart against his that made him so faint; but it was his own life ebbing slowly away through the wound Queen Esther had given him.

Meantime Tahmeroo urged her companion forward with an impulse sharpened by the sounds of conflict which followed them. Half-mad with contending feelings, Jane Derwent struggled in her conductor's hold, and would have rushed back in search of those she had left, could she have freed herself. But the young Indian kept a firm grasp on her arm, and dragged her resolutely toward the boats, regardless of her entreaties. They were too late; the canoes had put off.

When Mary saw her sister on her way to safety, she turned back and went in search of her grandmother, whom she found at bay on the hearthstone. She seized her by the arm, and pointing to the cellar door, dragged her down the ladder, closing the entrance after her. A hatch door opened into the garden, and through this the old woman and the girl fled into the open air.

The savages were rioting there, whirling firebrands snatched from the hearth, and striving to kindle the heavy logs into a conflagration. They saw

Mary, in her floating white dress, and fell back, gazing after her with dull awe through the smoke of their smouldering brands. Her deformity saved the old woman, for to them it was a mark from the Great Spirit, and to harm her would be sacrilege.

So the old woman and the angel girl passed through the savages unharmed; but there was more danger from the Tories, who shamed the heathen red men with coarser barbarities than they yet knew, for family ties were sacred to the Indian.

As the two females fled shorewards, many fugitives ran across the outskirts of the island, hiding among the vines and willows, or recklessly aiming for the eastern shore.

Among the rest, two men passed them; both were white and one was pursuing the other with desperate fury. One faltered and fell as he passed her, staggering to his knees as the other came up.

"Brother—brother! In the name of her who bore us, do not kill me!" shrieked the wretched man, looking with horror on the uplifted tomahawk. "I will be your slave—anything, everything, but do not kill me, brother!"

"Infernal traitor!"

The words hissed through his clenched teeth; the tomahawk whirled in the air, and came down with a dull crash! The fratricide fled onward—a brother's life had not satiated him.

Mary turned sick with horror.

"On, grandmother, on!" she called; "they will kill her, too, our sister!"

Jane saw them coming, sprang to her sister's arms, and began to plead in a voice of almost insane agony.

"Oh, Mary, let us go back and try to find him; we may as well all die together—for they *will* murder us!"

Tahmeroo parted them abruptly, and springing into the water, waded to a log which lay imbedded among the rushes, and rolled it into the current. It was scarcely afloat when a party of Indians came in sight, and, with a fierce whoop, rushed towards the little group. Tahmeroo sprang back upon the bank, pointing to the log.

"See, it floats! Fling yourself upon it—I will keep them back!"

She did not wait to see her directions obeyed, but walked firmly towards the savages.

Those three females made their way to the floating timber! Mary and Jane forced the old grandmother on it first, then placed themselves firmly on either side of her, and with a branch of driftwood, which Jane snatched from a thicket, pushed out on the deep river. The current, swift and strong, bore them onward, and with a terrible sense of vastness, they floated off into the night, leaving shrieks, the rattle of shot, and red flames, roaring and quivering where that old home had been.

The night had set in, but that red conflagration kindled up the waters and the dense woods with its lurid glare, which played about the bridal garments of the young girl, and that beautiful head, crowned with flowers, in fantastic contrast. The battle was over, but the yell of some savage, as he sprang on his victim, sounded horribly through the gathered stillness, and made those hapless females shrink closer together on their frail support.

Shuddering, and half-paralyzed by these horrors, and those they had just escaped, the little group drifted hopelessly on. But now a new fear crept over Mary, for she alone noticed the danger. As the pores of the timber gradually filled, its size became insufficient for their weight; every moment it was sinking lower and lower in the water. At first she was appalled, but after a moment the sublime bravery of her soul came back. The timber was heavy enough for two—the old granddame and that beautiful sister should be saved—as for her——

She looked down into the waters—deep, deep; the crimson of the distant fires warmed them up like blood; she could not give herself to them there; it was like bathing in a new horror. But soon the log floated nearer the shore, and carried them into deep shadows.

"Grandmother—Jane!"

"What, Mary, dear—are you frightened?" said the old woman.

"You speak strangely—has the cold chilled you through, sister?" questioned Jane, shivering herself in the chill night air.

"Grandmother—sister—you know where to go; when you come opposite Kingston, do your best to get on shore; run to Aunt Polly Carter's tavern, and hide till there is some chance of escape over the mountains. Do you listen, Jane?"

"Yes, yes; but you are with us—you will tell us how to act then."

Mary did not speak for a moment; a sob rose to her lips, but made no sound.

"It is well to understand," she said, faintly. "Grandmother?"

"Yes, Mary, but hold on; your arms fall away—you will slip off—hug me closer, Mary."

This Rock marks the spot where Queen Esther
slaughtered the Patriots in the battle of July, 1778.

The arms clung around her with sudden tightness; that pale face fell upon her shoulder, and a kiss touched her withered neck; one hand groped farther, and caught eagerly at Jane Derwent's dress.

"Jane—oh, sister Jane!"

"Don't, Mary; you almost pull me off."

The hand fell back.

"Mary—Mary—for mercy's sake, hold tight! Oh, dear—oh, Mary—Mary!"

"What—what is it? Grandmother, you make me tremble with these cries. Mary, don't frighten her so—she's old."

"She's gone—God forgive us two—she's gone—slipped off—drowned!"

Jane uttered a wild cry, and seizing the timber with both hands, strove madly to hold it back; but the current had them in its power, and mercilessly bore them on.

A cloud of white rose upon the water as they swept downward, sending back cries and shrieks of anguish. It sunk and rose again, this time nearer the shore. Then some human being, Indian or white, dashed through the brushwood, leaped into the stream, striking out for that mass of floating white. A plunge, a long, desperate pull, and the man was struggling up the bank, carrying Mary in his arms.

It was the missionary! He held her close to his heart; he warmed her cold face against his own, searching for life upon her lips, and thanking God with a burst of gratitude when he found it.

Mary stirred in his embrace. The beat of her arms on the waters had forced them to deal tenderly with her; and the breath had not yet left her bosom. For a moment she thought herself in heaven, and smiled pleasantly to know that he was with her. But a prolonged yell from the plain, followed by a slow and appalling death-chant, brought her to consciousness with a shock. She started up, swept back her hair, and looked off towards the sound. There she met a sight that drove all thoughts of heaven from her brain. A huge fragment of stone lay in the centre of a ring, from which the brushwood had been cut away, as an executioner shreds the tresses of a victim, in order to secure a clear blow. Around this rock sixteen prisoners were ranged, and behind them a ring of savages, each holding a victim pressed to the earth. And thus the doomed men sat face to face, waiting for death.

As she gazed, Queen Esther, the terrible priestess of that night, came from her work on Monockonok Island, followed by a train of Indians, savage as herself, and swelled the horrid scene. With her son's tomahawk gleaming in her hand, she struck into a dance, which had a horrid grace in it. With every third step the tomahawk fell, and a head rolled at her feet! The whole scene was lighted up by a huge fire, built from the brushwood cleared from the circle, and against this red light her figure rose awfully distinct. The folds of her long hair had broken loose and floated behind her, gleaming white and terrible; while the hard profile of her face cut sharply against the flames, like that of a fiend born of the conflagration.

Mary turned her eyes from this scene to the missionary: he understood the appeal.

"I will go," he said; "it may be to give up my life for theirs."

"And I," said Mary, with pale firmness—"God has smitten me with a great power."

She touched her deformed shoulder, as an angel might have pointed out its wings, and sped onward towards the scene of slaughter—her feet scarcely touched the earth. The missionary, with all his zeal, could hardly keep pace with her.

Queen Esther's death-chant increased in volume and fury as the chain of bleeding heads lengthened and circled along her tracks. Life after life had dropped before her, and but two were left when Mary Derwent forced herself through the belt of savages and sprang upon the rock.

"Warriors, stop the massacre—in the name of the Great Spirit, I command you!"

She spoke in the Indian tongue, which had been a familiar language since her childhood; her hand was uplifted; her eyes bright with inspiration; around her limbs the white garments clung like marble folds to a statue.

Queen Esther paused and looked up with the sneer of a demon in her eyes. But the Indians who held the men yet alive withdrew their hold, and fell upon their faces to the earth.

The two men crouched on the ground, numb with horror; they did not even see the being who had come to save them.

The missionary bent over them and whispered:

"Up and flee towards Forty Fort."

They sprang up and away. The Indians saw them, but did not move. Queen Esther heard their leap, and ended her chant in a long, low wail. Then she turned in her rage, and would have flung her tomahawk at the angel girl, but the Indians sprang upon the rock and guarded her with their uplifted weapons. Superstition, with them, was stronger than reverence for their demon queen.

The rage of that old woman was horrible. She prowled around the phalanx of savages like a tigress; menaced them with her weapons with impotent fury, and, springing on her horse, galloped through the forest by the smouldering fort and across the plain, until she came out opposite the little island where her son was buried. Her horse paused on the brink of the stream, white with foam and dripping with sweat, but she struck him with the flat of her tomahawk and he plunged in, bearing her to the island. Here she cast her steed loose, staggered up to the new-made grave, dropped a reeking tomahawk upon it, and fell down from pure physical exhaustion, bathed with blood, as a fiend is draped in flame.

As the aged demon took her way to that grave, the angel girl turned to her path of mercy. For that night the massacre was stayed. To the Indians she had appeared as a prophetess from the Great Spirit, who had laid his hand heavily upon her shoulder as a symbol of divine authority.

CHAPTER XXVIII
THE ISLAND GRAVE

The morning broke, with a quiet, holy light, through the thicket of crab-apple and wild-cherry trees which overlaced the spring in the centre of the island; and there, upon the blooming turf beneath, lay the form of Catharine Montour. Her eyes were closed, and the violet tint of exhaustion lay about them. The feathers which composed her coronet were crushed in a gorgeous mass beneath her pale temple, and her forehead was contracted with a slight frown, as if the serpent coiled around it were girding her brow too tightly. Ever and anon her pale hands clutched themselves deep into the moss, and her limbs writhed in the agony of her wounds. The pale, haggard face of Grenville Murray lay upon the moss where he had fallen when she dropped away from his arms, as it had done the whole night; and Varnham, the missionary, sat a little way off, looking mournfully on them both. There was a solemn and awful sorrow in his silence; yet something of cold sternness. He could not look on that pale, haughty man so near his wife, without some thought of the evil that had been done him.

On the swell of the bank, a short distance from the spring, crouched another miserable being. Tahmeroo sat upon the ground, looking upon her mother, in dreary desolation.

The expression of pain gradually cleared from Catharine Montour's face, and at last her eyes unclosed and turned upon Murray. She saw the death-drops on his forehead, and, struggling to her elbow, took his cold hand.

"Lady Granby, speak to me! In the name of God, I pray you, speak before it is too late. Say that I am forgiven!" he murmured.

There was a depth of agony in that voice which might have won forgiveness from the dead. Catharine Montour strove to speak, her lips moved, and her eyes filled with solemn light. Murray fell back and gave up her hand. Must he go into eternity with a doubt upon his soul!

"Caroline," said a low, broken voice, and a face full of anguish bent over her, "forgive this man, as I do, before he dies."

The hand which Varnham took was cold, but it moved with a faint clasp, and her eyes, which had opened again, turned with a confident and gentle expression upon the missionary's. A soft and almost holy smile, like that which slumbers about the sweet mouth of an infant, fell upon the lips of Catharine Montour, and a pleasant murmur, which was more than forgiveness, reached the dying man's ear.

"Great God, I thank thee that thou hast vouchsafed me the grace to forgive this man!" burst from the missionary; his face fell forward upon his bosom, and he wept aloud, as one who had found the great wish of a lifetime.

Murray turned his eyes, now freezing with death, upon Catharine's face; he saw that smile, and over his own features came a light that for one moment threw back the ashen shadows gathering there.

Varnham moved gently to his side, took the cold hand, and held it till it stiffened into the marble of death. Catharine watched his face as it saddened, shade by shade with the ebbing pulses that quivered under his touch. When she saw that all was over, a cold chill crept through her frame, the lids closed heavily over her eyes, and she was almost as lifeless as the man who had been her destiny.

Varnham laid the hands of the dead reverently down, and, lifting Catharine Montour in his arms, rested her head upon his bosom, while he called on Tahmeroo for water. She ran down to the spring, formed a cup with her two hands, and sprinkled the deathly face. But there came no signs of consciousness. She seemed utterly gone. Varnham knew that her heart was beating, for he felt it against his own, and for the moment a faintness crept over him; he forgot where he was, and that death lay close by; all the years and events that had separated those two souls floated away like mist; he bent down and whispered: "Caroline, my Caroline!" as he had done a thousand times when she was insane and unconscious as then of the love which had not died, which never could die.

"Caroline, my Caroline."

His head was bent, and his trembling lips almost touched her forehead; he heard nothing, saw nothing; an exclamation of surprise and alarm broke from Tahmeroo, but he was all unconscious of it till the form of Catharine Montour was torn from his arms by the chief, Gi-en-gwa-tah, who folded her to his broad chest, casting a look of sovereign disdain over his shoulder as he bore her away. A company of fifty Indians had followed him to the island, and when Varnham rose, dizzy with the sudden attack, they swarmed around him, offering no violence, but cutting off his retreat. When they left him at liberty again, he was alone with the body of his forgiven enemy.

In a little out-house that had escaped the flames Varnham found a spade and pickaxe. He left the body with Tahmeroo, and, going down to the old cedars, dug a grave with his own hands. Then, with the assistance of the Indian girl, he bore the body away, and laid it in the cold earth with unuttered prayers and awful reverence. The sods with which they heaped the earth that covered him were green, and the night dew was still upon them. But a drop fell upon that grave more pure than all the dew that trembled there. It was the tear of a man who had learned to forgive, as he hoped to be forgiven.

There was no hope for the people of Forty Fort, the stockade at Pittston had surrendered, Fort Jenkins was already taken, and from Wilkesbarre the inhabitants were fleeing to the hills. Thus, helpless and hopeless, the fugitives who had succeeded in reaching the fort with the women and children already there, had no choice between the terms of capitulation offered by Colonel John Butler and another massacre.

While the plain was strewn with the dead bodies of men who had marched forth from those gates so valiantly the day before, they were thrown open that the triumphant enemy might pass in. At the command of their colonel, the patriots came slowly forward and stacked their arms in the centre of the stockade. The women and children clustered in miserable groups, and stood in dead silence, waiting for the murderers of their sons and husbands.

The victors approached with beating drums and flying colors, divided in two columns. The Tories were headed by the Butlers, while in at the south gate marched the savages, with Queen Esther and Gi-en-gwa-tah at their head.

The faces of the Whigs were marked by the Indians with black paint, in order to insure their safety. The children retreated from this savage kindness with loud outcries; the pallid women passed before their captors, shrinking with horror from their touch.

"Ain't you ashamed, wimmen of Wyoming?" cried Aunt Polly Carter, marching boldly up to the tall savage who distributed the war-paint. "What are ye skeered at? I never expected to have the mark of Cain sat on my forehead by a wild Injun; but if I must, I must! Here, Mr. Copperhead, make it good and black. I don't want no mistake, if any of your chiefs should take a notion for more scalps; and I say, Mr. Injun, hold your head down here, while I whisper something. If you could just put an extra dab on, to let your men folks know I'm engaged, if they should want to marry any of our wimmen, I'd be much obleeged to you."

The Indian, who did not comprehend a word of all this, crossed his blackened stick on her cheek, gave her a push, and was ready for the next trembling creature that presented herself. As Aunt Polly took her place among the marked women, a little boy pulled her by the dress, and whispered that he had just seen Gineral Washington with an Injun on his back.

"Gineral Washington—my hoss—you don't say so?"

"Yes, Aunt Polly, his own self, with a big Injun a-riding him."

"He shan't ride him out of the fort, anyhow," exclaimed Polly. "Captain—Captain Walter Butler—I call on you to help me get my hoss back. One of them 'ere red fellers has stole Gineral Washington right afore my two eyes."

"I am afraid you will have to buy him back," replied Butler, laughing. "What can you give?"

"Give! I shan't give nothing for what's my own now I tell you."

"Then, I am afraid, you and the General will have to part."

The savages began to march out of the fort, and Aunt Polly followed in hot haste.

"Captain! captain!" she shrieked, "make the bargain for me—do; that's a good soul!"

Butler addressed a savage near him in his own tongue, and turned again to the old maid.

"Give him some money, Miss Carter, and you can have the horse."

"Money! pay money for a hoss that I've owned these twen—this long time!— Wal, that is a purty how-de-do, I must say."

But Butler's remonstrances and the sullen look of the Indian proved that she could not obtain the faithful animal on any other terms. That moment, the General looked towards his mistress, and, recognizing her with a low neigh of delight, Aunt Polly could not withstand that appeal. She put her hand in her bosom and drew forth an old shot-bag, as ruefully as if it had been her own heart, untied it, and took out the two guineas, her chief treasures. She eyed them ruefully, and was about to thrust them into the bag again, when the General, sagacious animal, whinnied. Aunt Polly grasped one of the pieces, and thrust the rest into her bosom.

"Perhaps you could persuade him to take a string of beads, or some gew-gaw instead," whispered Butler, rather pitying her distress.

"Lawful sakes," cried the old maid, joyfully. "I've got just the purtiest string; stand in front of me, captain, and turn your back, while I loosen my dress, so as to get 'em off."

Butler obeyed, laughing heartily, and Aunt Polly hurriedly untied a string of bright blue glass beads, and held them up before the Indian, who gave a humph of delight, and snatched them from her hand, at the same moment. Aunt Polly darted towards the General, slipped the bridle over her arm, and rushed back into the fort with the old horse trotting behind her; she reached a safe corner, and sat down on the ground, fairly hysterical with tears and laughter.

"Oh, Gin'ral, Gin'ral Washington, I should have died if I'd lost you—I know I should! He! he! only to think how I cheated the feller—poor old Gin'ral, you're thin as a shad! A string of old blue beads, that wasn't worth ten coppers—try agin, when you want to cheat a born Connecticut woman, you red varmint you."

When the Tories and savages had fairly disappeared Aunt Polly was among the first to leave the fort.

"Wal," she said to the bystanders, as she mounted on the General, with the aid of a broken bench, "I've lost my saddle; but, thank goodness, I can ride bare-back. But where's Captain Slocum? he hain't said a word about that 'ere rum."

The unhappy inmates of the fort were too much occupied with their own griefs to heed these pathetic lamentations, and Aunt Polly rode briskly away, muttering confusedly of her losses, and her delight at rescuing the General at so little cost.

Her heart sank when she drew near her own house, for she had passed nothing but smoking cabins all the way; but a sudden rise of ground revealed it, standing and unharmed. As she galloped up to the door, Sim White, looking really glad, came out to meet her, while Mother Derwent and Jane appeared in the doorway.

"All safe!" cried Aunt Polly, springing to the ground. "Where's Mary, and the minister?"

"Mary is on the bed, worn out with last night's work," began the old lady, but Aunt Polly did not pause to hear her out.

"Sim, take the Gin'ral, feed him well—and, Sim—you may kiss me. I don't care if Grandmother Derwent and Jane do see you."

Sim gave her a hearty embrace, and they all entered the house, where Aunt Polly related all that had happened, and, bringing out a blacking-brush, insisted on marking all their faces like her own.

But this quiet lasted only a few hours. The Indians, in total disregard of the terms of the capitulation, began plundering and setting on fire all the houses in the district.

CHAPTER XXIX
THE DOUBLE WEDDING

In a few hours after Aunt Polly's return home, the missionary came to the tavern, looking more haggard than he had ever appeared before. He inquired in a tremulous voice after Mary, and when he found her lying pale and exhausted on Aunt Polly's bed, but with an expression of sublime thankfulness on her face, the tears absolutely swelled into his eyes.

"Are you ill—are you hurt?" inquired the young girl, reaching forth her hand.

He shook his head mournfully.

"And the lady—that beautiful white queen—did you find her at last? I was almost sure that she passed me as I ran towards the river; but you could not believe it. Oh, tell me, did you hear nothing about her or the Indian girl?"

"I saw them both; one is unhurt, the other——"

"The other—not her, not her! Oh, do not tell me that she has come to harm!"

"I found her wounded—not mortally, I hope and believe; but she was forced from me while insensible, and carried away by the savages; but God is merciful, my child, and she has learned to trust in Him."

Mary had turned her face on the pillow, and was weeping bitterly.

"Mary, my child, be comforted."

His voice thrilled her soul with its sorrowful tenderness.

"My child! Oh, that is a sweet, holy word. She called me her child in the same way, and my heart trembled within me, as it does now."

The missionary stretched forth his arms, as if to gather the gentle girl to his bosom, but checked himself with an effort that shook his whole frame, and seating himself by the bed, began to talk hopefully to her.

"You are safe here, at least for the present," he said. "Young Butler has taken this house under his protection from some kindness to the landlady; but your sister Jane will endanger everything. Clark has escaped to Wilkesbarre; he must not rest there—Butler would burn every house in the village to reach him. Tell your sister to be in readiness for instant flight. I will seek for Edward Clark, bring him here, and perform the marriage ceremony, that they can depart in company, and join the unhappy fugitives that are now in the mountains."

Mary arose at once.

"We will be ready," she said, with quiet firmness.

"No, not you, or the old lady; for you, there is no danger."

"But my sister?"

"She will be with her husband, and I have need of you."

A faint flush rose to Mary's cheek. Spite of danger and death, her heart would betray its secret in that delicate color.

"I have great need of you, for we must seek out that strange lady together."

Her eyes brightened.

"Seek her? can we ever hope to know who she is, and why she affects every one so strangely?"

"Yes. You shall learn everything soon, Mary—only be patient and trust in me a little longer. Now, farewell for an hour or so. Tell Jane to have all things in readiness against my return."

"We will obey you," she replied; and without speaking to the rest, he left the house.

When Aunt Polly heard the object of his visit she was greatly excited. If it were dangerous for an individual to remain single in such perilous times, she thought, for her part, that one person was just as much to be considered as another.

She wasn't so certain of her house being kept over her head, and if her visitors couldn't feel safe without getting married, she certainly should be scared out of her seven senses. Just as if Butler wouldn't have as much spite against any other single woman as Jane Derwent—indeed!

Sim, who had just come from the barn, where he had bountifully provided for General Washington, heard the latter part of this speech with some dismay, but recovered himself immediately, and signified that he was ready to stand up to the mark whenever Miss Carter spoke the word.

Directly there was such a rummaging in the old chest of drawers, upstairs, as hadn't been known since they first held that setting out. Half a dozen old silk dresses were taken out and tried on; a new pair of morocco shoes were fitted over the fine homespun stockings, provided for this interesting occasion thirty years before, and, after a reasonable delay, the energetic spinster made her appearance clothed in a light green silk, with a waist three inches long under the arms, and a skirt gored like an umbrella cover. The dainty fashion with which she entered the room where Jane Derwent sat, in her soiled and dreary-looking white dress, would have made even the missionary smile, had he been there, heavy as his heart was.

"I calkerlate they won't find us back'ards in getting ready, Jane," she observed, seating herself with great dignity; "you don't happen to know if Mr. White has gone upstairs—do ye?"

Here Sim appeared at the door, with his best homespun coat on, and a broad ruffle, plaited by Miss Polly's own fingers, fluttering from his bosom like a fan.

Aunt Polly rewarded this prompt devotion with an approving nod, settled the skirt of her dress, and observed to Jane that the minister seemed to be a long time in coming.

Jane answered with a faint smile that deepened to a look of sorrowful delight as she saw Edward Clark and the missionary coming through the door-yard gate. Mrs. Derwent and Mary came in, and a brief ceremony united the couple whose wedding had been so fearfully disturbed the day before.

Then Aunt Polly arose, and observed to the minister that, seeing as everything was so unsartin in wartime, he might as well kill two birds with one stone.

The missionary was too much troubled for a smile, but gravely performed the required ceremony which made Miss Polly Carter Mrs. Simon White, and placed that inestimable lady on the pinnacle of human felicity, even in that region of death and sorrow.

Two horses had been provided for Clark and his bride, and within half an hour after their marriage they were on their route to the mountains, over which half the inhabitants of the valley were wandering, houseless, wretched, and desolate, soul and body.

Aunt Polly, whose fears had entirely left her after she became Mrs. White, insisted upon supplying Jane with a warm shawl and a homespun dress, with a pillow-case full of biscuits, dried beef, and doughnuts. Indeed, that little ceremony had so completely opened her heart that she made no objections when the missionary proposed to fill a flour-bag with similar food, which he would place upon the back of General Washington, and himself convey to the mountains, for without such help he knew well that starvation must fall upon the unhappy fugitives.

A few hours after, the newly married couple and the missionary were deep in the Pocono Mountains—the young people flying for their lives, the minister eager to carry help to those who were ready to perish. It was after dark when they came upon the great body of fugitives, and oh! it was a terrible sight! More than a hundred women and children, with but one man to guide them, were struggling up the steep ascent of the hills, some pausing to look upon the valley they had left, which their burning homes made a wilderness of fire, others rushing wildly forward towards the gloomy swamp where so many were to perish, afraid to look behind them lest some savage might spring from the thicket and snatch the little children from their arms. Women, so young in widowhood that they could not yet realize their loneliness, would turn with vague hope to see if the beloved one was not following them into the wilderness. Old women, more helpless than the little ones, would toil up those steep ascents with uncomplaining patience.

Among the group came a mother carrying a lifeless infant in her arms, where it had died against her bosom. She could not stay behind long enough to dig a grave for the little one, and so folded the precious clay to her heart and toiled onward. These wretched women had fled from their burning homes without time for preparation; most of them were without food, and now the pangs of hunger gnawed away the little strength that terror had left to them. One by one the faint and the feeble dropped off and were left to perish. Children wandered away into the swampy grounds, and never came forth again. Old people sat down patiently on the rocks and fallen trees, and saw themselves abandoned without complaint.

As the missionary and his companions penetrated the mountains, they found these wretched beings perishing in their path. The minister raised them up, fed them from his stores of food, and let them ride, by turns, upon the horses, from which the young and strong dismounted.

When they came up with the main body, it had halted, for rest. The little ones were clamoring for food, while the widowed mothers had nothing but tears to give in answer to their cries.

Into this scene of misery the minister brought his horse, laden with food, and while the tears stood in his eyes, distributed it. This kindness gave life and hope to them all.

At midnight the whole company lay down to rest, and the sleep of exhaustion fell upon them. Then, in the stillness of the woods, rose a wail, the faint, faint voice of a human soul born in the midnight of the wilderness, amid tears and desolation. It was a mournful sound, the first cry of human innocence trembling along that track of human guilt. When the weary sleepers awoke, and prepared to move on, that pale mother folded this blessed sorrow to her bosom, and prepared to keep her place with the rest, but Jane gave up her horse to the sufferer, and toiled on, side by side with her young husband, made happy, almost for the first time in her life, by conferring help on others.

At daybreak the missionary, having distributed his last morsel of food, bade the unhappy wanderers farewell, and returned, with a heavy heart, to the valley.

At last the Tories, accompanied by their leaders and a greater part of the Indians under the command of Gi-en-gwa-tah and Queen Esther, marched out of the valley. Mingling with the mournful savageness of the scene there was much that was droll and ludicrous. The squaws who followed the retiring invaders were decked with the spoils taken from the burning houses, the more fortunate wearing five or six silk and chintz dresses, one over the other, and above these dropped the scalps taken from their victims, which served as hideous fringes to their new costume. Many of them were mounted on stolen horses, and one old woman rode proudly in advance upon the identical side-saddle which had so long been the chief treasure of Aunt Polly's mansion; upon her head were perched half a dozen head-dresses of every size and hue, the old maid's immense bonnet crowning the whole, its yellow streamers floating out on the wind with every movement of the delighted wearer.

Catharine Montour, still in the dull delirium of fever, was carried on a litter in their midst, but neither the chief nor Queen Esther ever approached it. The old queen, from time to time, cast glances of malignant passion towards the unconscious victim of their cruelty, while Gi-en-gwa-tah rode on in stern impassibility.

Tahmeroo rode by her husband's side, and as he smiled upon her, she forgot all the suffering and horror of the past days, looking up into his face with proud affection, and bending to catch each passing glance. Butler treated her kindly now, and her love for him had recovered its first bewildering intensity; but at length her presence wearied him—he wished to converse with the chief and Queen Esther. Before the discovery of the secret which made her so precious to him, Butler would have sent her rudely away; but now he employed art instead of cruelty.

"You ought not to leave your mother so long," he said; "she may rouse up and require something."

"I have been cruel," said Tahmeroo, with a pang of self-reproach. "Will you ride back with me?"

"I will join you very soon, my red bird; but now I must talk with the chief."

Tahmeroo looked disappointed, but he patted her cheek and smiled so kindly, that she would have gone to the ends of the earth at his bidding. Without a word she rode back to the side of her mother's litter, and kept her station there.

Butler's eyes followed her, and his glance rested with malignant cruelty upon the litter.

"They say she is better," he muttered; "why didn't she die, and make an end of it? Then Tahmeroo would have been Lady Granby, and I an English landholder, with an income that dukes might envy. She shall not stand between me and this fortune; I'll pay her off, too, for all her scorn and hatred!"

He galloped up to Queen Esther as she rode, in gloomy silence, at the head of her warriors. The fury still smoldering in her eyes showed that her vengeance was not yet satisfied. Bloodshed only made her crave more, and she awaited a new opportunity to wreak her hate upon the people who had deprived her of a son.

"They tell me Catharine Montour is better," Butler said, abruptly, as he drew his horse close to hers, that their conversation could not be overheard.

Queen Esther did not reply, but her lips compressed until the hooked nose and projecting chin almost met.

"You must be satisfied now that my suspicions are true—she is a traitress, and was from the beginning."

"And will meet the fate of all traitors!" returned Esther, in a voice of terrible composure.

"But the chief is so blindly attached to his wife that he will not allow you to punish her as she deserves."

"Allow me!" The gladiator rushed into the woman's eyes. "I am Queen Esther; who dares dispute my will? I would drive Gi-en-gwa-tah himself out of the tribe if he opposed me!"

"Pleasant old devil!" muttered Butler; "I think I shan't have much trouble in waking her up!" He bowed his head, saying aloud: "I know that Queen Esther is all-powerful."

"You leave us soon?" she asked, without heeding his flattery.

"Yes. I must accompany my father and his men to Niagara—we shall find work enough there."

"Go; if you return with new victories, you will be welcome."

"Never fear; I shall do my best. Tahmeroo stays behind; she would only be in my way. I hope when I get back I shan't find Catharine Montour with all her old insolence and power opposed to you."

Queen Esther laid her hand on his arm; her lips moved, but she checked her utterance, though the light in her eyes revealed the murderess in her soul. Making a gesture to Butler, signifying that their conference had ended, she rode on, followed by her troops.

On the fifth day the armies separated; the Tories, under the command of the two Butlers, marching in the direction of Niagara, while the Indians continued their course towards Seneca Lake.

Tahmeroo was wild with grief at parting from her husband, but he promised a speedy return, and quieted her with elaborate kindness. After he had left them, Catharine required all her care, and she had little time to brood over her loneliness.

Catharine Montour's condition was a most critical one, and for days she hovered between life and death; but the chief never inquired after her, or paused, except for their accustomed rest. When Catharine came back to consciousness, she was far away from Wyoming. For a while she believed that all had been a dream; but at length thought came more clearly back, and with it remembrance. She started feebly up, with a faint cry for her child.

Tahmeroo heard the voice, and parting the curtains of the litter, said:

"I am here, mother."

"Not you," murmured the sufferer—"it is not you I call for."

She fell back on the pillows, too weak for words, powerless even to think collectedly. Day after day she remained thus, with life struggling feebly for supremacy, listening to Tahmeroo's conversation, or the hollow tramp of the savages who bore her swiftly on. She only remembered that Murray was dead, his cold face seemed lying forever on the pillow close to hers. She had a child—a husband—both lived, and she was separated from them, perhaps to all eternity. It was better thus, she felt almost a sense of relief in that rapid retreat—another meeting with husband or child, or even a clear thought of one who had been so closely linked with her past history, would have brought back the madness which a free life in the forest had so long kept at bay.

What mournful hours she spent thus! Unable to wrestle with her anguish, it lay like a weight upon her heart—every beautiful hope that had brightened her other life was dead, eternally dead, now. It was well that she could look upon her early years almost as another existence, and the broad ocean which rolled between her and that distant home as the tideless sea that separates time from eternity. When her fever would return and fill her mind with strange fancies, she believed that it was indeed eternity in which she groped; that the darkness must be everlasting. At such times she would call aloud upon Mary, her angel child, and, as that face seemed to rise before her in its loveliness, she would grow calm again, and fall asleep, taking those features into her dreams to brighten their dreariness. A fortnight elapsed before they reached the settlement at Seneca Lake. Catharine was borne to her house, accompanied by Tahmeroo; but Queen Esther went directly up to her gloomy palace, and the chief joined the general encampment of his tribe.

The summer months waned and deepened into the gorgeous brightness of autumn before Catharine Montour was able to leave her house. After that, accompanied by Tahmeroo, she would take short rambles in the forest, or the Indian girl would pile a bed of skins in her canoe, and row her about the lake for hours, seeming by instinct to understand her mood, talking to her in that pleasant young voice, or bending over her oars in silence, and allowing Catharine to recline in thought upon her couch whenever she saw her disinclined for conversation.

The girl became dearer than ever to the chastened woman, but Catharine would not think of her as her daughter—with that name rose the image of the pale girl far away, and her heart yearned towards her with all its remaining life. Tahmeroo was henceforth her friend, her young sister, but never again her child. To her, the thought was sacrilege.

Catharine's strength came slowly back, but her hard, proud nature was gone forever. She had grown meek and humble as a child; grateful for affection, almost timid in her new womanliness. Gi-en-gwa-tah was absent, and Queen Esther kept aloof. This was a great relief, for in the silence of her home she could sometimes forget the reality around her. She suffered continually, but it was no longer the stern, bitter conflict of former days— her heart bowed beneath the rod of the chastener and found solace in new and holier aspirations.

Keen self-reproach she was also forced to endure, though her marriage with the chief had been an innocent one, for she had solemnly believed her husband dead, it pressed upon her soul like a premeditated sin. Besides, Murray's terrible death tortured her continually. In the stillness of that awful night he had told her of his regrets, his broken life and loveless age. His wife and child were dead, and with the curse of unrest upon him, he had come a second time to America, accepting a commission from the ministry, but with no belief that she was yet alive.

Since the day of his marriage he had never seen her, and when the fact of her existence, and of the terrible sacrifice she had made for his sake, was so coarsely revealed to him at the table of Sir John Johnson, he had started at once to find her and crave the forgiveness without which he could never hope for rest.

He had reached Seneca Lake two days after the tribe set forth for Wyoming, and following rapidly as possible met her there; but only to die.

With mournful distinctness Catharine remembered every word those dying lips had uttered. She knew that her husband had appeared with the first dawn, and that they three were together again, sitting silently in the valley of the shadow of death. These terrible memories kept back her strength. Queen Esther's poniard seemed still in her bosom, rusting closer to her heart each day. She had but one wish on earth, an unquenchable thirst for the company of her child. To accomplish this, she would go on her knees to Varnham, and then die.

Late in the fall, while Catharine was yet very feeble, she was startled by the sudden presence of Butler in the settlement. He had come with a troop of soldiers to convey his wife into Canada, where she was to be left under the care of Sir John Johnson and his lady, while his father's troop lay on the frontier.

Butler did not deign to soften this cruel blow to the woman whose child, and sole companion, he was tearing away; but sent for Tahmeroo to meet him at her grandmother's mansion. The young wife, selfish in her joy, ran eagerly to Catharine's chamber.

"Oh, mother, he has come; I shall see him this very hour—he loves me, he loves me—and will take me with him now."

Catharine listened in pale silence. Was nothing on earth to be left for her? Must she be utterly deserted and alone with her sorrow?

Tahmeroo's better nature arose at once.

"But my mother; how can I leave you, so ill, so sorrowful? Tahmeroo will not forsake her mother."

"You will start to-night!" said Queen Esther, abruptly entering the lodge.

"It is sudden—I am not prepared to part with Tahmeroo at an hour's warning," said Catharine.

"You go to-night," repeated Esther, addressing Tahmeroo as if her mother were not in the room.

Tahmeroo's proud spirit revolted at this tyranny, and she replied with flashing eyes:

"Tahmeroo is the chief's daughter. Queen Esther has no power to drive her out of her father's tribe; she will not go if Catharine Montour wishes her to remain."

"Traitor, and child of a traitor," muttered Esther; but Tahmeroo turned to her mother.

"Shall I go or stay, mother? I will do as you bid me."

Catharine looked at her with sad affection; she saw the wild hope breaking through all the anger in those flashing eyes, and would not quench it.

"Go where your heart is," she replied, "and be happy."

"But you will miss me?"

"I shall know that you are happy; it will not be for long—you will soon come back again."

Queen Esther turned abruptly and left the lodge.

An hour passed in sorrowful conversation. Then they were disturbed by the appearance of Butler's soldiers, leading Tahmeroo's horse in their midst. The girl clung, weeping, to her mother.

Catharine pressed her once more to her bosom.

"Go," she murmured; "and if we never meet again, remember how fondly I have loved you, and all that I have said."

Tahmeroo sprang on to her horse with a burst of tears, and rode away. Catharine stood watching her from the door of her lodge. As the train reached a turn in the path, Tahmeroo checked her courser, and looked back, waving her hand in a last farewell. Catharine returned the signal, and the band disappeared, leaving the childless woman gazing sorrowfully after them through the windings of the forest.

Still Gi-en-gwa-tah was absent with the body of his warriors, which, at Colonel Butler's request, were active on the frontier of Canada. For the time Queen Esther was supreme in the settlement.

CHAPTER XXX
THE FATHER AND THE DAUGHTER

An Indian war-trail lay along the southern bank of Seneca Lake, scarcely discernible now that the snow was deep, and the trees shivering in the wind; but a man accustomed to the woods might have found sure indications of a path in the deep notches cut in the larger trees at equal distances, and in the broken boughs of hemlock and pine that fell here and there like banners over the buried path.

Through the still woods, and across the glittering snow, came a small party on horseback, toiling onward with a dull, patient movement, which was evidently the result of a long journey and severe weather. The party consisted of three men and a female, so muffled in fur, and shielded from the cold that it was impossible to judge of their condition. The female seemed like a little child, she sat so low on the horse; but the face which looked out from its hood of dark blue silk was more like that of a cherub than a human being.

Two men rode in front; one was evidently a guide, the other led a horse on which a canvas tent was packed, while the third, who seemed master of the party, kept close to the female, and every moment or two caught her horse by the bridle when he sank through the snow, or carefully folded the fur mantle about her form, that she might not be chilled by the keen wind which kept the naked trees above them in a continual wail and shiver, inexpressibly saddening.

"Are you very cold, my child?" inquired the man, looking with tender anxiety into that lovely face.

"Cold—no. This fur mantle is warm. I am not near so chilled as I was yesterday, when the storm overtook us," she replied.

"Do not be discouraged. This stretch of snow is like a desert, but the guide says we cannot be more than twenty miles from the settlement now, and part of the way is along the shore, where the Indians will have beaten a path. If our horses do not break down under all this heavy toil, we shall be there to-night."

"My father," said Mary Derwent, with a slight quiver in her voice, for her heart rose painfully with the question, "who is the lady whom we are searching for? Was it her name you called upon when we seemed perishing in the storm? Why is it that my breath comes quick when I think of her, and that I seem so lonesome when you speak as if she might be dead? Who is she, father—what am I to her?"

"She is your mother, Mary."

"My mother?"

"She is your mother, and was once my wife; for, as truly as there is a God to bless you, Mary, I am your father, not in name alone, but in the sight of Heaven."

Mary was not even surprised, she could not remember the time when the man supposed to be her father had been half so dear as the one before her. She reached out her hand, took that outstretched by the missionary, and, bending forward, kissed it with tender reverence.

"My father!"

The word never sounded so holy and sweet before; tears swelled to the missionary's eyes; a drop or two trembled on Mary's lashes, and froze as they fell away like pearls thrown up by the troubled waters of her heart.

"And now may I talk of my mother?—my mother," she repeated, with a gush of ineffable tenderness—"that is a new word."

"It is a holy name, my daughter; when you were born it kept me from thinking if the angels had any music as sweet."

"But my mother? I cannot understand—Jane—my grandmother?"

"They have been very kind, and Jane believes you to be her sister. The old woman kept my secret faithfully; Derwent was my loyal friend to the last."

"But why was it a secret—why did this lady, my mother, let me live all these years and never speak to me but once?"

"She did not know that you were alive. She believed you resting in the tomb of her family in England, sent there by her own hand."

"But why should any one keep a parent from her child—a poor, little girl, so helpless as I am, from the sight of her own mother?"

"I could not find her. For years and years I travelled through these forests, searching for her in every savage tribe, for she was not in her right mind, Mary, when she fled from her home; and I would have given my life to have carried her back to her country, and guarded her helplessness again. But she had taken another name—the name which that terrible Queen Esther had cast off, but by which she was still known among the whites. At first I hoped to find my lost wife in this Catharine Montour, but they spoke of her as a half-breed, already grey with age, and it was not till the council-fire at Wyoming that I found your mother bearing the cast-off name of that terrible woman."

"But you saw her then?"

"Yes, as the dead might come back and find the living forever lost to them. She had heard of the shipwreck in which I was reported to have been cast away, and believed herself free. Mary, she must have been insane still, wildly insane, for against her own wishes, and fired with terrible magnanimity, she became the wife of Gi-en-gwa-tah, the Shawnee chief—the mother of that wild girl who came to us on the island."

Mary shuddered. "Oh, this is terrible! My mother, my mother!"

"She believed me dead—she believed that you, my child, had perished by her own hand, for in the wild fancy that you were an angel that could help her up to heaven, she seized you in her arms one day and dropped you from the high window of the room in which we had confined her. We took you up, crushed and senseless, maimed, hopelessly maimed for life."

"And she—did my own mother do this?" said Mary, looking down at her person. "Was I straight like other children before that?"

"Paradise itself had not a more lovely child. She never saw you again till you lay upon her bosom at the spring on Monockonok Island, without knowing that you were her own child. I did not tell her then—how could I say to the wife of that stern chief—to the mother of that wild forest maiden: 'Behold! here is the husband and child whom you believed dead, rising up in judgment against you for this unnatural marriage?' It would have driven her mad again. Still, I would have done it, after prayer and reflection—for it was a solemn duty; but when I sought for her at the foot of Campbell's Ledge she was gone. Mary, I was ill after that, very ill for a long time, and unable to follow her; but we met face to face in that terrible massacre, and I told her all."

"Then she knows that I am her child; she will be wondering where I am, waiting for me."

"Mary," said the missionary, regarding her excitement with a troubled look, "Mary, your mother was terribly wounded on the island that night—wounded twice—for while the battle was raging she learned that her husband and child lived—then Queen Esther's poniard struck her down."

"Oh, my mother—my mother!" cried Mary.

"Let us be calm; I have heard from her twice; she was slowly recovering."

"Oh, God is very good to us! In a little time I shall see her! we will take her away from these savages; no one shall tend her but myself; I am her oldest child; never till now did I know what a mother was; how pleasant the sound, when you can say father, and know it has a meaning. Father, when I was so lonely, why did you never say: 'Mary—Mary Derwent, you are my own, own child?' I could have borne everything after that."

"I dared not. The love of one being had filled my soul with the sin idolatry; God allowed me to be smitten through my heart and through my pride; but I could neither cast off the love nor the resentment which a wrong that has no name, and which you could never understand, fastened like a viper on my heart. I dared not give up my soul to another worship, and thus offer a feeble service to my God. Besides, but you will not comprehend this, the very sight of you filled me with a tenderness so painful that I had no power to speak. Until I had ceased to hate my enemy I could not love her child without a pang of self-reproach."

"But you love me now?"

The missionary smiled.

"Love you! I thank my God there is nothing but love in my heart—love and forgiveness. I ask but to place you in her arms, and leave the rest with Him."

Mary looked eagerly forward; the night was closing in; and through the leafless hickory and beech trees a red sunset streamed along their path.

"It cannot be far off," she said, with kindling eyes; "let us keep on, father—all night, if it takes so long. I shall never get warm again till her arms fold me. Look, the moon is rising; shall we get off and walk by its light? the snow-crust is strong enough to hold us, though our horses sink through it. Father, I feel as if some one wanted me and I must come."

Varnham dismounted, and left their horses with the guides. He, too, was stricken with a sudden impulse to press forward and penetrate towards the lake. They walked on at a rapid pace across the gleaming snow-crust, where all the naked branches and innumerable twigs of the forest were pencilled by the moonlight; the hacked oaks guided their way; and the winds in the distant hemlocks moaned after the father and child as they passed.

The first snow of winter had fallen, and lay heavily upon the forest. The lake was frozen, till it shone like a sheet of rock crystal. The Indians left behind by the chief amused themselves in skating, and catching fish through holes cut in the ice. Gi-en-gwa-tah had not yet returned, and Catharine received no tidings of Tahmeroo. Once she sent to Queen Esther's house to make inquiries, but the old woman vouchsafed no answer; and Catharine was left alone with her feebleness and her weary heart.

One day she sat in her lonely lodge, looking out upon the lake. The wind moaned through the forest; the air was keen and sharp with sparks of frost; flakes of snow came down at intervals, but it was too cold for a heavy fall. Catharine Montour was more oppressed than usual; there was a strange trouble at her heart, and she felt that danger menaced her—or, possibly, her child, in some more terrible form. For herself she did not fear; but the thought of harm to Tahmeroo or Mary wrung her heart with anguish. The day wore on, and the night followed cold, still and icy. The moon was high in heaven, flooding the frozen lake with silver, and turning the snow-wreaths to garlands of pearls. Still Catharine sat looking forth, listening to the dirge-like moan of the pine forest with dreary thoughtfulness.

All was strangely still; the silence had something awful in it. The coldness about the watcher's heart grew deeper, till it seemed as if the frosty air from without had penetrated to her soul. The silence became insupportable at length; she arose and passed through the different rooms; not an attendant was in sight; she looked out, searching for the guard which always surrounded her lodge; it had disappeared; not an Indian was to be seen.

The stillness seemed to increase—even the low wind died away, and the beating of her own heart sounded to Catharine like the ticking of a clock in the gloom. The fire had died down, and the apartment was lighted only by the moonbeams that crept in at the casement, and poured their ghostly pallor upon the floor.

Catharine could endure it no longer—torment, death, anything, were preferable to that fearful suspense. She folded a fur mantle about her and went out, taking the path which led to the settlement. Midway between the Indian village and Queen Esther's mansion she saw the flame of a council-fire turning the snow golden with its brightness; seated about it were the old men of the tribe, whom the chief had left behind, with Queen Esther in their midst.

Catharine drew nearer, and from the rise of ground upon which she stood looked fearfully down upon the scene.

It was a strange sight: that blazing council-fire streaming far up in the heavens; that circle of stern warriors gathered about it, silent and motionless, with that grim woman in their midst, evidently speaking, though she made no movement or gesture. In the outskirts of the group hovered some young men and women of the tribe, with signs of awe breaking through the natural impassibility of their features.

Catharine drew closer still, and concealed from view by a massy hemlock, listened to what was passing.

"Drive her forth!" said the old queen, in her low, terrible voice; "a traitress and a craven. She has wronged your chief, and now only waits to sell his tribe to the rebels."

"She shall die!" exclaimed the prophet of the tribe, who had always been Catharine's secret enemy; "the great medicine has had a vision—the white woman shall no longer stay in the tribe she wishes to sell!"

"Let her die!" echoed a score of stern voices.

"No," returned Esther, "sudden death were too sweet; drive her forth into the wilderness; let the cold and the wild beasts destroy her, and leave her bones to bleach without a grave."

"The queen speaks well," returned the prophet; "it shall be so."

"This very night!" exclaimed Esther. "Let the tribe go in a body to her lodge—let her be dragged forth and driven into the forest, followed by the curses of the people whose queen she has braved—whose chief she has betrayed."

A low murmur of approval ran through the group, and the whole tribe gathered nearer the council-fire, like a pack of wolves on the scent of blood.

The warriors rose in a body and filed into rank; but before they could take a step in advance, Catharine came out of the shelter of the tree and confronted them.

"You need not seek her like wild beasts hunting their prey," she said; "Catharine Montour is here!"

There was an instant hush as Catharine Montour stepped, with that calm, sad face, into their midst. Even those savage hearts were awed by her fearless dignity; but Queen Esther was less human, and her voice woke again the fierce passion which her artful address had aroused.

"She braves the Shawnee chiefs because they are old!" exclaimed the fiendish woman. "She comes among you with her hands dyed in the blood of your people—Gi-en-gwa-tah's brother fell by her treachery."

Catharine lifted her hand. "I have done you much good; my wealth has been freely spent in your service; will the chiefs listen?"

"That gold," cried Esther, "belongs to Tahmeroo, the daughter of your chief; but while this woman lives she cannot touch it. When she is gone the young white brave will give you all. She has kept it to herself—her lodge is full of bright things, which she shares with no one, not even with the widow of your old chief. Your queen speaks no lie, ask her if Gi-en-gwa-tah's step has sounded in her lodge since we fought at Wyoming. Let her be driven forth!"

The women took up the cry, crowding about the handful of warriors, and forcing them on. Catharine stood calmly confronting them—nearer gathered those stern faces—horrible eyes glared into her own, but she met them unflinchingly.

"Away with her!" shrieked Esther; "the voice of her agony will be sweet to the murdered brave."

"Let it come; I have not sought death, but life is a burden to me now; you thought to revenge yourself, but I thank you for this release from heavy trouble; what matters the way? it is brief at best."

"Drive her forth!" cried the old queen, roused to insane fury by the composure of her victim.

The whole tribe rushed towards Catharine with yells and execrations. She made no effort to fly, but was borne helplessly along by the heaving mass. Balls of snow and ice were hurled at her, the sharp fragments struck her on the temples, but she made no outcry. Her long hair broke loose and streamed on the wind, while the serpent that girded her forehead flashed in the moonlight, the raised head with its open jaws seemed to hiss defiance at her pursuers.

Her silence and her meekness only added to Esther's rage, though the chiefs began to feel respect for her courage.

"Faster," shrieked the queen, "faster! drive her deep, deep into the woods, where no trail or path can lead her out again."

Thus fiercely urged, the savages swept on, dragging their victim rudely over the snow. They passed the outskirts of the settlement, and plunged into the forest, sinking kneedeep into the crusted snow at every step. When all her strength was exhausted, and they were compelled to drag her forward like a corpse, they flung her down upon the white earth and retreated, singing a low death-song as they left her to die.

She had fallen in the depths of a hemlock grove; thick green branches wreathed with snow drooped over her, swayed heavily by the sobbing wind. No moon could penetrate there; even the snow looked inky in those dense shadows.

A savage, less fiendish than the rest, came back, planted his burning torch in the snow, and went away; its red light streamed over her locked features. She felt the warmth, and struggled to get up. The motion shook the jewelled serpent from her head which uncoiled itself from her temple and lay writhing upon the snow like a living reptile creeping away from the flame.

She could not stand erect; she had no strength to cry aloud; but as all the terrors of that lonely death fell upon her, struggled fully, and answered the wind with her sobs. They had torn the fur mantle from her shoulders, and left her wrapped only in that crimson robe. The cold penetrated her to the heart, sharp particles of frost cut across her face. Her blue lips quivered above her chattering teeth. She crept towards the torch, and holding her purple hands on each side of it in piteous helplessness, strove to warm them; but they fell numbly down, and with a faint instinct she drew them under the flowing sleeves of her robe, and lay motionless, with death creeping steadily to her vitals.

"What is that, father? what is that shining like a fallen star through the hemlocks? See how that little column of smoke trembles through the leaves?"

Varnham turned from his path and the two bent their steps to the hemlock woods, following the light. Why did that pale man hold his breath as he moved forward? Why did Mary shiver audibly beneath her warm mantle? They had not yet seen that deathly face, the serpent scattering its mocking brightness on the snow, or the crimson robe that lay in masses over those frozen limbs. But a few steps more, and the torch revealed all this. The father and child looked at each other in mute horror. It lasted but a moment. Varnham swept back the hemlock branches and lifted his wife up from the snow. Mary took off her mantle and folded it around those heavy limbs, while the strong man gathered her to his heart and strove to warm that purple mouth with the life that sobbed and quivered through his own lips.

It was all in vain. The love which possessed no power over her youth, though it shook his soul to the centre, had not force enough to arouse his wife from that numb death-sleep. She opened her eyes once, after he bore her out to the moonlight, and, for an instant, Varnham felt her heart beat against his own. A cry of exquisite pain broke from him, then a tender young voice sobbed out:

"Mother—mother!"

A gleam of light stole over Catharine's face. It would have been a smile, but those features were frozen into marble, and had lost all power of expression; but the eyes had meaning in them still. They turned upon that angel face, and, filling with lovelight, froze in their sockets.

"Mother—mother!" cried Mary, falling on
her knees beside the lifeless form.

Mile after mile Varnham carried his marble burden through the forest and across a bend of the lake, till he stood, in the grey of that cold winter's morning, in the hall of Queen Esther's dwelling.

A troop of Indians, fresh from the warpath, were drawn up before the entrance, and among them was Gi-en-gwa-tah, mounted on his war-horse. The chief never would wear paint, like meaner men of his tribe, and those who looked on him attentively, saw that his face was haggard and his eagle eyes heavy.

Queen Esther met him at the door.

"Mother," he said, "you and the young brave have talked with serpent tongues. The Great Spirit has been whispering in my heart, and it beats loud. Gi-en-gwa-tah will be just. Let his white queen speak for herself."

As he spoke, Varnham glided by him, bearing the dead body of Catharine Montour in his arms. The Indians who had come out of the lodge with Esther sat down and covered their faces with signs of penitence, but the old queen stood up, cold and firm as a rock.

"Gi-en-gwa-tah is weak, like a girl, but Queen Esther can take care of her son's honor. See, yonder is the woman whose serpent words killed his brother. Last night the Council drove her out to die like a wolf."

The chief sprang from his horse, and, striding into the hall, fell down before the body of Catharine Montour; the anguish quivering in that stern face struck pity even into those savage bosoms; his chest heaved, his eyes grew large, wandering from the dead to his mother, with such wild sorrow that even she turned away, half-repenting what she had done.

All at once he fell upon his face, and burst into a passion of grief which shook his frame like a thunder gust. Once and again the storm swept over him, then he arose, terrible in the majesty of his grief, and, passing the old queen, mounted his war-horse. A small golden bugle, the gift of Catharine Montour, hung over his bosom; he lifted it and sent forth a blast which brought every warrior in the settlement around him.

"Warriors," he said, "this is no longer my home. That woman is not my mother, but the murderess of my wife. Let every man who went with her into the forest last night step to her side. Neither they nor their leader are longer of our tribe. I leave her to the Great Spirit, whose curse shall hang about her as lightning strikes an old hemlock dead at the top. Warriors, let us depart."

The chief wheeled his horse, the tribe fell into order, and while Queen Esther stood like a pillar of stone, with the last human feeling in her bosom struck dead at the root, the whole tribe save those who had partaken of her crime, filed into the war-trail, from which they never returned again.

CHAPTER XXXI
THE INHERITANCE

"Look, look, Tahmeroo, yonder is your home! To the right, to the left, on either side, from horizon to horizon the land is yours!"

It was Walter Butler's voice, exultant and loud, addressing his wife as they came in sight of Ashton.

Tahmeroo leaned out of the carriage, and looked around with a glow of proud delight. How different this scene from the broad forests of her native land—how calm and beautiful lay the hills and fields, rolling westward from the eminence upon which they had paused! A thousand blossoming hedges chained them together, as it were, with massive and interminable garlands. She saw clumps of trees, vividly green cascades and brooks meandering towards the one bright stream which cut the lands in twain. Upon the opposite hillside stood a mansion, vast, stately and old, towering upwards from a park of fine oaks, and chestnuts heavy with flowers. A prince might have looked proudly on a domain like that without asking for more.

"And is this all mine—my own, to do with as I please?" said Tahmeroo, turning her brilliant eyes from the landscape to Butler's face. "That pretty village, the old church, and all?"

"Yes, my red bird, you are mistress here—everything is yours."

"Not so," answered Tahmeroo, and her bright eyes filled. "What is Tahmeroo without her husband? it is his, everything—Tahmeroo wants nothing but his love."

"But words cannot convey property, my bird; it takes yellow parchment and wax, and the signing of names, to change an estate."

"But there must be plenty of parchment in that grand old house, and, thank the Great Spirit, Tahmeroo can write beautifully, like Catharine her mother. She will not shame the white brave in his new home—he shall yet be a great chief among these proud people."

"And you will do this willingly, my wild-rose?" cried Butler, with a glitter of the eyes, from which even the confiding wife had learned to shrink. "It will be easily done; the entailed portion of the estates are large enough for any woman; as for the rest——"

"Let the man drive quick, that we may find the parchment," answered Tahmeroo, eager to sacrifice her wealth.

Butler repeated her orders to the coachman, and the carriage, with its outriders—for Butler took state upon himself immediately on reaching England—dashed forward, and soon drew up before the lordly old mansion. The door swung open—a crowd of servants stood ranged in the hall, and as Tahmeroo entered the mansion a score of voices hailed her as the lady of Ashton.

The next day Butler went back to London, in order to take legal steps for the transfer of his wife's property. For three weeks Tahmeroo wandered restlessly through the apartments of her new home, which had all the loneliness of the forest without its freedom. She was like a wild bird, and fled with shy timidity from the attendants when they came to take her orders. How often during those weeks did she sigh for her own savage home at the head of Seneca Lake.

At last Butler returned, accompanied by a couple of the worst class of London lawyers, and a company of reckless young men, who he persuaded Tahmeroo were necessary witnesses to the transfer she was so anxious to make. These men, who came down more out of curiosity to see the wild forest girl who had turned out a countess than from any other motive, were assembled in the library, a vast apartment, whose tarnished gilding and faded draperies bespoke the long disuse that had fallen upon its magnificence.

Tahmeroo, in her wildwood innocence, received her husband's guests with genuine Indian hospitality. She was eager to complete the deeds which would make her lord a chief among them, and was bright with thankfulness for this opportunity to prove her love.

The entail of the Granby estates covered only an unimportant portion of the property, and when Tahmeroo was so eager to sign the deed which put Butler in possession, she was divesting her rank of all its appurtenances, and sweeping the property of a proud old family into the hands of a profligate and ruffian.

Still it was a beautiful sight when that true-hearted woman came into the room, arrayed with just enough of her former gorgeousness to give effect to her modern garment. A band of her own raven hair wreathed her head with a glossy coronet; her robe of crimson brocade, scattered over with bouquets of flowers, flowed in warm, rich folds about her person. She came in with all the stateliness of a queen, and the wild grace of a savage, her cheeks glowing like a ripe peach, and her eyes bright with affectionate triumph. She gloried in the sacrifice when the legal men told her how important it was.

A few smiling dashes of the pen, and the great bulk of Tahmeroo's wealth was swept away, and with—more terrible for her—all the power she possessed over the kindness of her husband.

That night—that very night—while the ink was scarcely dry upon those parchments, he turned sullenly from her when she spoke of the happy life they should lead in that beautiful home, and muttered something which cut her to the heart about encumbrances being attached to everything he touched.

When the deeds were signed which made Tahmeroo her husband's slave again, the young landholder and his guests sat down for a grand carouse, over which that queenly young wife was to preside.

The very presence of these men in the house was an insult to its mistress; but what did she know of that? With all her pride and natural refinement she had yet to learn that civilization sometimes exhibits phases at which the savage would blush. But ignorant as she was of all this, with the intuition of a delicate nature, she felt the coarseness of their manners and the absence of all that respect with which her father's tribe had ever surrounded her. Looking upon her as a beautiful wild animal, the guests put no restraints upon themselves, but following their host's example called on her to fill their goblets, and made free comments on the beauty of their cup-bearer, recklessly unconscious of the proud nature they were attempting to degrade.

No squaw of burden in her tribe could have been treated with more coarse contempt than Butler heaped upon that noble young creature before that reckless group rose from the table. At last, wounded and outraged, she scarcely knew how or why, the young Indian turned from them with a hot cheek and eyes full of indignant tears and left the room, refusing to come back when Butler, flushed with wine and insolent with triumph, called after her.

The rioters about the board set up a drunken shout, and levelled coarse jeers at their host.

"By Jove!" said one, "she moves off like a lioness in her jungle; you will find her hard to tame, Butler."

"What a haughty glance she cast back upon us," said another, looking at Butler over his wine-glass as he drained it; "you'll find that handsome animal difficult to break in."

"Shall I?" answered Butler, hoarse with rage; "she has given me the whip-hand to-night; come, see how I will use it."

They all started up and reeled from the table, crowding into the hall.

Tahmeroo, urged by the force of habit, had flung open the outer door with her own hands, and was going through into the night air. She could not breathe within doors; her proud spirit was all in arms against her husband's guests; even yet she never dreamed of blaming him; it seemed so natural to be his slave.

As she stepped on the stone terrace, followed by a stream of light from the hall, the young men came out of the saloon, and, seeing her, were about to advance; but, as they looked beyond, the outline of two carriages dimly appeared in front of the mansion, and a group of five persons were at that moment mounting the steps.

Tahmeroo sprang forward with a cry of delight, embraced some one passionately, and fled to her husband's side with the swiftness of a deer.

"It is the white angel! the beautiful—beautiful——"

She broke off, all in a glow of delight, for that moment Varnham entered the hall, leading Mary Derwent by the hand. They were followed by a young man, with a female leaning on his arm, and behind them all came an old lady, who looked half-terrified by the magnificence into which she had been introduced.

Butler looked on this intrusion dumb with astonishment, for the whole group was known to him. At last, rage brought back his speech; with a flushed face and unequal step he advanced to meet the young couple, for there his fury concentrated itself.

"Edward Clark, and you, Jane Derwent, I do not know what has brought you here, or how you have crossed the Atlantic, but permit me to say that this house is mine, and it receives no guests whom I do not invite."

Before Clark could answer, Varnham stepped back and confronted the angry man, with Mary on his arm.

"You mistake," he said, gently; "this house belongs to Lady Granby's daughter; you cannot be its master."

Butler broke into an insulting laugh, and beckoned Tahmeroo with his finger.

"It did belong to Lady Granby's daughter; but my squaw will tell you that it is now deeded to me, and these gentlemen can prove that it was done by her own free act."

"Indeed," said Varnham, casting a compassionate glance on Tahmeroo; "but she will fail to give you any claim here. This young lady is Lady Granby's daughter, born in her first and only legal marriage; even your wife has no right at Ashton, save as the half-sister of the young countess."

Here Mary reached out her hand towards Tahmeroo, with a look of tender humility, as if she begged pardon for being the elder and the legal child of their common mother.

Tahmeroo did not take the hand, but drew close to Butler; she could not quite comprehend the scene.

Again Butler laughed, but hoarsely and with a troubled abruptness.

"And you expect me to believe this; you——"

"Not without proof; one of you," said Varnham, turning to the servants that now came crowding into the hall, "one of you call the housekeeper, if she is yet alive."

An old woman, whose hair was folded, white as snow, under her cap, came into the hall, and, shading her eyes with one hand, fell to perusing his features with a disturbed manner.

"Mrs. Mason!"

She knew the voice; the hand dropped from her eyes, and tears began to course down her cheek.

"My master—my master!"

The oldest servants, who had held back till then, crowded forward, smiling and crying in the same breath.

"The master—oh, the master has come back!"

Butler grew pale; the very earth seemed slipping from under his feet.

"Who are you, and what right has this crooked imp at Ashton?" he demanded.

"I am the husband of Caroline Lady Granby; you see, these good people all recognize me."

"We do—we do—every one of us; his hair has grown white, and his forehead is not so smooth, but there is the old smile, and the old look of the eye; God bless the master."

"And you will know this face, too," said Varnham, removing Mary's bonnet, and allowing the golden hair to fall over her shoulders; "she is my child—little Mary."

The servants began to weep; some covered their faces; others came forward on tiptoe and tenderly examined those beautiful features. The old housekeeper sunk to her knees, and drew the face down to her bosom; then she looked up wistfully at Varnham; he understood all she desired to ask, and turned his eyes sorrowfully on his child's mourning-dress.

A quiet awe stole over the group of servants; they asked no more questions.

Gravely and quietly, like one who takes up a pleasant duty, the young countess of Granby assumed the great power of her birthright. Her father had spent half his life in striving to introduce the blessings of civilization among the savages; but in remedying the evils which civilization had yet left untouched in that rich domain, both he and the gentle Mary found ample scope for all the benevolence of their great hearts.

While Edward Clark managed the estates, and his young wife brought all her sprightliness and beauty into the household of her sister—for so she still called the Lady of Ashton—the lovely girl herself moved about her own mansion, in her simple dress of black silk or velvet, more like a spirit of mercy than the mistress of a proud name and broad lands. Her tastes continued simple and child-like as ever, and when she appeared in public it was to be greeted with such love as a beautiful spirit—let the form which clothes it be what it will—is sure to command from the good.

CHAPTER XXXII
THE ASHES OF POWER

After a few weeks of desperate struggle, Butler gave up all hopes of maintaining the rights he had so haughtily assumed, and departed abruptly for America, leaving his wife at Ashton, for a time unconscious of his desertion.

But when she knew that he was gone, no wild bird, torn from its mate, ever became so restless in its thralldom as she did in that princely mansion. She pined without ceasing, and, refusing all food, sat down with her face shrouded, after the manner of her race, and refused to be comforted.

In vain both Varnham and Mary strove to persuade the unhappy young creature to stay with them, and share the wealth which Catharine Montour's violent death had undoubtedly prevented her dividing. The forest girl could not be made to comprehend the value of property. As for gold, she scarcely knew its use, or that the beautiful objects with which her mother had been surrounded, did not come naturally to those whom the Great Spirit favored, as leaves grew upon the summer boughs. She pined for the presence of her husband, and smiled with scorn when any one sought to console her for his absence with gold which she did not want and lands that bore blossoms and grain, rather than the mighty old forest trees, under which her father's warriors had hunted all their lives.

At last a strange belief came upon her that Butler had not intentionally left her behind. She had known him called away suddenly to battle, when he had no time to warn her. Was not this occasion urgent, as those had been? She would not doubt it, in the faith of her great love she trusted in him still. One morning, when Mary went up to her sister's chamber, hoping to comfort her, she found the room empty. Tahmeroo had left Ashton in the night, and followed after her husband.

Across the ocean she came into her own beautiful, wild country. She was told that Butler might be found in the Mohawk Valley, leading his Indians on to battle again; and to that point she bent her way. Wherever a fight had been, or a body of savages gathered, she came in breathless haste, searching for the man who had cast her off.

In October, 1781, the poor Indian wife found herself on the banks of a creek, deep in the forest, with an escort of two or three Indians who had been detached from their companions, and were glad to take charge of their chief's daughter.

There had been a skirmish on this stream during the day, and from some of the fugitives Tahmeroo had learned that her husband was in command of the Indians. Without a thought of the dangers she was sure to encounter in a running fight of this kind, the young wife kept on her route, led forward by scattering shots, till the woods, now dun with withered foliage, were filled with the cold gloom of the coming night. As she moved on, the wind rose, filling the air with dead leaves, and above that came the rush and flap of wings. The patter of stealthy feet, and the low growl of wolves, disturbed by the approach of human beings.

A little hollow was before her, full of shadows, and with a black cloud of crows gathering over it.

Tahmeroo rode to the brink of the hollow, and looked down, stooping over the bent neck of her horse. From the side of a rock, around which a little stream of water was creeping, three ravens soared upwards, flapping their heavy wings, and roosting on a tree-branch sullenly eyed her approach. She did not heed them, for by the rock was a mass of blackness more terrible than the ravenous birds to her. She dropped slowly down the side of her horse, crept across the rock and bent over.

When her escort reached her, she lay with her face downward, and her eyes open, as they had looked on the dead body of her husband, but those eyes saw nothing, and when the savages lifted her up, she felt nothing—all the world was dark to her then.

As if Gi-en-gwa-tah's curse had fulfilled itself, the settlement at Seneca Lake had atoned for the massacre of Wyoming, and now lay desolated; the beautiful grounds were black with ruin, the charred trunks of the dead trees rose in black groups where life and greenness had been. Heaps of stone lay where the houses had stood, and a few bark wigwams, in which the broken remnants of Queen Esther's followers still sheltered themselves, were all that Sullivan's avenging troops had left to the old queen.

The mansion which she had called her palace was a heap of ruins, but some of the walls remained, and one of the largest rooms had been roofed over with plank and slabs, thus giving shelter to that terrible woman, who lay like a sick lioness on a buffalo skin in the centre, smitten by her son's curse, and struggling with that dogged old age which chains the passions it cannot quench.

On the broken door-step sat a group of savages, looking gloomily into the yawning hall. They dared not intrude on the sick woman without a summons; but sat listening, not for moans or complaints—those they never could expect—but for a sound of the death rattle, which must soon follow the appalling stillness in which she rested.

As she lay thus, picking perpetually at the fur on the buffalo robe, with a keen glare of the eyes, as if that work must be done before she could enter eternity, a figure glided past the Indians on the door-step and entered that death-chamber. It was Tahmeroo, her grandchild, but so haggard and lifeless that the Indians, whom she passed, had not known her.

The old woman turned her eyes that way, but kept picking, picking, picking at the fur.

All at once she seemed to comprehend that one of her own kindred stood beside her. She raised herself up on one hand; the snow-white hair swept back from her face, leaving it stony and ashen. Up and up, inch by inch, she struggled, shaking like a naked tree in the winter, till she stood upright.

"Tell him that you saw his mother die upon her feet. He struck her with a curse, but death is not so strong. I grapple with him, face to face, tooth and tooth; but a child's curse who can bear!"

She reeled heavily, flung out her clenched hands, striving to balance herself, but fell with a dull crash. There was a sound in her throat, like the muffled rattle of chains in a dungeon, and the old queen lay across her buffalo robe stiff and dead.

All that day and night a death-chant rose and swelled through those ruins. The blackened trees, dead, like their owner, shivered as the wind passed them burdened with that mournful wail. That little group of Indians, broken off from the great tribe by the curse of their chief, buried their queen among the blackened ruins, covered her grave with ashes, and sat down by it in patient desolation.

Then Tahmeroo glided among them like a ghost. "Old men," she said, in the gentleness of solemn grief, "sit no longer in the ashes of my father's curse. Gi-en-gwa-tah will listen to Catharine Montour's child when she tells him all the sweet words which her mother left behind. Gather up the dried fruit and corn in your wigwams, and follow me to the great-waters, where the tribe are planting young trees and building new lodges."

The Indians arose in dead silence and filed away. As they gathered the scant provisions from their wigwams, the death-chant was hushed, but when they struck into file again, and Tahmeroo placed herself at their head, it broke forth once more, and went moaning down the banks of the lake, deeper and deeper into the wilderness, till a sob of wind carried the last sound away.